THE
NEIGHBORS

For additional books by Hannah Mary McKinnon,
visit her website, www.hannahmarymckinnon.com.

THE

NEIGHBORS

HANNAH MARY McKINNON

mira

If you purchased this book without a cover you should be aware
that this book is stolen property. It was reported as "unsold and
destroyed" to the publisher, and neither the author nor the
publisher has received any payment for this "stripped book."

Recycling programs
for this product may
not exist in your area.

ISBN-13: 978-0-7783-1100-3

The Neighbors

Copyright © 2018 by Hannah McKinnon

All rights reserved. Except for use in any review, the reproduction or utilization of this work
in whole or in part in any form by any electronic, mechanical or other means, now known or
hereinafter invented, including xerography, photocopying and recording, or in any information
storage or retrieval system, is forbidden without the written permission of the publisher,
MIRA Books, 22 Adelaide St. West, 40th Floor, Toronto, Ontario M5H 4E3, Canada.

This is a work of fiction. Names, characters, places and incidents are either the product
of the author's imagination or are used fictitiously, and any resemblance to actual persons,
living or dead, business establishments, events or locales is entirely coincidental.

® and TM are trademarks of Harlequin Enterprises Limited or its corporate affiliates.
Trademarks indicated with ® are registered in the United States Patent and Trademark Office,
the Canadian Intellectual Property Office and in other countries.

For questions and comments about the quality of this book, please contact us at
CustomerService@Harlequin.com.

MIRABooks.com

BookClubbish.com

To the loves of my life—Robert, Leo, Matt and Lex

THE
NEIGHBORS

THEN: JULY 18, 1992
ABBY

"HELP."

The faint voice floated toward me. Gliding smooth as a paper airplane from somewhere in the midst of the fog swirling through my brain. Orange lights flashed in a steady rhythm and—

"Please."

I wondered if I'd uttered the words, but I hadn't moved my lips. Hadn't moved at all. Couldn't. It hurt too much. Everything hurt too much.

Moments passed, and I tried to string together the few wispy fragments my mind allowed me to cling to. My arms, chest and legs were pressed against something hard and uncomfortable—the ground, not my soft bed—but the reason why I found myself in that position escaped me entirely. And I was too exhausted to care.

A breeze softly brushed across my cheek. The pavement beneath me felt warm, and despite the distinct taste of rust invading my mouth, I could smell freshly cut grass. Hadn't I been—

"Help me, Abby."

The voice was too low to be mine. A man's then—it had to be. Why wouldn't he let me sleep? My eyes felt heavy and impossible to open, so I let my thoughts start pulling me away, ever so slowly, to the deliciously inviting state of unconsciousness.

"Abby."

Rest would have to wait. Against my better judgment I raised my head, each millimeter expending energy I didn't think I had and causing pain to shoot through every part of my body like a thousand burning hot pins. I tried, but my legs and lower back stubbornly refused to budge even the tiniest amount, as if I'd been nailed to the ground.

I forced my eyes open.

And I saw him.

"Tom." My own voice this time, barely a whisper. "Tom." A little stronger, louder.

My brother lay a few meters away in what had been my blue Ford Capri, but which was now an upturned carcass of broken glass and mangled steel. The flashing of the hazard lights illuminated Tom's bloody face and body every few seconds, a perverse freak show. He hung upside down. Unlike me, he was still in the car, somewhere between the front and back seats, his arms and legs bent at impossible angles. Eyes wide and glazed. Staring at me. Desperate. Begging.

"Abby," he said once more, and I watched as he attempted to lift his arms, tried to reach for me. "I can't get out." Tears rolled up his forehead, mixing with a steady stream of blood from the deep gash above his eye that looked like a second mouth. "I can't get out."

"Tom," I said again, before my eyes closed despite my efforts to keep them open. Fighting the beckoning darkness felt like a struggle I'd never win.

The light from the wreck somehow became brighter, warmer, too. Somewhere in my brain it occurred to me it wasn't the sun—couldn't be the sun—it was still so dark. Wasn't it? My mind started drifting away.

But then the pungent smell of smoke and petrol filled the air.

I wanted to move. I needed to get to him. But I couldn't.

"I'm sorry," I whispered, my eyes open again, staring into his. "Tom. I'm so sorry."

The last thing I heard were the screams, Tom's and mine, as the car burst into flames.

NOW
NATE

WHEN THE U-HAUL van arrived next door, I did what most sensible human beings would do: I ignored it. Once I'd made sure it was just the new neighbors moving in, not some crazy person stealing lingering Christmas decorations, I cranked up the fire, flopped back down on the sofa and buried my nose in my copy of *I Am Ozzy*, marveling at how the guy had lasted so long.

As far as I was concerned, moving in February, undeniably the coldest month of the year, was a ridiculous notion. And I wanted nothing to do with it.

The house was my peaceful kingdom that blustery Saturday morning. Abby had gone to pick up Sarah from a sleepover, and they'd planned on a Mum and Daughter shopping spree in town. Bad weather and potential conflict be damned.

I think Abby had her eye on the winter jacket sales, and knew Sarah wanted a pair of Steve Madden combat boots. I could tell from my daughter's look she'd been impressed when I said I knew who Steve Madden was. In reality, I'd only heard about him when I'd finally got around to streaming

The Wolf of Wall Street, belly-laughing as Jonah Hill struggled to pronounce the designer's name whilst high on a bucket of quaaludes. Abby hadn't been impressed by the film, not even by Margot Robbie in *that* scene. Well, never mind Margot's perfect breasts. Apparently Abby didn't like Steve Madden's boots either.

"They're awful," she'd whispered last night as we lay in bed. Then she must have remembered Sarah was out because she said, more loudly, "Grunge, punk or whatever the hell gone bad. I hate combat boots."

I lowered the stack of papers I'd promised myself I'd look over as soon as I got home but had barely made a start on. "I hope you didn't tell Sarah."

Abby pulled a face. "God, no, 'course not. I said they were great, and I might get a pair, too. Figured reverse psychology would stop her from wanting them."

"Did it?"

"Nope. She gave me one of her looks."

I laughed. "I think they're pretty cool." When Abby raised an eyebrow I added, "The boots, not the looks. And it's her money. She saved up for them. Let her do what she wants."

"Yeah, I suppose." She wrinkled her nose.

"I'd wear them if they didn't make me look like a middle-aged has-been."

Abby smiled, rolled on top of me and kissed my neck. Her hair tickled my face and smelled of something vanilla and cherryish. She always smelled nice, even when she'd been on one of her insane, million-mile runs.

"You're not a has-been, Nate," she whispered.

I wrapped an arm around her, slid my other hand underneath her T-shirt, ran my fingers up and down the soft skin of her back. "And what about the middle-aged part?" I said before nibbling on her neck.

She raised her head and looked at me with one eyebrow arched, and a sly smile playing on her lips. "Let's see…"

As her mouth traveled down my chest, I shoved the papers off the bed, letting them slide to the floor in a heap. Reviewing Mr. Rav Ramjug's superior programming skills could wait. Frankly it had been a while since Abby and I last got busy. People say it's normal for a couple's sex life to disappear for a while after having a kid. What they don't tell you is the vanishing act repeats once said kid hits teenage years because she a) doesn't go to bed at seven and sleep like a dead man until dawn, and b) has the hearing of a greater wax moth.

I groaned as Abby kissed my stomach. Despite us having the house to ourselves and the entire night ahead of us, we ended up in a frantic quickie, with Abby collapsing onto my chest afterward, the two of us breathing heavily.

"I think we both needed that," she said, before sliding off me and getting up. I never had the chance to moan about my wife wanting to spoon endlessly after sex. Three minutes in and she was about as cuddly as a piece of Lego.

I propped myself up on one elbow and watched her get dressed. I did that sometimes—watch Abby—and mostly she was unaware of it. When she was baking and I pretended to be engrossed in a book or—another favorite—when she was going over the monthly bills, hair scrunched up in a messy ponytail, brow furrowed at the latest phone statement, lips moving silently as she checked the numbers.

I liked to look at her, I mean *properly* look at her. Study her as if she was a Miró at The Tate I could stand in front of and ponder, cocking my head to one side, pompously tapping my lips with one finger, wondering what the *artiste* meant to express with the masterfully applied strokes and splashes of paint. Not that I had a bloody clue about art. I could barely tell a Picasso from a stick man even if the latter tapped me on the shoulder and kicked me in the nuts.

So I silently perused Abby's long, slim legs with the scars she hated so much but were a huge part of her, the arch of her back, her elegant, swan-like neck. A classic masterpiece.

"What?" Her voice pulled me out of my trance. She'd turned around, and I'd missed it. *Busted*.

"Nothing," I answered with what I hoped was a charming grin, and shook my head slightly. "Just looking at you."

As she smiled her blue eyes sparkled, and her long blond hair settled in that sexy, tousled bed-head look, the one that screamed, "Oh, yeah, I got some." I let my gaze linger as she went to the bathroom and closed the door behind her.

I lay back in bed and thought about my wife the way you do in a fuzzy postcoital state. Abby could give Jennifer Aniston a run for her money anytime. At forty-four she looked at least six years younger. It put me, with my slight paunch that I swore every January (the last one being no exception) I'd get rid of, to absolute shame. I wasn't overly proud of the thinning spot on the top of my head either. But what can you do? I was almost halfway between my forty-sixth and forty-seventh birthday. Jesus, *forty-seven*—it had sneaked up on me like my *slight* paunch. I stretched, sighed and soon felt myself drift off to sleep, only stirring slightly when Abby climbed into bed a while later.

Back in my warm living room, I reluctantly dragged myself out of the memory, cleared my throat and concentrated on Ozzy's extravagant tales. They kept me entertained for a further ten minutes, before, mug of fresh coffee in hand, I meandered to the window, fully intent on spying on who was moving in next door.

I sipped my drink and watched three jacket-, hat- and glove-clad figures slowly lugging boxes from the van to the house. Not professional movers, I decided. Not brisk enough. Difficult to tell for sure from the angle, but they looked like a standard family. Woman, bloke and, from what I could see, a gangly-legged teenage boy, hunched over, moving slowly, his body language screaming "get me out of here." I couldn't blame him. Like I said, moving at this time of year was a ridiculous notion.

I picked up my phone from the coffee table and sent Abby a text. Neighbors moving in. Look normal. How's the shopping? Should we re-mortgage the house?

A few seconds later my phone buzzed.

HAHA. Haven't left Camilla's yet! Are you helping them? You'd make a good impression.

Shit. I hadn't thought this through. Why did I send a message in the first place? Now I'd be a dickhead if I didn't do my share of carrying. I walked back to the window.

The teenager stood at the back of the van, gesticulating to someone inside the vehicle, his arms flying around. He appeared to cross them over his chest, and, although I could only see the back of his black-and-yellow hat, which made his head look like a giant and slightly angry bee, I'd have bet money he'd stuck out his chin, too. The woman walked over and put a hand on the teen's shoulder before waving her arms around, too, pointing to the house, the inside of the van and back to the house again, shaking her head.

I sighed loudly and made my way into the hall, where I pulled out my coat, boots and hat. I looked at the photograph of Tom, my wife's brother, whom I'd *almost* met before he died, and gave him a nod. "You think I'm a crazy bugger going out there. Don't you?"

He stared back at me with his forever boyish grin and early '90s boy band haircut, which made him look like he'd stuck a fluffy palm tree on top of his head.

"Yeah, exactly," I said, then opened the front door. The cold air whipped around my face, and the gravel scrunched beneath my feet, protesting each of my heavy steps. "Jesus, my balls will turn to ice cubes," I muttered as I pulled my hat past my ears and trudged to the van.

"...telling you. There's no way we can lift it, Liam," I heard the woman say to the person in the van when I got within earshot. "It's not happening. It isn't."

Her voice was soft yet determined. It reminded me of Abby, and what Sarah and I secretly called *the tone*. My daughter and I knew there wasn't an inch of wriggle room left when Abby used *the tone*. Capitulation was the only option. Capitulation or certain death—probably. We'd never dared find out.

I looked in the back of the van and saw the guy—Liam, apparently—put down the side of a green sofa. As he straightened his back he caught sight of me and smiled.

"Hey," he said, tilting his head. "Can I help you?"

I smiled back and shrugged. "I was going to ask you the same thing."

The woman and Beanie Boy turned around. I guessed him to be around the same age as Sarah. The woman smiled; he didn't. No surprise there. There's nothing quite like the downer of amputated teenage happiness.

"I'm Nate." I pointed to our house. "From next door. Thought you might need a hand."

The woman's smile broadened, showing off immaculate

teeth. Brown curls stuck out from underneath her fire engine-red bobble hat. She stood around the same height as Abby but looked as if she weighed a few kilos more. It suited her—it was hard not to notice just how well.

"Thanks," she said and held out her hand to shake mine. "I'm Nancy. Nancy Jefferson." She pointed to the guy in the van, surrounded by boxes neatly marked Garage, Bedroom, Living Room—FRAGILE and so on. "That's my husband, Liam, and this is our son, Zachary."

"Zac," the teenager said, rolling his eyes around in his head so hard they started to look a lot like marbles. "I'm Zac." He shook my hand, too, and now that they'd stopped their dizzy spin, I noticed he had his father's intense eyes.

Liam jumped down from the van and gave me a hard clap on the shoulder. "Cheers," he said. "Appreciate it. The removal company got delayed, so we decided to bring a few things ourselves. A couple of people helped us on the other end but now, well…" He whistled. "You're a lifesaver." He smiled again, revealing teeth as white as his wife's.

I figured these people were either dentists or had a great family discount. Either way, Liam's jaw was what my mother would have called "strong," and his cheekbones probably had their own exclusive page in *Esquire*. When he discarded his winter jacket, and although he wore a fleece, I could tell he was no stranger to the weight bench.

"Happy to help," I said. Then I did that male-pride thing—sucked in my gut, straightened my back, all the while wishing I'd been a tad more diligent with my sit-ups in recent months. "Let's start with that sofa."

Liam and I made a couple of trips from the van to the front door, where Zac and Nancy took over dispatching boxes to the appropriate rooms.

"So where did you move from?" I asked Liam as we carried a TV the size of a small country up the driveway. The bloody thing felt as solid as a slab of gold and probably cost more. "You don't sound local."

"Lancashire. Preston area." He navigated us toward the front steps. Christ, he didn't even seem to be sweating while I could already feel my shirt sucking mine up like a sponge.

"Really?" I straightened the TV slightly so we could get it through the door without scratching it. "My grandparents lived in Longton."

"Yeah? You grew up there?"

"No. We went north almost every summer, though." We put the television down in the living room, my back screaming a silent *thank god*. "But my wife grew up near Preston. She moved here after we met."

"Seriously? What's her name?"

"Abigail—Abby—Morris." He shrugged so I added, "Sanders before we married."

Liam looked at me for a few seconds, then blinked. I thought I saw a flicker of something pass over his face, but it disappeared all too quickly, so I figured I'd imagined it.

I laughed. "Don't tell me you know her?"

"No." He turned and headed for the front door. "The name doesn't ring any bells."

In hindsight I should have stopped him. Questioned the look. At least asked what it meant. If I had, then perhaps none of what was to come would have happened.

And maybe, just maybe, I'd still be with my wife.

NOW
ABBY

"THEY'RE MOVING IN TODAY?" Camilla wiped her flour-covered hands on her apron. "That didn't take long to sell, did it?"

I nodded, and peered past her up the stairs, wishing Sarah would hurry up. Now that Camilla and I both worked at Sterling Engineering, seeing her on weekends could be, well, a bit much. She gossiped a fair amount and somehow got people to say more than they should despite themselves, including me if I let my guard down.

"The house was only empty a few weeks," I said. "Not surprising, considering the price they were asking." I heard Sarah and Claire giggling upstairs and imagined them speaking in hushed whispers about boys, music and music by boys. They'd declared themselves BFFs on their first day of school, but Nate always said nowadays they were more like conjoined twins.

"Let's go, Sarah," I called out, "We'd better get a move on if you want those boots."

Sarah's answer was a casual, "Yeah, coming," and I pictured

her rolling her eyes and Claire putting a hand over her own mouth—maybe my daughter's, too—stifling another laugh.

"So who are the new neighbors?" Camilla raised her eyebrows. "Some hot guy who can mow the lawn for you?"

I scrunched up my face. "Hardly. Nate just said they look normal. And he cuts the grass."

Camilla laughed. "Well, if a fit bloke moves in next door you might want to rethink that. But," she said, "enough of my fantasies. In any case, they can't be worse than Barbara, right?"

I knew exactly where this conversation was heading. Camilla always wanted the skinny on our neighbor's latest antics, and there had been plenty to entertain her with in recent months. "I bet you're glad they dragged her off to the home," she continued, "and—"

"That's a bit unfair. She wasn't well, you know? We all need to—"

"I know, I know." Camilla shrugged. "You're going to tell me to be more compassionate. Someday I'll be old and senile and glad of people being patient with me." She laughed. "But even *you* have to admit she was a nightmare. Sarah said she's refused to go near the old bat for *years*. You never told me it was that bad."

I opened my mouth in contradiction, then closed it again. After all, I could hardly deny it, Barbara Baker truly had been a nightmare. She'd been our neighbor since we'd bought the house in Bromley almost seventeen years earlier. At first she'd been charming and eloquent, brought us succulent mince pies at Christmas and soul-warming chicken-noodle soup when both Nate and I got the flu. She'd babysat Sarah whenever we'd desperately needed a night out—and even when we hadn't. The perfect neighbor. Except, over the years, as Barbara slowly lost each of her cats and most of her marbles to old age, she'd gradually morphed into a shrieking banshee who wore the same white flannel nightie that had taken on a distinctly yellow sheen under the arms. It was sad, it really was, and we helped her as often as she would allow, which, lately, had been hardly ever.

Camilla leaned in and only slightly lowered her voice. "Did she honestly shout, *'Eff off and die, you shits'* at you before she left?" Her eyes were wide, anticipating the latest morsel of gossip.

I nodded. "We'd been counting the days until she left for the home." Why had I said that? Now Camilla would tell everyone we hated our old neighbor.

Camilla laughed. "You mean the godforsaken place where you come out stiffer than the box they shove you in, isn't that what Barbara always called it? And Sarah said she threw the contents of the litter tray over the fence, too? God." As she stopped to catch a breath, her face flushed, and I couldn't tell if it was information overload or something menopausal.

"Yes, she did." I'd have to educate Sarah again on the lost art of discretion, not that I was exactly leading by example. I cleared my throat. "But Barbara wasn't well, the poor love."

"So sad," Camilla said, floury hand on hips, her voice grave. "Old age is a friend to no one."

"Absolutely," I said, determined to change the subject. "So how's Josh?"

Camilla clicked her tongue. "Oh, fine. Out with his bowling league again. Some tournament or something. Can't keep track where."

I smiled. "Isn't it great that you have your own interests? When you don't have to live in each other's pockets?"

Camilla's eyes narrowed. "Yeah. Fantastic. So do you still work out as much?"

"Yeah." Sensing an impending interrogation, I called out, "Sarah, forget it. The weather's horrible anyway. We'll go home instead."

My daughter immediately appeared at the top of the stairs, her bag in her hand. "Nu-uh," she said, pushing her blond hair away from her face. "I'm coming. I want those boots." She hugged Claire, then kissed her on the cheek with a big, lip-glossy *mwah* noise. "Bye, thanks for everything." She bounded down the stairs, patted Camilla on the arm, walked directly past me and opened the door. "Come on then, Mum. What's keeping you?"

I refused the bait, said my goodbyes and followed my daughter outside, wondering how we'd make it through the day without wanting to throttle each other.

NOW
SARAH

Dear Diary,

I think Benjamin Franklin said, "Guests, like fish, begin to smell after three days." Well, me and Mum would *never* make it that long. We stink after three hours.

People say I'm like her. I suppose we have the same hair, nose and maybe eyes. But that's it. Thank god my personality's much more like Dad's because Mum's a nightmare.

For example, even though I was shattered this morning, I was still looking forward to spending time with her and getting my boots. That lasted about thirty seconds until we got in the car. First of all, Mum had a go at me about the Word of the Day calendar she gave me for Christmas. The conversation (not that it was a proper conversation) went something like:

Mum: Why aren't you using it? Don't you want to be a journalist? I thought it would help.

Me: I haven't had time.

Mum: Oh, come off it, Sarah. You spend forever on that phone of yours.

Ugh!

And when I tried on the combats, Mum went all passive-aggressive with eye rolls and huffs. We studied the behavior at school when Ms. Phillips tried to show the class how pathetic it was, hoping we'd stop. Except of course we didn't because we knew how much it peed her off.

So, when I asked Mum what was wrong she huffed again and said the boots were "aggressive looking" and "not very feminine." I told her not to worry. That during the summer I'd only wear flip-flops and micro shorts where half your bum hangs out.

Me: What do you think, Mum? Those shorts are *really* feminine.

Mum: You will *not* be wearing those, young lady. Absolutely not. Over my dead body.

She even used *the tone*. God. I'd meant it as a joke. Like I'd ever be seen dead with half my bum hanging out. Not that it's a bad butt. Actually I think it's a quite okay butt, thank you very much, *but* (and that's a lot of buts, ha ha) I wouldn't walk around with it on display. I thought Mum would get the joke. I mean, doesn't she know me at all?

Anyway, I bought my combats (black leather, funky, sassy, kick-ass and 60% off, yes!). Mum found a coat (black wool, single-buttoned, boring, predictable, 40% off, still not bad). And then, of course, we couldn't agree on lunch. I wanted a burger. She wanted sushi. We ended up at Pret. Sandwiches must be the gastronomic equivalent of neutrality. Hey, that's not a bad line. Must remember that one for my next essay.

We're home now, and she said we should visit the new neighbors. She texted Dad, and he's helping them put furniture together or something. Hardly a surprise. Dad's always fixing stuff. I thought he was Bob the Builder until I was six. Might

even have called Mum Wendy once (oops!). Speaking of, she
told me to hurry up again. I'd better go before she flips her lid.
Later,
Sarah x.

PS. Word of the day: *fantod*, noun.
1. *plural* a: a state of irritability and tension.
b: fidgets.
2: an emotional outburst (fit).
As in: *Going shopping with my mother gave me the fantods! Hahahaha!*

NOW

ABBY

"COME ON, SARAH." I stood by our front door with a bottle of chilled white wine in my hand. Nate always said people liked chardonnay. I hoped he was right. Sarah trudged down the stairs in her new boots at a glacial pace before giving me an uninspired look.

"Why do *I* have to go?"

I stifled another sigh. "It's the polite thing to do."

She glanced at the bottle. "What if they don't drink?"

"I'm sure it'll be fine."

"*You* don't drink."

My eyes darted involuntarily to Tom's photograph. "No, I don't," I snapped, then took a deep breath. Sarah hadn't had anything to do with the accident—she hadn't even been born.

"But what if they're recovering alcoholics?" she gasped and put a hand to her mouth in a deliberately dramatic gesture. "Or Muslim? Or *Amish*?"

"Don't be a smarty-pants, Sarah."

"Wowzers, Mum. I can be smart without even trying."

I counted to ten in my mind. Slowly. I knew exactly what

she was doing. She thought if she annoyed me enough I'd lose my temper and tell her to stay at home. Too bad for her, I used to play the exact same game with my mother. For once I was half a step ahead of her.

I smiled. "Yes, you can be. Come on. Time to go."

She pouted as she pulled on her jacket, and I made sure I kept my expression neutral to avoid another feud. A minute later we plodded over to the neighbors and rang the doorbell.

A teenage boy who looked like he'd been stretched like a rubber band opened the door. "Can I help you?" His voice was deep, gravelly and a little on the husky side.

"Hi." I smiled. "I think you still have my husband."

He gave a blank look, then flicked his shock of chocolate-brown, gold-streaked hair.

"Nate from next door," I offered, and put a hand to my chest. "I'm Abby. This is Sarah."

He smiled. Sort of. "Oh, yeah. Come on in," he said in a monotone, then turned and called out, "Mum, it's the neighbors."

A woman's voice came from the back of the house. "Great. Bring them in, Zac."

"Go on through." Zac gestured with his hand.

I walked into the eccentrically wallpapered hallway, which always reminded me of The Who's *Magic Bus*. Barbara had loved bright colors and flowers, and almost every room was papered in a different pattern. She used to say it meant spring sprang eternal in her home. We always assumed she'd eaten a lot of magic mushrooms in the seventies.

As we made our way down the hall, the sweet perfume of apples and cinnamon filled the air, warm and inviting. Zac disappeared up the stairs, and Sarah and I continued to the kitchen. A candle—one of those scented ones—glowed in the middle of a table otherwise covered in stacks of plates, glasses and cutlery.

Nate leaned against the fridge with his arms crossed and a half-full Heineken in one hand. "Hey." He smiled.

A woman with long, curly brown hair in an untidy pony-tail took two steps toward us. When she smiled, her face lit up like a very pretty fairground.

"Hi." She threw a rag on the counter and wiped her hands on her jeans before stretching one out toward me.

"This is Abby." Nate winked at me. "Abby, this is Nancy."

"It's great to meet you." Nancy shook my hand, and I noticed how warm and silky her skin felt. "Nate's told us so much about you already. And your daughter." She looked past me. "You must be Sarah. It's such a pleasure, really, it is." I didn't know the woman, but she seemed incredibly nervous, almost desperately keen to make a good impression.

"Uh, hello," Sarah mumbled back. She still got embarrassed when introduced to strangers. It concerned me sometimes, especially if she wanted to follow her dreams and become a journalist. Nate always said she'd be fine; she'd make her own path. I worried she'd never find it to begin with.

"Liam—that's my husband—went out for more beer." Nancy laughed. "We only had two in the house. Not nearly enough to get rid of the pain from lifting all those boxes."

"I told you we had some." Nate grinned at Nancy. It was his charming smile, the one he used to disarm people, the one that made them feel comfortable. I swear he never noticed how effective it was. Sometimes I didn't think he realized he was doing it.

"No way." Nancy waggled a finger. "You've already helped

so much. We couldn't take your beer, as well. It would add more abuse to your injuries, or whatever the expression is."

"Insult to injury." I caught Nate's look. I often did that. Corrected people, even when it was irrelevant. Such a bad habit. I plastered my own smile on my face and mouthed, "Sorry," at Nate. I waved the bottle of wine around in mid-air. "I brought this. Hope you like chardonnay."

"Absolutely love it." Nancy took the bottle from me and set it on the table. "That's so sweet of you. And thanks for lending us your hubby." Nancy pointed at Nate. "He's a hero, you know. Helped us carry the heavy things inside and even fixed the leaky toilet upstairs." She laughed again. It was a warm laugh, nervous perhaps, but kind and genuine. I had a feeling I'd like her husband, too, if he had a personality similar to hers. She clicked her tongue. "It would have taken Liam six months to get around to it. But Nate? He rolled up his sleeves and voilà."

When Sarah hummed the *Bob the Builder* tune, I poked her in the ribs, and she huffed as if I'd deflated her like a balloon.

The front door opened. "I'm back," a man called out. "Who needs a drink?"

A shiver shot down my spine. That voice. That unmistak-able voice. Deep and silky. Sexy. You never forget a voice like that. Not when the memory of words spoken, even after all this time, still made my knees buckle. I tried not to gasp, and bit my tongue as images flashed into my mind, the ones I tried hard not to think of when I was in bed with Nate. Arms and legs entwined. Gasping, groaning, sweaty backs and my cries of, "Fuck me, Liam. Harder. *Harder.*"

It's not something I'd ever said to Nate. He probably would have blushed.

The footsteps were coming down the hallway, had almost reached the kitchen.

And there was nowhere for me to go.

No escape.

No place to hide.

THEN
ABBY

IT WAS NEW YEAR'S EVE, and I'd decided if the last few minutes were anything to go by, nineteen ninety-two was going to be absolute crap.

My boyfriend of eight months, Dwayne Mazerolle, had just—literally *just*—dumped me. Standing in the middle of Rowley's Irish Pub with a group of his friends, he'd pulled me to one side.

"...so...tell you...going...buy land." His voice boomed in my ear, making me wince. I couldn't make out what he'd said because EMF's "Unbelievable" blared from the loudspeakers. Turned out the song was quite fitting.

"What?" I shouted back. "Why are you buying land?"

"*Thai*-land," he yelled. "I'm going to *Thailand*." He held up two thumbs, swaying a little, not to the music, but because of the many vodka and Cokes. "On a trip."

"Thailand?" I felt my face scrunch up into a puzzled look. "When?"

Dwayne pulled me to one side of the bar and away from the

speaker where it was marginally quieter. "Day after tomorrow," he said, taking a sudden interest in his size eleven feet.

"Eh? You're kidding!" I wondered if he was going to start making fun of my expression, tell me it was all a joke. If it was, I didn't get it.

He lit up a Benson & Hedges and blew the smoke out of his nostrils, kind of like a cartoon bull. "It's a spiritual trip," he said. "You know, to reconnect with nature. I need to *find* myself."

"*Find* yourself?" He was twenty-three, worked as a mechanic at a local garage, lived with his parents. Where, exactly, had he *lost* himself?

"We'll start seeing each other again when I'm back." He dragged deeply on his cigarette, the orangey glow lighting up his face. I'd always hated the smoky taste when he kissed me, even after he'd munched his way through half a packet of mints.

"When *will* you be back?" I tried to keep the whine out of my voice.

"I don't know, babe." He blew out a steady stream of smoke, then pulled me closer. "When I feel at one with Mother Nature. Or when I run out of cash."

"But when did you decide?" I shouted as the music switched to R.E.M.'s "Shiny Happy People," telling us to throw our love around. Oh, yeah? The only thing I wanted to throw was a slap in Dwayne's direction.

He shrugged. "I booked it last month. I—"

"Last *month*?" This time there was definite whining, and I cringed.

"See." Dwayne shook his head, and I realized he must have confused my self-directed contempt for emotional upset related to his imminent departure. "This is why I didn't bring it up. I knew you wouldn't understand." And then he actually pursed his lips.

God, I hated it when he sulked. Come to think of it, over the past few weeks I'd hated pretty much everything he'd done. A few days ago I'd told him I was ill so I didn't have to endure *The Last Boy Scout*. I'd watched *Fried Green Tomatoes* alone that night instead. The week before I'd said my period had come early because I wasn't in the mood. Again. In fact, I couldn't remember the last time I'd been in the mood. But all that aside, dumping me on New Year's Eve was a shitty move by any standards.

"You know what, Dwayne? Have a great trip and a happy bloody 1992."

I pushed past him, fully intent on retrieving my coat from the back of the bar so I could go home, curl up in bed and ignore the rest of the world's celebrations. But the bar's resident DJ Joe had other plans. The music stopped.

"Okay, everybody," he said into his mike. "Grab your partner—or whoever you'd like to have as your partner *tonight*—and get ready. Only a few more seconds. Gird your loins, people, because… Here. We. Go!"

Everybody chanted, "Ten…"

As I pushed past a few more sweaty bodies I felt a hand on my arm.

"Nine…"

I was ready to turn around and tell my now *ex*-boyfriend to let me go. But when I heard a man's voice in my ear, it wasn't Dwayne's.

"It's bad luck to start the New Year without a kiss."

"…eight…seven…"

Oh, come *on*. Did I have a Lonely Hearts Loser sign stuck to my back? Nice voice, though.

"…six…five…four…"

I turned around. Eyes, those *eyes*. Gray. Clear. Mesmerizing. I couldn't help but stare.

"…three…two…"

"I'm Liam," he said. His face moved closer. He put his index finger underneath my chin.

"…one."

"And I've wanted to kiss you all night."

I didn't recall hearing the shouts of, "Happy New Year."

All I could remember were his arms sliding around my waist, mine around his neck, and the multicolored fireworks going off in my head when our lips touched.

NOW
ABBY

HE STOOD IN the doorway of Barbara Baker's kitchen. Liam. My ex. The one man I'd loved more than life itself. I'd walked away from him, twice, and the last time I'd told him we'd never, *ever* see each other again. And yet, here he was. Living in the house next door.

"Hello," he said, and swallowed. He looked at Sarah, then at me with those gray eyes. Wolf eyes, I used to call them. Hypnotic, hungry, searching.

I took a deep breath, realizing I'd held it since I'd heard his voice. My legs were planted firmly on the ground, heels pushed in, my arms crossed. A statue. What the hell should I say?

"Hello," I muttered. "I—I'm…pleased to meet you."

Had I said that out loud?

After a second he turned to Nate and shrugged. "I'm sorry." He smiled, and I noticed his laughter lines had become a lot deeper since we'd last seen each other, but they suited him. "I'm hopeless with names." He looked at me again. "Nate told me, but I'm afraid I've forgotten."

"Abby," Nate, Nancy and I said together, my voice twice as loud as theirs combined.

"Abby," Liam said slowly, deliberately. "So sorry. I'm Liam."

"Well, yes, we—" I stopped myself. We knew each other. Of course we did. I wanted to laugh, make a joke about it being a small world and wasn't it a strange coincidence, ha, ha, ha. But I kept quiet. I should have said something. Made it abundantly clear there was history between us. A shared past. I had the opportunity. But I didn't say anything. I didn't *want* to say anything.

Liam held out his hand, and when I shook it I swear an electric current passed between us. It flowed out of him and into me, washing over my entire body like a surfer's wave. I hadn't felt his touch for so long, but it was as if every pore of my skin remembered him. I looked into his eyes, tried to gauge his reaction, wondered if he'd felt it, too. He must have, surely. It had been too intense to ignore.

"Pleasure to meet you, too." He let go of my fingers, his eyes giving nothing away, and turned to my daughter. "You're Sarah?"

Sarah nodded.

"Can I get you a Coke?" Liam asked, and she nodded again. "How about you, Abby?" He held out a Stella, and I watched a drop of condensation run down the bottle neck and onto his hand. I wanted to reach out and touch it, but instead I cleared my throat.

"Water would be great."

It seemed impossible to take my eyes off him as he grabbed a can from the fridge and handed it to Sarah. When he passed me a glass of water his fingers seemed to linger that little bit too long. My mouth went dry as old toast, so I swallowed a big gulp to compensate, almost emptying the entire glass in one go.

He'd hardly changed since I'd seen him. He always used to keep in shape—ran four or five times a week along with frequent visits to the gym. His dark blond hair had grayed slightly at the temples, and I liked it cut in that style, short at the back and slightly longer on top. Something I could run my fingers through when...

"So, Abby." Nancy smiled brightly, plucking my mind away from the restricted area. "Nate said you grew up around Preston?"

"Uh...yes."

"How funny," she said, smile brighter still. "Like we told Nate, that's where we've moved from."

"Really?" I tried not to look at Liam but noticed my voice sounded a little shrill.

"Broughton," Liam said.

"And Nate mentioned you're from Hutton, Abby?" Nancy said, and all I could do was nod.

"Don't let her accent fool you," Nate said. "She's a Northerner, born and bred. You might even know some of the same people, maybe—"

"Look," I said, "I'd better get back and start dinner. I just wanted to say a quick hello."

"Oh, don't worry." Nancy waved a hand. "We ordered pizza. There'll be enough for all of us. Should be here any minute. You'll stay, won't you?"

"I can't," I said quickly. "I've got some work to finish."

"Babe." Nate frowned.

"What do you do?" Nancy asked.

"I'm an accountant for Sterling Engineering but—"

"It's Saturday night," Nate said. "Can't it wait?"

"No. But you and Sarah can stay and—"

"Mum," Sarah half whispered out of the side of her mouth, giving me the evil eye at the same time. "*Don't* leave me here."

I ignored her, and everybody else. "I have a bit of a headache anyway."

"Oh, no." Nancy furrowed her brow and tilted her head to one side. "I hope you feel better soon."

"I'll come with you." Nate put down his beer.

I had to get out of there. Alone. "No need. I'll just lie down for a bit. See you later."

Nate smiled and blew me a kiss. "Later, hon."

"I'll see you out," Liam said.

"I'm fine."

"I insist."

As we walked away from the kitchen where Nate and Nancy had started talking about the abysmal winter and how they couldn't wait for spring, Liam whispered, "God, Abby, this is a surprise, I—"

Zac came down the stairs, nodding his head to the music coming from his bright orange headphones. We watched him make the peace sign toward us before disappearing into the kitchen.

I spun around to face Liam. "What the *hell* are you doing here?"

He stared at me and held up a hand. "Hang on. I could ask you the same thing."

"I've lived here. For *years*."

"I didn't know."

"Are you sure?"

Liam exhaled. "Abby, please."

"So why here?"

"Why are you being so hostile?"

I pressed my fingers over my eyelids until I saw stars, then looked at him again. "Why *here*?"

Liam ran a hand through his hair and lowered his voice. "Internal promotion at the bank. Nancy found the house. It was a good deal. She wants to redecorate and—"

"That's it?"

"What do you mean?"

He was so close to me now. I could barely stop myself from pulling him toward me. I stepped back until my shoulders touched the wall, hoping I might disappear into the garish paper. "You honestly didn't know we lived here?"

"No, I didn't. Christ, it was such a shock. When Nate said his wife's name was Abby Sanders and that she was from Preston…well…I decided it couldn't be you. Too much of a fluke, you know…" I blinked rapidly and he put a hand on my arm. "I'm sorry I didn't say anything in there. It was a gut reaction."

"I know. Me, too."

Liam swallowed. "Should we go back and tell them? We could say we only just recognized each other."

My eyes widened. "No," I whispered. "That's crazy. Not after…" I couldn't bring myself to say it. "No."

He leaned in a little closer. I could smell a hint of his aftershave. I wanted him to reach out and touch me, but instead he put his hands in his pockets and said, "It's good to see you. Completely surreal and unexpected, but good."

My shoulders dropped a little. "You can't stay here, in this house."

"Abby." He smiled that bloody gentle smile of his. "We don't have much of a choice. Whether we like it or not, we're neighbors now."

Head shaking, I said, "I can't see you. I told you last time… And before when…when Tom…" My eyes filled with tears, and I willed them to dry instantly. I had to be strong. I couldn't give Liam an excuse to comfort me, however much I wanted him to.

"Oh, Abby." He looked at me. "You're not even close to getting over losing Tom, are you? Even after all these years." When I looked away Liam sighed. "Listen—"

My eyes flashed back to his. "No. *You* listen. We have to stay away from each other."

"Hey…" The hurt in his eyes almost took my breath away and made me want to put my arms around him, hold him close and whisper I was sorry.

"Keep away," I seethed instead as I glared at him and yanked open the door. Once outside I filled my lungs with gulps of crisp, cool air.

And then panic took over. I'd left my husband and daughter with my ex-boyfriend. Should I go back in, say I'd miraculously recovered from my headache? No. I couldn't be in the same room as Liam. I'd told him to stay away, but they were just words. Words to convince myself the feelings spilling out of my heart weren't real. But I knew him—all of him—inside and out, and he'd never say anything to Nate. He'd never say anything to anyone.

I ran back to our house—the one I shared with my *husband*— my heart pounding, and all I could think of was Liam. Liam. Liam. *Liam.* I tried to slow my breathing as I stepped inside and flicked on the light.

"Tom." I looked up at the picture of my brother. "Oh, shit, Tom. What am I going to do?"

But all I got in return was his permanently youthful smile, and I imagined him shrugging and saying, "I don't know, Shabby. You're really fucked this time."

THEN
ABBY

WHAT AN IDIOT. An absolute, dumb, stupid, moronic *idiot*. Me. Not Liam.

We were five days into 1992. Five days since I'd met Liam at Rowley's. Five days since he'd kissed me. Five days since I'd seen him. *Five*.

It may as well have been five hundred.

Lying in bed wrapped up under my blankets, I could still feel his lips on mine, his hands pressing into the small of my back, pulling me closer. The scent of his musky aftershave lingered on the scarf I'd worn that night, and I'd slept with it ever since. I closed my eyes as I nuzzled it, rubbing the fabric against my cheek. God, he was *hot*. But that wasn't all— he was *nice*, too.

I wanted to call him. I would have if I hadn't been such a dumb, stupid, moronic *idiot*. I'd said he should take my number. Insisted on it, in fact. Why? Because I was sure he'd phone? I shook my head. No. More like because I was sure he *wouldn't*. If I didn't have his number it meant I couldn't call him. And if I couldn't call him, I wouldn't look like an imbecile when he made some crap excuse about not seeing me again, like "my dog died," or "I'm running away to join the circus," perhaps even "sorry I'm being abducted by aliens tonight." I hadn't heard all of those before, but a couple came pretty close.

"You're so beautiful," Liam had whispered after our first kiss at Rowley's, and I couldn't believe how genuine he sounded. But guys like him were never genuine. Everything about him seemed too good to be true, from his dirty blond hair that fell slightly into his gray eyes, to his apparent kind, gentle nature. He couldn't be real. In my experience, guys like that always turned out to be phonies.

In any case, I'd already decided I wouldn't be going home with him. If, *if* the chemistry between us turned into a long-term thing—and how, after knowing him for all of an hour, was I so sure it would—I didn't want to be the girl who had sex on the first night. Quite a departure from my usual open-to-pretty-much-anything self.

He'd taken my hand, and we danced together in the corner, arms wrapped around each other, moving slowly even to the fast songs. We barely spoke. Nothing needed to be said.

"Hey, mate." Dwayne had appeared next to us and put a hand on Liam's shoulder. "What the hell," he'd yelled over the music, "are you doing with my girlfriend?"

"*Your* girlfriend?" Liam had shouted back, shrugging off Dwayne's grip, towering over him and frowning. He took my hand and held it over his heart. "Sorry, *mate*. But you must be mistaking her for someone else."

Dwayne's eyes narrowed but he took a step back. Then he looked me up and down as his lips curled into a sneer. "You're only doing this because I'm going to Thailand." He turned back to Liam. "She's all yours, *mate*." He stomped away with the scent of another Benson & Hedges trailing in his wake.

Liam looked at me and shrugged. "Why's he going to buy land?"

I laughed. And that was the moment I knew I was in trouble. Big trouble. I'd heard about love at first sight, feeling like you'd been struck by lightning, that it was meant to be and all those other clichés. I'd heard about it, but I'd never actually believed it. It was no secret I had trouble keeping hold of relationships—any kind of relationships—something my kid brother pointed out on a fairly regular basis. But even he agreed he'd gone too far the last time.

"You've broken another guy's heart? Jesus, Abby, I bet you're like Dad," Tom had said a few months back. "He's probably on his tenth ex-wife by now. You two are destroying both sexes for the rest of us."

I didn't speak to Tom for a week. Not until he came over to my flat and apologized, groveling with two bottles of my favorite wine and a very large curry.

But now, here I was. Lying in bed in my little flat above the Kettle Club Tea & Coffee Shop. Almost *five days* after kissing the most handsome and interesting guy at the pub, wishing he'd call. And then the phone rang.

"Hello?" I held my breath.

"Shabby!"

I groaned. "Don't call me Shabby, Tommy."

"Then don't call me Tommy, Shabby. I'm not three."

"Okay, Golden Child, Oh, Chosen One."

Tom made growling noises down the phone, and I grinned. Most of our calls started off this way.

"What are you doing?" he said.

"Lying in bed."

Tom laughed. "You're not still nursing your New Year's Eve hangover, surely?"

I sighed. "No."

"Still no news from eye-guy?"

"Nope."

He sniffed. "Maybe his beer goggles wore off."

"He wasn't drunk." At least I was pretty sure he hadn't been. Oh, god. Maybe he had. Maybe he didn't even remember me. Maybe—

"Well, in that case he must've thought you're a rubbish kisser," Tom continued, obviously enjoying himself. "What did you eat that night? Onions? Garlic? *Snails?*" I opened my mouth but couldn't think of a clever answer quickly enough before he said, "Or I suppose he could have lost your number."

"Yeah. Let's go with that." I rolled my eyes. "At least it'll make me feel better."

"You said his name was Liam? Short for William?"

"Yeah."

"Jefferson."

The words hung in the air for a while.

"How did you know?"

Tom cleared his throat. "You must have told me."

"I did *not*. I know I didn't." I laughed. "Come on. How did you know? Spill. Or else."

The grin in Tom's voice was audible. "William Jefferson." He let out a half snort. "Sounds like a future Prime Minister. Anyway, his phone number is…"

My head spun as he reeled off the digits. I grabbed a pen from my bedside table, smoothed out a tissue and scribbled the digits, trying not to rip the Kleenex in the process. Then I stopped. I knew my brother, practical joker supreme, far too well.

"Okay," I said. "You got me."

"What do you mean?" His voice sounded strangely honest, and I pictured him scrunching up his face like the time I'd explained algebra to him. "I'm not kidding or anything."

"Yeah you are, you bastard of a little brother." I laughed. "I bet that's the number for a Chinese restaurant."

"No, it isn't."

I think my heart skipped an entire tune, let alone a beat. "A pizza place then? A strip joint? The police station?"

"Nope. Nope. And nope again."

Pause.

"So you're not making this up?"

He sighed loudly. "Negative, Shabby. I happen to be very resourceful. A friend of a friend of a friend was at Rowley's, too. Apparently Liam said he met a cool girl there on New Year's Eve, then lost her number. Been looking for her since."

"No way!"

"But, thinking about it," he chuckled, "that can't be you, can it? He said a *cool* girl."

"Sod *off*!"

Tom laughed. "Apparently he's searching the entire area. Asking everybody if they know an Abby Sanders." He sniffed. "Well, *I* know an Abby Sanders."

"Seriously?"

"Cinderella, my darling," he said in a high-pitched voice, "you *shall* go to the ball."

I wanted to stick my arms through the phone and hug him. "You're the best, Tom."

"Anything for you, my dearest, most favorite sister ever."

"Hey!" I grinned. "I'm your only sister."

"Yeah, I know. Even though I asked for a different one every Christmas."

If we'd been in the same room I'd have punched him. Not hard, just hard enough.

"So are you going to call him?" he said.

"No!"

"Why the hell not? After all that?"

"I can't. It's not…it's not…" I hesitated, before very quietly adding, "ladylike."

Tom burst out laughing. "Oh, come *on*. It's nineteen ninety-*two*, not the fifties. And since when are you a lady?"

"Ha, ha."

"He wouldn't track you down if he wasn't interested. Trust me." I couldn't deny the solidity of my brother's reasoning. The little smarty-pants. "Anyway, it's your call. No pun intended. So…and I'm pretty sure I know the answer, but I'll ask anyway. Are you coming over for dinner tonight?"

"Uh, I don't think so."

"Jeez, Abby, are you and Mum ever going to kiss and make up?"

"Negative, Tommy. Is Sophia coming?"

"Not sure." Tom's voice changed from happy to sad in an instant. "Haven't spoken to her for three days."

"Again?" She was such a bitch. He deserved better.

"I know what you're thinking," he said. "Sophia's a bitch. I deserve better."

"No, I wasn't," I lied. Sometimes our connection even freaked us out. "I, uh…"

"Yeah, you were. Look, come over. Mum said she'd like to see you."

I snorted. "No, she didn't. Speak to you later?"

"Will do, sis. But put Liam out of his misery and call him, yeah?"

"Yeah." I paused. "Tom?"

"Yeah?" When I didn't reply for a few seconds he said, "Love you, too, big sis."

As I dropped the phone to the floor and pulled the blankets over my head, I let out a scream and kicked my legs. Once partial dignity was restored I retrieved the phone, took a few deep breaths and dialed the number on the tissue. Being a lady was vastly overrated anyway.

"Hello, this is Liam." His voice sounded as delicious as a hot chocolate on a cold winter's day. I wanted to stay in bed, wrapped up under the blankets, and listen to him speak for hours. Then I decided I'd better say something before he rang off.

"Hi, uh, it's Abby."

"Abby? Not *the* Abby from New Year's Eve?"

I smiled. "Well, that depends."

"On what?"

"How many Abbys you kissed at Rowley's."

He laughed. "One, promise. God, I'm so glad I found you."

"Well," I said, trying to hide my smile, "technically, I found *you*."

"I would have called days ago, but I lost your number," Liam said quickly. "And I've been cursing myself ever since. I'm such an idiot. A moronic *idiot*." He cleared his throat and I grinned. "Anyway. Can I see you again? Today? For lunch? I can pick you up."

I whipped the blankets off and stood up so fast my head spun again. "Give me an hour."

NOW
NANCY

"THANKS AGAIN, NATE. Lovely to meet you, Sarah. Hope Abby's okay. Night." I closed the front door with a contented sigh and turned toward Liam, who stood behind me. I thought I saw a frown cross his face but as soon as my eyes met his, he smiled.

I put my arms around him and squeezed, relishing how our bodies still fit together perfectly, despite being married for so long. Liam kissed the top of my head, and I couldn't help noticing how he didn't really hug me back. I decided he was probably exhausted from the move, so I squeezed harder to make up for it.

"I have a feeling we'll be very happy here," I said.

"Still no regrets about moving, then?" he said.

"I already told you," I said with a smile. "The most important thing is that I'm with you. Still, can you believe we've been here a day and we've already got such amazing neighbors?"

"Yeah, great," Liam said, with less enthusiasm than I'd expected as he extricated himself from my embrace. "Although Zac didn't seem too impressed."

"Really? I thought he was quite taken with Sarah."

Liam laughed softly. "No, he wasn't. He hardly talked to her."

"Pah. That's his usual nonchalant way. But I know he liked her."

"Oh, boy," he said, heading toward the kitchen. "You're going to tell me it was your women's intuition again, aren't you?"

I forced a laugh. "You know my track record. I'm never wrong." He had no idea how desperately I wanted that to be true. I'd always been proud of my ability to pick up signals everybody else seemed oblivious to, but I was petrified I'd been wrong once, years ago. Only Liam would have been able to reassure me otherwise, and even imagining him not being able to do so made my palms clammy and my heart speed up. I pushed the thought back into a remote corner of my mind, willing it to keep quiet and hold still. "Anyway," I said casually as I followed him down the hall, "what did you think of Abby?"

He turned away with a shrug and picked up the remaining slice of pizza nobody had had the courage or inclination to polish off. "Shall I chuck this out?"

"Here, put it in this for Zac. He'll have it for breakfast." I handed him a plastic container and wondered if I should let the Abby question go. Comparing myself to other women was an old habit I'd never been able to break. A bit like eating sweets, and singing in the shower, or having two sugars in my tea, even when I went on a diet, which seemed to be every other Monday. "So, what did you think of her?"

He shrugged again. "She wasn't here long enough for me to form an opinion."

"She's pretty." I kept my gaze on him to see if there was any kind of reaction but got nothing at all, which wasn't overly surprising. I'd always said he'd make a killing at poker. Sometimes I wished I could crawl into his brain to find out what was really going on in there. Then again, it was probably better I didn't. What if I found something I didn't like?

"Pretty, huh?" he said. "Did you think so?"

"Well, not chocolate-box pretty, but *very* attractive. And she has a great figure."

He looked at me. "Far too skinny. But now you…*you* have a great figure."

His words were like aloe vera on a sunburn. "Yeah, and I bet I look fab after lugging all those boxes around." I clicked my tongue and rolled my eyes more at myself than at Liam because, while I continually craved his praise, believing it had never been my strong suit. Even after he'd told me, years ago, that doubting his compliments was akin to calling him a liar, I still had trouble accepting them.

Liam smiled. "Honestly, love, you look great. And I'm not the only one who thinks so. Nate's eyes grew stalks when he first saw you outside."

"Stop it. You're being crazy," I said, even though I secretly agreed. I'd noticed Nate's reaction, too. And I had to admit, only to myself of course, that I'd liked it, especially when I'd met Abby. She was the kind of woman who made people trip over their own two feet. The kind who needed five minutes in the morning to look gorgeous, when it took us lesser mortals an hour, and even then we never achieved the same impossible standard. Abby made me feel inferior just by breathing, so the fact that her husband had even glanced at me made my heart rate quicken. The fact that Liam had noticed it too made me practically want to burst.

"You went a bit quiet when you came back with the beer," I said. "I thought maybe Abby had made a huge impression on you."

What was wrong with me? I was basically forcing him to find her attractive, pushing him to admit something that would make me feel terrible as soon as he uttered it, but I really couldn't help myself. I'd done it at school, too. Pointed out the prettiest girl to the boy I liked, then pretended not to be disappointed when he'd asked her on a date instead. But I'd known they'd want to be together, it was only a matter of time. Why bother putting myself through unnecessary heartache? And although I'd got the most handsome boy in the end, it wasn't so much that I was surprised Liam had chosen me, it was the fact that he'd stayed. Even as he moved into his late forties, Liam was still a catch. He and Abby were comparable to a fine and expensive Château Lafite, whereas Nate and I, while perfectly okay really, were more of a reasonably priced Montepulciano.

I realized Liam hadn't answered, and I knew that was his way of signaling he had nothing more to say on the subject. It infuriated me sometimes, the way he decided—via his silence—when our conversations were over. Then again he'd told me a million times how he found me attractive. It really wasn't his fault I never accepted it.

"It's been a long day. I'm going to bed," he said. "Are you coming?"

"Only if you'll inaugurate our new bedroom with me." I smiled as I cocked my head to one side and raised my eyebrows, images of our naked bodies pressed together flashing through my mind. "What do you say?"

Liam shook his head. "Not tonight, love. I'm knackered."

"I'll be up later then." I tried to keep the clipped tone out of my voice, the one he'd accused me of using when he last refused me. He didn't say no often, but whenever he did, it felt like a rejection—which it was, of course—but I always thought his reasons of being too tired or having to get up early were an excuse, and that in reality there was something wrong with me. I was getting fat, unattractive, or he was bored of me. Sex meant my husband still wanted me, desired me, loved me. Why did he have trouble understanding that?

"Good night, then." Liam turned away without kissing me.

And as I stood there for a few seconds, watching him leave the kitchen, I suddenly had an awful sinking feeling that maybe this time, his refusal had nothing to do with me at all.

NOW

NATE

BY THE TIME Sarah and I got home from Liam and Nancy's, Abby was in bed, curled up like a cat, snoring gently. I backed out of the bedroom and plonked myself in front of the TV downstairs.

"Night, Dad." Sarah gave me a hug before vanishing upstairs, clutching her phone. Claire was probably on Snapchat standby, waiting to hear all about next door's additions. I gave a laissez-faire shrug. My daughter would be lucky to get to sleep before dawn and would spend most of Sunday lounging around like I used to when I was her age.

She'd seemed pretty comfortable after Abby left us at Liam and Nancy's. She'd even told them about a school project she was working on—the most efficient way to recycle used tires, of all things. While I chatted with Nancy about the neighborhood, I heard Liam ask Sarah tons of questions about her project. Not only was he a good-looking bloke, even I had to admit that, but an intelligent and articulate one, too.

I'd kind of wanted to dislike him. Actually I'd pegged him as a prat when I first saw him in the back of the van. Make that a pretentious prat. The way he'd taken off his jacket and flexed his muscles—he might as well have whipped out his *bratwurst* to mark his territory. But actually, he was okay. From what I'd seen, he had the makings of a good neighbor. I could even picture having a beer with him, kicking back and playing some pool. And I'd been the reigning champion at university, so at least I'd beat Muscle Man at something.

I stretched out on the sofa, extended my arms and legs as far as I could, then yawned loudly. I had two episodes of my favorite zombie show to catch up on, something best done alone. Sarah had said it was lame, and the undead always freaked Abby out.

Years ago, when we saw *28 Days Later* (my pick, her nightmare), Abby had spent the entire time hiding behind a pillow. It surprised me all the more when she'd announced she was going to be tough and suggested *World War Z* for one of our anniversaries. Not as surprised as she'd been when those zombies looked like they were on speed. I swear she had an entire escape route planned from then on. If there was ever a zombie apocalypse, I'd survive providing I could keep up with Abby. Fat chance. My brains would be their first snack.

After making sure the hero lived to fight another day, I had a brief shower and slipped between the cool sheets. I thought about making love to Abby but remembered her headache, so instead I gently kissed the nape of her neck. When she didn't stir, sleep came quickly and soundly for me, too.

Early light spilled into our room when I woke up Sunday morning. I groaned, realizing Abby was kneeling between my legs, her bare nipples softly brushing against the inside of my thighs. And I was harder than a cricket bat.

"Shhh," she whispered when I groaned again. "I want you."

"Uhhh," was about all I could manage, and when I thought

I was at the point of no return, she stopped, climbed on top and slid me inside her.

"It's my turn now." She grabbed my hands and pulled them onto her breasts. I felt her fingers between her legs, rubbing and touching. It drove me crazy. I had no idea if she still had a sore head, and frankly right then I didn't care.

But she whispered, "Fuck me. Come on, baby, fuck me. *Hard*."

God knows how, but some of the blood got diverted from my dick to my face to the point where I felt my cheeks glow like a beacon. Now, I'm no prude, but Abby, well, I didn't like *fucking* her. Yes, having sex with my wife was awesome. Better than beer, pool and England winning three World Cups in a row (I imagined). I'd heard some guys got tired of being with the same woman, but Abby still drove me crazy every single time. I'd taken care of her ever since I'd laid eyes on her, and *fucking* her seemed too…rough, uncaring, somehow.

I thrust a little faster, and she drove herself down onto me, eyes closed, back arched. It was savage; there was no tenderness at all. I felt like I could have been anybody, or that maybe I was surplus to Abby's requirements. As I wondered even more what the hell she was doing, I almost started to go limp. When she climaxed and collapsed on top of me, I held her as she gasped quietly.

"Did you come, too?" she whispered.

"Of course," I lied.

She raised her head and looked at me for a second, then slid off me and went to the bathroom. I rolled over and, when she came back a few minutes later, pretended to be asleep.

NOW
NATE

IT WAS JUST after six on Wednesday evening, and Abby and I lay on the floor. We hadn't made it to the bed—deeming the extra few meters an unnecessary obstacle course, a waste of precious time. When I'd got home from work, she'd surprised me by walking down the stairs dressed only in emerald green, satiny underwear.

I'd fleetingly wondered what had gotten into her, but then realized we could have sex for the second time in four days. Seeing as my performance hadn't been great on Sunday morning, I stopped wondering and started *doing*.

Afterward, I stretched my arms out, momentarily too exhausted to get up, exhaled deeply and pulled some clean towels from a plastic laundry basket barely within my reach. I covered Abby's shoulders with the warm fabric. She shivered and raised her head from where it had been nestled on my chest.

"Hey," she said, smiling, "I just folded those."

My fingers traced the length of Abby's back, and she sighed as she propped herself up on one elbow. I noticed the shadows under her eyes and realized she probably wasn't sleeping well again. Before I could ask her what was going on, she said, "How was your day?"

"Ugh," I groaned, not wanting to spoil the afterglow with stories about the office.

"That bad?" She wrinkled her nose.

"Nah," I said. "Business as usual, you know? Got another deal done today. That's four in less than a fortnight."

"Congrats, Nate," she said and kissed my chest. "Fantastic."

I had to agree it was a pretty great result. I'd worked in recruitment for more than two decades, started fresh out of uni. But it was hardly earth-shattering stuff. I couldn't say I hated my job, nor was I exactly passionate about it. I'd always been envious of people who said they loved what they did, or they'd always known what they wanted to do with their lives, what they wanted to *be*. On the other hand, I made good money, was a recession veteran, had worked my way up the corporate ladder to IT Sales Director. I could hardly whine.

My fingers slid through Abby's silky hair. "How about you? You okay?"

She blinked three times. Slowly. "I'm fine." A small smile. "Everything's fine."

She looked about as fine as I did when my brother, Paul, set fire to my hair at church one Christmas. Accidentally, of course, or so he'd claimed. "You sure?"

I should've bet money on her answer.

"Yep."

Ka-ching!

She got up and reached for my hastily discarded boxer shorts, which now dangled off the side of the bed. As she passed them to me her face relaxed again, and she winked. I smiled back and watched as she slipped on her underwear,

T-shirt and jeans. When Abby bent over to pick up the towels I'd pulled out of the basket, I clung to mine as if it had the makings of a magic carpet.

Abby was a bit of a neat freak. Okay, a lot of a neat freak. She was the epitome of the saying, "A place for everything and everything in its place." Except her version included family, friends and, I'd come to accept after all this time, feelings. She was better at keeping the lid on stuff than Tupperware. I'd acknowledged a long time ago I'd never completely know my wife, however much I wanted to, or tried.

"So Sarah's at Claire's again?" I said. "They working on that tire project?"

"Oh, Nate." Abby laughed. "You're so wonderfully naive. I bet you five pounds they'll gossip far too late and barely make it to school on time."

I grinned. How our daughter continually pulled A's out of her bag was a mystery to me. She definitely got her brains from her mother because I'd battled like a bastard for every B I'd brought home.

Abby dumped the briefly used towels into the laundry basket (neat freak alert), then said, "I don't feel like cooking tonight. Shall we get some food in? I fancy Indian."

I gave her two thumbs-up and made an attempt to move. "Deal. I'll go."

She held out a hand in a stay-put gesture. "I'm dressed. You chill out, okay? There's some wine and beer in the fridge."

"Thanks." I grabbed her hand and kissed it. "How kind of you, my beloved."

"Anything for you, husband dearest." She curtsied and laughed.

And with that, she was gone, leaving me lying on the floor with a tepid towel, wondering why her laugh had somehow sounded a touch too loud.

NOW
ABBY

AFTER CLOSING THE front door behind me I cast a surreptitious glance toward Liam's house, hoping he was outside and I'd catch a glimpse. Seconds later I cursed myself for thinking about him again and got in Nate's car before easing it out of the driveway, forcing myself to keep my eyes—and all of my thoughts—away from Liam and on the road.

A few minutes into my trip to the Funky Bombay restaurant my shoulders dropped. I switched on the radio and hummed along to a tune that sounded suspiciously like what once had been Sarah's favorite boy band, but whose name I could never remember. I grinned and thought I'd better not tell her or she'd make fun of me until Christmas, chastising me for never knowing what was and, more important, what wasn't trendy.

The band had lost its prime position on Sarah's bedroom wall years ago, replaced by some young actor who sported a curly mop of long, dark hair and a sullen expression. I told Sarah I thought he was *smokin'*, and she'd looked at me with wide eyes until I'd laughed, saying at her age I used to think my mum was dead from the neck down. Although in my mother's case it might actually have been true.

Sarah and I had been getting along far better the past couple of days, especially after she'd let slip what she thought of Zac.

"Honestly, Mum," she said Monday after school, "he's an idiot. You should have seen the way he looked at me on Saturday. Really, he's, like, a total douche."

Normally I might have said, "So is he *like* a total douche or *is* he a total douche?" But instead of making a snide remark about her grammar I tried not to punch the air. "Sounds like you weren't impressed." I crossed my fingers and hoped she'd keep talking.

She did. "I mean, he's okay-looking..."

My heart sank a little. "Even with the fluffy brown hair and caramel highlights?"

"I know." She tutted. "*Highlights*, but they looked *good*. And I'm pretty sure every single supermodel in the world would kill for his cheekbones, *and* that he can stuff his face with five slices of pizza and be that fit."

"*Five?*"

"Uh-huh. I counted. God, if I ate that much my bum would be bigger than Wales." She exhaled deeply. "Anyway, so he's, like, on his third slice already and I comment on his T-shirt. He had that *Call of Duty* one, you know?" I shook my head and Sarah continued, "Anyway, I said it was cool..."

"Let me guess, he didn't like the compliment?"

"Hah. Worse. He goes, *Yeah, it's a game.* Like, duh. So I roll my eyes and say, *I know. I play loads of games.* And do you know what he said? He said he meant *video* games. Not *board* games. Can you believe it? God, like I bet he was picturing me playing *Detective Barbie* or *Clue* or something. And he made wide eyes at me, too."

I tried not to laugh. "So, what did you say?"

She sniffed. "That being a girl and liking fashion *and* video games aren't mutually exclusive."

"Good comeback."

"I know, right? I said Dad practically raised me on *Tomb Raider*. Told him I dressed up as Lara Croft for years." She laughed. "Remember the rucksack I filled with Medipacks we made from empty toilet rolls? I spent hours with that thing strapped to my back upside down, running around the garden with water pistols."

I smiled as I recalled the memory, a time when things had been so much easier between us. "And you won best Halloween costume at school."

"*Twice.*" Her smile disappeared all too quickly and was replaced with a frown. "Seriously, Zac's such an *idiot*."

"He definitely sounds arrogant," I said, making sure to tread carefully. "And just because he lives next door doesn't mean you have to have anything to do with him."

She crossed her arms. "I couldn't care less if I never see him again. Him living next door will have *nugatory* effects on my life."

"Nugatory?"

"It means trifling, inconsequential," she said proudly. "I got it from that Word of the Day calendar you gave me."

After that, she asked me for advice on her homework. And when she read her presentation out to me, her eyes and voice eager for praise, I gave it to her by the bucket load. She was probably wondering about the source of my continually sprightly mood, and, knowing the somewhat cynical view of the world I'd bestowed on my daughter, she maybe even speculated I had a bag full of uppers.

I sighed. Now that I'd driven far away enough from home

I could admit the truth to myself. The past few days had been hell. At first I'd been in a state of panic after seeing Liam on Saturday, then it had given way to curiosity, which was worse because everyone knows the saying about what it did to the cat.

For the past three mornings, I'd either left even earlier than usual, or made sure Liam's car was gone before I ventured outside. As soon as I got home Monday evening, I'd tidied up the garage so I could park my car in there, avoiding a chance encounter. When I saw him again it had to be on my terms. I wanted—no, *needed*—to be prepared.

Of course, I knew my attempt of grabbing the upper hand was window dressing. I reasoned if I was able to control my actions, then maybe I'd become master of my thoughts, too. I'd hardly stopped thinking about him. Where was he? What was he doing? Was he thinking about me? About us? What would he say the next time I saw him? Because, inevitably, there would be a next time.

At night I lay in bed awake, wondering if he was making love to Nancy, and it made my stomach churn. I imagined his lips and fingers gliding over her skin and her silky soft curves, the memory of me a transparent ghost floating somewhere at the back of his mind, whispering to him, demanding attention yet remaining entirely ignored. Then again, maybe while he was thrusting into her he imagined she was me. Like I did when I was with Nate.

The surprised expression on my husband's face when I'd walked down the stairs in my new underwear a while earlier had quickly given way to a look of utter devotion. It almost made me rush back to the bedroom and pull my clothes on. But it wasn't cheating, not technically. And I wanted…well, not Nate, not exactly, but I needed to feel his desire for me, both physical and otherwise, so I could keep pretending it was enough.

That it had ever been enough.

THE NEIGHBORS

NOW
NATE

THE DRAUGHT GOT to me a few minutes after Abby left, so I forced myself up. I grabbed the tartan pajama bottoms Sarah had given me one Christmas, and rescued my badly crumpled Genesis T-shirt from the floor. I was pulling on my left sock when the doorbell rang.

"Oh…hi, Nate." Liam smiled when I opened the front door, and I noticed how sharp he looked. His long black coat, charcoal gray suit, blue shirt and paisley tie made me feel like a hobo. He indicated behind him with his thumb. "I'm in luck. I thought I saw your car leave."

"Abby must've taken it. She's gone to get Indian for dinner."

"Yum." He patted his flat middle. Funny, I'd imagined he thought carbs were witchcraft.

I frowned. "So…?"

Liam cleared his throat. "Yeah, uh, I'm glad I caught you." A slight shrug. "Uh…do you know any good repairmen? The, ah, heating's a bit…weird."

"*Weird?* Has it turned into the TARDIS or something?"

He laughed. "No, but that would be cool. It made these, uh, clunking noises last night. Nancy didn't hear a thing. Never does when she's asleep. But I don't want it dying on us, you know?"

"Want me to come and have a look at it?"

"Oh, no." He held up his hands. "I don't want to put you out."

"Come in for a sec." I waved him inside. "You'll freeze your nads off." As I closed the door behind him, I added, "I don't mind giving you a hand. Doesn't make sense to call a repairman if it's an easy fix."

"Well...only if you're sure?"

"'Course. I'm playing volleyball tomorrow. How about Friday evening?"

"Yeah, great, thanks. It'll give Nancy another reason to cook you dinner."

"Oh?" That sounded intriguing.

"Yeah, she wants to invite you all over soon." He grinned. "Keep you in our good books. I've always had two left hands when it comes to anything manual. Much to her despair."

Of course that was why Nancy wanted me to come over. Why else would it be? I laughed at my stupidity. "No worries. I got my DIY knowledge from my grandfather. Taught me everything I know." I nodded toward him. "Looks like you're just getting back from work."

"Yeah." Liam stretched out his neck and loosened his tie, then stuffed it into his coat pocket. "Long day."

"Finance, isn't it? That's what you said the other night?"

"Yup. Typical banker, I'm afraid. But I'm one of the good guys. Honest." He held up his fingers in a Boy Scout salute.

I grinned, thinking some male company might not be too bad for a while, seeing as I was permanently outnumbered in my house. Even our dead cat had had a pair of ovaries, for Christ's sake. "Got time for a beer?"

He seemed to hesitate again. "Won't Abby mind?"

"'Course not. And she won't be back for half an hour anyway. She probably went to the Funky Bombay."

Liam laughed out loud. "The Funky Bombay?"

"Yeah. It's farther away but worth it. I'll give you the address if you like. Dump your coat on the banister and go on through to the back."

As we walked across the hall I saw Liam look at Tom's picture. His steps slowed, and I wondered if he'd ask about the guy in the picture. It happened sometimes, and the photograph was the first thing Abby had hung up when we'd moved in. "I want it on the landing," she'd said, handing me the hammer and nails. "So I can say good-morning and good-night to him when I walk past. You don't mind, do you?"

Of course I didn't mind. Although, and I knew this was a selfish bastard attitude, I sometimes resented Tom, but at least I felt like a prick for thinking it. He still had such a solid grip on Abby, unrelenting and strong. I wanted her to move past the accident. Not forget—you can't forget something like that—but I wanted her to forgive herself.

I was relieved when Liam kept walking. Once in the kitchen, I handed him a Heineken from the fridge.

"Thanks," he said. I watched as he took a sip, leaned against the counter, then crossed his arms. He was at least three inches taller than me and I could see the faint outline of his biceps through his suit. Fit fucker. He leaned to the side and pointed to the conservatory. "Is that a pool table?"

"Yeah. Fancy a game?"

"Love to. I'm a crap player," Liam said as he took off his

jacket and unbuttoned the cuffs of his shirt, rolling the sleeves back in preparation for battle. "But you're on."

"Are you guys settling in okay?" I said as I racked up the balls and broke, potting two of them instantly and trying not to grin too much.

"Nice shot. Yeah, we're getting there. The new job's pretty busy, so Nancy's doing most of the unpacking. She reckons it's a good thing." He grimaced. "She says I'm a big tree who gets in the way."

I half snorted as I lined up my next shot, which I stupidly missed. "Abby wouldn't let me touch the kitchen when we moved in. Said she'd never find the tin opener again if I did." I stood up and surveyed the damage.

Liam smiled. "You guys have been here awhile?"

I picked up my beer and swallowed a mouthful, then realized I'd adopted the same pose as Liam, arms crossed, leaning against the pool table. Mirroring—a classic wannabe tactic. I shifted around and stuffed one hand in my pocket, wishing I was wearing a suit. "Almost seventeen years."

"And you grew up around here?" He took a shot but missed. *Amateur.*

"Wembley, where Mum was from. Dad moved south for work after he left school."

"They still live there?"

"No." I paused. "Mum's been gone sixteen years now. Two years less than Dad."

Liam stopped moving and looked at me. "Oh, shit, sorry, mate."

I looked at his furrowed brow, saw his head slightly tilt to one side. Something made me continue. "Dad was in the police force for over thirty years." I drank more beer. "Boasted about how he never took a sick day. Then he keeled over in the garden a year before he was supposed to retire. Can you believe it? Massive heart attack. Dead before he hit the ground. So much for never being ill." I walked around the table, potted another ball.

"Jesus," he said, "that's rough."

"Yeah. And cancer got my mum. It was shit." I shrugged. "Even my brother, Paul—"

"He died, too?"

I laughed. "No. He moved to Wales. Married with twins. What about your family?"

Liam shrugged. "Only child. Parents are still around, but we don't see them much. We, uh, don't exactly see eye to eye."

"Sounds like Abby," I said without thinking.

"Oh?" Liam raised his eyebrows. "How so?"

I hesitated, but only for a second. "Her relationship with her mum is messed up. Always has been. And her dad walked out when she was little. Can't imagine doing that to a kid." Why had I told him that when I knew how private Abby was about her life? She'd have my balls on a plate. "Anyway." I cleared my throat, shrugged and drained my beer. "What can you do?"

Liam didn't speak for a while. He took a couple of shots, which, I had to admit, weren't too bad, then said, "Family's really important to you, isn't it, Nate?"

I looked at him. It was such an odd thing for one guy to say to another, especially since we'd only just met. But the way he'd said it was even odder. Gentle, almost apologetic. A few seconds passed, and when he still didn't make eye contact, I said, "The most important thing in the world. Nothing else really matters, does it?"

He nodded slowly and finally looked up. "I suppose not."

As I shook my head I added, "Abby's estranged from her

parents by choice. Not necessarily hers, mind you, but me and my family?" I waved a hand. "Death and geography."

He nodded again but didn't say anything, then finished his beer, too.

"Another drink?" I said.

Liam looked at me and smiled. "Yeah, why not?"

NOW
ABBY

THE CAR IS filled with the warm aroma of cardamom and ginger, and yet, I shivered. My phone rang just as I pulled into our driveway, and I recognized my mother's number immediately. I sat quietly, holding my breath as if she'd know I was there if I moved, and waited for the beep that indicated a new voice mail.

"Hello, Abigail." My mother's tone was typically stern, almost businesslike, not what most people would expect from their own flesh and blood. "I need to speak to you. It's important. Please call me at your earliest convenience. Thank you."

I rolled my eyes. No way in hell would I call her. It had been a long time since we'd last spoken, a few years at least since we'd had a proper conversation that went beyond strained civilities. And I wasn't about to change that now, not after the way she'd treated me. I stabbed at my phone to ensure her message was deleted, gone forever. I took a deep breath, grabbed the paper bags and headed toward our front door.

Once inside, I placed the food on the stairs, slipped off

my boots and turned to hang up my jacket. That was when I spotted the long black coat casually draped over the banister. I reached out and touched the soft lapel, closed my eyes as I breathed in the familiar earthy scent of aftershave.

My heart pounded as I picked up the bags and walked toward the conservatory.

Nate's voice floated toward me. "…of course at that point I'd met my exes at a university party, a bar and a launderette."

"Well, the launderette sounds kind of original." Liam's voice, deep and gravelly. Manly, sexy. My stomach did a few flips, and I cursed under my breath, willing it to keep still.

"Ah," Nate said. "That's what my grandmother said, too, until she found out I'd been moderately wasted. Anyway, I'd better shut up or I'll bore the crap out of you." His laugh, a sound that had once made my stomach flutter gently, now left me lukewarm.

"He's a good man," I whispered to myself. "Nate's a *good* man."

"It sounds like you were really close to your family," Liam said.

I swallowed. How long had Liam been there? Had he been watching us from his window, waiting for me to leave so he could get to Nate? And if so, why? He'd been a little jealous when we were dating, sure, although he'd never seemed the vengeful type. But so many years had passed since we'd seen each other, I couldn't be sure I still knew him at all. And yet, everything about him, his voice, his laugh, the smell of his aftershave, was familiar. More than familiar. In so many ways it was as if we'd never been apart.

"Yeah, really close," Nate said before clearing his throat. "Like I said, my grandfather was my hero. I was devastated when he died. Going to his funeral was one of the saddest days of my life."

"I suppose after that you didn't go north much?"

I put a hand on my stomach in an attempt to stop it from lurching. Why was Liam asking all these questions? What did he want? And what was Nate doing, talking about his family to someone he'd just met?

"I wasn't planning on it at first," Nate said, and I wanted him to stop talking so I quickened my step, almost running down the hallway as Nate continued. "But destiny, fate or whatever the hell you want to call it decided otherwise because on the night of the funeral—"

"I'm back," I said as I charged into the room, my glance darting from Nate to Liam, whose beautiful gray eyes stared straight back into mine.

Nate, who was bent over at the waist, by the look of it about to pot the black, turned around. "Oh, hi." He put his cue down, walked over and took the bags from me before softly kissing my cheek. "I didn't hear you come in."

"Huh?" I swallowed. Had Liam tensed at Nate's romantic gesture or had I imagined it?

Nate frowned. "You okay? You were gone for ages." He went to the kitchen and put the bags down on the table.

"Uh, it was busy." I tore my gaze from Liam's and focused on my husband. "And, uh, then a rabbit or something ran in front of the car."

"Shit, did you hit it? You okay?" Nate put an arm around me, and I wanted to shake it off.

"No, and I'm fine," I said instead. "Spooked me a bit, that's all."

Liam cleared his throat. "I'd better go."

A few seconds ago I wished he wasn't in my house. Now

I almost told him to please sit back down and have another drink, but I managed to keep my mouth closed.

"Thanks for the beer and the games," he said to Nate. "Appreciate it, even if I was a crap opponent."

Liam, a crap opponent? He could have gone professional when we were going out. The local pool club had hailed him a prodigy, and ran under-the-table bets whenever he showed up. Why was he lying about that?

"No sweat," I heard Nate say as they moved into the hallway. "And I'll stop by on Friday."

Friday?

"Sorry?" Liam turned, and I saw his blank expression that probably matched my own.

"Yeah." Nate laughed. "You know, the heating?"

Liam smacked his forehead with his palm. "Brain overload. Yeah. Friday. Thanks." He looked at me. "Bye, Abby. Nice to see you again." He lingered for a moment, and I half expected him to say something else, but then he walked out, so I fled to the kitchen.

I'd barely started functioning again when I heard Nate's footsteps coming toward me. I tried to make myself look busy and normal by grabbing plates, cutlery and glasses.

"Mmm… This smells delicious." Nate ripped open the paper bags. Why did he have to tear into them like an animal? He could have easily lifted the containers out, then folded the bags and put them in the recycling bin.

I suppressed what would have been a churlish sigh and smiled instead. "Samosas, lamb korma and chicken vindaloo," I said, plopping paper napkins on the table.

"Korma *and* vindaloo?" Nate raised an eyebrow. "I didn't think you liked either."

Another smile. "They're your favorites. I wanted to do something nice for you."

His grin was so genuine and full of love, I could feel a lump rising at the back of my throat. I turned and grabbed the jug of lemon water from the fridge, then sat down when I was sure my eyes weren't glistening anymore.

Once we'd filled our plates, as casually as I could I said, "What's this about Friday?"

Nate waved his fork around, then swallowed. "Problem with the heating. I told Liam I'd have a look."

"I thought Barbara only had it installed last year? It'll be under warranty, won't it?"

Nate shrugged, dipped a samosa into the little plastic container of green sauce. "Maybe they don't know. I'll remind him. It's probably nothing anyway. He sounded a bit vague."

The knife in my hand felt like it weighed a ton, so I put it down. "What were you talking about when I came in?" I tried not to snap, telling myself for the twentieth time that day Nate was not at fault, he'd done nothing wrong. He never did anything bloody wrong.

"My family."

I sat a little straighter, reminding myself to breathe. "What did you say?"

"Not much. Told him a bit about Nana and Granddad, that's all."

It dawned on me that Liam must have been trying to size up the competition. Then I almost laughed out loud at how obsessive that sounded, as if I were the center of everybody's universe. Still... "You told him about your grandparents? Why?"

When Nate shrugged it made me want to slap him. If his attitude was any more laissez-faire, he'd be permanently horizontal. "It was a conversation, Abby. We had a couple of beers, played some pool. We got to talking. Why are you so bothered?"

"I don't like him."

"Liam?" He raised his eyebrows. "You've only known him five minutes."

I swallowed hard. "He's smug. I get this bad vibe from him."

How long could I keep this pretense up? Was I such a good actress that Nate couldn't see straight through my lies? Then again, it wasn't the first time I'd kept things from my husband. Secrets he'd never know about, could never know about. Secrets that would destroy him.

"Ah, crap." Nate mopped the sauce running down his chin with a napkin. "Well, you're going to have to give him another chance."

"Why?" My heart thumped wildly again as I wiped my clammy palms on my trousers.

"He said something about Nancy planning on cooking for us and—"

"I don't want—"

He held up a hand. "Nothing's planned yet. And it's just dinner. It's not like they asked us to move in. They seem nice to me. Give them a chance. Let the kids hang out, too."

"No." My voice came out louder than I'd intended. "No," I said, more quietly this time. "Sarah told me she hates Zac."

Nate laughed. "Sure she does."

"What's that supposed to mean? Did she say something to you?"

"No, but he's a good-looking kid, and—" Nate must have caught my startled look because he leaned over the table and put his hand on my arm. "Seriously, are you okay?"

I tried a smile, feeling like one of those clown dolls with a permanently painted-on grimace. All I needed was the ruffled shirt and polka dots to go with it, maybe a monkey with a pair of cymbals. "Yes, fine. Headache."

"Again?" Nate frowned.

I cleared my throat. "I think I had some trail mix with hazelnuts at work. You know how bad it can get when I eat those."

"I'll run you the bath after dinner."

"You don't need to, Na—"

"'Course I do."

His kind smile made me want to scream at him, shout that I didn't want him to run me the *fucking* bath and could he please, for once, not be so *fucking* nice and stop trying to *fucking* fix me all the time. Instead I said, "That would be lovely. Thanks, Nate."

As I desperately tried to stop my mind from rushing back to the past and everything it represented, I wished my husband could prepare a container of sulfuric acid for me to slip into instead.

THEN

ABBY

SIMPLY RED'S *STARS* played softly in the background of the Kettle Club Tea & Coffee Shop, lending the place a slightly cooler atmosphere than it actually deserved. Tom sat at the old wooden bar, a mug of steaming hot chocolate in front of him, complete with marshmallows, whipped cream and chocolate drizzle. I watched him sink his spoon into the fluffy top layer, take a big scoop and put it in his mouth.

"Mmmm." His eyes closed for a second. "Despite your dubious music choices, you make the best bloody hot chocolate in the world, Shabby. No wonder Stu asked you to run the place."

"Thanks," I said, thinking that at almost twenty-two, perfect beverage-making was about the only thing I could put on my anorexic-looking list of work experience. "You know, you'll give yourself a heart attack with that stuff," I added, then told myself to shush or I'd sound like our mother before my next birthday.

Before Tom could comment, the door opened and an elderly couple walked in. I watched as the man held the door for his companion before popping their umbrella into the copper stand. He slid out her chair, helped her sit down, and as he said something to her, she chuckled and covered her mouth with her pale, slim fingers.

I walked over to their table. "Good afternoon," I said with a smile.

"Good afternoon to you, young lady." The man's blue eyes were bloodshot and watery, but surrounded by laughter lines that could tell a thousand tales.

"Can I get you some coffee, or tea?"

"Two cups of tea, please, love," the woman answered softly as she set her purple knitted beret on the chair next to her and patted her gray curls back into place. "And two sticky buns if you have any. Our George gets grumpy if he doesn't have his sticky bun."

I grinned. "Well, we can't have that now, can we? Two teas and sticky buns it is. Back in a sec." As I turned I noticed how they'd reached for each other across the table, their worn fingers already entwined. Six months ago I would've demanded Tom pass me the sick bucket. Now all I saw was Liam and me in sixty years. It was crazily weird. *Wonderfully*, crazily weird. As if he'd found a treasure chest of feelings buried so deep in my heart, even I hadn't known it was there.

After I'd brought the couple's order over to them I returned to the bar from where Tom eyed me with a barely concealed grin as he licked his spoon. "I saw how you looked at them," he said.

I popped some dirty cups in the sink. "No idea what you're talking about."

"Yeah, right. You're going all mushy… Anyway, how are things with Liam?"

"Great. He's busy with work. The bank's given him more responsibility already."

"Has he told them about losing his license?"

"Yeah. He didn't have much choice seeing as he's supposed to travel to the different branches. God, he was so worried and—"

"No kidding. I still can't believe how much over the speed limit he was, he—"

I waved a hand. "Yeah, yeah. Anyway, they didn't give him that much grief in the end. Obviously it can't happen again, but they still think he's amazingly talented." Ugh. I was *gushing*. I cleared my throat. "How's Sophia?"

He waggled a finger. "Oh, no, don't change the subject. Have you asked him yet?"

"No. I don't want to spook him."

"Pah, pah, pah." Tom put up his hands. "You're in love with him, aren't you?"

"Yeah, but—"

"And you're practically living together anyway. He hates his flatmates. He'll never live with his parents again—"

"Not likely. I've never met such bigots. If you live south of the river they think you're a foreigner."

"Well, then," Tom said. "It's simple. Ask him to move in. Think of the money you'll save."

"Sounds like *you* want to move in with him."

Tom flicked his spoon at me and I ducked, narrowly avoiding a well-aimed chocolaty milk blob that splattered on the floor. "I wish I could move out, believe me," he said. "And as soon as I've finished this bloody economics degree, I will. Until then…"

"You get to live with the Wicked Witch of the East." I

grinned, wiping up his deliberate spill with a piece of kitchen paper.

Tom laughed. "Mum's not that bad."

"Not to you, she isn't." My smile disappeared. "She hates me."

"Knock it off. She doesn't *hate* you."

"Yes she *does*." I took a breath. "Because I remind her of Dad."

Tom pulled a face. "You've said that before. But if it was true, she'd hate, uh, I mean she wouldn't *get along* with me. I'm the guy. I must remind her way more of Dad than you do."

"I don't think gender has anything to do with it." I paused. "I'm pretty sure I have his mannerisms, you know? Facial expressions, gestures, that kind of thing. At least that's what Mum accused me of." I plopped a tea bag into a mug. "But I'm not like him. I've never been unfaithful. I wouldn't cheat on Liam. I don't have a gambling habit. And I'd definitely never walk out on my partner." I sighed. "I love Liam."

He grinned. "Told you. You're going all mushy."

"I'm being serious. I mean I *really* love him. And it scares the hell out of me."

"Why?"

I threw up my hands. "Why *not*? What if this is another relationship I mess up? I don't want that to happen… I'd do anything for him, Tommy. Anything."

Tom tut-tutted and rolled his eyes. "Except ask him to move in with you."

I flicked him with my dishcloth. "We've not even been going out six months. Anyway… How *is* Sophia? And I mean *really*." He pulled a face and I raised my eyebrows. "Arguing again?"

"Yeah."

"So she's still possessive, paranoid and, well, a bit odd?"

"Sounds about right." Tom laughed.

I flung my hands into the air again. "Why do you bother? You hate conflict."

"Well, that's not surprising, is it?" Tom put a hand over his heart. "My poor soul's been badly traumatized by all the fights you and Mum had."

"And that's exactly why I moved out. Five years later and I can still hear her shouting at me." I nudged Tom with my elbow. "But Mum loves you, so her heart's only half made of stone. Or maybe it's two sizes too small." Tom didn't grin like I thought he would, so I added, "Like the Grinch who stole Christmas. Dad used to read us that book. Remember?"

He kept his eyes downcast and his shoulders hunched, looking like an abandoned puppy standing in the rain waiting to be let inside. "I wish I remembered *him*," he said quietly. "Properly, I mean. I wish we knew where he was."

"I know. So do I."

I shook my head as I recalled the day my father had walked out, which had been ordinary in every other way. Everything about that day was still vivid, almost as if someone had etched it all, right down to the tiniest detail, permanently in my mind. A definitive marker of the day everything changed.

It happened during the school holidays, a few weeks after Tom's ninth—my tenth—birthday. It seemed "Upside Down" by Diana Ross was on a constant loop on the radio, and I knew all the words by heart, singing them as loud as I could at every opportunity.

"Stop singing that!" Tom had moaned the day before, flicking me on the back of the neck each time I broke into the chorus. But it was one of those earworms you couldn't get out of your head. Even walking around the house, humming

The Muppets tune didn't help. Although—and this delighted me—I noticed Tom couldn't stop humming that now, which was payback for flicking me in the first place.

The boy I liked sat on the park swings with me the day Dad left. Derek Stokes stood barely taller than me despite being almost two years older. But he had big, emerald green eyes and the cutest half-moon dimples I'd ever seen. I greedily snatched up any and every glance he threw my way, storing them so deep in my memory, I could still recall them over a decade later. Derek really did turn me inside out, and made all my feelings go around and around.

Even my recollection of the weather was clear. I could almost feel the drizzle that had softly fallen on my cheeks as Tom and I walked home from the park. See the billowing clouds that hung around in the air until the evening, when, finally, the sun broke through. Whenever that happened I thought it meant good things were on the way. After all, if the sun always won against the rain there had to be hope for everything else. There had to be.

We ate supper. The four of us—Mum, Dad, Tom and I—sat at our square table with the vase of daffodils in the middle, and the red-and-white-checkered plastic tablecloth, which had a cigarette burn on the left side, three squares up. I couldn't say what we had to eat the evening before, or the one after, but that day we had bowls of steaming homemade tomato soup, buttered bread, thick slices of cheddar cheese and sweet gherkins. Lots and lots of sweet gherkins.

Mum wasn't unusually quiet. Dad didn't shout. In fact, they had a perfectly civil conversation about politics. My mother had trouble believing an actor could be the President of the United States, whereas my father insisted Reagan was the man to rule the Land of Opportunity.

Tom and I didn't care about politics. We pulled faces at each other when our parents weren't looking and chattered about what to do with the rest of the summer holidays. Neither of us wanted to go back to school; it would get in the way of playing hide-and-seek until the streetlights came on—later if we could get away with it—or playing circus with Mrs. Bennett's golden Labrador and my silver-and-pink-striped Hula-Hoop.

"Let's go outside," Tom said as he licked his bowl clean of the last remnants of soup, leaving an orangey moustache above his lips. "On our bikes. We can roll over the smiley ball."

He didn't need to ask twice. As soon as Mum had given her approval in the way of a curt nod, we hastily shoved our dishes in the kitchen sink and ran to the front door, ignoring our mother's instructions to be careful.

Tom had found a yellow ball a few days earlier, and we'd drawn a big smiley face on it with black felt-tip pen. We'd pushed the ball into a hole in the middle of our street, so only the top half stuck out, then we'd driven over it again and again, laughing and wobbling on our bicycles. We both knew one of us would fall. That was the whole point. The question was who would first. My brother probably had a bet on with the other kids it would be me. He was right.

The seventh time I drove over the ball that night it burst with a loud *ka-boom*. I jumped. The bike swayed, my hands hit the brakes too hard and I lost my balance and tumbled to the ground.

Tom laughed until he heard me crying and saw the blood on my knees. He jumped off his bike and ran over.

"Gross," he said, looking at my leg.

I cried harder, big fat tears rolling over my cheeks.

"I can see a bone," he said and I gasped, then howled. Tom laughed again. "Nah. It's a pebble."

"Not funny," I wailed.

He grinned at me. "You'd better stop crying or Mum will cut your leg off."

I wiped my runny nose with the back of my hand, leaving a wet streak from my knuckle to the middle of my arm. "Not crying. Help me up."

Despite Tom being a year younger, he was already freakishly tall and strong, too. He put his hands around my waist and pulled me up. I tried to ignore the blood leaking out of my knees and running down my legs, staining my dusty socks.

"I'll take your bike," Tom said. "Okay?"

"S'fine," I said and limped home. And that's when we saw Dad coming out of the house with a suitcase in each hand. He looked up at us and stopped walking, then put the luggage down and held out his arms.

"Where are you going?" Tom said as he hugged Dad.

"Away for a while."

"Can I come?"

"No, little fella." Dad ruffled my brother's hair. "You need to stay here. Look after your mum and your sister for me."

I looked at my father, frowned when I noticed the tears in his eyes. "When are you coming back, Daddy?"

My father pulled both of us close and kissed the tops of our heads. "I'm not sure, sweetheart. Soon." His eyes quickly traveled toward the front door. "I'd better go."

He released us from his grip and stuffed the suitcases in the trunk of our old VW Beetle. Another hug, another smile. More promises he'd see us soon, and then he left, sticking his arm out of the rolled-down window, waving as he drove away.

It was only as he disappeared around the corner that I realized he hadn't stopped to question the blood running down my leg, hadn't asked if I was okay.

Tom and I raced inside to find Mum where we'd left her, sitting at the kitchen table, which had already been cleared and wiped down. When she looked up at us, her face void of expression and with what appeared to be a fresh coat of makeup, the only thing she told us was, "Time for bed."

"I suppose Dad must have had his reasons for not contacting us," Tom said quietly, snapping me out of the memory and back to the coffee shop.

I smiled at him. Tom, my baby brother who was exactly a year younger than me—to the day. He'd spent his first few weeks in an incubator because he'd arrived two months early. When he told people it was because he'd been in a rush to meet his big sister, it made me feel so proud.

I was about to reply when the elderly couple got up. The man pointed at the change he'd left on the table next to their used plates and cups, and they both waved at us as they walked out, leaving the shop empty except for me and Tom.

"Mum probably told him never to set foot on her doorstep again or she'd turn him into a toad or something." I shrugged. "Or maybe he just didn't care."

"Do you think he's still alive? People don't disappear like that, do they?"

"Well, with the amount of money Mum said he owed... I don't know. Maybe we'll find out one day." I patted his arm. "In any case, she still lives in the same house, so it's not like we're difficult to find."

The coffee shop door opened, and Liam stepped inside, his shirt speckled with rain droplets. As he walked toward us, my heart thumped against my rib cage like a beating drum.

"Ask him to move in with you, or I'm telling," Tom hissed out of the corner of his mouth.

"Do that and you'll go straight to hell," I whispered back through clenched teeth.

"No worries, Shabby," Tom said with a laugh. "I'll see you down there."

I laughed, too, as I hugged Liam, thinking there was no way Tom would ever go to hell.

But something inside me whispered that I probably would.

NOW
NANCY

"HAVE YOU SEEN anyone from next door lately?" I asked Zac and Liam as we cleared up after dinner together, me putting leftovers in the fridge, Liam washing up and Zac—under usual duress—haphazardly drying the dishes. Neither of them responded at first so I asked the question again.

Zac shrugged. "I see Sarah at school sometimes."

"Oh, *do* you?" I said in an attempt to be the fun mum, which backfired immediately.

"It's not like that," he said with a huff, puff and eye roll. "I mean I see her *around*. In the corridors and stuff."

"You could walk to school together," I said. "You might have something in common."

As Zac turned and put the glass dish on the counter I saw him meet Liam's eye. "We're not five, Mum," Zac said. "You'll be trying to arrange playdates for me next."

Liam chuckled quietly, and I clenched my teeth. Why couldn't he be on my side? It hurt when he made me feel like the odd one out. As for Zac, I was almost used to his verbal jabs and remembered being the same with both my parents at his age, but I missed him being the cuddly little boy he'd once been, always willing to wrap his arms around me like Mr. Tickle, whether his friends were watching or not. Time had passed so quickly, and these days I was lucky to get a hug on Christmas morning. My son was growing up, pulling away from me—and rightly so—and yet the legitimate distance it created between us hurt like sandpaper on an open wound.

I smiled breezily and looked at Zac with my head tilted to one side. "Playdates, that's a good one. No, I just meant that I think Sarah's—"

"Nancy," Liam said, and I thought he was about to ever so politely tell me to back off, but he did a one-eighty. "I thought I'd take you out for dinner over the weekend."

"That would be lovely." I smiled back, a bit surprised yet delighted at the prospect. "The three of us haven't been out for ages."

"Actually," Liam said as he flicked the kettle on, "I meant just the two of us."

"But what about Zac? You want to come with us, don't you, honey?"

"Like I said, I'm not five," Zac snapped. "I'll be perfectly happy on my own."

"Watch your tone, Zac." Liam pulled the rubbish bag out from under the sink and held it out toward him. "First of all, don't speak to your mother like that. And second, empty the rest of the bins around the house."

"But I'm drying—"

"Just get it done."

Zac snatched the bag from Liam and stormed out of the kitchen, and within seconds I heard him stomping up the stairs.

"Thanks, love," I whispered, glowing at the fact that Liam

had sprung to my defense. "And by the way, I know he's in touch with Sarah. They're connected on Facebook."

Liam pulled out the jar of coffee. Despite the fact that I'd bought one of those fancy machines, he hardly used it. According to him there was nothing wrong with instant. I smiled to myself, grateful that, despite his successful career, he'd remained a man of simple tastes. My heart fluttered, as it often did when I thought about him, about us, but then it almost stopped when Liam looked at me with his brow furrowed, eyes narrowing, judging me.

"And how do you know that?" he said.

I turned away so he couldn't see my face flush. "I've been looking."

"*Nancy.*"

"I'm his mother. I'm perfectly entitled to—"

"Snoop?"

We'd had this discussion before, and never agreed. He thought it was an invasion of Zac's privacy. I thought it was good, old-fashioned common sense. Everybody looked at what their kids were doing online these days.

"Call it what you want," I said. "It's my job to keep tabs on him. Make sure he doesn't—"

"You don't need to keep tabs on him. He's a good kid. He's never been in any trouble."

I crossed my arms. "You're forgetting the incident at his last school."

Liam stirred his coffee with more vigor than I thought necessary. "He didn't start it."

"Yeah, well. Anyway...while I was on Facebook I connected with Nate."

"That's nice."

I knew he wouldn't ask me why or show any signs if it

bothered him. Honest to goodness, my husband was a smart man, but didn't he realize a little bit of jealousy from his side would make me feel better? More confident and safe—more desired? But if I raised it he'd almost certainly counter that the ring on my finger should be enough reassurance.

It never had been. Not really.

I told myself to stop being so petulant and smiled again. "You know what, though? I couldn't find Abby. I looked on Facebook, Twitter, Instagram—"

"Sounds laborious."

"—but I couldn't find her anywhere. Doesn't that strike you as odd in this day and age? What deep, dark secrets do you think she's hiding?" I'd meant it as another joke, but judging by Liam's tone and expression, he didn't find it funny.

"You know she lives next door, right?" he said. "If you have such a burning need for information, why don't you go over there and ask?" His words stung as much as the look he threw my way.

"Baby, it's not—"

"Some of us don't want to spread our lives over the internet for all to see," Liam said.

I stiffened. "What's that supposed to mean?"

"Nothing, dear." Liam sighed.

"Don't 'dear' me. I hate it when you do that. So you think I post too much online?"

"Look." Liam used his placid voice, the one that could calm me down or light my fuse in a second, depending on the situation. "I mean this in the nicest possible way, but I wonder if anybody's interested in the paint colors you're thinking of using, or the lunch you've made or..."

"I've got to share those things with *somebody*," I snapped. "You're not around much these days, are you?"

"Nancy…"

"The few girlfriends I have are back home, so I can't see them. I've asked you to look at the plans for the house, but you're either too busy or not here. You hardly take an interest—"

"I've taken on a new role at work, Nancy. More responsibility. More direct reports. You knew I'd be swamped for a while when you agreed to us coming here."

"Sure, but I didn't expect you to be so distant and preoccupied. Downright ratty, actually. And don't even get me started on our sex life." I glared at him, for once unwilling to back down and appease him, which felt surprisingly good.

Liam threw his arms into the air. "Where the hell did that come from? Actually, no. It doesn't matter. I'm not having this conversation again. I've got work to do."

"Of *course* you do," I said icily as he turned and left.

Zac came back into the kitchen and plonked the full binbag on the floor. "There. And so you know, Mum, the walls in this house are really thin. So if you and Dad are going to argue about your, uh, *sex life*, can you do it when I'm not around? *Gross*."

And just like that I stood alone in a half-cleaned kitchen with a full rubbish bag at my feet. This wasn't exactly how I'd imagined starting our Easter weekend. There was no way I'd go out for dinner with Liam now. It would serve him right for being so rude. I picked up the bag and took it outside, grateful for the moment of fresh air. I briefly considered getting my jacket and going for a walk without saying anything, but it was cold, and I doubted Liam would notice I'd left.

"Bugger it!" I said out loud.

"Hey, Nancy." Nate's head popped up from the other side of his car and as I dropped the bag into the container and walked over, he wiped his hand on a rag. "Everything okay? Haven't seen you in ages."

Something inside me lit up a little when I saw his smile. Maybe it was just the sting from Liam's indifference, but there was definitely something sexy about a man working on his car. Something a bit rough, primal, almost.

"Fine, fine," I said. "The usual. Keeping busy."

"Doing anything special for Easter?" He leaned against the car, still wiping the grease from his hands.

I hadn't noticed his hands before. They looked strong, solid, with long fingers. I forced my gaze up to his face. "Uh, not really. More of the same, sorting stuff out, I suppose. You?"

"My brother, his wife and their twin girls are coming for the weekend." His smile grew, positively beaming at the mention of them. Clearly the thought of spending time with his family was a good one, and I suddenly wished we had people visiting, too. I could have done with the company.

"That's great," I said. "Sounds like fun."

"Yeah. It will be. So, uh…" Nate cleared his throat.

An awkward silence surrounded us as we looked at each other. It made me feel like an embarrassed teenager again, trying to come up with something intelligent to say.

Nate nodded toward his house. "I'd better go inside. I promised Abby I'd sort out some shelves in the spare bedroom before everyone arrives tomorrow."

"She's lucky to have a husband who's so good with his hands," I said, and winked at him. "Very lucky, indeed." As the heat prickled the skin on my face, I wondered what on earth had gotten into me.

Nate laughed. "You tell her that next time you see her, okay? Put in a good word for me."

"I will," I answered, thankful he was oblivious or not willing to take the bait. He gave me a wave, and I watched him walk back to his house and disappear inside.

As I wandered toward my front door, a thousand thoughts racing through my mind, I decided I was done going unnoticed in my own home. My husband had to start paying more attention to me.

And I'd just found the perfect person to help make that happen.

NOW
SARAH

Dear Diary,

It's the school holidays, but I wish I could go back to class. Mum's so grumpy, it's like she's got her period *all the time*. She bit my head off yesterday when I asked if she knew where my phone was. *Aren't you old enough to look after your own stuff, Sarah?* It was only a question!

Even Dad's been treating her with thicker kid gloves than usual. Sometimes I wish he'd tell her to *fuck off*. Like on Tuesday night, when I overheard this:

Dad: Did you pick up a chocolate Easter bunny for Sarah?

Mum: No, I forgot. *(Huh? The Oracle of Details never forgets anything!)*

Dad: Any chance you could get one?

Mum: I've done the shopping and it'll be mayhem at Tesco's. You go.

I hoped Dad would say something about *the tone*, but he didn't. He's just too nice. Later on Mum told me she didn't get me a bunny because she thought I was too old, and did I mind? I said I didn't care, so we both lied which makes us equal. I know it's stupid and, yeah, I'm sixteen, but I thought it was kind of a tradition and it's not like we have many of those.

At least Uncle Paul, Lynne and the twins are coming this weekend so the house won't be like a funeral home for a few days. I mean, it's usually only Dad, Mum and me for holiday weekends and stuff. It's not like we have much family around.

Anyway, last week Dad suggested we invite the neighbors over soon. Both Mum and I said *NO* straight away. I don't want to spend time with *idiot* aka Zac. He tried to start a conversation with me the other day. Ugh. Like we have anything remotely in common.

Mum told Dad they were probably still busy getting themselves organized after the move, and we should leave them time to settle in. It was the first sensible, non-snappy thing I'd heard her say for ages, and I thought maybe she was back to normal.

But then I got into an argument with her because I want to go to a party on Saturday with Claire and her new boyfriend, James. I told Mum James would drive, which is true, and there wouldn't be any alcohol, which definitely isn't. So Mum said I could go, and she'd take us.

Me: But I said James can drive.

Her: And I said I'll take you. I'll pick you up at eleven.

Me: *Eleven?* That's way too early. There's no point in going. I'll look like a baby!

Her: Don't go then.

Me: Why are you being like this? You're not being *fair*.

Her: Fine. Decision made. You're not going. Paul and Lynne are here anyway.

Me: But—

Her: The answer's no.

Gah! Sometimes I *hate* her! I mean *really* hate her.

Right, I'd better do my homework. Mind you, it's not like I've got anything better to do on f#&%ing Saturday night now, is it?
Later,
Sarah x.

PS. Word of the day: *otiose*, adjective.
1: producing no useful result.
2: being at leisure.
3: lacking use or effect.
As in: *Trying to change Mum's mind about the party will be an otiose debate!*

NOW
ABBY

NATE AND SARAH were out, and I'd spent the morning preparing the house for Paul and Lynne's arrival, tidying up, doing the washing and getting the spare room ready. I knew Nate was happy to see his brother again, and Sarah adored her aunt Lynne.

I smiled as I thought about the twin girls, Rachel and Rosie. It had been ages since we'd seen them, and I couldn't wait to pick them up and nuzzle my nose against their heads. Babies and toddlers were so uncomplicated, nonjudgmental and easy to please.

I headed upstairs to Sarah's bedroom with a basket of fresh laundry. She'd inherited my need for tidiness and kept her space immaculately neat, something Camilla often lamented Claire was incapable of. Camilla said she'd once found three plates and a half-eaten sandwich under her daughter's bed. At least she'd thought it was a sandwich. It had been so green and furry it may have been Kermit's remains.

The sun bounced off Sarah's multicolored bedspread, lighting up the room like a rainbow. I didn't go in there often anymore, and it felt unfamiliar somehow, as if I was entering an area with a specific time limit.

I used to read to Sarah every night, as I'd done with Tom. But by the time she was eight, Sarah already preferred to read alone or make up her own stories. Fierce independence was another trait I'd given my daughter.

The highly volatile peace treaty between Sarah and me was well and truly over. Days later, the argument about her going to the party still made me feel bad. Not bad enough to change my mind—I wouldn't go back on my word—but she'd stayed up late to work on school assignments for weeks. She was a good kid, and I often thought I should cut her more slack.

After setting her clean clothes on the bed I turned to leave. I'd stopped putting Sarah's washing away years ago, often repeating she didn't live in a hotel and had to pitch in, but in light of everything that had happened, I decided to make an exception.

I popped her T-shirts and jeans in the cupboard, then started putting her underwear away. And as I slid her socks into her drawer and pushed a purple bra aside, I saw it. Sarah's blue diary with a white leather buckle and a golden dragonfly on the cover. The one I'd given her for her birthday.

As soon as I saw the journal, I swore I wouldn't touch it. It's something my mother would've done, had I ever been diligent enough to write about my teenage angst. I put Sarah's clothes away, shut the drawer and made it as far as the top of the stairs before turning around and walking back to Sarah's room. With every step I took I tried to talk myself out of what I was about to do. But as I eyed the diary, then let my hands pick it up, I'd already convinced myself it was for Sarah's own good. I could protect her in case she got messed up in drugs, mixed with the wrong crowd or had questions she was too embarrassed to ask. It was for her benefit, and would make me a better mother. It had absolutely nothing to do with spying.

And so I sat on my daughter's cheerful bedspread and read. At first my breathing quickened as my eyes scanned the pages. Then I had to tighten my grip. The bolt of anger soon gave way to sadness, and I managed to turn away just before a fat tear could land on Sarah's angry scribbles.

I brushed the tears away with my sleeve so I could read on, and as I went over my daughter's diary a second time, the affection she felt for her father and the distaste for me practically leaped off the pages and scurried down my throat.

Thank god my personality's much more like Dad's because Mum's a nightmare.

I mean, doesn't she know me at all?

Sometimes I wish he'd tell her to fuck off.

Gah! Sometimes I hate her! I mean really hate her.

I shook my head and wondered how I'd become so much like my mother even though I'd distanced myself from her as early as I possibly could. How was it, despite my best efforts, my daughter and I couldn't get along?

I should have been thrilled Nate and Sarah were close, that she'd taken so much after him, if not in looks, then certainly in character. I knew Nate's tenacity had held us together all these years. He was a little bit like Play-Doh or plastic wrap, molding himself around me, over every ugly lump, bump and pimple.

At times I wanted to shout, "Save yourselves, it's too late for me." But I'd end up alone. I didn't want to be alone, although it would be well deserved. I slipped Sarah's journal underneath her underwear, removed the clothes I'd carefully put away and set them in a neat pile on her bed.

As I walked downstairs, I stopped to look at Tom's photograph. He'd truly been blessed by the God of Good Genes, and girls had gone crazy over his deep blue eyes and infectious smile. He could have had almost anyone if he'd wanted to. As it happened, he'd believed in true love and saw the goodness in all people, whereas I was the miserable cynic.

"There's no way you'd have let me become so much like our mother," I said out loud. "You'd give me hell for being such a bad mum." I gently touched his one-dimensional cheek with my fingertips. "Sarah would have loved you. Just as much as I do."

I closed my eyes to stop the world from spinning out of control, and imagined how different all of our lives would have been if only I hadn't chosen to be so reckless.

THEN
ABBY

"WE'RE MEETING THEM for drinks at Humpty Dumpty's?" Liam called out from behind the shower curtain.

"Yeah," I said, applying a second layer of mascara. "Sophia's picking up Tom, and they'll head straight there."

Liam pulled the curtain back a little and stuck out his head. Although I wasn't focusing on his face. Instead I watched the water run over his tight stomach, giving *washboard abs* a whole new meaning entirely.

"Abby?"

"Huh?" I slowly raised my head. "What?"

He laughed. "I said, what time are we meeting them?"

"Eight." I grinned. "God, don't you listen to anything I say?"

"Look who's talking. And for the record, I listen to everything you say. What time is it?"

I glanced at my watch. "Just gone six thirty. Plenty of time."

"Yeah." Liam smiled and opened the shower curtain fully. "Plenty of time. And you look like you need a wash."

"You cheeky git. I *had* one."

"Nu-uh. I'm sure you didn't. And there's room in here. Take your clothes off?"

I giggled. *"Liam."*

"Do it." He smiled again, then added, "Please?"

He didn't take his eyes off mine as I unzipped my dress and let it fall to the floor. Then I unhooked my bra and shimmied out of my knickers. He exhaled deeply, and I could already see how much he wanted me.

"You know we'll be late," I said as I stepped into the bath. "And—"

He silenced me with a slow kiss that could have lasted forever. His mouth slid downward, pausing for a little while on my breasts before traveling south again, to tease and please, until I was perched on the edge of ecstasy. Back arched, legs trembling, my hands pushed against the wall to stop me from falling.

"Don't stop." My words disappeared amid the noise from the running water, so I said them again, louder this time.

But he did stop, then stood up slowly, turned me around and slid deep inside me. He whispered my name as he thrust deeper and faster, his fingers in all the right places, his mouth on the back of my neck. I called out his name again and again as he took me to the brink and pulled me back, only to do it once more. Then we both gasped in unison, almost collapsing in a heap in the bath, panting, our hearts racing.

"I love you," Liam whispered as he wrapped his arms around me. "I love you."

I took a deep breath, patted his hand. "You know the rule. Ten minutes before and after doesn't count."

A small sigh, which I mistook as an expression of afterglow pleasure, until he quietly said, "Don't."

I frowned. "Don't what?"

"Make flippant comments when I tell you how I feel."

"I never do that."

Liam kissed my shoulder. "Yeah, you do." He ran his fingers down my arm and kissed me again. "Almost every time."

I shrugged him off. "Yeah, well..."

He pulled me back toward him. "It's okay. I know why."

"I'd better get ready or we'll be late." I slipped away from his arms, stepped out of the bath and closed the curtain behind me.

As I grabbed a towel and wrapped it around myself, Liam said, "Just because your dad left and your mum's a...because she's *difficult*, doesn't mean you don't deserve to be loved."

I was about to snap at him, tell him to stop psychoanalyzing me. But, quite unexpectedly, the anger vanished. My shoulders dropped as I finally realized he *got* me. *All* of me. The good, the bad and the downright ugly. Yet miraculously he still loved me. I pulled the shower curtain open again, little droplets of water splashing onto my face. Liam stared at me, started holding up a hand, apparently ready for my icy rebuttal.

"Move in with me," I said before I lost my nerve.

"What? I—"

"I love you," I said quickly. "I think about you all the time. I've never felt like this about anyone." I couldn't meet his eyes. "Actually, I've, uh, never loved anyone this much, not properly." I laughed apologetically and raced on. "Except for Tom, of course, but he's my brother and that's different but—"

"Abby—"

"—he thinks you're great. He says so all the time, and it makes me love you even more. And I want to go to sleep at night and wake up with you every morning, you know? That

probably sounds corny, but it's true. So what do you think?"
I looked at him for the first time since I'd begun my pathetic
monologue and immediately registered his raised eyebrows.
"It's too early. It is, isn't it? It's only been six months. Ridiculous. Never mind I—"

"Yes."

My face fell and I forced a smile. "I know. Too early. Okay
then. Sorry about that, I—"

"No." He switched the water off. "I mean, yes, I'll move in
with you." Liam reached for me, pulling me back into a damp
embrace. "I feel the same way. From the first time I saw you."

I laughed as I threw my arms around him, covered his face
with kisses. "I wanted to ask you ages ago."

He grinned. "I know. Tom told me."

My mouth dropped open. "He *what*? The little shit. I'll
kill him."

"Please don't." Liam shivered so I rubbed his arms. "There
was so much beer involved he probably doesn't remember. I
think it went something like, 'My shishter lovesh you, mate.
She really, *really* lovesh you. She wansh you to move in wiv
her but she'sh shcared to ashk.'"

"*What?* Why didn't you say anything?"

Liam stroked my cheek with his index finger. "Because
you needed to figure it out in your own time. There's no
rush, is there?"

"No." I tilted my head to one side. "But when *will* you move
in?"

A grin crept over Liam's face. "Sunday?"

"My birthday?"

Liam grinned. "Good present?"

I hugged him again. "Best present *ever*."

We were in the middle of another passionate kiss when the phone rang.

"Leave it." Liam nuzzled my neck, his hands pulling on my towel. "Stay here with me."

"Can't." I reclaimed the towel and pushed him away gently. "It's probably Tom. Bet you they're late again. You know they live on Sophia Mean Time." I sprinted to the living room and snatched up the receiver. "Hello?"

"Abby, it's me."

"I knew it." I huffed. "Don't tell me. You won't make it until nine."

"Not exactly." Tom's tone was quiet, subdued. "We had another fight. A big one this time. It's over. I'm done."

I wanted to jump up and down, skip around the flat singing Hallelujah. Instead I muttered, "Oh, bollocks. What happened?"

"Remember a couple of weeks ago, when I had a rotten cold? And *she* went out with her mates from the salon?"

"Yes," I said quietly, worried I had a feeling where this might be going. "I remember."

"Well, she went off with some bloke that night. Had a quickie in an alley somewhere up against a stack of beer crates."

"*What?*"

"*Jesus*, sodding beer crates! And she tells me two days before my birthday."

"But she was always the one accusing you of—"

"Tell me about it."

I sank down on the sofa. "How did you find out?"

He snorted. "She was acting all nice and lovey-dovey…"

"Well, that's not like her."

"Exactly. And when I asked her what was going on, she started crying."

"*She* cried?"

"Yeah, as if *that* would make me feel sympathy. And then she told me." He took a deep breath. "She says it meant nothing, and she can't even remember his name. Can you believe it? She doesn't even know who she screwed."

"Bloody hell. What a—"

"*Bitch?* Yeah. I'm so *mad*," Tom said. "What the hell did I see in her? Two-faced *slag*."

"Listen," I said gently, "forget stupid Sophia. Forget Humpty's. Come over. Liam's here. We can get pizza and watch our old *Dukes of Hazzard* videos. What do you say?" When Tom didn't answer I added, "Go on. It'll take your mind off *her*."

He sighed. "Actually, do you mind if we go out? Just you and me, for a while? No offense or anything, but I don't want to watch you two all loved up on the sofa."

"Okay, no problem."

"But I'll have to make it cheap 'cos I'm broke."

"Fair enough," I said. "I'll pick you up in about an hour. We'll go to Humpty's and Red's."

"Ugh," he groaned. "Maybe not Red's. What if Sophia's there shagging someone else?"

"Okay. But tonight's my treat. I'll drop you back home, too, and you can save the taxi fare. What do you think?"

He exhaled. "Thanks, sis. And fair warning. I'm planning on getting absolutely shit-faced."

I laughed. "No problem. I'll look after you. Promise."

"See you later then," Tom said. "Tell Liam I said hi and sorry for stealing you."

"Everything okay?" Liam asked as he came out of the bathroom, and after I'd quickly explained, he hugged me, kissed the top of my head and said, "Tell Tom I'm sorry and to enjoy himself. I'll go to the flat, have a couple of beers with the guys and start packing my stuff."

I grinned. "I can't wait."

"Me neither," he said. "I might catch up with you for a drink at Humpty's later tonight, okay?"

"Okay, great."

"If I don't show up, then I'll call you tomorrow morning and we'll get your car if you leave it there." He laughed. "By the sound of what you two have planned, you probably should."

THEN
NATE

AT TWENTY-FOUR I considered myself pretty lucky when it came to encountering death. Compared to a lot of my friends I'd been relatively untouched by it. But two funerals only twelve months apart meant the Grim Reaper and I were no longer on amicable terms.

Nana had passed away first, and now, almost exactly a year later, Granddad was gone, too. In my humble opinion trips to Northern England were officially to be considered an utter pile of bollocks, and now there'd be no real reason for me to come back.

I needed a change of scene after the funeral, so I called the number on the piece of paper my brother had slipped into my hand at the end of the service. "I've got a mobile phone," he'd said with a wink. "It's brilliant."

No surprise Paul had the latest tech gear. When I'd started in recruitment, he was one of the first people I'd placed at IBM where, in his own words, he "was seriously going places." But unlike the stereotypical IT nerd, Paul was confident, outgoing and could have starred in a Calvin Klein advert, sandwiched between Kate Moss and Christy Turlington. And they'd have loved him, the good-looking bastard.

I listened to the phone ring a few times and had to hold it away from my ear when Paul answered. "Nate," he yelled. It sounded like he was in a wind tunnel. "We're in my car. Can you believe it? Mobile phones are the future, mate. They really are. Anyway, you all right? Everything okay?" He must have moved the phone because his voice became distant. Not distant enough, though, because I still heard him say, "Hold on, Stacey, finish me off later, yeah?"

Stacey. I'd been racking my brains for her name. I bet none of the men at the funeral—and perhaps even some of the women—could describe her face. We'd all been too heavily focused on her chest, an almost welcome distraction given the reason for us being there.

"I know I said I wasn't going to bother, but do you fancy going out tonight?" I yelled, unsure if Paul could hear or focus on what I was saying, particularly if Stacey was doing to him what I thought she was doing to him.

"Sure, no problem. Any preference?"

"Chiapparelli's. Definitely. Nothing outrageous. Good food, one beer. That's it. And no talk of death and funerals, okay?"

"Gotcha. I'll call and book. See you there in an hour." He hung up.

I went back to Granddad's, where I was staying with Mum and Dad, and had a shower before setting off down Liverpool Road in my trusty old Fiat, my favorite David Bowie album, *Let's Dance*, blaring out of the crackly sound system. It almost felt like a normal weekend visit to Preston, and by the time I parked my car along Fishergate, my spirits were higher than they'd been since we'd got the call about Granddad. I was looking forward to spending the evening with my big brother, even though our characters were more like a pea and a herring in a pod. Our parents didn't understand how we got along so well—no one did, really. But we were family. We clicked. Simple as that. What more was there to it?

Paul was already at the restaurant and waved to me as I walked in. "Hey, little brother." He stood to hug me. "You look better than you did at the funeral. Ah, bollocks. I wasn't supposed to mention it."

"About that," I said as we both sat. "Stacey?"

"What about Stacey?" he said, eyes raised in a masterful but totally fake air of innocence.

"Let's just say, when you showed up in a red convertible—"

"Love that car—"

"—and another blonde with, uh, *assets*, none of us blinked. And I bet Granddad appreciated the gesture, you livening his funeral up like that."

He grinned. "She's gorgeous, isn't she? And sexy. Have you seen that smile?"

"She has a *head*?" I kept my face straight. "I think the vicar's going straight to hell."

Paul winked at me. "Don't get too attached."

"Surprise me."

He counted on his fingers. "Too clingy. Too needy. Too jealous—"

"Shocker."

"—and she gave me hell for blowing her off for you tonight."

"Aww…" I gave him a sarcastic look. "And after she blew you, too."

For a moment I had the pleasure of seeing Paul speechless.

"How the...? Bloody mobile phone. I need to figure out how to use the mute button."

"My brother, ladies and gentlemen," I said, holding out a hand. "Easily distracted, quickly bored and, thus, destined to be a bachelor forever. If only—"

He laughed. "Fuck off."

The rest of the evening didn't progress to more serious topics. No, people couldn't understand how I got along with England's answer to Casanova, but right then Paul's unashamedly carefree view of the world, a ham-and-cheese pizza and a beer were exactly what I needed.

Unsurprisingly, Paul drank too much, ate too much and swore too often, and after we'd finished our nosh we headed for the nearest pub. It wasn't overly busy, and I nursed a couple of Cokes while Paul had another two pints, then bought a gin and tonic for last orders.

"Good job I'm getting a bloody cab," he said, bleary-eyed, as he finished his final drink. "I'm fucking wasted."

I looked at my watch. Almost eleven thirty. Time to head back. "I'll drive you."

Paul waved a hand. "No need. Hotel's in the opposite direction anyway. And don't forget, I've got this." He fumbled around in his jacket pocket and fished out his mobile phone. It looked a little heavy to be lugging around, but I couldn't help marvel at the technology all the same. Making calls from anywhere? Brilliant. Maybe they'd catch on.

I stayed long enough for a cab to arrive and made sure the driver understood Paul's instructions because it sounded like his tongue had grown a size too big for his mouth.

By the time I got back to my car the streets were almost deserted. I'd been going a little more than ten minutes when I saw the fire. At first I thought some idiot had set a bonfire on the side of the road or something, but as I got closer, I saw it was far more serious.

It was a car in flames.

I hit the brakes hard and jumped out.

"Hey," I shouted, trying to get closer. The car lay upside down, most of the vehicle already engulfed. The roof resembled a squashed pop can, and pieces of glass from the shattered windshield and windows lay strewn across the ground, glistening like shards of ice.

"Hey!" I bent over. "Jesus Christ!" Was there someone in the back or was the light playing tricks on me? As I tried to get closer I felt the heat on my face. "Shit! *Fuck!*" I jumped back. "Help!" I shouted, my voice barely traveling beyond the blaze. "Help!"

I whipped my head around, desperately searching the street for oncoming headlights. Or a cyclist. A dog walker. *Anyone.* But I was alone.

I remembered the fire extinguisher my father always insisted I carry and legged it to my car, grabbing the can from the trunk and turning back. Jesus *Christ!* What had been a vehicle a few moments ago was a fireball now. Aiming the nozzle, I felt as if I'd stumbled into a sick nightmare I'd wake up from at any second. But moments passed, and I was still there. And it was pointless. I might as well have tried to blow the fire out. As I emptied the extinguisher the flames grew higher. Red-and-orange demons taunting me, daring me to try again.

"Fuck it!" I shouted as I threw the canister on the ground. "Fuck *you!*"

I bent over, trying to see inside the car properly. Even through the stench of burning petrol I could smell searing flesh. Vomit rose to the back of my throat, and my heart pounded as I realized there was definitely someone in there.

Was he—was it a he?—still alive? Everything else in the car was wreathed in billowing smoke, but there was a chance. And if I could get to him, *if I could just get to him*, I might be able to pull him free.

Images of burn victims flashed through my mind, and a small part of me thought he might be better off gone. I tried to get closer to the wreck, but when the hair on my arms singed and my face scorched like an instant sunburn, I jumped back, patting myself harder than I needed to.

The flames were even higher now, hotter, too, forcing me to retreat another few steps. I let my arms drop, ready to admit defeat.

No. Goddamn it. *No!* There had to be something I could do. I looked around again.

And that was when I saw her.

She lay a few meters away to the side of the blaze, face down on the road, dress pulled midway up her thighs, what had to be blood seeping out of her legs. Her body lay eerily still. How come I hadn't spotted her before?

"Get away from the car!" I screamed as I ran toward her, my arms flailing. "Get away!"

As I fell to my knees beside her the heat almost knocked me over again, and my eyes welled up with smoky tears. She was too close—far too close—for me to leave her there. I tried checking for a pulse, but my fingers trembled so badly, I couldn't tell if the thud-thudding I felt was hers or my own.

I knew if I moved her, and she was alive, I risked doing her more damage. But the alternative was too horrific. I got up, put my arms under hers, trying to ignore how her head lolled around like a rag doll, and dragged her away, surprised at how light she felt. Once I was sure we were far enough from the car I got her into the recovery position. I pulled off my sweater and put it under her head, brushed her matted hair out of her face and away from her closed, swollen eyes.

And then I talked to her. Told her everything would be okay. To hang on. Hang on. *Please hang on.* I continued talking, even as I heard the sirens in the distance, and right up until a paramedic the size of a sumo wrestler gently told me to move out of the way.

"Sir," he said. "It's okay now. Sir? You have to let us take care of her."

Somehow I let them guide me to the back of an ambulance and check me over, put a mask over my face, ask me what happened, if I knew the people involved, what had I seen, exactly? The paramedic came back and made me lie down with my legs up, muttering something to someone else about me not going into shock. From my new vantage point I watched as the firefighters worked on putting out the blaze, reducing what had once been a blue car to a smoldering steel shell. The smell of burning rubber filled my nostrils, and when more saliva collected in my mouth I worked hard to hold down my food.

The police blocked off the road and put up tarps so the wreckage and body were no longer visible. And over and over again I told myself: if only I'd done something differently.

If only I hadn't let Paul get so pissed he needed me to pour him into the cab.

If only I'd walked back to my car more quickly.

If only I'd put my foot down and gone through that yellow light.

If only…

I wondered, fleetingly, how many times my father had been at the scene of accidents like this one. How many families he'd visited in the middle of the night, standing on their doorstep in his police uniform, waking them up to tell them their loved one was gone. Dad never spoke about that side of his job. He liked to say he kept his cards close to his chest. More like the entire deck. Paul and I had always known when he'd had a bad day at work. He'd hug us that little bit tighter at night, sit on the end of our bed and ask us how our day had been, ignoring Mum when she reminded him for the fourth time that we needed to go to sleep.

A tall, bandy-legged police officer with the name tag G. Cook came to take my statement. His ginger hair peeked out from under his hat, and I noticed his eyes were so bloodshot, they resembled complicated road maps. Mine were probably no better.

The officer nodded silently, allowing me plenty of time to answer his questions, while he scribbled in his notebook. "So you don't know who was in the vehicle?"

I rubbed my hands over my face. "No. But what about the girl? Where did they—"

"Preston Hospital."

"He's dead, isn't he?" I swallowed. "The guy in the back. They couldn't save him."

Officer Cook lowered his notepad, put a hand on my shoulder. "No," he said quietly. "There was nothing we could do."

I smacked my fist against my chest. "*I* should have done something. I should have—"

"Listen to me," he said.

"But I—"

"*Did* do something. You stopped. You got out of your car.

You tried to put out the fire." I opened my mouth again, but he held up his hand and continued, "You pulled that young lady to safety. You stayed with her. You're helping us work out what happened." He paused. "I'd say you've done quite a lot, wouldn't you?"

"No," I said, looking away. "I did exactly *fuck* all."

NOW
NATE

"BLOODY HELL, IT'S good to see you, man." Paul's bear hug had the same warmth and power as our dad's. He stepped back, cursed and hugged me again. "It's been too long," he said. "Far too long."

"Come here, you." Lynne put her arms around me and squeezed. I noticed how easily I could clasp my hands behind her back, and she laughed. "Not quite the same size anymore, am I?"

Paul grinned as he caught my expression. "Don't look at me," he said. "I know better than to comment on my wife's girth more than once."

"Well, to be fair—" I turned to Lynne "—you had twins in there."

"God." Her face lit up with one of her effervescent smiles. "Please don't remind me. I was the size of a house *after* they fished them out. Before that people thought I was an estate."

"Stop it!" Abby walked up behind us and gave both Lynne and Paul one of her breezy, noncommittal hugs. "Where are those gorgeous creatures anyway?"

"Sleeping, thank Christ," Paul said, pulling a face. "If I had to listen to another *Mr. Men* song I think I would have lost my shit."

Abby laughed, then hummed the theme tune. Lynne and I joined, the three of us getting louder and louder until Paul held up his hands. "Argh! Enough." He clapped me on the shoulder. "I need a beer or three."

"No, you don't." Lynne grabbed her husband's arm. "We can't leave the girls in the car."

"Why not?" Paul shrugged. "Whoever takes them will bring 'em back in five minutes."

Lynne put a hand firmly on his chest. "Kids. Bags. Fetch. Now."

He saluted. "Yes, ma'am."

"I'll give you a hand," I said, grinning.

It was still a bit odd, seeing Paul utterly and completely devoted to one woman. Not as strange as seeing him with kids, though. That, I had to admit, had come as a shock to everyone.

He'd finally surrendered what he'd sworn was his eternal bachelor card three years ago. At almost forty-six he'd shown no signs of ending his mission to shag every woman within a hundred mile radius of London. Actually, by that point he'd possibly expanded that to a hundred and fifty. We'd agreed he'd only introduce me to his latest conquest if they'd been seeing each other for more than a month, and he hadn't done so in years. Then things changed, and it all got very strange, very fast.

Paul phoned one Friday morning, and I could tell something was up from his tone.

"Uh-oh," I said. "Another bunny-boiler on the loose?"

"No," Paul said. "Uh, it's, uh…"

"Someone's dad's after you or—"

"*No.* If you must know, I, uh, got dumped."

"You *what?*" I said. "Well, that's a first."

He sniffed. "She said she wanted to go out with someone younger."

I cleared my throat, trying not to laugh. "How old was she?"

"Twenty-seven," he said with a sigh. "Apparently me being more than twice her age grossed her out."

"She *actually* said that?"

"Yeah." He sighed again.

"Did you say twice…?"

"Yeah, smarty-pants. *Twice*. As in *two times*. It's messed up, man. Properly messed up."

"Did you love her?"

"Fuck, no." His big belly laugh almost took my ear out. "And you're missing the point."

I scratched my head. "What *is* the point?"

The click of his tongue was probably accompanied by an eye roll. "I'm getting old—"

"Sod off!"

"—so I want to drown my sorrows with an overpriced lunch and a beer. You up for it?"

"'Course."

"Great. I'll pick you up now."

"Now?" I said. "It's not even eleven yet."

"Yep. But I've finished a meeting, I'm thirsty and we'll get a good table."

Bang on schedule Paul arrived at the office five minutes later looking decidedly suave in his blue pin-striped suit and shoes he'd no doubt instructed one of his many lackeys to shine to perfection. As we stood in the hallway waiting for the lift he elbowed me gently in the ribs, indicating toward the left with his head. "Who's she?"

I groaned inwardly. He'd been dumped five minutes ago, and yet he was on the prowl already. I looked over, wondering how I could alert his next victim before it was too late. I could do without the hassle of a colleague crying on my shoulder for the next few weeks because he never returned her calls. It wouldn't have been the first time.

"Which one?" I said, frowning as I looked at the three women deep in conversation. "Two of them are blondes."

He shook his head. "Neither. I meant the short girl with the dark hair."

I squinted. "Lynne? Seriously?"

"Uh-huh."

"She runs the Cardiff office. And with respect, she wouldn't put up with your bullshit. She'd have your balls on a... Hang on." I grinned as I looked at him. "Are you...*blushing*?"

Paul shrugged. "She's, uh, cute."

I'd never heard my brother say the word *cute* before in relation to a woman. *Goddess, hot stuff, fun bundle, amusement party, very bad kitty and*, increasingly frequently, *MILF*. Yes, pig that he was, he regularly used all of those, and some, but *cute*? This was turning out to be a day of firsts.

"Fine," I said, "I'll introduce you. But don't say I didn't warn you when she tells you to get lost."

Turned out, I was wrong on two accounts. While Lynne wasn't Paul's usual pneumatic blonde archetype, she did turn out to be the love of his life. Within a year Paul had moved to Cardiff and they were married. My brother happily reminded me on his wedding day that you should "never judge an armchair by its upholstery, my friend." Then quickly added, "I'm talking about myself, man. I'm not saying my wife looks like furniture."

Nine months later the twins came along—totally planned— at least the getting pregnant part had been. Paul had said when he saw two fuzzy-looking blobs swimming around on the ultrasound screen he didn't move again for three days straight.

He was too busy watching the rest of his life flash in front of his eyes.

And now the four of them were spending Easter with us, and I'd finally get to have more than a fifteen-minute phone conversation with my big brother, a discussion usually peppered with demands for Daddy, Daddy, *Daddy*. Squared.

"So how are things?" I said as I lifted a sleepy Rachel—at least I think it was Rachel—while Paul tackled Rosie's seat belt, cursing under his breath about it being some kind of Mensa test.

"How are things?" he repeated. Then he lowered his voice to a whisper, giving a furtive glance around him. "Oh, man. It's tough, really tough. We're permanently exhausted. Why didn't you warn me?"

I laughed. "If I had you wouldn't have believed me. And you've got twins."

"Christ, if it's like this now," he said, "what will it be like when they're teenagers?"

"Absolute hell. Having girls is penance, you realize that?"

He rolled his eyes. "Tell me about it. I've already told Lynne if they show any signs of being like me they're getting chastity belts for their thirteenth birthday."

We took the kids into the house and gave them to Abby and Lynne, then returned to the car to unpack the trunk.

"And the amount of stuff you need," Paul said, hoisting two travel cots and a bag the size of a small elephant over his shoulder. "It's frigging ridiculous."

"Yep." I wondered whether I should point out he'd started saying "frig."

"I mean," he continued, "I used to throw a toothbrush and a pair of pants in a bag and take off for the weekend. Actually, the pants were optional. Now we pack half the sodding house."

I grinned. "Welcome to parenthood, my friend. It gets better. For a while at least."

"Oh, yeah?"

"Yeah. And in another twelve years they won't want anything to do with you anyway."

Paul put his head in his hands and groaned, but I could tell he was laughing, too.

"Hi, Nate."

I turned around. Nancy had arrived in her driveway next door and was in the process of unloading her car. As she bent over to pick up a couple of bags, her blouse fell forward, and I caught a glimpse of something sky blue and floral. I gave my head a slight shake, concentrated on her face and held up a hand. "Hey, Nancy. How are you?"

She put the bags down and strolled over, her long brown hair bouncing like one of those women in a shampoo advert. From nowhere, an image of her standing in the shower, water running over her breasts and thighs, darted through my mind, and I could feel my face getting warmer despite the miserable temperatures.

I hadn't seen Nancy in a few weeks, not since I'd checked out their heating, which turned out to be absolutely fine. Abby had insisted on leaving our new neighbors loads of time to settle in. When I said I was going to offer them my tools and maybe help put a few more things together, she hadn't been impressed.

"Leave them to it," she'd snapped. "You don't have to always fix everything, you know. I'm sure Liam is perfectly capable." Her mood hadn't improved for ages, and as I looked at Nancy's warm smile I couldn't help but wish Abby were as relaxed, instead of being as tightly wound as a pocket watch.

"How's the house coming along?" I said.

"Oh, great. I already started a few projects." She smiled. "I have *loads* of ideas."

I smiled back, trying not to focus too much on the dimples in her cheeks. I hadn't noticed them before. They were... *cute.* I cleared my throat. "Nancy, this is my brother, Paul. Paul, Nancy."

"I can see the resemblance," she said to Paul. "It's nice to meet you."

"You've just moved in?" he said.

"Last month. We moved down from Preston and—"

"No sh...*way*?" Paul said, turning to me. "We know the area well, don't we?"

"I've heard all about it." Nancy laughed. "We seem to be congregating around here. First Abby, now us. Do you live locally, too?"

"No, we're here for the weekend," Paul said. "I live in Cardiff now. That's where my wife's from."

"Oh, that's nice," Nancy said. "We went to the castle once when I was a kid. It was fun. Great city, isn't it?"

Paul nodded. "Yeah, not bad. But, uh, we won't be there much longer."

"You're moving back here?" I raised my eyebrows. "It's about time. That's fantastic!"

Paul looked a bit sheepish. "Er, no. We, uh, we're moving to Zurich in June."

"What?" My eyebrows practically slid down the back of my head. "You mean Zurich as in Zurich, *Switzerland*?"

"Yeah." He grimaced apologetically. "I only found out last night."

"But you never said anything." I felt like a bit of an idiot, having this discussion in front of Nancy, but *Switzerland*? What the hell?

He shrugged. "Didn't see any point. The company had a one-year contract going, so I applied thinking nothing would happen." He paused. "Next thing I know I've got a job in the land of cheese."

"Well, I think it's fantastic," Nancy said. "Switzerland? Wow. Nate, what a great excuse to visit." She looked at us both. "You'll have lots to celebrate this weekend. I should leave you to it."

"Join us." I just about stopped myself from scratching my head as I wondered why I'd extended the invitation so swiftly. Maybe the glimpse of her bra had messed with my mind.

Nancy looked at me, her head tilted sideways, her forehead in a slight frown. "Sorry?"

"I mean, you, Liam and Zac," I said, feeling the need to clarify. "Why not come over tomorrow night?"

"Oh, well—"

"The weather's supposed to be good. Paul's a master at the old barbecue. And we've got so much steak we could re-build a cow."

Nancy grinned. "Sounds great."

"Yeah?"

"Absolutely. We don't have any plans. You sure it's not too much trouble?"

"No trouble at all," I said. "The more the merrier. How does six thirty sound?"

"Great. Okay then. I'm not sure about Zac, but Liam and I will definitely be there. I'll bring an apple pie, if that's okay?"

"Apple pie's my favorite," Paul said.

"Oh, good. Thanks so much, Nate. It'll be a relief to get

away from looking at color schemes and fabric swatches." She turned to Paul. "Nice meeting you. See you tomorrow."

"Look forward to it," Paul said, giving a slight bow.

We watched Nancy walk back to her car, although we both pretended we didn't. As we pulled the rest of the bags from the back of Paul's car, he said, "She likes you."

"What?"

"She *likes* you, you daft prick."

I laughed. "Wait till you see her other half, then you'll see how stupid that sounds. He says he works at a bank but I reckon he moonlights as a Chippendale or something."

Paul gave me a look. "I may be married, but I'm not stupid." He lowered his voice. "And I saw the way you looked at her. You be careful there, sunshine. Believe me, shagging the neighbor never ends well."

I harrumphed and picked up a bag, wondering if Paul could possibly be right. I couldn't remember the last time someone other than Abby had shown any interest, let alone flirted with me.

My wife had pointed out a couple of times when waitresses made doe eyes at me, then laughed when I asked her if she was delirious. Abby reckoned my radar had been permanently shelved when we got married, that if a woman came up and snogged me—tongue and all—I'd still pass it off as a case of mistaken identity. I told her it had actually happened once. In a dark corner at a Saturday afternoon disco with Heather Kitchen when I was thirteen. As first kisses go, it had been a bit of a letdown when she'd realized I wasn't my mate Justin.

I walked back toward the house, considering the possibility of an attractive and quietly sexy woman like Nancy finding me even remotely interesting. It put so much spring in my step, I could have done with a couple of weight belts.

"How's Abby?" Paul said, bringing me back down to earth.

I stopped and lowered my voice. "I'm not sure. She's been a bit...*off* these days."

"*Off?*"

"Yeah. Grumpy. Moody."

"Have you asked her what's going on?"

"Hah. Do you ask Lynne when she's in a mood?"

"Not if I think it's my fault. She once said if I couldn't figure out what I'd done wrong, then she couldn't be bothered to tell me."

"And did you figure it out?"

"Oh, yeah. I'd forgotten it was the anniversary of the day we met. I told her men can only remember one anniversary. It's a genetic thing. But she waved my phone in front of my face and said, 'There's an app for that, Techno Man.'"

"I think it might have something to do with Tom," I said. "Abby was shouting in her sleep again. She hasn't done that for ages."

"Anniversary's coming up soon, isn't it?"

I half shrugged. "Kind of. July."

"There's your answer then. Can't be easy, celebrating her birthday and commemorating her brother's death." He opened the front door. "Especially seeing it was Abby's fault."

"What was my fault?" Abby stood in the hallway.

"Uh..." Paul's eyes darted from me to Abby and back again. "That I got married and ended up with twins. You helped me pick the ring, remember?"

Abby smiled, but her jaw seemed to remain clenched, and I hoped she hadn't heard the rest of our conversation. "I ran into Nancy." I closed the door and set the last of the mammoth luggage collection on the floor. "I invited them for the barbecue tomorrow night."

"What? Nate—"

"She seems nice," Paul said before Abby could finish. "And Nate said her husband's a bit of all right."

Abby frowned. "Well—"

"Actually." I laughed. "Abby thinks he's an—"

"Okay guy." She finished the sentence for me. "But I wish you'd given me more notice," she said with another tight smile, her eyes sending a clear message she didn't want Paul to know how she felt. Couldn't say I blamed her. Paul had never exactly been known for his discretion. When I was eleven he told one of the teachers about my crush on her. I pretended to have a fever for three days, sticking the thermometer on the radiator when Mum wasn't looking until she threatened to take me to hospital.

"Don't worry," Paul said to my wife. "We'll fetch whatever else we need. And I've got a Texas marinade recipe I—"

"A Texas marinade recipe?" I rubbed my chin. "Who *are* you? Gordon Ramsay?"

He winced as he picked up the bags. "Trust me, he'll be breaking the door down when he gets a whiff."

As I watched my brother walk up the stairs I glanced at Tom's photograph. Remembering Paul's comment about the anniversary, I put my arms around Abby. "I love you," I whispered in her ear. "I'm always here for you. Okay?"

"I know," she said, and I couldn't help noticing her hug wasn't nearly as tight as mine.

NOW
ABBY

SHIT. SHIT. *SHIT*.

My husband, the person who, by his own admission, only haphazardly organized any of our social events, had invited Liam and Nancy for dinner. And they were coming over this evening. For dinner. Not a *drink*. I could have maybe managed a *drink*. That would have meant seeing them for an hour, give or take. But dinner, especially with Paul and Lynne, would go on until the next morning. What the hell was I going to do?

I'd hardly slept at all, too many thoughts and scenarios buzzing through my head. I'd finally dropped off at around four, only to be woken by the twins two hours later, and now all I wanted to do was curl up in a ball and hide.

I'd been doing a lot of that lately. Avoiding Liam for the past month had been relatively easy. I'd continued setting off for the gym or the office earlier than usual, and came home late, too, taking on extra work without hesitation—my boss probably wondered if I was vying for her job. And at home I made sure either Nate or Sarah was with me when I stepped outside. It was ridiculous. It had to stop.

I looked at myself in the bathroom mirror, thinking I'd have to emerge at some point or a search party would come knocking. I knew I wouldn't be able to hide forever, not today in the downstairs loo, and certainly not forever in the house. Spring was here, a time I'd always looked forward to, when winter finally released us from its clutches, its parting gift longer days and promises of sunshine.

But this year Liam would be tackling Barbara Baker's unkempt lawn and overgrown trees on the opposite side of our fence, playing Happy Families with his cheery, button-nosed, curly-haired wife.

I'd figured I had another couple of weeks to get over myself and accept the situation, give me the time to tame the beast within. As it stood, I had a few hours.

I wondered if I could feign another illness, but swiftly decided I couldn't use that excuse again. Liam would no doubt see straight through it, Nate would pester me about how I should take it easy and Lynne would force-feed me foul-smelling homemade remedies.

My heart was pounding, and I made myself take a few deep breaths. I'd been short-tempered around Nate and Sarah, had even snapped at Paul and Lynne twice, despite trying hard not to. Most of the time I felt like a hormonal teenager, oscillating between wanting to scream at someone or yell at myself in the mirror instead.

It couldn't go on. It *couldn't*. I had to accept that Liam lived next door—short of moving, which I'd tentatively explored with Nate one night only to be shot down with loud protests—there wasn't anything I could do.

Liam and I were married, I repeated to myself again for the millionth time that day. To *other* people. My feelings—

any feelings—were irrelevant. Nothing was going to happen. Nothing *could* happen. I'd make sure of it.

Another deep breath, a flick of my hair, a perfectly poised smile and I walked back into the kitchen. Lynne greeted me with a couple of limes and a paring knife in her hand. "Oh, there you are," she said. "I took the liberty of starting on the G&T's. I don't suppose you want one?"

"No, I'll stick with water."

"You still don't drink?" She poured a generous helping of gin into the glass, added the tonic and a slice of lime.

"No."

"Never, ever?"

"No. Never, ever."

"God, I couldn't do my job without alcohol. I'm sure Nate has told you when you work in recruitment, you need booze." She laughed. "But now I know your secret."

"Secret?" I cleared my throat. "I don't have any secrets."

She took a sip of her drink, the ice cubes making a clunking sound against her glass, and gestured toward me. "Your amazing figure. Before the girls, heck, even when I was *sixteen*, I was never as trim as you."

"Oh." I shrugged, trying to disguise the relief on my face. "I'm careful. No bread or pasta. No chocolate or cakes. I go to the gym and run at least four or five times a week."

Lynne grimaced. "God. That sounds way too punishing. I'd die without crumpets. And chocolate. I can't do without my daily fix or two."

I forced a smile. "You get used to it."

"So these new neighbors?" Lynne said before sipping her drink. "Anything I should know about before they come over? Uncovered any horrible skeletons in their cupboards yet?"

I could feel my cheeks flush, so I quickly crossed over to

the fridge, retrieving the lettuce, tomatoes and spring onions. "No." I tried to press my forehead on the milk jug without her noticing. "They seem pretty normal. You know, mum, dad, teenage boy."

"How old?"

"Midforties?"

She laughed. "I meant the boy."

"Oh. Seventeen, maybe?" I knew exactly how old he was, remembered how, years ago, Liam had showed me a picture of his baby. I refused to let my mind elaborate on the memory, and shoved it back into the deepest darkest corner of my mind, inside the box I'd marked Do Not Open. I ran the tomatoes under the water and put them on the wooden chopping board.

"Is he cute?"

I rolled my eyes and picked up the knife. "He's a bit young for you, Lynne."

She laughed. "Don't be silly," she said, waving her glass. "Not for me. For Sarah. She doesn't have a boyfriend, does she?"

A shiver traveled down my spine. "She's too young."

Lynne snorted. "She's sixteen. How old were you when you had your first boyfriend?"

"That's different."

"How?"

I slammed the knife down a lot harder than I'd intended. "It just *is*, okay?"

"Uh, is everything all right?"

I exhaled. "Yes. Sorry. A bit tired, that's all."

She looked at me. "Well, we won't make it a late night then. I'd better go and check on the girls."

I didn't see the ruby-red smears until she'd gone; I hadn't

even felt the blade pierce my skin. Swearing under my breath, I dug out a plaster and wrapped it around the gash in my finger, my mind racing.

Lynne's suggestion of Sarah and Zac liking each other wasn't new to me. The idea had kept me awake many times. I'd even dreamt about it, waking up amid sweaty shouts of "No!"

I shuddered at the image of them together and quickly batted it away. When I'd asked Sarah—*again*—what she thought of Zac, she'd been dismissive, waving a hand and muttering about him already being Mr. Popular at school, but as far as she was concerned, still an idiot.

I'd checked her diary to be sure. And as I read the pages, the feelings of disgust I felt toward myself actually made me feel better. It meant at least part of me was still a decent human being.

I forced my mind to go blank while I finished making the salad, then peeled the potatoes Nate and Paul had bought that morning. I could see them through the window, standing outside in the garden, no doubt discussing lawn mowers, beer and, in Paul's case anyway, probably the approximate weight of Kate Upton's individual breasts.

Nate looked up and waved at me with a big grin on his face. I raised my hand to return the gesture, but remained unable to even half match his smile.

I jumped when my mobile rang, and I snatched it up, hoping it was Nancy or Liam, canceling the dinner. Then I remembered neither of them had my number, and when I looked at the phone, my heart sank. It was my mother again, and I let it go to voice mail.

I listened to her curt message, instructing me to call her, that she really needed to talk. A shiver of satisfaction slid down my back as I pressed the delete button. I didn't care about what she wanted to say; I already had enough emotional turmoil dragging me in all directions. Why would I allow the person who despised me the most in the entire world make me feel even worse? She'd never forgiven me for what I did. What she didn't know was that I hadn't either.

THEN

ABBY

TOM WAS DEAD.

They hadn't said so at first, but it was obvious from the looks on their faces. The nurses had kept their eyes down and their voices low, telling me over and over I'd be okay.

I'd be okay. I'd be *okay*? I'd never be okay again.

Tom was dead.

I was alone in my room again after my mother had been asked to leave. She'd arrived a few hours before, probably as soon as the police had told her both her children had been in an accident. I heard her screams in the corridor. "My baby's dead! He's dead." Someone must have asked her to please calm down because Mum shouted, "How can I? My son is *dead*!"

Things went quiet for a while. I drifted in and out of consciousness for a few seconds, and when I opened my eyes Mum stood at the bottom of the bed. The sun was barely up, yet she'd pinned her hair into an elaborate bun. Her cheeks glistened with a mix of rouge and tears, but her waterproof mascara clung stubbornly to her long lashes. I noticed how her starched, white shirt had been precision pressed to the point where it could have marched around by itself. I'd always been amazed at how quickly she could get herself together, but given the circumstances it disgusted me.

"Mum," I said. "I…I…"

"Tom's dead." She crossed her arms protectively over her torso, her eyes focusing steadily on mine. "He's gone."

"I know… I—"

"You were driving."

"I…I think so. I can't remember but—"

"And drinking." She raised her chin. "Weren't you?"

"I'm sorry, Mum. *Please*," I whispered. "I'm so sorry."

"I can't see him, Abigail. They won't let me."

I swallowed. "I know. I asked to see him. They said… They said he… There's…"

"Nothing to recognize."

I watched her eyes well up. "They gave me this." She opened her palm to reveal Tom's necklace, the one with the engraved dog tags I'd given him for his eighteenth birthday. It was no longer silver, but badly blackened and charred. "This is all I have left."

I wanted to hold her, her to hold me. Feel the warmth she'd always shown Tom, and the strength that made her so independent, strong but equally cold and distant. Instinctively I held my arms out. She didn't move.

"There's nothing to recognize," she repeated, her eyes hardening again. "Nothing at all, Abigail. Tom's gone."

"Mum, I'm—"

"He's gone," she whispered, as she put her hands over her face, her shoulders shaking. *"Gone."*

I willed myself to disappear. Wanted the floor to crumble, taking me, the bed, the drip and the beeping machines with it. I'd fall, fall, fall. Continue falling until I vanished completely.

That was what I deserved. To be gone, too. But the ground stayed firm and neither of us spoke. Mum kept perfectly still and stared at me until the doctor walked in.

"Remember me?" he said, then turned to Mum. "She was pretty out of it a while ago. I'm Dr. Raj Patel." He held out his hand.

"Dolores Sanders," she said, giving his hand one deliberate shake. "Abigail's mother."

He came over to me, bending slightly at the hips as he listened to my chest with his stethoscope. "How's the pain?" he asked gently.

"I can't feel anything." I looked away. I didn't want to see the empathy and concern in his big brown eyes. I deserved none of it.

"You were lucky," he said quietly as he hung the stethoscope around his neck and took my pulse at the wrist.

I snapped my head around. "Lucky?"

He patted my hand. "Lucky you were ejected from the car. Lucky how you landed. And very lucky someone stopped. Otherwise you—"

"Someone stopped?" I said. "Who?"

"A young man, I think." He cleared his throat. "The bruises will fade. The fracture in your leg will heal quickly—it was relatively easy to fix. But both legs will be badly scarred from all the lacerations. They were pretty deep. Again, you were lucky you didn't hit an artery."

I wanted him to stop saying I was lucky. My brother was dead because of me. How did that make me lucky? "I don't care about scars."

Dr. Patel nodded slowly and I noticed he had one himself, above his top lip, in the shape of a boomerang. Maybe he was Australian. I suddenly wanted to giggle. Tom would like that joke. I made a mental note to tell him before I remembered, with a sharp tightening in my chest, that I'd never be able to tell Tom anything again.

Meanwhile, the doctor had continued talking. "…so skin grafts may be a possibility in time. They do marvelous things with plastic surgery these days. You'll be as good as new and…"

I looked away again, studied the bland, gray metallic blinds that covered the windows, noticed how immaculately clean they were. Not a speck of dust anywhere. Sterile, devoid of life and the possibility of life. I shook my head. The scars would stay.

"…so call the nurse if you need anything." Dr. Patel squeezed my hand. "Anything at all."

"How about a drink?" Mum said. She'd been so quiet I'd almost forgotten she was there.

"She can have water or juice," he replied with a smile. "I'll ask the nu—"

Mum half laughed. "What about vodka?"

Dr. Patel's brow furrowed. "Excuse me?"

"Or was it gin?" She put her hands on her hips and looked at me, her blue eyes colder than a winter's day. "Or beer? Or wine? Maybe all of the above?"

"Mrs. Sanders, I don't think—"

"She drank." Mum spat the words in his direction but didn't take her gaze off me. "My daughter drank. Then she drove and—"

"Perhaps we—"

"—now her brother, my *son*, is dead."

I closed my eyes, once more demanding the floor to open up. Please *open up.*

"Mrs. Sanders," the doctor said, "I understand this must be incredibly difficult for you—"

"Do you? *Do* you? It's her fault." Mum pointed at me, and the intensity in her voice surprised even me. "She *killed* him."

"Mum, please." Tears slid down my cheeks.

"It was an accident," Dr. Patel said. "And—"

"You *killed* Tom," Mum shouted at me. "You fucking *killed my son*."

I'd rarely heard Mum swear. It sounded so ugly coming from her mouth. But that was nothing compared to the look of rage and absolute revulsion on her face. She didn't need to tell me she hated every single bone in my body, begrudged every breath I took, wished it were my charred remains in the morgue. She didn't need to tell me. And I wished it were me, too.

"You need to leave, Mrs. Sanders," the doctor said as he put a hand on her arm, firmly guiding her toward the door. *"Now."*

I watched as Mum regained some of her composure, shaking off his grip, taking deep breaths, her mask of perfection sliding over her face once more.

"Oh, don't worry, Doctor," she said with a terse smile. "I'm leaving." She strode toward the door, then turned, her face ashen, her lips tight. "I'll never forgive you for this, Abigail. *Never.*" And then she left, the click-clacking sound of her heels following her down the corridor.

Dr. Patel raised his eyebrows, exhaled deeply and gave a tentative smile. "Your mother will come around. We've seen this before, unfortunately. But she'll forgive you. She needs time."

I let go of the breath I'd been holding as if it were a life jacket, and immediately felt like I was drowning again. "Yeah." I gave a halfhearted nod. "I'm sure you're right." It was easier than telling him he was wrong. Easier than trying to explain the complicated relationship my mother and I had endured.

Dr. Patel opened his mouth to say something else, so I turned my head, focusing on the cleanliness of the metallic blinds again. After a few seconds I heard the door shut quietly, and I was alone.

"Abby? Abby?" The voice was gentle, quiet, familiar.

"Tom?" I said, eyes half open, trying to focus on the shape next to me. "Tom?"

"It's me, baby. It's Liam." His voice sounded different, hoarse, and I noticed he'd been crying. "It took me ages to find you. Oh, baby, look at you." He kissed me softly on the cheek, his fingers cupping my face. "Look at you. I'm so sorry."

"Tom," I whispered. "He's...he's..."

"I know," Liam said as he tried to wrap his arms around me but stopped when I let out a soft moan. "Oh, my god. I'm so sorry, Abby. I'm so sorry."

I cried again. "I...I don't remember anything."

He pulled away slightly. "What do you mean? You know me, Abby, I'm your—"

"No, I meant about last night." I took a deep breath. "It's all fuzzy."

Liam swallowed, then blinked and quietly said, "What do you remember?"

I covered my eyes with my palms for a second, trying to magic the memories back into my head. "You and me in the shower. Tom calling about Sophia." I paused. "Picking him up and going to Humpty's. I...I think I wanted to go to Red's, but he said no. He wanted to go home."

"And then?"

"That's it. That's all I can remember." Tears streamed down

my cheeks, their dampness pooling in my ears. "Then... nothing... Nothing until I woke up here." I searched his face, tried to figure out what he was thinking, then I frowned and reached for the swollen bruise on his forehead. "What happened to your face?"

Liam shifted in his seat. "Abby, I—"

With a sharp knock on the door, two police officers wearing sullen expressions stepped into the room. "Abigail Sanders?" the tall one with ginger hair said. The dark purple bags under his eyes made me think he hadn't seen a bed in weeks.

"Yes." My voice sounded small and pathetic, and I was sure they could hear my heart pounding against my ribs like an increasingly manic drum solo.

"I'm Officer Cook." He pointed toward the other man, who was significantly shorter, his smooth skin an indication his police career was a recent thing. "This is Officer Marsh. We'd like to ask you a few questions."

"Can't it wait?" Liam said. "She's been through a lot."

"I appreciate that," Cook said slowly. "But the doctor cleared her for questioning, and sooner is better than later." He turned to me, and I tried to disappear into my pillow. "We understand the passenger in the car was your brother, Thomas?"

"Tom," I whispered. "He hates being called Thomas."

"We're very sorry for your loss, Miss," Marsh said. "Very sorry."

I swallowed, thinking again I didn't deserve any sympathy. Punishment—that's what should be on the menu. Now, and for every single one of my days to come.

"Sir," Cook said to Liam. "Could you wait outside, please?"

"Liam's my boyfriend," I said, grabbing hold of his arm. "Please let him stay."

"Uh, shouldn't you have a lawyer?" Liam said as he eyed the policemen.

Cook and Marsh looked at each other, then at me.

"I don't need a lawyer, Liam," I said quickly. "There's nothing to hide."

"Abby, you don't—"

"It's fine. I'll be fine."

Cook cleared his throat. "What can you tell us about last night?" he said, pulling a notebook from his pocket.

I burst into a monologue, trying to get everything I could think of out of my head. Tom calling me about Sophia and the beer crate incident. Me telling Liam I'd take Tom out for some drinks instead of the three of us going out. Liam not minding the change of plans. "He's a wonderful boyfriend," I said, looking at Liam, the certainty of him now being too good for me wrapping itself around my neck, gently starting to squeeze. "If only I'd asked you to come out with us." I tried swallowing the lump in my throat. "You'd never let me drive if I was off my face. Never."

"Abby..." Liam held my hand, but I couldn't return the pressure from his fingers.

"It's our birthday tomorrow," I said as I rubbed my eyes, trying to squeeze the tears back in. "Tom's and mine."

"You're twins?" Marsh said gently.

"No. Tom's a year younger. It's his twenty-first." Liam squeezed my hand again as I continued. "And his present is hidden away at the back of my cupboard." I swallowed once more. "A Viking cue. The Stars and Stripes one. Tom loves—" I stopped, blinked. "He *loved* America."

The tears were impossible to hold back this time. Liam handed me another tissue, and I continued my ramblings. I told them about us having beers at the pub, playing a few games of darts, me suggesting we go to Red's, him asking the barman to rack up another round of B-52s instead. "Tom almost slid off the stool, and I laughed so hard I almost pe—" I exhaled, thinking everything had seemed hilarious last night. Right up until this morning, when somebody I'd never met before, their hands stuffed deep into the pockets of their white lab coat and a grave expression on their face, told me my baby brother was dead.

My shoulders shook and Liam stroked my hair. "Nothing's ever going to be funny again," I sobbed. "Nothing." After a few moments I looked up at the policemen, ready to submit to their judgmental, contemptuous stares. Instead I saw empathy in their eyes and looked away.

"So you'd agree you had a fair amount to drink?" Cook's voice was even, his eyebrows raised, his pen poised, ready to permanently record all my deadly sins.

"Yes, but I can't remember exactly how much," I whispered and looked down at my hands. "I never drink and drive." My eyes met Cook's again. *"Never."*

"I'm afraid it only takes the once," he said. "And the blood test showed an alcohol level well over the limit."

I started sobbing again, salty tears running into the corners of my mouth as I said, "How could I be so stupid? I'm such a bloody *idiot*."

"What else do you remember?" Cook's gentle question pulled me from the edge of the deep black hole I was staring into in my mind, wishing it would suck me into oblivion. "What about leaving the pub?"

"No."

"Or the drive?"

"I can't—"

"You were on Liverpool Road, heading to Hutton. Where Tom lived."

"Nothing," I said as I looked at Cook and registered his half frown. "I don't even remember getting in the car. I've tried, honestly I have." I closed my eyes until the click of someone's tongue made my temper flare out of nowhere. "I'm not lying," I said loudly as I looked at the policemen and lifted myself up. "I'm *not*. The doctor called it, uh, he said..."

Cook clicked his pen, and I realized that was where the sound had come from. "Retrograde amnesia," he said, and I sank back down onto my pillow.

"What's that?" Liam said. "Is it serious? Please tell me it's not—"

"No, it means I can't remember anything before or after the accident," I said. "Dr. Patel thinks it's because I went through the windshield." I blinked. "On the way to hell."

Cook cleared his throat and looked at Liam. "And where were you, sir?"

"He was packing his stuff." I started to cry. "We're supposed to move in together."

Marsh looked at us both. "Do you remember if you drove anyone else?"

My hands dropped to my sides as if they'd instantly filled with lead. "Was there somebody else in the car?" My heart sped up, and I wiped my palms on the blanket. The possibility hadn't even crossed my mind.

"Well—"

"Please," I croaked. "Please say there was nobody else."

"No, Abby," Cook said. "Nobody else in the vehicle. Nobody else involved." I took a deep breath, tried to slow my racing heart as he continued. "But we're curious about one thing. Why was Tom in the back seat?"

"Abby," Liam said. "I—"

"Liam," Cook said firmly as he held up a hand. "Let her answer the question."

My eyes flooded with tears. "Tom had a thing about sitting in the front passenger seat," I whispered. "He always insists...*insisted* on getting in the back."

"Why?"

I held my breath for a second. "He's done it since we were kids. Never wanted to sit in the front. Always said he felt safer in the back. I used to tease him all the time, but he didn't care. That's Tom for you. Stubborn as hell."

As Cook scribbled something in his notebook I forced my memory again, trying to make the little pieces I could almost, *almost* grab hold of fit together. "What happens now?"

They looked at each other, and Marsh spoke softly. "Our specialists have attended the scene, and they're trying to work out what happened."

"How?" Liam said. "If nobody else was there?"

"Tire marks on the road, positioning of the car and so on," Cook said. "We'll also make an appeal for witnesses to come forward. We're not expecting much, but we'll talk to the young man who stopped and helped. See if he remembers anything."

"You didn't tell me someone stopped," Liam said, looking at me and then at Cook. "Who was it? We have to thank him."

"We'll give Abby the details once we've spoken to him again, and if he wants us to," Cook answered, then looked at me. "That's all for now. Thank you."

"I'm going to prison," I said, staring at him. "Aren't I?"

"That's not for me to decide," he said quietly.

My eyes darted around the room, then landed on Liam's face, which had turned the light green shade of the walls. I felt his hand tighten on my shoulder.

"Abby," he said as we watched the policemen leave, quietly conferring with each other on the way to the lift. "Jesus, I should have… I wish I'd… I'm so sorry."

But I closed my eyes, didn't want to listen to another person saying how *sorry* they were. He'd begun despising me for what I'd done, I was sure of it. Somehow he was being different toward me. He'd already started pulling away. And I couldn't blame him. How could he love me after what I'd done? How could anyone?

"I'm tired," I said quietly, turning my head away from him. "Let me sleep. I'll call you."

He bent over and kissed my forehead. "You rest."

I sobbed quietly after he left. Rage, denial, fear, hopelessness—impossible waves of emotion smashed into me, churning me back and forth, back and forth, as if controled by some psychotic sadist.

Twelve hours ago Liam and I had decided to live together. But now we may as well have been stranded on different planets.

The pain in my legs woke me, and I wasn't sure how long I'd been asleep. The nurse with short blond hair and fake eyebrows mercifully pumped me full of morphine again and told me to rest some more. Seconds after she left, Liam walked into the room carrying a spoon, three pots of chocolate pudding and a plastic-wrapped sandwich.

"Have you been awake for long?" He held out the food. I shook my head, and when I didn't reach out he put the items on the tray in front of me. "Shall I open something for you?"

"I'm not hungry."

"You have to eat."

"No, I don't," I snapped. "I really don't."

He looked at me for a while. "I've been thinking about what should happen next," he said. "I mean, after...you get out of here. And, uh, Tom's funeral." Long pause. "I can still move in."

"With me?" I raised my eyebrows. "You still want to?"

"Yes. Nothing has changed and—"

"How can you say that?" My voice went up a few notches. "Everything has changed. Everything!"

Liam took a step toward me, but when he touched my hand I pulled it away.

"You'll need help around the flat," he said. "Let me be there for you. I feel so...responsible. We could—"

"Don't, Liam."

"Don't what?"

"Pretend everything's going to be okay. Pretend that playing house will help."

"Baby, we'll get through this and—"

"How? I killed Tom. I don't see how I'll ever get through this. Ever."

"You need time," Liam said. "I'm here for you. I'll always be here for you."

"I'd like to be alone." My voice came out as a strangled whisper. "Please, I—"

"Abby. I love you."

"Please." I turned my head away from him. "Go. I do need time. Alone. I'll call you when I'm ready, okay?"

I didn't open my eyes for ages, not until I was absolutely sure he'd left. And while the drugs had helped the pain in my body subside, the agony traveling throughout my soul and into my heart was unbearable. I wanted to scream, howl, swear and rant, climb out of bed, get a barrel full of morphine or whatever I could find and pump it into my veins.

Liam and I were meant to be together, everybody said so. For the first time I hadn't kept parts of me compartmental- ized, denying him access, like I'd always done before. I told him everything, to the point where sometimes he had to kiss me to shut me up. We fit together, like in those unrealistic, sappy Hollywood movies. Except in our case, none of it was scripted.

In so many ways Liam had become my savior. The only person apart from Tom who'd stopped me from giving up on relationships—with boyfriends, girlfriends, family. But now Tom was gone, and it was all because of me.

The punishment a judge and jury would impose didn't frighten me. I welcomed it. Nothing could be worse than the lifelong sentence I'd handed myself anyway. Knowing my brother had burned to death because of what I'd done. No other sentence would even come close.

Lying in that hospital bed in the clean room with the ster- ile blinds, I vowed I'd make myself pay for the rest of my life. If Tom couldn't live, I didn't deserve to be happy. My shoul- ders dropped as the finality of my decision crystalized in my mind. It had to be this way. It had to. After all, Liam would soon see me for what I truly was.

A monster.

I barely moved for hours, not until a man with a full head of gray hair, thin wiry spectacles and a freckle-dashed face entered the room. He was dressed in a somber suit and held a shiny black briefcase with a silver buckle under one arm.

"Miss Sanders?" he said, and as he smiled his nose bent slightly to the left.

"Are you another policeman?"

"No, no. I'm Sean Joyce. From Cascio, Joyce and Blunt."

The name rang a distant bell, but when I didn't answer he added, "I'm a solicitor."

"I'm not sure I understand. I didn't call—"

"Your mother did. My partner, Mr. Blunt, handled her divorce."

That was where I recognized the name from. "But why..."

"She said you'll need legal help."

I looked down, felt the heat spreading across my cheeks. "I can't afford to, um..."

"Oh, don't worry." Mr. Joyce tapped his briefcase with his index finger. "It's been taken care of. Your mother, she—"

"I can't accept her money. We don't... I don't deserve it, we... She hates me and—"

"Miss Sanders, *Abby*," Mr. Joyce said gently but with a firmness that made me look up at him. "Your mother was very clear that she doesn't want to see you in prison. The fees have been taken care of. So let me help you." I nodded slowly, and he pulled up a chair.

"First of all," he said as he patted my hand, "I'm so sorry for your loss. I won't ask how you're feeling emotionally. I find the question abominable, given the circumstances."

I half smiled. "Thank you."

"But how are you physically?" he continued. "Do you need anything? Are you in pain?"

"My legs... They hurt."

Mr. Joyce squeezed my hand. "Shall I ask the nurse to—"

"No," I said loudly, then dropped my voice. "The pain makes it more real."

He looked at me with his pale blue eyes, and I wondered what he was thinking.

"I never met Tom," he said after a moment. "But your mother speaks highly of him."

"Yes. He's wonderful." I bit the inside of my lip. "Was."

Mr. Joyce opened his briefcase and balanced a thick, yellow legal pad on one thigh. "Let's start from the beginning. Tell me everything."

He made copious notes as I talked, gave me tissues for my tears and patted my hand when I sobbed so hard I couldn't speak. He asked pertinent questions, probing as gently as I imagined he could, and never once, or so it seemed, passed judgment. It was like talking to a saint.

"Take your time, Abby," he said softly, and on more than one occasion. "We have all the time in the world."

I got to the end of my story. "So," I said, exhausted from the range of emotions I never thought would be possible for any human to go through in such a short time, "how long will I be in prison?"

Mr. Joyce patted my hand again. "There are no prior convictions. No history of alcoholism, correct?"

"No, none."

"Well, a large part of the sentence will depend on how far over the alcohol limit you were. A custodial sentence is mandatory, I'm afraid."

I swallowed. "What's that?"

He cleared his throat. "Prison, potentially." He held up a hand before I could say anything. "But under two years can be suspended. People tend to see this kind of situation with a more compassionate eye. After all, your only brother died in an accident you allegedly caused."

"I caused it, Mr. Joyce. I'm guilty. You don't need to tiptoe."

"Right. Well, they'll look at how you were driving, too."

"What do you mean?"

"The police could determine your actions contributed to

the accident in some way. If you were speeding, for example. But there'll have to be some form of physical evidence showing you were at fault. Do you understand?"

"Other than the alcohol, you mean?" I said. "But what will the consequences be? Surely there'll be some?"

"Well, I'll try my best for a suspended sentence. You'll likely lose your license for at least two years. Probably obligatory endorsement and compulsory extended test." He must have seen my face. "It means you'll have to re-sit your driving test."

"I don't care about that."

He smiled. "Of course not. Look, I realize the whole situation is terribly frightening, but I'll help you through this. You're not alone." Mr. Joyce ran a hand through his thick hair. "It'll take a few months to get this sorted out, hopefully no more than a year. But we'll get there." He stood up. "Is there anything else I can do for you now?"

"No. But thank you."

Mr. Joyce smiled. "It was nice to meet you, Abby. I only wish the reasons were different."

He held out his hand. It felt soft, warm, and I wanted to keep on holding it, snuggle up in his palm, ask him to please keep me safe for a little while longer, but it was time to let go.

Dr. Patel stood at the bottom of my bed when I woke up.

"How are you?" he said. "I hear you slept for hours and haven't asked for more morphine."

I yawned and rubbed my eyes. "What time is it?"

"Twenty past ten." When I frowned he added, "Sunday morning."

A fleeting smile crossed my lips. Then a wave of nausea grabbed hold of my gut, turning it inside out and around and around. From nowhere, Diana Ross's voice popped into my head, and all I could think of was Tom flicking me, telling me to stop singing that song. And then all I could see were images of *The Muppets* and I wanted to laugh and laugh, not because it was funny, but because it was so overwhelmingly *sad*.

Dr. Patel looked at me. "Abby, I'm going to arrange for you to see the hospital's grief counselor as soon as possible. To talk."

"Okay."

Dr. Patel kept looking at me but remained silent until the spiky-haired nurse arrived. I let them move me around as they checked me over and looked at my legs, removing dressing, inspecting stitches, talking in medical terms I didn't understand.

"Everything looks good," Dr. Patel said as the nurse left, then he crossed his arms in front of his chest. "Have you remembered anything more about the accident?"

"No. Everything's still blank."

"That may never change. But give yourself time."

Time. That word. That theory again. If I gave myself enough time, everything would be okay. *Time heals all wounds*. How wrong. How impossibly wrong.

Once I was alone again, I attempted to swallow the food that had been left for me while I'd slept. The bread stuck to the roof of my mouth. The coffee tasted bitter. The yogurt bland. My eyes welled up, and I wanted to retch after every bite.

"Thank goodness you're eating." Liam came into the room holding the biggest bunch of flowers I'd ever seen. White lilies had always been my favorite. He set them down and hugged me. "How are you?"

"Tired of people asking me that question," I snapped, then mumbled, "Sorry."

"It's okay. I brought you some magazines. It'll give you something to do."

He kissed my forehead, and I wanted to wrap my arms around his neck, ask him to carry me away, take me somewhere safe. But then I looked at him, and all I could see were moments we'd shared with Tom. Playing darts or pool at the pub, them gently making fun of my music choices, or debating the best football teams. I'd told them more than once they should've been dating each other, and I was so happy I'd found someone who'd love my brother almost as much as I did.

"You shouldn't have come," I whispered. "I said I'd call."

"I know, baby." Liam stroked my cheek. "But it's your birthday. I didn't want you to be alone—"

"But that's the point. I have to be."

He clenched and unclenched his fists hanging by his sides. "Abby. I—"

"Listen." I swallowed, then looked directly into his beautiful wolf eyes. "I want you to leave," I said loudly, straightening my back.

"What—"

"And I don't want you to come back."

Liam frowned. *"Why?"*

"I can't be with you."

"You don't know what you're saying." He took a step back, the hurt etched in his face. "I'll come and see you tomorrow. And the day after and—"

"No." I took a deep breath. "Don't you get it? I don't want you to come back. I can't be with you at all. Ever."

He drew a sharp breath as the realization of what I was saying hit him. "You're ending this? Now? You can't."

I wanted to scream no, but instead I said, "Yes, I can. I have to."

"No, you *don't*. You're overreacting and—"

"Overreacting?" I shouted, inexplicably wanting to hurt him. "I can't be around you," I said, every syllable a dagger sure to pierce his heart. "Every time I see you I think of Tom. And he's dead. The person I loved the most is gone because of me." I balled my fists, and my voice dropped to a strained whisper. "Please. I don't want to explain. I'm exhausted. But I can't make you happy anymore. So go...just go."

"But, Abby—"

"Go!"

Liam stared at me. "Fine. I'll go. Give you some time. But I'm calling you tomorrow."

"Don't you get what I'm saying?" I was shouting again and I saw the blonde nurse pop her head in through the doorway. I shook my head at her, and she retreated. "I don't need time. I need you to leave me alone. I hate myself, and you're making it worse. Don't make it worse. If you love me, then *go*."

Liam stuck his hands in his pockets, opened his mouth to say something, but he must have thought better of it, because he suddenly turned and walked away.

As I pulled the blankets up to my neck I kept my eyes shut tight. This was the way it had to be. I knew that as my body healed, Liam's compassion would turn into resentment, hatred and then, worst of all, indifference. And I couldn't bear to see the ugly transformation begin.

NOW
ABBY

WITH OVER AN hour to spare, I'd set the table. Nate took over the kitchen duties, so I fled upstairs to shower. After completely redoing my makeup and fussing over my hair, I changed into the long blue dress with the plunging neckline I knew showed off my figure. I avoided looking at myself in the mirror for too long. I didn't want to stare at the person pretending the effort was exclusively for her husband.

When the doorbell rang, the necklace I'd been trying to put on slipped through my fingers and landed on the carpet with a dull thud.

"Can you get the door, Sarah?" I heard Nate call out.

"No problem, Dad," she yelled back, her footsteps going toward the front of the house.

If I'd asked her she'd likely have answered, "In a minute" or "I'm reading"—or perhaps she wouldn't have responded at all. There was no denying her clear preference for Nate over me, though I supposed that shouldn't be much of a surprise, particularly when the little voice in my head reminded me about how I'd betrayed Sarah by reading her diary.

Muffled voices and laughter traveled up the stairs. Although it was time for me to go downstairs, my feet were glued to the floor. I looked at myself properly in the mirror, taking in the low-cut dress that perfectly framed my cleavage and my toned arms. I swallowed. Shaking my head, I changed back into my jeans, pulled on a white T-shirt, and rubbed the blusher off my cheeks with the back of my hand.

"Abby?" Nate stood in the bedroom doorway. "Are you okay?"

I jumped and turned around. "Yes, I'm fine."

"You coming?" He paused. "What's up?"

"Nothing."

Nate walked over and put his arms around me, pulling me closer as I tried not to bristle. "You'll have to do better than that. What's going on?"

"I told you. I don't like him very much."

"Well, they're here now. Give him a chance, okay? And Nancy seems great. It's just them for now. Zac will pop by later." He took me by the hand and led me downstairs to the kitchen where Paul, Lynne, Nancy and Liam stood chatting to each other with the apparent ease of old friends. Nancy already had one of the twins balanced on her hip, gently rocking her.

Paul looked over. "There she is. We thought we'd lost you."

I smiled but said nothing.

"Hi, Abby." Nancy hugged me with her spare arm, and I know I bristled because she let go of me as if she'd scorched herself. "Thanks for having us over." She smiled a bit too brightly. "It was *lovely* of Nate to ask, but are you sure it's no trouble?"

When my eyes met Liam's I didn't need to force myself to look happy. I couldn't have stopped myself if I'd tried. I rubbed my hands together. "None at all. What can I get you to drink?"

An hour of small talk went by. I carefully avoided finding myself alone with Liam, made sure I paid attention to Nate, looking at him intently when he talked, touching his arm or his leg when I spoke, acting the perfect wife.

I had to admit Nancy was fun, regaling us with stories about when she'd worked as cabin crew for British Airways before she'd had Zac. And all her tales had the right amount of self-deprecation and perfect timing of the punch lines.

She finished off another anecdote "...and that's why we never gave him peanuts again." Liam laughed. I expected him to put his arm around her, which would have instantly made the green monster within me snarl, but he didn't and I secretly cheered. Nancy didn't seem bothered. "Sit next to me at dinner, Nate," she said, "and I'll tell you how I broke my nose while surfing the aisle on a serving tray."

"Great," Nate said. "You can tell me now because the food's ready. I'll get Sarah."

The nine of us settled around our chunky wooden dining table, with Rosie and Rachel sitting in the purple-and-green plastic booster seats Lynne and Paul had brought with them. The dishes with salad and mashed potatoes were passed around. Nate served everyone barbecued steak that smelled hot and spicy, and made our mouths water.

"Jamie Oliver's already texted me for the deets," Paul joked. "He said it smells *wicked*. But Ramsay told him no fu—I mean, *frigging* way."

Liam sat next to me, and our hands touched for the briefest moment each time I passed a plate to him. I wanted to put my hand on his leg, rest my head on his shoulder and whisper a private joke into his ear. I imagined standing up, shouting out loud we'd been lovers and still would be, if only things had been different. But instead I sat still, anticipating each touch, trying to find reasons to hand him the mash a third bloody time.

Nate sat opposite me, and when our eyes met he winked and I smiled back, hoping he wouldn't see through the cracks in my expertly plastered facade.

"Can I go?" Sarah said after finishing her food. "I've got homework to do."

"'Course you can," said Nate. "I'm sure we've already bored you enough."

When she disappeared upstairs Nancy touched Nate's arm, leaning toward him as if she were about to share a secret. "She's beautiful. And polite."

Nate laughed and I had to join in. "Thanks."

"She's got your wonderful charm, Nate, but she looks like you." Nancy pointed a finger at me. "Sorry, Nate. It's probably because she's a girl. Everyone says how much Zac looks like Liam. Same eyes, you know?"

I opened my mouth, feeling the need to justify. "Well, I—"

Nancy cut me off. "Didn't you want more kids then? You're such great parents."

Nate looked at me, and I could tell he was about to jump in and save me like he usually did. But I stopped him. "I can't," I said.

"Oh." Nancy covered her mouth. "I'm sorry, I didn't mean to—"

"There were complications." I cleared my throat. "Placenta previa, you know, when the placenta covers the cervix?" Nancy opened her mouth so I pressed on before I could change my mind. "We planned a C-section because of it, but I went into labor." I was talking quickly now, the words tumbling out. "We almost lost Sarah. Actually, they almost lost me, too—"

"God…"

"—and I had a hysterectomy." I exhaled. "So, there you go. That's why we only have one." Everybody was staring at me, including Liam, but I didn't dare look at him, so I smiled instead and focused on Nancy, deliberately blocking out everybody else. "Did you two ever think of having more kids?" I picked up a dish. "More salad?"

"Uh, that's the mash," Nate said, taking the plate from me.

I laughed, then saw Nancy's shoulders drop, too. "No," she said. "We only ever wanted one, didn't you, Liam?" He can't have noticed the unmistakable jab because he nodded without taking his eyes off me. Then Nancy said, "I'm so sorry about what happened to you. How awful."

"I've never heard Nate so panicked," Paul butted in. "When he called me from the hospital and—"

"Okay," I said, holding up a hand, "let's not get overly dramatic. It was—"

"The worst day of my life." Nate looked at me, and for a moment everybody around us disappeared. "The birth of your child is supposed to be one of the best, but it was…horrific." He reached over the table and grabbed my hand. My throat tightened; I couldn't breathe. I suddenly wanted to wrap my arms around him and tell him I was sorry. For everything.

But Nate grinned as he looked around the table. "Then again, we don't exactly have a history of making things easy, do we, love?"

"Oh, do tell." Nancy leaned in toward Nate again. "I'm intrigued. I bet it was romantic."

"It's nothing," I said quickly, frowning. "We—"

"You know how most people meet at a bar, work or, nowadays anyway, online?" Lynne said, nodding toward Nate and I. "Well, these two lovebirds met at a car crash."

I had to stop the conversation. "Who wants—"

"No way!" Nancy said, eyes wide. "Did you bump into each other or something?"

Nate opened his mouth, but Paul wagged a finger. "Oh, no. My brother, the hero, came across Abby's burning car and pulled her away. Saved her life."

I held up a hand. "I'm sure that nobody wants to—"

"Seriously?" Nancy's voice went up three notches. "When I said I bet it was romantic, I didn't think it would be *dramatically* romantic. Nate, you're a dark horse, aren't you? How *interesting*."

"Nancy," Liam said, "you shouldn't—"

"Well, don't leave me hanging," Nancy said as she ignored Liam and turned her back on him. "Tell me what happened next. Was it bad? How did—"

"Nancy." Liam's voice was loud this time, loud enough to make everyone stop talking. He smiled at her. "Where did you put the dessert?"

She stared at him. "Kitchen," she sniffed, and sat back in her chair with her arms crossed.

"Well," Liam said without missing a beat, "dinner was really delicious," and everyone around the table murmured their agreement.

"You were right, Paul. That's the best steak I've ever had. You're an *amazing* chef," Nancy said, obviously recovered from her scolding. "Thanks so much."

"Don't thank me," Paul said. "One of my exes was American."

"Just the one?" Lynne laughed, an eyebrow raised. "Nancy,

I think you'll find my husband has toured the US without even setting foot on the continent, if you know what I mean."

Nancy almost spurted her mouthful of wine over the table. She turned to Lynne. "You'd better tell me more or you'll forfeit your piece of apple pie."

"I'll help you clear the table," Liam said quietly as he pushed back his chair.

When Nate reached for one of the dishes, I shook my head and said, "You know the rule. He who cooks the most clears up the least. It's okay, we've got it."

"More beer or wine, anyone?" Nate asked, looking around the table.

Nancy's and Lynne's heads bobbed up and down in unison, and Paul added, "Another Stella for me, please."

"I'll get it," Liam said. "Fridge, right?"

"Thanks," Nate said, then turned toward Paul and mentioned something about Zurich.

I picked up more plates and headed to the kitchen, acutely aware Liam was two steps behind.

"Thank you for stopping her," I said. "I—"

"Abby," Liam said. "What you said about Sarah's birth. God, I can't imagine... I..." He exhaled and pinched the bridge of his nose. "Look. I know this is hard, but we need to talk."

I turned away, set the dishes down next to the sink and put my palms flat on the counter. "Why? There's nothing to say."

"There's plenty." He was behind me now, his hands on my shoulders, gently turning me around.

I looked up at him, my head tilted to the side. I remembered when we first met, standing in the middle of Rowley's and how everything—Dwayne, the crowd, the music—had become a distant buzz. All that had mattered at that precise moment was him and me. Us. And here we were again, this time in my kitchen, with everything around us fading to black.

I wanted to kiss him. Instead I cleared my throat. "I'll fetch more dishes." He let go of my shoulders, so I deftly stepped past him and went back to the dining table.

Nancy looked up. "Do you need any help?" Her voice had a slight slur I hadn't noticed before, and her cheeks had taken on a pinkish sheen.

"Yes," Lynne added, her eyes shiny, too. "At least let us give you a hand with dessert."

"No, no. Stay put. Liam's helping me anyway. You two keep Nate and Paul company."

"Okay, if you insist." Nancy smiled slowly, and I headed to the kitchen, where Liam was opening a bottle of white wine.

"We've finished two already," he said as he pulled the cork out. Then he put everything down and swallowed hard. "You've been hiding."

I lifted my chin. "With good reason."

Liam stared at me for a moment. "Yes… So, uh, have you ever been back to the Cotswolds?" When I didn't laugh he said, "Shit. I'm sorry. I can't believe how nervous I am." He rubbed the back of his neck. "When Nancy said Nate had invited us over…" He shook his head. "I wondered what plausible fake illness I could come up with."

I managed a small laugh this time. "That makes two of us, I—"

"Liam." Nancy walked in, looking at Liam, then me with a sugary smile. "We're parched out there."

"I'm coming." Liam picked up the bottle of wine as he walked over to Nancy. She grabbed his free hand and smiled at me before leading him out of the room.

I realized how fast my heart was beating, so I took a deep breath and closed my eyes, before opening them again when I heard someone come back into the kitchen.

"Forgot the beer." Liam pulled a Stella from the fridge, then moved so close I could almost feel his breath on my cheek. "Can I see you tomorrow?" he said quietly. "Please?"

I leaned in toward him, our fingers almost touching. "It's Easter, and with Paul and Lynne here..."

"So when?"

"I don't know, Liam, I—"

"Monday? In the morning? Or lunch?"

"It's a bank holiday."

He swore under his breath. "Tuesday then. Let's talk, okay? We have to."

I looked at him. He was right. We had to have a conversation that forced us—whether we wanted to or not—past this awkward stage. I grabbed my mobile from the counter. "What's your number?"

He rattled off the digits, and I swiftly entered them in my phone. Then I sent him my details, all the while wishing my heart would slow down, and chastising myself for feeling like a giddy schoolgirl who'd been asked out on her first date.

"I'll call you Tuesday morning." Liam smiled at me. He reached out and gently tucked a stray lock of hair behind my ear, then turned and walked out of the kitchen, leaving me standing among the dirty dishes, my skin tingling where his fingers had been.

When I felt my legs and hands were steady enough, I put Nancy's perfectly baked apple pie on a tray, added a jug of custard, some plates and spoons, and joined the others. Sarah was at the table again, and now Zac was seated next to her. They leaned toward each other, engrossed in conversation, their body language screaming too many things I didn't want to hear. I let go of the tray a little too soon, and it clattered onto the table.

Zac looked up. "Hello, Mrs. Morris."

I smoothed down my hair. "Zac." My face must have looked like a cross between an overly eager door-to-door salesman and a knife-wielding psychopath. "You're just in time for dessert."

"Cool," Zac said as he turned back to Sarah. "Mum's apple pie is sick."

I watched as they closed themselves off from everyone again. Returning to a conversation in which nobody but them had a place. How long had I been out of the room? And since when did those two enjoy each other's company? I feigned interest in another of Nancy's stories, half registering how she touched Nate's arm for the third time in under three minutes. As I nodded and made the occasional "uh-huh" noise, I listened to the conversation between Sarah and Zac, trying not to look at them.

"What's the scoop for the school newsletter this month?" Zac said, and when Sarah didn't answer he added, "Come on, throw me a bone."

"If you must know," Sarah said, "it's about being LGBT at our school."

"Really? Why?" Zac said, and I was glad he'd spoken before me or they'd have noticed how intently I was listening.

"Because it's important, *duh*!" Sarah said. "We think it's accepted, but it isn't. People get bullied all the time. Like, a few weeks ago a kid got beaten up on the way home. Three guys jumped him, called him a faggot and almost sent him to the hospital." Her voice got louder, so I turned my head to look at her, noticing how red her face was. When she saw me staring I quickly looked away, and she lowered her voice. "It's disgusting."

"Right, uh," Zac said, "how does your…girlfriend feel about you writing it?"

Girlfriend?

Sarah sounded equally surprised. "Sorry?"

Zac cleared his throat. "Isn't that why you're doing the article? Because you're gay? Isn't Claire your girlfriend?"

"*Claire?* No," Sarah said. "But if she was, would you have a problem with that?"

"'Course not," Zac whispered. "None of my business, is it? And I don't have a problem with that stuff."

"That *stuff*?" I sneaked another glance. Sarah leaned back in her chair and crossed her arms. "Okay, *Zac*, what would *you* have done if you'd seen the kid being hurt?"

He didn't hesitate. "I'd have stopped it. Or at least tried to. I've done it before."

"What do you mean?" Sarah gasped. "What happened? Tell me."

Zac laughed. "You're sensing a story, aren't you? Okay, I helped a kid at my last school. Thirteen-year-old. Same thing. A couple of idiots beat him up because he was gay. So I gave them a taste of their own medicine."

"Wow." Sarah sounded breathless. "Did it work?"

"Yeah." He snorted. "And I got suspended."

"But that's not fair!" Sarah said.

"Well," Zac said, "according to the headmistress, I should have asked a teacher for help."

"But—"

"I know. Like I was going to run and get a teacher while a kid who's already on the floor gets the shit kicked out of him." He snorted again. "I don't think so."

"What did your mum and dad say?"

"They argued with the headmistress, defended me—"

"Well, that's great—"

"—but I got suspended for three days anyway. And afterward I got notes shoved in my locker. Threats and comments about how I'm a gay lover, that kind of crap."

"Unbelievable. That's not why you moved, is it?"

Zac harrumphed. "Please. I have a black belt in tae kwon do. At that level they do stuff behind your back, not to your face. Cowards."

"Can I interview you about this?" Sarah asked. "Properly, I mean? For the article?"

I hoped Zac would say no, but he answered, "Sure. I don't mind."

When neither of them spoke for a minute I thought their conversation had petered out, and Sarah would go back to thinking he was an idiot, but then he said, "Uh, I'm going to Manchester University next year. Computer science."

"Cool," Sarah said. "I'm going to be a journalist."

"Shocker. And, uh, are you really a gamer? I mean a *proper* one."

"Yes, a *proper* one." Sarah's tone flipped back to indignant. "So?"

"Nothing," he said quietly, "it's…cool. Different."

I waited for Sarah to challenge him, ask him to explain what he meant, as I knew she would have done had I made that remark. But instead she said, "It's because of Dad. We used to play all kinds of stuff on the Wii. *Chick Chick Boom* was my favorite."

"Chick whaty-what? Never heard of it," Zac said.

"You've never…" Sarah pushed her chair back. "Come on. I'll show you."

My heart thumped loudly as I watched them leave, remembering the emotional roller coaster I'd leaped on when I was Sarah's age and a boy showed interest in me. Nate said something about getting coffee, and I stood up and crossed my fingers, silently praying Sarah wouldn't start hiding her diary somewhere else.

NOW
NATE

EASTER SUNDAY HAD been filled with egg hunts in the garden, mountains of chocolate and way too much other food. Now Paul and I were almost the last men standing. Abby was still up, doing some work in our bedroom, so I played a couple of games of pool with my brother.

"Great night yesterday," Paul said, accidentally potting the white again, and I couldn't help feeling a tiny bit smug. "Your neighbors are fun. And I still think you should watch out for Nancy. She was all over you."

"Don't be ridiculous." I laughed. "She's just one of those touchy-feely people."

"Yeah, maybe," Paul said. "But I don't know what you meant about Abby being grumpy. She seemed fine to me."

I frowned as we sat down. "Didn't you think it was out of character, you know, how she brought up the hysterectomy?"

He shrugged. "Not really. It was traumatic. Women talk about that kind of stuff. And speaking of traumatic, sorry again that I didn't tell you about the Zurich job before." I looked at him with one eyebrow raised, and he held up his hands in self-defense. "I wasn't sure I'd get it, okay? Or that I'd take it."

"Why wouldn't you? Leading the IT security team is massive."

"I know. So's the salary." He grinned.

"I'm surprised Lynne's okay with it. I mean, she wouldn't even think about leaving Cardiff when you met."

"You should've seen her face when we flew over a few weeks ago."

"On your—" I made air-quotation marks "—Swiss mini-break aka fact-finding mission?"

"Yeah, well, she loved it. One of the only times I've seen my wife incapable of talking. It's a beautiful place, it really is."

"Ah, well, at least the contract's only for a year."

"Yeah… About that…it's not contract."

"But you said—"

"I said that's what I applied for, but after the interview, they changed the spec."

"So it's a *permanent* role? Well…bugger me."

Paul grimaced. "I know. It's a big step."

"A big step? It's bloody…*gargantuan.*"

He laughed. "Bigger than Kate Upton's boobs."

Thankfully Abby and Lynne weren't in the room, or they'd have smothered him with a pillow. I took a swig of my beer. "No kidding. And I've said a thousand times how the boss kisses the ground your wife walks on. I swear Kevin tells me at least once a week the Cardiff office would crumble without Lynne. Shit, he'll flip his lid when she resigns."

"He'll cope. And she's looking forward to spending more time with the girls."

"Hmm… So where will you live?"

"The company's relocation people will help sort us out.

But Lynne doesn't want to be in the city. So somewhere in a village with cowbells and chocolate, I expect."

I laughed. "Yeah, where nobody speaks any English and—"

"Who cares? We'll take German lessons."

God, he didn't have a clue, did he? "They don't speak *German*. It's *Swiss*-German. Some dialect only the locals understand. And they have weirdo laws."

"Oh, yeah, like what?"

I counted on my fingers. "Like no standing up to piss after 10:00 p.m. if you live in a flat. You can't mow your lawn or take stuff to the recycling on Sundays, and—"

"Oh, sod *off*." Paul laughed.

"It's true."

He crossed his arms and stared at me. "Since when are you an expert?"

I cleared my throat. "I may have Googled a bit."

"A *bit*? Well...I don't give a shit about the dialect or weirdo laws. And it's for the girls as well, you know. Give them some international exposure. Raise them multilingual."

"Multi... Jesus, they're not even two years old. They can barely manage a sentence in English yet."

He shook his head, and for a moment he looked like Dad. "It's happening, Nate—"

"I know."

"—middle of June—"

"I *know*."

"—and I'll make sure we get a place big enough so all of you can come and stay."

I squinted at him. "You fucking traitor. Dad, Mum and now you, all abandoning me."

Paul put his head back and laughed his deep, throaty laugh. "And I love you, too, little brother." He leaned forward and patted my head as if I were the two-year-old. "Tell you what, the first time we need more people, I'll call you. Let you do all the recruitment. How's that?"

After mumbling another obscenity I felt slightly better. "Okay. Time for bed."

I walked up the stairs to the bedroom, thinking a trip to Switzerland might be exactly what Abby and I needed. I'd tried talking to her the night before, after Liam and Nancy had left. But when I asked if she was okay she said she didn't want to talk, rolled over and pretended to sleep.

"Did you finish your stuff?" I said as I entered the room. Abby was lying on our bed, fully dressed, flat on her back and staring at the ceiling. I sat down beside her. "What's going on?"

Her lips moved, but no sound came out.

"Is it me?"

She shook her head.

"Is it us?"

A blink. A shake of the head.

"Is it Tom?"

Abby hesitated, swallowed and nodded.

I sighed. Then reminded myself Abby's happiness had always been paramount. Taking care of her was the one thing that mattered the most in the world. And as I put my arms around my wife and held her tight, I started formulating a cunning plan, an entire deck of aces I'd whip out from my sleeve and surprise her with.

I'd fix this. I'd fix everything, just like I did when we'd first met, and every day since.

THEN
NATE

IT TOOK ME all of three seconds to fall in love with Abigail Sanders when I saw her again. Who was I kidding? It wasn't even two and a half.

By the time the paramedics and Officer Cook let me leave the scene of the accident, the sky was a light shade of pink. When I got back to Granddad's place, I let myself in. Mum and Dad would be up soon, so I crept to the bedroom and sank onto the bed.

Attempting sleep felt ludicrous, like riding a bicycle through a field full of cats with a bucket of fish balanced on my head. Doable if someone pressed a gun against my temple, but otherwise utterly pointless.

The accident kept replaying in my mind, over and over again. A bad horror movie I was forced to watch on an incessant loop. Except it had happened for real. A man had died, and I'd been powerless to stop it. Every time I closed my eyes I saw the car, the flames, heard imaginary screams, saw the woman's clothes on fire, even though they hadn't been.

At some point I must have fallen asleep because the next

thing I knew Mum stood over me, shaking my shoulders gently.

"Nate, wake up." The words were urgent. "Come to the phone. It's the police."

I shot up, rubbed my itching eyes, wondering if the smoky, sweaty smell came from me.

"What's going on?" Mum said. "What happened?"

"There was an accident—"

"Oh, my god, are you okay? What about Paul? Is he—"

"He's fine, Mum. I stopped to help someone. Hang on." I stepped around her. "Let me speak to the police, and I'll tell you." I half stumbled into the hallway and grabbed the phone. "Nate Morris."

"Mr. Morris. This is Officer Cook."

I wanted to swallow, but there was nothing to bring down. "Officer. Is something wrong?"

"No, no," he said quickly. "But I'd like to go through your statement again. Make sure we didn't miss anything. Could you come down to the station this afternoon? Say, three thirty?" He gave me the address. "Thank you, Mr. Morris. We'll speak later. Goodb—"

"Hold on." I scratched the back of my head, registering how thick and dirty my hair felt, then noticing the dusty blackish sheen that had attached itself to my fingertips. "The woman? Did she... I mean, is she okay?"

The smile in his voice was audible as his tone softened. "Yes, Mr. Morris. I'm told she'll pull through, thanks to you."

When I put the phone down and turned around, Mum and Dad stood in the hallway, watching my every move.

"Sounds like you had a rough night, son," Dad said.

I exhaled. "You can say that again."

Mum rubbed my arm. "I'll put the kettle on."

★ ★ ★

The interview at the police station felt far less intimidating than I'd expected, and I blamed my negative preconceptions on watching too many episodes of *Law & Order*. I had visions of me sitting in a barren room, tape recorder on the table, two policemen smoking, leaning over me, playing good cop, bad cop. As it happened, Officer Cook and I sat in a brightly painted area with a Mickey Mouse clock on the wall, and two mugs of tea and a packet of Jaffa Cakes in front of us.

Officer Cook took me through the details again, I signed my witness statement and was free to go. "Thank you," he said as he walked me out of the building. "Thank you again for stopping. You saved Miss Sanders's life."

It was shortly after five, and I thought it best to head back and pack up my things. My boss wasn't expecting me for a week, but after Granddad's funeral and the accident, I felt like I'd been whizzed around in a blender for a month.

I decided I'd make an early start home the next morning. try to return to some degree of normalcy. And if it meant sitting in the office, poring over candidate details and writing job ads for Visual Basic gurus, then that predictability was fine by me.

But as I drove to North Road I spotted a sign for the Royal Preston Hospital and, on impulse, followed it. Officer Cook had assured me Miss Sanders—*Abigail*—would be okay, that the injuries weren't life-threatening. It was hard to believe. There had been so much blood on her face, arms and legs she'd looked like Carrie at the prom.

I parked close to the hospital and went to the front desk. Three wrong turns, a pit stop at the gift shop, two lifts and one long walk later I arrived on what I hoped was the correct floor.

"Excuse me," I said to a tiny nurse with spiky blond hair. "I'm looking for Abigail Sanders."

The nurse's eyes narrowed and her hands went to her hips. "Name?" She raised her penciled-on, clown-like eyebrows.

"Nate Morris."

"Are you family?"

"Uh, no, I…"

She kept staring at me, and I tried not to focus on the crazy eyebrows. I almost snapped my fingers. *Ronald McDonald.* That's who they reminded me of. I attempted a disarming, charmingly reassuring smile, but Nurse McNugget wasn't having any of it.

"I can't let you see her if I don't know who you are," she said. "She's had enough trouble from her…" She cleared her throat. "So…?"

I shrugged again. "I'm just the bloke who stopped at the crash and I wondered—"

The nurse's mouth dropped open, and she clapped her hands. "That was *you*? Oh, my gosh. Why didn't you say so? You're a hero." A megawatt smile lit up her face. "I'm sure Abby will be pleased to see you. She's in there." She pointed to the door closest to her station. "But go easy, okay? No need to tell you she's had a tough time."

"I won't stay. I only wanted to make sure she's okay, you know?"

"I understand," my new best friend said, her expression soft, her voice gentle. "I understand completely."

I stood in the doorway, looking at Abby for those two and a half seconds, falling in love with her. Her blond hair was still matted with blood, her forehead a mosaic of plasters, and even from under the covers, her right leg looked twice as thick as her left. But despite all that, or perhaps because of it,

I could tell she was a fighter. There was no doubt she could do anything she put her mind to.

Her eyes were shut, her head turned slightly toward the window. As I stared at her delicate cheekbones and the gentle slope of her ski-jump nose, I wanted to trace a finger down the side of her face, tell her how amazingly strong and resilient she was. Instead I cleared my throat.

"Just leave, will you?" Her voice sounded hoarse, distant. "I told you to go."

I wasn't sure what I'd expected, but this definitely hadn't been it. "I'm sorry." I retreated toward the door. "I'll, uh, I'll leave you to it then."

"Wait." Her head was facing me now as her eyes searched mine. "You must have the wrong room," she said, turning away again.

"You're Abigail Sanders?"

She looked at me, then at the bunch of yellow daffodils draped over my arm. "It's Abby. And I didn't know the police brought flowers."

My laugh bounced around the room and stopped when I clocked her expression. "I'm not from the police." I put a hand to my chest. "I'm, uh..." I didn't want to sound like a pretentious prick. "I'm the one who stopped. At the...at the crash."

She frowned as she stared at me, the effort of her thoughts visible on her face. What was I thinking, coming here? They'd probably drugged her way past her eyeballs, had her drifting higher than a satellite. No doubt she had a ton of family and friends already fussing over her. A boyfriend, too, *definitely* a boyfriend. Maybe even a husband. She didn't need me, a total stranger, showing up with a bunch of overly sprightly colored flowers.

"You're the one who found us?" she said, and her bottom lip quivered.

"I'm sorry," I said as my shoulders dropped, and all of a sudden I almost didn't dare look at her. "I'm so sorry."

"Sorry? Why?"

I paused. After a few beats I looked her in the eyes and whispered, "I couldn't get to him." I put the flowers on the table. "The man in the car. The flames...the heat... I couldn't save him. I'm *sorry*." Silence enveloped the room, and I stood there, wringing my hands until I quietly said, "Do you mind, uh, can I ask who he was?"

When she looked at me again the pain in her eyes was unbearable, and yet I couldn't break her gaze. "My brother, Tom."

"I'm so sorry." The offering sounded pathetic. Insignificant. "I'll leave now."

"Please don't," she said, holding up a hand. "Could you... stay? For a bit?"

She seemed so small and lost, like a kid who'd woken up from a nightmare and had asked for her teddy. As I walked over to the bed I wanted to scoop her up and hold her close. "I'm Nate," I said. "Nate Morris."

"Thank you, Nate." She managed the tiniest of smiles that made her look beautifully sad, like a princess from an old fairy tale or something. "You saved my life."

I inhaled and exhaled deeply. "Do you know what caused the accident?" I said gently. "I don't mean to be rude but... well... I wish..."

"It was me." Her eyes closed for a second. "I must have lost control."

"Do you mean you don't remember?"

"Nothing. But you…you were there. Tell me what you saw. Please. When you got there, was he…was Tom still alive?"

I couldn't be sure; I'd never be sure. But she didn't need to know. "No. He was already…gone."

She covered her mouth with her hand and, despite the tears, didn't break eye contact. "Thank you," she whispered, although I wasn't quite sure what she was thanking me for.

"What about your injuries?" I said. "Will you be okay?"

She rattled off a list and finished with, "The doctor said I'll be fine." She looked away. "Physically anyway."

"I'm sure you'll—"

"Can we talk about something else?" she said quickly. "Something that doesn't have to do with anything…"

"What do you—"

"*Anything.* Something stupid so I can pretend it's a normal day… Could we?"

"Of course, absolutely." I wanted to ask about her brother, what he'd been like, what he'd looked like. I pulled up a chair and leaned forward. "We could be typical Brits and discuss the weather." *Pathetic, Nate, pathetic.* I smiled. "Or you could tell me your favorite film of all time."

"Actually," she replied, patting my arm with fingers that felt like they'd been carved from ice, "I'd rather listen. What's yours?"

"Easy. *Big.*"

Abby squinted a little. "With Tom Hanks?"

"That's the one."

Her brow furrowed further. "Why?"

"The scene with the piano on the floor? And when he shows up at a black-tie do in a white tux and nibbles the mini corn on the cob? Genius." A hint of a smile made her lips twitch, but it disappeared all too soon. I vowed to make it reappear, for longer next time.

"Where are you from?" she said. "Not around here. Your accent's too posh."

I allowed myself a small laugh, unsure of the protocol to follow when talking to a woman who'd just lost her brother. "London," I said, "Wembley."

"What are you doing here? Visiting family?"

"Kind of." I pulled a face. "My grandfather died and—"

"Oh, god, I'm so sorry. Were you close?"

"Very. And he was only seventy-five." I crossed my arms. "My grandmother died last year and he never got over it. It's like he lost his way, like he no longer had a purpose, you know and—" I stopped. "Christ, I can't believe I said that."

"It's okay—"

"No, I'm a dickhead. I'm sorry."

"It's fine, honestly. You're taking my mind off...stuff." I thought she was going to cry, but she swallowed hard and added, "Did he live in town? Your grandfather?"

"No. Longton. I had dinner with, uh—" I was going to say *my brother* but reconsidered "—a friend in town last night and I was on my way back when...when..."

"When you found us." She closed her eyes for a few seconds, tears spilling from the corners. "And you saved me."

"I didn't see you at first." My voice trembled slightly and I watched her wipe her cheeks. "I was trying to get to...to Tom. When I saw you I thought you were dead. I've never been so scared in my life." I took a deep breath, and she grabbed my hand.

"Thank you for stopping," she whispered, and squeezed my fingers. "I'm...grateful."

I almost asked her if she meant it. Something told me she

wished she could swap places with Tom, but I'd never say that out loud. "It was nothing," I murmured. And somewhere not too deep inside me a voice told me it wasn't nothing. It had become *everything*.

Abby didn't pull away as I thought she might when I kept hold of her hand, but curled her fingers around mine. I didn't dare move as we continued talking until her eyes closed and opened increasingly slowly.

"Would it be okay if I came to see you again?" I asked as I stared at her, trying to memorize her features in case she said no. "Before I go back home?"

Abby nodded as her eyes closed again. "I'd like that," she whispered. "Thank you, Nate. You make me feel…safe."

I held her hand and watched her sleep for another fifteen minutes before standing up slowly and slipping out the door.

THEN
ABBY

THE NEXT FEW days went by in a blur. My fractured bones were healing, the stitches would come out in two weeks, and I'd have to spend a couple of months in physiotherapy. The yellow daffodils Nate brought hadn't yet started to wilt, and I wished they would. When he'd asked me if I liked them I'd said yes, they were my favorite. It wasn't true. I still hated daffodils.

I tried not to think about Liam too often. He'd respected my wishes and stayed away. If he hadn't, I wasn't sure I'd have been able to stick to my plan. I missed him. I missed Tom. Part of me even missed Mum. At least until the nurse Nate called "McNugget" told me my mother had phoned, briefly asking how I was, but declining the offer to talk to me herself.

"She thought it was for the best," the nurse said, eyes downcast, head shaking slightly, before she retreated to the safety of her station.

Dr. Patel came in the afternoon, and I noticed the concern in his eyes had lessened. "You've seen the grief counselor?" he said.

"Yes. It was helpful." When he stared at me I forced a smile. "Very helpful."

Actually, it had been hell. An entire hour where I was expected to talk about myself to a complete stranger I'd never see again. I hadn't known where to start. I didn't want to speak about my father abandoning us, my mother's bitter resentment or my brother's accident. We wouldn't have left but the tiniest of scratches in the surface of those beasts. What was the point?

Instead, I talked about Tom. How he made me laugh, how smart he was, how he'd run the fastest mile in school, a record, people prophesized, which would remain unbeaten for at least a decade. "He's really, really good at sports," I said to the counselor with a smile, which immediately disappeared when I realized I'd referred to Tom in the present tense again. I hadn't said much more afterward.

"Abby," Dr. Patel interrupted my thoughts. "As we discussed yesterday, I'm happy to release you today, if you're ready to go home?"

"Yes," I said. Getting away from everybody was finally within my reach. "Please."

"Can someone come and get you?" He raised his eyebrows when I shrugged and added, "It'll be tricky with your things and the crutches, you know?"

"I'll be fine."

"Good grief, you're the most stubborn patient I've met in a long time." He paused. "And that's why I know you'll continue to recover. Make sure you take the pills I prescribed, and I'll see you in two weeks for the stitches. And take it easy," he added, crossing his arms and frowning like an overprotective headmaster speaking to his student. "That's an order." Then he walked over, and for a second I thought he'd give me a hug, but he shook my hand and left me to start gathering my things.

After a few minutes I decided he was right—I needed help. Not many people had visited me over the past week, although a handful had called. With an uncomfortable knot in my stomach I realized I didn't have many close friends. Keeping people at a distance came with stark consequences, and recently it had been all about Tom, Liam and me.

So, I had two choices. Mum—the option almost choked me—and Liam, equally impossible. As I sat on the hard, plastic chair, I decided there was a third possibility.

Although I hadn't expected—let alone asked—him to, Nate had come back to the hospital every day. He'd stayed for more than an hour each time and had done most of the talking. I'd been surprised by how much I enjoyed his company. It helped me feel less alone, and took my mind off things for a while, although I knew that soon he'd be going back to his normal life and I'd have no choice but to get on with mine.

"I'm definitely leaving on Friday," he'd said yesterday afternoon, sitting in his usual uncomfortable plastic chair, his legs stretched out, his brown cowlick sticking up at yet another angle. "But I'm glad I stayed this week."

"Did you get a lot done?"

"Yeah. Most of Granddad's stuff, you know, things at the house, the last legal bits." He paused. "I don't know if I'll have to come back again."

"Up north?"

"Uh-huh. But I hope so and—" he cleared his throat "—can I call you when I'm here? Or before, even?"

I looked at him. His gentle blue eyes, funny-looking hair, three-day stubble and slight shadows under his eyes. Although I hadn't known him for long, I could tell he was a kind man.

Solid. The type who wouldn't mess you around. He'd make whoever he ended up with very happy.

"I'm not, uh, expecting anything...*romantic*," he said quickly, apparently more than a little flustered by my silence. "God, that sounded crap." He rolled his eyes. "Look. I know you haven't had a boyfriend for ages—"

"Well—" I started to correct him, but remembered just in time how I'd said I'd been single for a while. How could I tell Nate about Liam when the mere thought of him made me want to bury my head in my pillow and sob? With Nate I could pretend I had a slightly different past. Use him as an escape from my real life. If I didn't tell him about Liam, if I didn't acknowledge his existence, then I'd never have to talk about him again. Never have to openly mourn the loss of our relationship either. Goodness knows I was barely coping with Tom's d— I couldn't even think the *d*-word yet. It was too raw, too painful.

"—so I'm not trying to pick you up, okay?" Nate had continued talking. "But I...I care about what happens to you, Abby."

"I don't think I deserve that."

"Of course you do. And you don't have to be alone. You said your mum isn't...well, you know. So let me be there for you." He smiled. "As a friend."

"A friend?"

"Everybody needs a friend sometimes." When I didn't answer he said, "Okay. Here's my number back home, and the one where you can get hold of me until Friday. Just in case." He tore a piece from one of my magazines and scribbled the digits, then pushed the note into my hands. And a little while later, when he'd given me a hug, kissed my forehead and walked out of the room, I'd been pretty sure I'd never see him again. But something had stopped me from throwing the piece of paper away.

I hobbled around as best I could and finally located the note under my shoes. After taking a deep breath, I picked up the phone and dialed Nate's number.

Within an hour I heard the noise of Nate's sneakers squeaking along the corridor, and as I took in the dampness of his hair and the scent of fresh aftershave, my stomach curled up at the realization that the effort might be for me.

"Sorry I'm a bit late," he said. "I was helping Dad clear out Granddad's shed. You should've seen the sawdust. The spiders down my shirt weren't particularly welcome either."

At that point I told myself to stop being so self-involved and grabbed my crutches, determined to make the trip to Nate's car without the wheelchair Dr. Patel had recommended.

"Do you have everything?" Nate asked gently.

I looked around. There were still Get Well Soon cards and a couple of bunches of flowers dotted around the room. Not many people had congratulated me on my birthday—which wasn't a surprise. "Yes. Everything I need."

"Would you like to take your daffodils?" Nate said with a hopeful look, and despite myself, I nodded. His face burst into a smile. "I'll get some newspaper."

As we slowly walked out of the room and down the corridor to the lifts, the nurse came out of a nearby room and rushed over, instructing Nate to take care of me. When she hugged me carefully, she whispered, "You'll get through this, Abby. I promise. It'll take time, but you will." I had to bite my lip to stop myself from blubbing, and wished she were my mum.

Except for me occasionally giving Nate directions, we were

both silent on the drive back to my cozy flat above the Kettle Club. I clutched the few things I'd stuffed into plastic bags close to my chest, and stared out of the car window. How could everything look exactly the same as before, when my entire world had changed?

"Thank you," I said as we finally made it up the steep flight of stairs to my front door. I slid the key in the lock and turned to Nate. "I'm grateful, really. But I can manage now. I know you've got to get going."

He smiled and held the door open while I hobbled through with my crutches. "Don't be daft. I'll make you a cup of tea."

"I don't think I have any milk."

He shrugged. "I'll pop out and get a pint."

I turned and looked up at his kind smile and smooth, clean-shaven skin. A little voice whispered I didn't deserve to have someone taking care of me, but I flicked the annoying creature away. "I think I should lie down for a bit."

"You rest, okay? I'll get some milk, then sit on the sofa and, uh—" he looked at the coffee table "—flick through *Cosmo*." He grinned. "I might learn something."

When I struggled up a while later I heard rustling and the sound of the kettle being filled. I limped into the kitchen to find Nate, who'd strewn a few empty plastic bags over the floor.

"Did you go…shopping?" I looked at the lettuce, apples and bread, the ham, cheese, tinned soup and baked beans on the kitchen counter. He'd even gotten two packets of Hob-nobs, and found a vase to put the daffodils in.

He shrugged. "Your cupboards were empty." I noticed a hint of a blush creeping up his neck. "And you can't pick much up with those crutches."

"Thanks, Nate. How much do I owe you?"

"Don't be silly."

I looked around. He'd put away the dishes and arranged my post in a neat pile, too; now he was busying himself by putting the washed apples in a bowl. "Are you secretly Mary Poppins?"

He put his head back and laughed. "You were out cold, and after learning about power dressing for work and, uh, other *techniques* from your magazine, I thought I'd help you get organized." He picked the plastic bags off the floor. "Do you want a cup of tea? Oh, and I also bought some big bags and string, so you can tie one around your leg when you shower. That way the water won't—"

"Nate?"

He took a deep breath and held up his hands. "You're going to tell me to stop fussing, aren't you? That I can't fix everything?"

"Sounds like someone already beat me to it."

He smiled and rubbed the back of his neck. "When Nana died I stayed with Granddad for a week. Helped him around the house, did his shopping. Bought him Hobnobs." I smiled back and he continued. "He patted my back one night and said how grateful he was, but fussing over him wasn't the only way to help myself feel better." He looked away. "I guess this is the same thing."

We said nothing for a while but stood in the kitchen until the kettle switched itself off and the pain started creeping up my legs. I hadn't been on my feet this long for a week.

"What are you going to do about work?" Nate said as I eased myself onto the sofa.

"I spoke to Stu yesterday." I winced as I lifted my leg onto a pillow, relieving some of the pressure. "The Kettle Club owner," I added when Nate shook his head. I kept forgetting we'd only known each other for a few days. "He wants me to take more time off, but I said I'll start Monday."

"What? Are you crazy?"

"I have to keep myself busy." I looked away.

"But don't you think—"

"Life's going to continue as normal whether I want it to or not. I'd better get used to it."

He gestured to my leg. "But how will you manage with that thing?"

"I suppose this is one of those times where living above work has its advantages. And Stu agreed I'll just cover the bar. He said he'd do the rest for a while." I waved a hand. "It'll be fine."

"God, you're stubborn."

"Yeah, Tom always says..." I cleared my throat. "Thanks for helping me."

"Abby—" he stuffed his hands into his pockets "—will you be okay at the funeral tomorrow?"

"I'm not going."

He walked over and sat down in front of me on the coffee table. "But you have to. It'll help with closure and—"

"With all due respect, Nate, I don't give a shit about closure right now."

"You say that now, but in the future you'll—"

"In the future Tom will still be dead, so what does it matter? Anyway, I can't go."

"Why?" When I didn't answer he gently put his index finger under my chin and turned my face toward his. "Are you worried about what people will say? Is that it?"

"No." I blinked back the tears. "Mum called the hospital and said I shouldn't come. She doesn't want me there."

"Jesus." Nate whistled as he got up and paced around the living room. "Where's the service?"

"I'm not sure. Mum didn't say."

"What's her number?"

"Nate, I—"

"Don't worry. I'm not going to give her hell. Just let me call her and find out where and when, okay? Then you decide whether you want to go."

"I *told* you, I'm not welcome."

"I'll take you. We'll get there late and stay at the back. Nobody knows my car. You can go all Audrey Hepburn style. Big hat and glasses." He paused when I didn't smile. "Tom's your brother. You have to go."

"Why are you doing this for me? Why are you being so kind?"

He walked over, knelt down and grabbed hold of my hands. "Like I said, I'm helping myself, too. Let me do this, okay?"

"I can't give you anything in return."

He squeezed my hands. "I'm not expecting you to."

"Okay," I whispered. "Okay."

He picked up the phone and I gave him Mum's number. I listened as he extended his condolences, saying he'd been at university with Tom, and could she please give him the details of the funeral because he'd like to pay his respects. His voice was soft and gentle, and I closed my eyes as I listened to him.

"Ten thirty tomorrow," he said after he rang off. "I'll pick you up at quarter to."

I had planned to go to the funeral, truly, I had. I'd managed to get up early, tie a bag around my leg, shower, stand long enough to put on makeup in an attempt to camouflage my cuts and bruises, pull on a black dress and find the biggest, darkest glasses I had. But when I opened my wardrobe and finally located my big blue straw hat with the white rim, I sat down on my bed, completely still, unable to move.

I clutched the hat close to my chest as if doing so would bring the memories back to life. Tom had given me the hat for Christmas three years ago. He'd wrapped it up in tissue paper and the biggest box he could find.

"A summer hat?" I said, as I pulled it out from the layers and layers of bright pink-and-purple paper. "Wow, thanks, Tommy." I raised my eyebrows to the heavens. "What a practical present for this time of year."

Tom had laughed. "Cut the sarcasm, you ungrateful little shit. It's a subliminal message."

"What? A reminder that I'm going to freeze my bum off for the next few months?"

"You're such a pessimist, Shabby." He plopped the hat on my head. "Remember you used to say you didn't care about the rain because the sun would always come?"

"Yeah." Since then my eternal optimism had taken such a beating, it had retreated into its shell like a turtle, expecting to be whacked on the nose each time it dared come out.

"Well." Tom crossed his arms and sat back on the sofa. "This is a reminder. Whatever happens, spring and summer will always come. Things will always get better."

The memories of the conversation first took my breath away, then tore my heart clean down the middle. I lay back down on my bed, not caring if my dress got rumpled or my mascara traveled in black smudgy rivers down my cheeks.

"Abby?" His soft voice startled me, and I turned my head toward Nate, who stood in the doorway. "I knocked but you didn't answer. The door was unlocked so I... Oh, Jesus."

Within a second he was next to me, his arms holding me tight, helping me sit up.

"I…" The words wouldn't come out. "I, uh… I…can't go, Nate." My voice was so low I wasn't sure he'd heard me. "Not with Mum and everybody… I…I *can't*."

"Abby…"

"It was my fault," I said, pulling away from him, suddenly needing him to hear the truth about what I'd done, wanting him to know exactly what kind of a person I was. "I drank and I drove." The words tumbled out before I could even try to stop them. "I was wasted. And I crashed the car. And Tom's dead. It's all my fault."

Nate looked at me for a second, then wrapped his arms around me again as more of my tears soaked into his shirt.

"It's all because of me," I whispered.

"But you didn't—"

"You don't get it." I pushed Nate away, angrily swiping at my tearstained cheeks with the back of my hand. "Tom's dead. I'm not. You see? I drove and I lived. It's not right. It's not fair."

"I'm not going to pretend I understand what you're going through," Nate said gently. "But both of you got in the car. You didn't force Tom. He could have called a cab, too."

"Yeah? Well, Tom's not here anymore so that exonerates him from any kind of blame, doesn't it? It's far more difficult to hate someone who's…not here anymore when there's a living, breathing person who'll fit the bill. Just ask my mother." I looked at him. "You can go if you want. You don't have to stay."

Nate shook his head and put his hands on mine. "I'm not going anywhere unless you tell me to."

Neither Nate nor I spoke on the way to the cemetery much later that day, and I was grateful he didn't keep asking me how I felt. I wouldn't have known how to put the tangled mess of emotions into proper words. I'd changed into a white T-shirt and my long, paisley-print skirt but still clutched the big straw hat to my chest.

I looked out of the car window and watched a kid on a skateboard weave his way in and out of the oncoming foot traffic. The flames on his shorts matched the color of the tightly wound spiral curls on his head, and his fluorescent green plaster cast on his left arm had a picture of what looked like a skull. A sudden pang of envy hit me in the chest, and I wished I could be that young again, oblivious to the shit-storm of complications that came with being a grown-up.

"I'll be right here if you need me." Nate's words made me jump, and I looked around. We were already at the ceme-tery, and he got out and opened my door. "Take all the time you need."

As I stood by Tom's fresh grave I looked at the trinkets and flowers that had been laid down for him only hours earlier— roses and chrysanthemums, candles, teddy bears and angel ornaments. Many, many people, it seemed, had come to say goodbye.

A headstone would follow, although that would be some-thing I wouldn't have a say in, something else decided on without my involvement. Mum would probably choose an over-the-top and garish stone, with harp-carrying cherubs. She'd always picked what she thought was best for Tom, even when he'd disagreed.

Pushing the thoughts of my mother aside, I wanted to kneel down, feel the soft soil and let it glide through my fin-gers. But the cast on my leg stubbornly prevented me from bending over, so I stood there, listening to the birds and the wind in the trees, and feeling the sun on the back of my neck.

I pictured Tom next to me, immaculately dressed in black from head to toe, hands clasped, head down—serious at first glance, but in reality he'd have a smile on his face. He'd have charmed everyone who'd come to wish him farewell. No doubt he'd even have told a joke or two.

"This is it then, Tommy?" I said out loud, starting an imaginary conversation with my brother, my voice strange and eerie, as if it belonged to someone else. "You're going forever?"

"Looks like it," I heard him say in my head. "But you'll be okay, Shabby."

"No. I won't, Tom," I whispered. "I'll never be okay without you. You were the glue that held everything together. You know that."

I heard Tom's laugh, pictured his wide grin. "Yeah, the Krazy Glue."

"No," I whispered. "The superglue."

"Liam will take care of you," he whispered back. "Although you know very well you can take care of yourself."

I brushed the tears off my cheeks. "I can't be with Liam. He'll end up hating me for what I've done."

"Then what about that guy?" Tom gestured with his head toward Nate. "He's been hanging around you a lot. He seems nice."

I looked over at Nate. "He is," I said quietly. "And he's the only one who understands, because he couldn't save you either."

NOW
ABBY

I WAS UP well before my alarm went off, my mind racing as I pulled away the covers. It was the Tuesday after Easter. The day on which Liam said he'd call. I shuddered, not from the chill in the air—I always insisted on sleeping in what Nate called subzero temperatures—but with a *frisson* of excitement. I looked over at Nate and immediately felt a lorry load of guilt being dumped on top of my head, making its way down my spine, causing every hair on my body to stand on end.

I crept into the bathroom, claiming it as mine for the next forty minutes. The house had an eerie stillness about it— quite the contrast in comparison to the last few days. Paul and Lynne had left the day before. Usually I would've been sad to see them go, but it had brought tomorrow, *today*, that little bit closer.

As I showered, lathering my body with thick, rich almond and cherry blossom shower cream, I wondered if Liam would get close enough to notice the fragrance on my skin, maybe even reach out and feel how soft it was. I told myself to stop. He'd said he'd call today, not that we'd meet. And even if we did meet, it was for closure, to get our heads straight and move on.

But as I carefully applied my foundation and blush, eyeliner and mascara, each brushstroke was a whisper about whom I was doing this for. *Me*, I repeated to myself, *I'm doing this for me*. It was to make myself feel good, more confident. That way, if Liam suggested anything, I'd be able to say no.

Fingers trembling slightly, I tied my hair in one of those messy updos I'd seen in a copy of *Good Housekeeping*, but had never bothered to try. They always made the hairstyles look effortlessly chic, and, as I finally dared to appraise myself in the mirror, I had to admit it looked good. My mother's genes had blessed me with a distinct lack of gray hair, and I still didn't need to resort to dying it and touching up the roots every few weeks.

Nate wasn't in bed when I returned to our room, and I let out a sigh. I pulled on the clothes I'd carefully laid out the night before, a black dress and a pair of matching shoes with a silver heel. It was a professional outfit that hugged my figure, but it wasn't low cut or short enough to scream *adulteress* at the top of its silky lungs.

Not that I had any intention of doing anything with Liam. I couldn't. If I got on that slippery slope again, this time I'd be whizzing down all the way to the bottom, without any opportunity of stopping or the possibility of catching my breath.

"Wow," Nate said as I walked into the kitchen.

Sarah looked up. "Yeah. That dress really suits you, Mum."

They sat next to each other at the breakfast table. Him with his Best Daddy Ever coffee mug she'd given him when she was four, her with a half-eaten piece of toast, both sharing the newspaper. Nate had claimed the sports section, Sarah the entertainment news. They seemed more like a married couple than Nate and I at times.

"You're not going to the gym this morning?" Nate said. When I shook my head he brushed some crumbs off his tie, folded the paper and asked, "Big meeting or something?"

"A new client's coming in, so I thought I'd smarten up."

Sarah stared at me, and I hoped my smile didn't betray me. I concentrated on my breathing, a technique a teacher once taught me. Focus on your breathing, and you'll stop blushing. It didn't often work but, thankfully, this time the warmth didn't seem to spread much beyond my neck.

"Are you off then?" Nate said, standing up. "I'll walk out with you."

"Okay." I looked at Sarah. "What are you doing today?"

"Uh." She fiddled with her hair. "I'm going out with Claire later. She wants to look at some clothes." She held up a hand. "And before you say no, I've almost finished all of my school projects for the holidays."

"I never even mentioned—" I quickly got my tone in check. "Have fun. Don't forget to lock the door."

She rolled her eyes. "I won't."

"It was the one time, love." Nate got up and made his way to the door. "Two years ago."

"I know." I smiled at Sarah, received nothing in return. "Enjoy yourself, and be back by six thirty for dinner."

"I will. Bye." She saluted, then waved. "Bye, Dad."

"Shall I pick something up for tonight?" Nate said as we walked outside.

"No, it's fine." I unlocked my car. "There's stuff in the freezer."

He handed me a brown paper bag. "I made you lunch. Chicken lettuce wraps and an apple."

Guilt and disdain flooded me in equal measure. "That's lovely."

"Anything for you, sweetheart." He kissed me softly as I swallowed the lump in my throat. "Anything at all."

I misfiled three sets of reports before nine thirty, and when I checked the payroll entries I got a different result four times. My mobile sat on my desk, set to silent, but vibrating at each new message and email that arrived. I kept staring at it, willing Liam to call, then checked it again to see if it was still working.

In the words of my daughter's generation, *WTF?* Here I was, a grown woman in my midforties, waiting for a guy to call. Why couldn't I pick up the stupid thing and phone him? But, I stubbornly decided, he'd said he'd call me, and I'd be damned if I caved.

When my phone finally burst into a twinkly display of an incoming call, I didn't move, watching it slowly inch its way across my desk, flashing and buzzing instead. After it had gone quiet I kept staring at it, and when it sprang to life again two minutes later I snatched it up.

"Hello?"

"It's Liam." His voice was a silky smooth scoop of raspberry sorbet on a hot summer's day. "How are you?"

My legs trembled, so I dug my heels firmly into the industrial carpet, thankful for my sturdy office chair. "I'm okay."

"When can we meet?"

I laughed. "Jesus, Liam. You're not wasting any time, are you? Cutting right to the chase."

"Sorry. I dialed a few times but hung up before it rang." He lowered his voice. "To be perfectly honest, I'm feeling like a hormonal schoolboy. I can't believe you still have that effect on me." I didn't say anything. I think I stopped breathing until he cleared his throat and said, "Abby Sanders—"

"Morris."

"Ah." His laugh sounded forced. "Yes. Excuse the Freudian slip." He paused long enough for me to come up with a hundred different variations of what he was going to say next. "Mrs. Morris, may I have the pleasure of your company for coffee or lunch?"

Coffee. Of course that was the way to go. A quickish cup of decaf at Starbucks, over which we'd reminisce about our relationship, deftly avoid talking about the Cotswolds, then agree to move on with our respective partners. We'd laugh about how we would become good neighbors, how we'd help each other out with cups of sugar or a ladder to put up the Christmas decorations. We'd end the conversation with a hug that felt more like a squeeze from a relative than an embrace from a former lover.

Coffee. Definitely coffee.

"Lunch," I said. "Lunch would be nice."

"Oh, I—"

"Unless you don't want to?"

"Lunch would be great, Abby, I didn't think you'd... Anyway... Want to choose where? I'm at the Market Square office today."

"Really? I'm on Harmony. Just around the corner." Neither of us spoke until I said, "How about Incognito?" I almost laughed at the implication, so I quickly added, "It's always busy at lunchtime. Can you meet at eleven thirty?" I gave him the address, heard him look it up on the PC.

"Incognito. Looks good. But...isn't it a bit close to your office?"

"Why?"

"What if someone sees us?" he said quietly.

"Liam, we're neighbors. We're having lunch. No big deal, right?"

"Right." He paused again. "I'll see you later."

We're having lunch, I told myself again, trying not to think of Nate and everything he'd ever done for me. For *us*. "It's just *lunch*," I whispered. Perhaps if I'd repeated it often enough, it might actually have been true.

NOW

NANCY

LIAM HAD LEFT for work early, evidently unable to wait to get out of the house. Away from *me*.

Zac was probably still in bed, too. My hangover had spoiled the rest of the long weekend, and I really didn't fancy continuing the renovations. I wanted to lie around, read a book and dig into some chocolate. I'd be sure to regret it later—especially when I stepped on the scales. I'd laughed with Lynne Saturday night, joking about how I'd lost at least forty kilos.

"*Forty?*" she'd said, her eyes wide with admiration. "Wow, good for you."

"Yeah. Shame it was the same two kilos twenty times." We'd dissolved into fits of giggles again. Lynne was a riot, her sense of humor as dark as mine, and we'd spent a lot of the evening talking. I didn't often click with women. Despite the cries of "Sisterhood Unite," I felt we could be despicable toward each other, and because of that I often preferred the company of men. But Lynne was different, and I imagined we'd have become great friends if they'd lived close enough. It was a shame Nate had married Abby instead of Lynne.

My pulse throbbed as I recalled the events of Saturday night. I'd had a cunning plan, taken extra time on my hair to ensure it fell in the softest curls. I'd applied just the right amount of makeup, and had worn the red wraparound dress I knew Liam loved. By the end of the evening I wanted him on his knees, begging me to take it off, which I would, but only after he'd begged again.

Despite looking better than I had in months, and even though I'd flirted with Nate all night, touching his arm and leaning forward when I dropped my napkin on the floor twice, neither he nor Liam appeared to notice. Damn it, couldn't Liam see what was right in front of his nose? Had I become that much of a routine to him, such a sure thing? When, exactly, had that happened?

I'd wondered if Abby would pick up on my antics, maybe look at me with raised eyebrows, send me a firm but friendly message to back off her husband, but she was far too distracted by Zac and Sarah, watching them like an overprotective lioness.

I didn't blame her. I was curious about what the two of them were up to, but I got the feeling she did it in the spirit of protecting Sarah. From what, I wasn't sure. Maybe she believed Sarah was too precious to go out with Zac. That thought pissed me off because Liam and I raised him to be a gentleman. Besides, kids were kids. At their age they were bound to experiment and try things—Lord knows I certainly had, and I'd been younger than him.

I stretched out, threw the covers back and padded to the bathroom. As I showered, I thought about Abby's story of Sarah's birth—which could have explained her wanting to protect her from everything—and how Nate had looked at her. His face had been full of love, tenderness, adoration. As if she were the most important human being in the world. And she was, to him, obviously, although exactly why eluded me. She was so distant and quiet, pretty but boring. Maybe she was great in bed although I couldn't imagine it. Wasn't she too cold for that?

In any event, Nate's affection toward her reminded me of when I watched romantic comedies, or read love stories. I wanted that. I wanted Liam to worship me like Nate worshiped Abby. Had Liam ever looked at me that way? I wasn't sure—if he had, it was a long time ago.

Abby had been pretty dismissive of Nate. It made me think she didn't deserve him, not really. If I had that kind of adulation thrown at my feet I'd at the very least have acknowledged it. I shook my head. Just like Liam, Abby didn't see how lucky she was.

I finished showering and looked at myself in the mirror, noticing the fine lines that had appeared around my eyes, as if from nowhere. I'd barely noticed the slow changes; I'd been so busy over the last seventeen years, looking after Zac, bending myself into a pretzel for Liam, giving up everything to become the dutiful housewife and mother. Not that Liam had ever put me under any pressure to do so. No, my personality had slowly been eroded entirely of my own accord.

"I need to feel alive again," I said to my reflection. "I deserve to feel alive again."

As I lathered my body in rich, sweet-smelling lotion I decided I would do whatever was necessary to be lusted over like the heroines in the novels I read. Fought for like the stars in the Hollywood movies.

And I decided if Liam wouldn't extend me that courtesy, then someone else would instead…

NOW
ABBY

BY THE TIME I'd walked from the office and got halfway to Incognito to meet Liam, my dress had grabbed hold of my sweaty back, my shoes felt like my feet had grown two sizes and my relaxed updo threatened to become a pathetic down-do any second. I cursed myself for getting dressed up, then swore at the foggy humidity, too. At least it had stopped raining for the time being.

What the hell had I been thinking? My usual combination of black trousers and a white shirt would have been perfectly fine, not to mention my trusty court shoes. It was penance, that's what it was. Payback for skulking around, going off to meet an ex-lover while our respective spouses went happily and unsuspectingly about their day.

As I turned the corner and got closer to the restaurant, my heart made its way up my throat with every step I took. I wiped my palms on my dress and fussed with my hair for the fourth time in thirty seconds.

I hadn't felt like this since Liam and I'd been going out together. It had always been this way during the six months we'd dated, and since then I'd almost convinced myself it was only because we'd been young and so carefree. But now, twenty plus years later, it felt exactly the same. If anything, it was more intense. The fluttering in the pit of my stomach, the giddy light-headedness, a smile I couldn't quash, not even if I tried for a million years. The anticipation of seeing him had never disappeared; it had merely been buried under years of absence.

My head was screaming at me to turn back. But like an unyielding judge, my heart overruled my brain and resolutely made my feet carry me forward instead. And I kept telling myself we'd have lunch, clear the air and that would be it. Lunch. Clear air. Over.

But then there he was. And as I looked at Liam I wanted time to stand still so I could observe him for a while. He stood under Incognito's black-and-gold awning, his gray jacket casually slung over his shoulder, and his shirt so white it could have starred in an OxiClean commercial. He spotted me and raised a hand. His gaze didn't waver as he watched me approach, and I barely managed to stop myself from wiping my hands on my dress again. He leaned toward me when I reached him, and kissed me gently on the cheek.

"Hey, neighbor." He pulled away. "Not that I usually kiss my neighbors."

I laughed and dropped my gaze, reminded myself we were there to sort things out, not make them more complicated. I had to stay focused, make sure I said what I'd prepared myself to say, not deviate from the script nor improvise, not even in the slightest.

We made our way to the restaurant, where a waitress with shiny butterfly clips in her mass of blond curls brought us glasses of iced water and handed us the menus before rattling off the specials, none of which I could recall.

"I'll have a Caesar salad," I said, trying to smile but sort of grimacing instead.

Liam folded his menu and handed it back to the waitress. "Same for me, please."

Neither of us spoke for a while. This wasn't how I'd rehearsed things in my head. In my version we were supposed to talk. Decide on a way forward. A *separate* way forward. I uncrossed and recrossed my legs, and took a sip of water to stop myself from twirling my wedding ring.

Liam broke the silence as he flattened out the serviette in his lap. "I don't know where to start either."

I let out a combination of a sigh and a laugh. "I think I'm still in shock."

"I never expected to see you again, Abby. Let alone live next to you."

"So how *did* you end up there…?"

"Nancy did all the research and—"

Panic gripped me. "Do you think she knows something happened between us?"

"Abby, come on. It was years ago…"

I shook my head. "Sorry, you're right, of course you are."

"She went to look at the house, then showed me pictures. But if I'd known…"

"What would you have done?" I searched his face. "Would you have moved in anyway?"

"No," he said quietly. "I don't think so."

I felt as if the wind had been knocked out of me and chastised myself. This was good. It meant he didn't have feelings, it meant—

"It's torture," Liam continued. "Living in that house, knowing you're next door...with him. *Nate*."

"I know what you mean." *Oh, shit*. Major script deviation.

He stared at me. "Do you?"

I couldn't help myself. "Yes."

Before either of us could say anything the waitress brought our salads. She asked if we wanted fresh pepper, which I accepted to buy myself some time, although Liam and I continued staring at each other while she twisted a huge wooden pepper mill that dwarfed her tiny frame.

"Thank you," Liam said to the waitress, finally breaking eye contact. She smiled at him and wished us bon appétit, and when Liam looked at me again, for once, I couldn't read him. "Nate seems like a good man." He fiddled with his glass. "Just the way you described him."

I swallowed. "He is. Nancy seems—"

"She is."

"So what now?" I said, unable to wait any longer. "Where do we go from here?"

Liam looked at me. "What do you want to happen?"

"You mean between us?"

He said nothing, continued to stare at me with a slight look of hope. Was it hope? I wanted to reach for his hand, get up, leave the restaurant and never go home. Images of a faraway beach flooded my mind. Us walking across a vast stretch of soft white sand next to a turquoise ocean, both of our bodies smooth and as brown as caramel, our hearts free from guilt and full of love. I looked outside at the gray skies and the damp umbrellas of the people walking by.

"Nate's my husband," I said. "And I love him."

"Are you certain?"

I made sure I held his gaze and stuck to the script. "Yes." I picked up my fork and attempted to stab a crouton.

Liam sat back in his chair. He hadn't touched his food. "Then nothing happens."

"So you're saying if I said yes, we'd have an affair?" I whispered. "That's a bit rude, don't you think?"

"It wouldn't be the first time." When I flinched, he exhaled, held up both hands. "Shit, I'm sorry. That was way out of order."

"Nothing like that ever happened again," I said, deliberately blocking the memory from my mind.

Liam swallowed. "It didn't for me either. I'm sorry."

I put my fork down, leaned in a little farther. "Does Nancy know you...cheated on her?"

He looked away. "No. Does Nate?"

"No."

"When's Sarah's birthday?"

The abrupt change of subject made me flinch, and I looked up at him sharply. His face had hardened, and I could feel mine do the same. "She's not yours, Liam," I said quickly. "She's *not*."

"Are you sure?"

"*Yes.*"

"When's her birthday?"

"February fifth."

He fell silent. I waited as he did the calculation in his head. "You were pregnant when..."

I had to look away. "Barely."

Liam leaned forward. "When I saw her, I wondered... For a second, you know?"

I kept my gaze steady. "She's Nate's. She's *his* daughter."

"She looks like you." He smiled. "I can see why Zac likes her."

My breath caught in my throat. "What do you mean?"

"They were texting each other last night. Didn't you know?"

"No! What did they say?"

"I don't know. I was in the dining room, doing some work, but Nancy picked up his phone when he went to the bathroom." He sighed. "It pisses me off when she does that, spying on him, reading his stuff."

My throat felt dry so I drank some water, my hands trembling as I held the glass.

Liam frowned. "Are you okay?"

"Did Zac say anything to you about Sarah?"

"He only said she surprised him, but that was about it. You know what teenagers are like. He communicates in grunts and huffs most of the time."

I stared at him. "I don't want them spending time together."

"Why? They can be friends."

"And what if it turns into more than that?" I shuddered. "With our past, it's just way too complicated. We have to make sure they stay away from each other. Okay?"

"Why not let things run their course? They'll lose interest in each other soon enough."

A trickle of sweat slid down my spine. "*No.* They can't be involved. I mean it."

He was smiling now. "Imagine if they got married. Jesus."

My fingers were squeezing the glass so tight it was in danger of shattering in my hand. I let it go and flexed my fingers. "It's not funny, Liam."

"Okay, okay. But I didn't come here to talk about the kids."

"Then why *did* you come?"

"I want to talk to you. Find out how you've been." He smiled at me again. "How are you? Tell me about where you work."

I sat back in my chair. "Well, I'm okay, I suppose. My job at Sterling's not bad. I preferred it at Hoskins, but it would have been an impossible commute from here. What about you? Still happy at the bank?"

"Yeah, definitely. The promotion has been…" He put his fork down with a clang. "I can't do this. I won't."

I frowned. "Do what?"

Liam shifted in his seat. "Pretend. Be all polite and civil and so bloody English about it when…it's just that—"

"Don't, Liam, we—"

"—you know how I feel about you." He moved his hand, and for a moment I thought—*hoped*—he might reach for mine, but he fiddled with his napkin instead. "Ever since I saw you at Rowley's all those years ago." He looked away for a second, then his eyes met mine again. "Saturday night was horrible, seeing you with Nate. And bloody worst of all, you seem quite happy."

My back stiffened, and I struggled to keep my expression even. "We are. *Very*."

"And I suppose I'm glad for you," he said. "Although I was hoping you weren't. That way I could scoop you up and take you away. Far away. Forever."

I couldn't stop a grin. "People don't talk like that anymore, do they? I feel like we're in the middle of *Gone with the Wind*."

"Give me a break." Liam laughed. "I'm rusty. And you know what I mean."

"I'm not going to risk twenty years of marriage for a fling."

He leaned forward, put his hand over mine, making my fingers tremble. "Who said it would be a fling?"

"That's enough." I snatched my hand away, waved at our waitress, indicating for the bill.

"Abby, look, I—"

"Friends, Liam." I reached for my bag. "That's all we'll ever be. I can't do that to Nate. Or Sarah. It's not fair."

Liam folded his napkin and put it on the table. We waited in silence until the waitress came over, and Liam insisted on buying lunch, never mind my protests. "I'll walk you back," he said, as we both got up.

The drizzle had stopped, and I squinted at the brightness outside, despite the clouds. I slipped on my jacket as we made our way down the street, our arms occasionally touching. We walked far closer than colleagues or friends would. Anybody who took the time to observe us surely wouldn't doubt we were, or had every intention of being, far more.

We walked around the corner where Liam stopped and turned toward me. Without saying a word, he slid one arm around my waist and gently tilted my head upward with his fingers. I held my breath as his lips came closer, unable to move away. My eyes closed, my hands moved up around his neck, and there we were, in broad daylight, only a short distance away from my office, completely lost in a kiss I wanted to go on forever.

When we finally broke away he looked at me. "Friends from now on," he whispered.

And then he walked away, leaving me breathless, and trying to remind myself of why I'd chosen to walk away from him and marry Nate instead.

THEN
ABBY

WE TALKED ABOUT our guilt sometimes. When I woke up screaming for the fifth night in a row, Nate held me. He wept when I whispered it wasn't his fault he hadn't been able to save Tom. He seemed so grateful, so overwhelmed I could forgive him, although there was nothing to forgive.

Nate. Kind, caring Nate, who'd returned to Wembley and called almost every day before coming back to see me a month later. I often thought about how we'd ended up in bed together that weekend. How we'd gone out for dinner and, afterward, I'd asked him to come back home with me. What had I been looking for? To thank him? Repay him with sex? No. I cared for him—not as much as he cared for me, that I knew, but there was an undeniable connection, as if ending up together had been inevitable.

The day the judge handed me a suspended prison sentence and took my license for eighteen months, Nate suggested I move to Wembley. "What do you have to lose?" he asked. Nothing, was the honest answer. I'd tried to make things work in Preston, but an invisible yet oppressive cloud had permanently settled over the area, the epicenter, the eye of the storm, firmly taking hold over the Kettle Club and my life there. I'd attempted to ignore the stares and whispers of some customers. Most of their comments probably had nothing to do with me anyway. But from some of their looks, it was difficult to imagine they were anything else.

"Yes," I said to Nate, "yes, I'll move in with you," and a week later we drove south.

Nate introduced me to his brother, and I instantly admired his carefree view of the world. "It must be so hard," one of Paul's numerous girlfriends said, fluttering her thick, mile-long eyelashes, "abandoning everything and everyone."

I smiled, tilted my head to one side and answered, "A little." A complete lie, of course. "Everything" consisted of a few pieces of furniture in my flat. "Everyone" meant my mother and a dwindling number of friends. And Liam, who I constantly had to shove to the back of my mind.

He'd left me countless messages, written letters, and I was sure I'd seen him on the pavement across the road from the Kettle Club numerous times. But when I'd gotten to the front door he'd disappeared. I didn't blame him. Actually, I thanked him. It made my decision to move south an easier one. After all, going away isn't difficult when you don't leave a void behind.

"Now you've been here awhile," Nate said three weeks after I'd arrived in his two-bedroom flat, with three suitcases and a couple of plastic bags. "What do you want to do?"

We sat in his kitchen, eating boiled eggs and toast, the only thing I made properly. "You mean for work?" I dipped my bread into the waxy yolk.

"Yeah. Not that there's any rush, okay? No pressure."

"I thought I'd apply to some coffee shops in town." When I noticed he'd stopped chewing I frowned. "What?"

"Coffee shops?" Nate was frowning, too. "Is that really what you want?"

"Well, not *really*." I shifted in my seat. "But I don't exactly have fantastic work experience, do I? My qualifications are pants."

He shrugged. "Then get some."

I harrumphed as if he'd told me to stroll up Mount Everest in a pair of rubber boots, backward. "It's not that simple, is it?"

"Why not? What would you have done if you hadn't left school so early?"

"Dunno." I stuck out my chin. "Anyway, I had to leave so I could get away from my mum."

"Sorry." He pulled a face. "I'm not trying to be a wanker. What would you *like* to do?"

"I used to help a friend of Mum's at her office during school holidays," I said quietly. "She taught me a bit about accounting."

"Accounting?" he said. "Seriously?"

"Yeah. I know it sounds boring—"

"Hey, I didn't mean—"

"—but I enjoyed it. Debit, credit. Making sure everything was where it needed to be, that the accounts balanced."

Nate smiled. "Great. Take a course then. You've got time during the day and—"

I laughed. "Er, *no*. I'm running out of money. I need to get a job."

Nate reached over the table. "I'll support you. I've still got some cash Granddad left me and—"

"Look, Nate, I—"

"Let me do this for you, Abby. Please. I want to."

I looked at him. "I'll think about it. Give me a bit of time."

"Okay." Nate popped a piece of toast in his mouth, trying not to grin.

As it turned out, "a bit of time" was a few weeks. Nate's neighbor helped me find an entry-level bookkeeper job with Hoskins Insurance where a bubbly girl called Olivia took one look at me and declared we'd be the best of friends. Five days later I signed up for an evening course at the Chartered Institute of Management Accountants, which sounded so overwhelmingly posh, I kept whispering it to myself.

Suddenly the next few years were mapped out for me—a situation both new and daunting, yet comforting at the same time. I'd started to *belong*.

As I got ready the evening of my first class, pondering if I should wear a skirt or trousers, Nate walked into the bedroom. He held out a large parcel wrapped in white-and-green-striped paper that made it look like a giant mint. "Happy first day at college," he said.

"What's this?" I took the gift and gave it a squeeze, trying to guess what was inside.

He grinned. "Open it and see."

I tore into the paper, revealing a royal blue box underneath. "What *is* it?" I repeated, laughing as I struggled to open the lid, then pushed the white tissue paper aside. "What have you...*wow*." My fingers slid over the smooth, brown leather satchel, glided across the brass buckle.

"I thought you needed something to help you feel the part." Nate reached for the strap and put the bag over my shoulder, nodding his approval. "It suits you. Definitely not yuppie and not nerdy either. It's perfect."

"Thank you, Nate." I put my arms around him, reaching for his lips with mine.

"You're welcome," he whispered as I pulled away. "Why don't you have a look inside?"

I frowned. "Wait. You didn't get me the pen I said I liked the other day, did you?" I flipped open the satchel, stuck a hand inside and rummaged around. "It cost a fortune and—" The rest of my sentence died in my throat as my fingers closed over a small box buried at the bottom.

When I looked at Nate again, he was on one knee, staring up at me with a smile. He gently lifted my arm out of the satchel and loosened my fingers to reveal the green velvet box in my palm. Nate opened the box slowly. My heart thumped and my throat went dry as I stared at the solitaire engagement ring inside, gleaming like a little ray of golden sunshine.

"Abby," Nate said, his eyes shining brightly, "I know you might think it's a bit sudden. But I know it's right. I *know*." He swallowed. "I love you so much. Will you marry me?"

I couldn't move. I couldn't speak. This wasn't supposed to happen. I didn't deserve this. I didn't deserve to be *happy*. But now Nate, a man who'd seen me at my absolute worst, supported and cared for me without asking for anything in return, wanted to spend the rest of his life with me. Nate had stuck by me, even when I'd pushed, prodded, stepped on and yanked every one of his buttons and levers I'd discovered since we'd met.

I looked at the cowlick in his hair he could never tame, his blue eyes that twinkled when he told a joke, his soft lips that kissed me better whenever I wanted to hide away from everyone.

I hadn't asked or expected him to fall in love with me. Nor had I even considered I'd ever feel what I did for him, or anyone else for that matter. It wasn't the explosive, all-consuming, passionate love I'd had—still had—for Liam. Nothing would ever come close. That was a once-in-a-lifetime thing, never to be repeated.

Was it even love I felt for Nate? Perhaps. Something like it anyway. He was patient, loving, caring. "But he's not Liam, is he?" the little voice in my head whispered, and I pushed the words away. Patient, loving, caring, I repeated to myself. *Patient, loving, caring.* Nate never did anything wrong. He always wanted to make everything right.

"Abby," Nate whispered, looking at me with his eyebrows raised. "Say something?"

He loved me enough for the both of us; he'd said it more than once. What I felt for him might not have been love, not exactly. But surely it was close enough? And I didn't want to end up alone. I had no family left, I realized, trying not to shiver as the thought of loneliness sneaked its way down my spine. Nate was all I had.

"Yes," I said. "Yes, I'll marry you." And then Nate was on his feet, cupping my face and kissing me softly, drowning out the whispers in my head that kept repeating I was a selfish bitch, and he deserved better.

NOW

SARAH

Dear Diary,

I think I'm going crazy. I mixed up my underwear drawer the other day and I never do that. Although I could be distracted because:

I put on a kilo over Easter. Argh!

Mrs. Cloisters emailed and said I got 98.5% on my math test. Double argh!

Zac likes someone. And it's not me. Triple argh!

Okay, okay. Let's take these in order. The weight—I'll starve myself for the rest of the week. The math test, *whatever*. I'll make sure I get 110% with the bonus question on the next one. So I can cope with the first two. But the third?

Zac came over for the interview. And what do you know? The boy speaketh in sentences! He was brilliant, really detailed, and I know my article's going to be great now I have a proper story. He even said I could use his photo.

We played *Chick Chick Boom* again (5-0 to *moi*), then he suggested watching a movie.

Me (bringing up Netflix): Comedy, drama or action?

Him (groaning): Anything but a rom-com. Nothing with Anne Hathaway or Amy Adams.

I told him whatever, they were both brilliant but he rolled his eyes and called me a princess. By now I've pretty much caught on to his straight-faced sense of humor. I punched his arm and continued flicking through the films until we both agreed on one.

It was funny how we laughed at exactly the same things. And it was crazy how comfortable I felt with Zac, like we'd know each other for ages. I think his air of superiority is just that. I bet you he secretly likes kittens and puppies, and thinks rainbows are magical. Hang on, now he sounds like a wishy-washy kind of guy, which he isn't. But there's definitely more to him than he lets on.

I'm glad it was the two of us at home. Otherwise Mum would've come in every five minutes asking if we wanted some crisps. Her voice would be all singsongy, as if Zac and I were a couple of four-year-olds watching *Teletubbies*. And it would only be to check up on us, make sure we weren't shoving our tongues down each other's throats.

Anyway, she needn't have worried because Zac started talking about Nicole Goyle. Bloody tall, slender, long and dark-haired Nicole Goyle, the new girl at school who jumped into the magic gene pool and got the looks *and* the brains. Zac wanted to know all about her. He didn't exactly come out and ask if she's seeing anyone, but that's what he was getting at.

So I put him out of his misery. Told him the truth. She's single. You should have seen the look on his face—triumphant, that's what it was. I could have lied, but what's the point?

So bollocks to it. I guess I'll be the oddball gal-pal who lives next door. Great. Oh, well. I didn't like him that much anyway.
Later,
Sarah x.

PS. Word of the day: *gravitate*, verb.

1: to move under the influence of gravitation.

2a: to move toward something.

b: to be drawn or attracted especially by natural inclination.

As in: *Why do all boys have to gravitate toward bloody, sodding Nicole GARgoyle?*

NOW

NATE

DESPITE THE PROSPECT of my brother and his family setting off into the sunset with an alphorn slung over their shoulders, the week had become an absoluhte corker. A couple of minutes ago I'd placed another two web designers on twelve-month contracts with my favorite client and posted the deals on our intranet.

I watched my boss saunter over with a grin on his round, fake-tan face. Even though Kevin was coming up to his sixty-fifth birthday, he still had a full head of hair so white we could have used it to light the way in a blackout.

"Christ, you're on a roll," he said, standing in front of me with his arms crossed. He made a circular gesture with his hand. "Can you get these other useless pricks to do the same? HR is 10 percent behind target, and don't even get me started on the finance group."

I laughed. "Do you want me to tell them recruitment is all about relationships?"

"Hah—"

"That they have to know what people need before they know it themselves?"

"Oh, boy—"

"How about people buy people from people?"

"Okay." Kevin pretended to hang himself with his Ralph Lauren tie. "Enough of my wonderful corporate bullshit." He leaned in closer. "Your bonus will be outstanding this quarter. But you knew that already."

Sure I did. I raised my eyebrows and said, "Is it?"

Kevin snorted. "And it's looking like the trip is yours, too, my friend. It's what? Ten weeks till year end? The other department heads will never catch up."

I leaned back in my seat, pulled down my sleeves. "Kevin, if I have anything to do with it they'll be choking on my dust."

He gave me two thumbs-up. "Like it, mate. I bet Abby's excited. Who wouldn't be? Amsterdam, Berlin *and* Rome?"

"Actually—" I smiled, ready to put my master plan into action "—can we swap Rome for Zurich?"

"'Course." Kevin rubbed his palms together. "You're on. Abby's idea?"

"I haven't told her anything about it yet. I want it to be a surprise."

Kevin's eyes widened. "Well, that's going to be one hell of a surprise. She's a lucky woman." He gave me a clap on the shoulder. "Now go and help the rest of 'em do some deals, will you? Please? The wife wants a fancy European trip, too."

On the train back home I rehearsed how I'd tell Abby and Sarah about the trip. "Guess what, ladies…" Cue huge drumroll followed by gasps of glee and thunderous hand clapping.

Abby wasn't a massive fan of traveling, and I'd never been to Berlin or Zurich. I'd visited Amsterdam once, on a stagweekend before Abby and I had met. Me, Paul and six of our barely post-pubescent friends had gotten off the plane and headed directly for one of the multiple coffee shops in the red-light district. The three-day weekend had disappeared in a hazy daze of weed, beer and, in Paul's case, a particularly persistent case of crabs.

Of course this time around would be far more civilized with trips to the Rijksmuseum, the Royal Palace and, if I could get away with it, a stint at the Heineken brewery.

Surely this trip would put a smile back on Abby's face because having one surly teenager in the house at the moment was quite enough. At times like these I wished for an overtly manly hobby, like model trains or CB radio, not to mention a shed—anything that would give me a safe place to escape the moodiness that seemed to follow us around these days.

I sighed. I knew what my hobby was. Fixing stuff. Shelves, the neighbor's heating and, of course, my wife.

When the woman diagonally across from me on the train coughed loudly I looked over and noticed the book in her hands. The title? One word. A scary word. *Menopause*.

My mind played the *duh-duh-duuuuuh* music and a lightbulb the size of a hot-air balloon went off in my head with a bang. I whipped out my phone, ran a search and wanted to stand up and shout, "Elementary, my dear Watson!"

Apparently, psychological symptoms of said men-o-pause included anxiety (seemed like it), poor memory (she'd forgotten to pay the phone bill, which never happened), depressive mood, irritability and mood swings (check, check, check—Jesus, had *Abby* written this?) and less interest in sex. The last one was only recent—she'd turned me down at least four times now—but everything else rang true.

I stuffed my phone back in my pocket and stretched out my legs again. Menopause, or at Abby's age, probably premenopause. Of course! Why hadn't I worked it out before? I shook my head, thinking I definitely should make more of an effort. And so, when I got off the train and into my car, I decided to stop at *The Flower Girls*.

"Mr. Morris." Mrs. Cuthbert put the red roses and green fuzzy stuff I could never remember the name of down on the counter and held out a wrinkled, fleshy hand for me to shake. "Haven't seen you for a while." Her chin wobbled as she waggled a finger. "How are you, dear?"

"Great, thanks. And how are you, Mrs. Cuthbert?"

"Oh, hanging on for dear life, my love." She laughed and tapped her lip with a stubby finger. "Let me guess. Yellow daffodils for Abby?"

I grinned. "Yes, please. They're still her favorite."

Mrs. Cuthbert headed over to one of the many metal buckets of flowers that were lined up in neat rows, like hopeful orphans waiting to be chosen. "Special occasion?" she wheezed as she deftly arranged an ornate bunch from the desirables.

"No. Just because."

Mrs. Cuthbert smiled, creases forming like empty river beds across her cheeks. "She's a lucky woman."

"You're the second person who's said that today."

"Ah, well—" Mrs. Cuthbert cocked her head to one side "—then it must be true."

I'd only been home for a few minutes when the doorbell rang. I gave up trying to find a suitable vase for the flowers and propped them up in the sink instead, then headed for the front door.

It was cool outside, but Nancy stood on our doorstep in a white T-shirt, and as I greeted her, I tried not to notice how sheer it looked.

"I hope I'm not bothering you," she said, rubbing her left arm with her right hand. "But there's something wrong with the dishwasher. It won't drain. I'd ask Zac to help, but he's out and Liam's still at work, so I wondered..."

"I'll come over." I grabbed my keys and closed the door behind me. "Lead on."

"Thanks, Nate," Nancy said as we walked over to their house. "Liam's not a great handyman at the best of times. But don't tell him I said that."

I laughed. "I think as far as he's concerned it isn't a state secret."

She opened the front door, and I whistled. "You've been busy."

"Oh. Yeah, I have."

I looked around, taking in the bare floor and the walls now stripped of Barbara's crazy wallpaper. "You took up the carpet, too."

"It smelled of cat wee." Nancy wrinkled her nose. "I'll order a new one, but I think I want to knock down the wall between the dining room and the kitchen first." She frowned as she wrapped a strand of hair around her finger. "That's a lot of work, though, isn't it?"

"It is. We did the same thing."

"I know." Nancy grinned. "That's where I got the idea from. I'm trying to convince Liam to let me redo the kitchen as well, but he's not keen."

"Oh?"

"Nah. We'd only finished our old house a few months before we moved, and that renovation took *forever*." She looked around. "But at least now I feel like I have some idea of what I'm doing. And I know you're right next door. You know... if I have any questions."

"I didn't know you're such an avid DIY'er."

She laughed. "I read a lot of magazines, and I've taken a few online interior design classes. But those don't teach you how to sort out petulant appliances, do they?"

We went through to the kitchen, where I kneeled in front of the dishwasher and tried to unscrew the filter. "So what else are you planning on doing?" I asked.

"Get rid of the wainscoting. I hate it."

"Really?" I wriggled the filter around, cursing silently when it wouldn't budge. "So did we, but ripping it off is a massive job. That's why we painted it," I said, looking up at Nancy who was now kneeling next to me. "But we got rid of the stucco ceilings."

"That's a great idea." She bent over to watch what I was doing.

I turned my attention back to the dishwasher and away from her cleavage. "Let me know if you ever need anything. Our garage is full of tools."

She put a hand on my arm and squeezed. "And you call *me* an avid DIY'er."

I grinned. "Ah," I said as I finally managed to open the rebellious filter. "I see what the problem is."

"What? Is it bad?" She leaned in so far I thought her breasts might graze my shoulder. Then she looked at me. I hadn't noticed how long her eyelashes were, or the heart-shaped beauty spot to the left of her nose.

"Something's stuck." I grabbed hold of the black material and gently twisted it free before holding it up. "It's a… oh…uh…"

"Oh, god, how embarrassing!" Nancy grabbed the tiny thong and stifled a giggle. "I wondered where the devil it had gone. Thanks, Nate," she said and squeezed my arm again.

I got up quickly—too quickly—because I whacked my head on the kitchen table with a thud. "Ouch!"

"Oh, shit," she said, a hand flying up to cover her mouth. "You okay?"

I waved a hand. "Other than my pride, yeah."

Nancy didn't hide her giggle this time. "Well, that makes us even then." She looked at me. "Are you in a hurry? Do you have time for tea or something? I could show you my plans for the house. I'd *love* to have your opinion."

Images of her in that teeny-weeny thong came out of nowhere, and I cleared my throat in a sort-of effort to get rid of them. "Sure." I shrugged. "Why not?"

"Great." Nancy went to fill the kettle while I tried to focus on the middle of her back, not lower down. Christ, I seriously needed to get a grip.

"I've put a folder together," she said as she shut off the tap. "Done some sketches and stuff." She switched the kettle on and slid a massive binder across the kitchen table. "Milk and sugar?"

"Milk, thanks." I flicked through the plans, grateful to have something to take my mind off her behind. I pointed to the drawing of her open-plan kitchen-diner. "This looks great, Nancy. But I'm pretty sure the wall's load-bearing."

"You think?"

"Uh-huh. At least ours was. We got an engineer in to be sure and had a beam put in."

"But look at your place now. I'm so envious. You did such a great job." She put a cup of steaming tea in front of me and smiled. Was it me or was she fluttering those lashes?

We spent the next few minutes going over the plans, then debated the merits of scraping a ceiling versus covering it with sheets of plaster board.

"I don't mind the scraping," Nancy said, "but I don't think I can keep my arms in the air for that long. I don't have biceps like yours." There was definite fluttering that time.

"If it hasn't been painted, then it'll come off easily." I turned a page so I didn't have to keep eye contact. "But a stucco remover's your best bet. I'm pretty sure one of my mates has one you could borrow."

"Oh, Nate, that would be fantastic." Nancy beamed. "When we bought the place I was happy to have a project to work on, but now I think I've bitten off more than I can chew…"

I took another sip of tea and, before I could change my mind, said, "I'll help you with the ceiling."

"Oh, no, no. I can't possibly expect you to do that."

"Why not?" I used my pretend-offended voice. "We finished our renovations ages ago. There's nothing left to do, and I kind of miss it."

"Well…if you're sure. I certainly won't say no." She looked directly at me, then wiped her lip slowly and, I was certain, quite deliberately with her thumb.

I swallowed. I had the beginnings of a hard-on. What the heck was I doing? "Nancy, look, I—"

"Oh, goodness, look at the time." She turned away. "I still have to get to the post office."

I was happy for the excuse to head out before things got even more awkward, and stood up quickly. "I'll see myself out."

"Goodbye, Nate." Her green eyes twinkled when she glanced at me again, and I suddenly wished Abby would look at me that way, too. "Looking forward to working with you. It'll be fun."

As I walked back to the house, I wondered how many people had dirty fantasies about their neighbors. Then I wondered how many acted on them.

And how many of those got caught.

NOW
SARAH

Dear Diary,

I haven't written for ages, have I? Sorry, but things have been happening. *Good* things.

I've met someone. Someone I really, *really* like. A lot.

I'd seen him around at school—he's a year older than me—but we'd only kind of acknowledged each other in the hallways. But today I was a total klutz because, bang in the middle of the hallway, I dropped my bag. Which I hadn't closed properly, *of course*, so my books and stuff went everywhere and I think I bent my laptop.

Anyway, the important thing is that, as I was on my hands and knees scrambling to pick everything up, Brian Walker knelt down next to me. *Brian Walker!*

Him (in his deep, sexy voice): Let me help you. Oh, were we?

I didn't get what he meant until he pointed to the book *We Were Liars* by E. Lockhart.

Me (totally blushing): I guess we all are, sometimes.

Brian smiled. God, he has a nice smile. Small dimples in his cheeks, perfectly straight white teeth. And those blue, blue eyes. They look like the pictures of the lagoons in the Seychelles, the ones I liked looking at in the travel magazines Dad used to buy. Pools of water you want to dive into and swim around in for hours.

He introduced himself and my face got all hot. I bet I was glowing like a humongous tomato. I mean, Brian's *the* coolest guy in the school. Not to mention *the* most handsome. He's captain of the fencing club, too. I doubt he's into video games, but nobody's perfect. I'd cope.

And then...

Him (looking deeply into my eyes): You're Sarah, aren't you?

All I could think was *he knows my name.* My tomato head got so big it was in danger of bursting and splattering all over him. I mumbled something incomprehensible, and stood up.

Him (still looking cool): I'd better help set up science lab, but I hope I'll see you around.

He walked away, then turned back after a few steps and smiled, just before Claire rushed over to me, saying, "Holy *shitballs.* What did he say, what did he *say?*"

She went all googly-eyed as I told her, her head bobbing up and down like one of those nodding dogs old ladies have in the back of their cars. Then she told me it was a good job I'd decided I didn't like Zac because she'd seen him kissing Gargoyle in the cafeteria earlier. *Gross.*

I looked at Brian, who'd stopped to talk to Mrs. Cloisters. And you know what? I don't care about Zac and Gargoyle. Like, *at all.* Brian Walker is way, *way* more *amazeballs* than Zac ever could be. I should ask Brian out. In fact, the next time he talks to me, I will. Although I'd better grow a pair first. And I'm not talking about tomatoes!

Later,

Sarah x.

PS. Word of the day: *boffin*, noun.

a scientific expert; especially one involved in technological research.

As in: *I bet Brian's a real boffin in the science lab!*

NOW
ABBY

ALTHOUGH WEEKS HAD PASSED, every single day I kept reliving Liam's kiss in my mind, over and over again. The perfect kiss with the perfect man. The one I wasn't supposed to be with. And I kept asking myself: Why shouldn't I? Why *couldn't* I? Then I chastised myself for being stupid, blinded by two decades worth of perfection projections, and tried to convince myself for the umpteenth time I didn't even know Liam anymore.

But I did. I'd always known him. Always loved everything about him.

When I got home that evening, a huge bunch of yellow daffodils stood on the table. And, selfishly, all I could think of was that if I were with Liam, they'd be lilies.

Later, when Nate gently kissed the back of my neck and slid his hands up my thighs, it felt like my skin was on fire. I pushed him away at first, then let him make love to me despite the fact that he wasn't the one I thought of while he was inside me. And I hated myself even more.

Once again I avoided Liam. It was easier that way. People

on a diet didn't continually stare at chocolate cake or pastries. Cravings passed, I knew that. This would be the same. It had to be. Nate was the man I'd married, I reminded myself. He was the one who'd taken care of me, picked me up and put me together again.

"I've offered to help Nancy with some of their renovations," he told me one evening.

I nodded. "That's nice of you. I might sign up for a boot camp at the gym."

He frowned. "Instead of going in the mornings?"

"No. As well as."

"What are you trying to prove, Abby?" Nate said, his face still in a frown. "And what for?"

I looked at him. After all these years he still didn't get it. It wasn't about proving anything to anybody. It was about punishing. That's what it had always been about. Disciplining myself for every single shortcoming, every aspect of myself I detested, every flaw, no matter how tiny, insignificant or downright invisible it appeared to everybody else. I didn't bother answering him. What was the point? He wouldn't understand. He'd strap on his tool belt and try to fix me instead, bring me more daffodils thinking he'd done something great—and it was my fault for letting him believe he had.

As all these thoughts raced through my mind, I sat in Sterling Engineering's lunchroom supposedly listening to Camilla. She'd talked for ten minutes straight, with me occasionally making an "uh-huh" sound. But then she said something that pulled my attention back to her.

"Hang on," I said, my mouth still half-full of quinoa and vegetable salad. "You and Josh are doing *what*?"

"Splitting up," Camilla said as she took another bite of her

BLT, a splotch of mayo splattering on her napkin. "Getting a divorce."

"But...but *why*?"

Camilla continued chewing and shrugged. "We're not happy, so what's the point?"

I'm pretty sure my mouth was still open. My spoon certainly hadn't moved. I looked around the room, leaned in toward her. "Have you met someone else?"

"Not yet." She winked.

"Has Josh?"

She shrugged. "Maybe. I don't know. He says he hasn't. But it wouldn't bother me."

I bit my lip for a second. "What about Claire?"

"Abby," she said after a sip of water, "she's sixteen. She'll cope. We'll be around for her as much as we've always been. Except we won't be living together. We're telling her tonight."

"So what's happening with the house?"

"Josh is moving out in a few weeks. He's already found a new place a few streets away. Simple." Camilla popped the rest of her sandwich into her mouth.

"Sounds like a divorce made in heaven."

She nodded. "You know what? It is."

"But I still don't understand why. You get along, don't you?"

"Yeah, we do... I suppose. But we don't have anything in common. Honestly, I don't think we were ever that suited. From the beginning, you know?"

"No, I don't. You always seemed so happy. I've never seen you argue."

"Well, we don't, not anymore at least. It's almost as if—" she lowered her voice "—we've shifted into tolerance mode. You know—we put up with each other because that's what we're used to. Well, screw it." She sat back in her chair, her voice louder again. "I'm forty-five. I don't want to live like this for the next forty years... Now ask me about the sex."

"Do I have to?" I shifted in my seat. Talking about other people's sex lives made me feel like a reluctant spectator at a free peep show. "It can't be that bad."

She shrugged and sipped her water again. "Can't remember. He's never had a particularly high sex drive, but the past few years... *God*." She waved a hand around. "You know the joke about Christmas coming more often? Well, let's just say in that case we're Jehovah's Witnesses. Sorry, but I'm too young to be celibate."

"I had no idea." I wanted to reach out and pat her hand, but ate another spoonful of my lunch instead.

"Thing is, I know exactly where we went wrong." Camilla crossed her arms and lowered her chin, her voice softer again. "When we first met, Josh was already into shuffleboard and bowling. I mean *properly* into it."

"Okay..."

"Well," Camilla continued, "I pretended I was, too. But I thought it was a pile of crap. I mean, calling a game you combine with copious amounts of beer and pork scratchings a sport? Please. They take themselves far too seriously. But I liked Josh and wanted to impress him."

"Makes sense and—"

"Wait, wait. You see, Josh pretended he was all romantic. Bought me flowers, took me to see all the Meg Ryan movies." She smiled. "He wooed me, and I thought he was the bee's knees. But after we got married, well, we stopped making the effort to impress each other."

"You're saying you're getting divorced over chick flicks and bowling balls?"

"Abby, you're missing the point. After we got married, we went back to being who we were before, our usual selves."

"But isn't that what most people do when they first meet? Be on their best behavior?"

"Being on your best behavior is one thing," Camilla answered, "but in hindsight, pretending to be something you're not is stupid. I reckon it's why one in two marriages end in divorce. You can't keep the illusion going forever. I think we've done well to make it this long." She tipped the rest of her water into her mouth.

"But what about wasting the last, what, twenty years you've been together?"

Camilla waggled a finger. "Ah…you're missing the point again."

"Am I?"

"Entirely. I can't do anything about the past. It's gone. Done and dusted." She paused for a second. "But the next twenty years? Those are the ones I don't want to waste." I must have had a puzzled look on my face because Camilla laughed. "You don't get it, do you? Let me ask you this. If you woke up one day knowing you're with the wrong person, would you stay?"

"Well." I cleared my throat. "I don't know, I—"

Camilla patted my hand. "I know it's hard to imagine. I mean, you and Nate are perfect for each other. He worships the ground you walk on. You're very lucky."

"Yes," I said, thinking about the flowers—daffodils or not—the notes, the lunches and all the little things Nate did for me. He'd never pretended to be something he wasn't. Not once.

"Josh and I, well…" Camilla continued, "it's taken us years to get to this point. We've had heated discussions and pretty nasty arguments about who we were before we got married versus who we are now."

"And…?"

She scratched her ear. "We came to the conclusion it's irrelevant. The fact is, neither of us wants to change. Neither of us wants to go back to being the person we pretended to be. So we decided, in a completely grown-up way, actually, that we'd be better suited to other people."

I sat back in my seat, thinking about the possibilities. Wondering if it was a debate I could have with Nate, an easy discussion that led to, *"Well, that was kind of fun but let's split up now. Bye."* I shook my head.

"You don't approve," Camilla said, mistaking the gesture for criticism. "We can't all be as happy as you and Nate, you know. Not everybody marries their soul mate."

I exhaled. "You don't know what you're talking about."

Her eyes widened. "Explain?"

"Sometimes…" I sighed.

"What? You're not happy?"

I looked at her. "Sometimes."

Camilla played with her napkin while she waited for me to speak, but I couldn't. If the words were out there, it made them real, it meant I'd have to do something. And I couldn't tell Camilla, not unless I wanted the world to know.

"You don't want to talk?" Camilla finally said.

"No. It's just a phase. I'm being hormonal. But thanks for asking." I put the lid on my plastic tub, picked up my bottle of water and smiled. "I'd better get on with the returns."

Camilla refused to break eye contact. "If you change your mind, you know where to find me."

Later that evening I went to the gym, planning on pounding out ten kilometers on the treadmill straight after my evening boot-camp class. I shut off the obscure music I'd let Sarah add to my workout playlist, opting instead to focus on my breathing, concentrate on my heartbeat and make myself put one foot in front of the other.

As I racked up meter after meter, a feeling of absolute fatigue spread slowly through my veins. It came from my fingertips and toes, crept up my arms and legs like a virus, higher and higher, until my breathing sounded raspy and my head spun. If I hadn't dropped the pace on the treadmill to a leisurely stroll they'd have wiped me off the back wall with a sponge.

I shut down the machine, gasped and tried to catch my breath as I walked over to the mats, where I flopped down on one side.

"Hey, Abby. Are you okay?"

Opening one eye I saw a black-and-red shape in front of me. Jake, one of the boot-camp trainers, slowly came into focus. He was bent over at the hips, staring down at me.

"I'm fine, Jake. Thanks."

"You sure?" He crouched down beside me. "You totally killed that class, but you're really pale now. Do you want some water?"

"I'm just tired. I'll head home in a minute." He gave me a look, and I added, "Honest. I'll be okay."

Jake stood up and crossed his huge arms, his red shirt straining at the seams. "Okay." He looked at me sternly. "I'll finish my pull-ups, but I'm keeping an eye on you."

As Jake walked away I moved into an iron cross stretch and closed my eyes again, focusing once more on my breathing. In through the nose, out through the mouth, over and over. My arms and feet stopped tingling, so I let myself relax until it felt like my body was dissolving into the mat. My mind started to drift. And for once I allowed it to rid itself of the hundreds of thoughts that weighed it down.

My father's abandonment. The pathetic excuse of a relationship I had with my mother, and who I now ignored. Nate's love for me, which I'd never truly deserved or could properly reciprocate. The fact that I was spying on my daughter, and unable to bond with her properly. Liam, the man I'd walked away from, and desperately wished I hadn't. And Tom, always Tom. My darling brother, for whose demise I'd forever be responsible.

I imagined a deep blue sky above me and let those thoughts go, one by one, as if they were helium-filled balloons floating upward, farther and farther, until they disappeared, leaving my mind empty and calm...

And as I lay there, in a semi-state of peace, it must have been the quiet humming of the other treadmills and the complete absence of chatter in my head that gave birth to the epiphany.

I finally offered myself up to the realization that had been calling out to me, quietly at first, then louder and louder, until it could no longer be ignored.

And at last I accepted I was tired. Worn out. Spent. The constant sadism—akin to self-flagellation, really—that I inflicted on my mind and body was too much, way too much. And for what? For *whom*?

Lying on the gym mat, stretched out as far as my limbs would allow, I decided there would be no more. It had to stop. It was enough. It was time.

Newfound energy seemed to flow back into my arms and legs, traveling through my weary muscles, across my back and chest. I gasped as I finally opened my eyes, feeling more alert than I had in weeks. Months. Probably even years.

I jumped up and bounded toward the changing rooms, giving Jake a thumbs-up. Then I grabbed my gear, walked out of the gym and straight into The Steam Room Café next door. As I stood at the counter, it dawned on me I'd never been there before. I'd always ignored the delicious scent of freshly baked scones, muffins and cakes, favoring my carrot sticks with "hearty hummus" instead, despite the fact that I loathed chickpeas.

"What will it be, love?" The waiter smiled at me. He was at least twice my width and the girth of his belly stretched out the letters of his black "Keep Calm—I'm A Barista" T-shirt.

I looked at the blackboard menu. If they'd served them, I might have considered asking for a gin and tonic. "A cappuccino, please. And, uh, can I have it with whipped cream on top?"

He smiled. "Absolutely. One cappuccino with whipped cream coming up."

As he turned away, and before I could change my mind, I pointed at the blackboard again. "Do you still have some sticky toffee pudding left?"

"Of course." He patted his midriff. "It's great. As is the chocolate mud pie."

"In that case—" I slipped off my jacket "—I'll have some of both."

I sat down and pulled out my phone, my fingers gliding through the contacts. "It's me," I said as soon as he picked up. "I need to see you."

NOW

NATE

"THIS LOOKS GREAT, NANCY." I put the paintbrush down and looked around the dining room. "I can't believe how smooth the ceiling is. You did a brilliant job."

Nancy smiled at me. Her jeans were speckled with droplets of paint, the smudges on her arms already cracked and dry. "I couldn't have done it without you," she said. "Thanks again for getting the sander for me. I'd still be at it if you hadn't. And look—" she made a big sweeping movement with her arms "—it's finished. And it's fabulous."

She was right. The stucco ceiling was now smooth as a mirror, and we'd painted the room in a pale gray color scheme I'd secretly questioned. Thankfully I hadn't shared my doubts with Nancy or she might've made me eat my words along with the leftover paint.

Although I'd initially volunteered to help with the ceiling, we'd stripped, sanded and painted, busted down a wall and ripped up more carpet. Come to think of it, I'd probably spent more time with Nancy recently than I had with Abby. And with the amount of projects Nancy still wanted us to tackle, that wasn't likely to change. I didn't mind. I liked feeling useful. And, if I was being completely honest, I liked the way Nancy harmlessly flirted with me, too.

Abby didn't seem to mind me spending time next door either. She had plans of her own. One night, as I read the paper after dinner, drooling over the pictures of the new Mustang—I'd always had a soft spot for American Ladies—Abby said something about me, running and mud. At least that's what I thought she'd said. I lowered my paper. "You want to sign up for a what?"

"A mud run."

"A mud run? I suppose it safe to assume there's *running* involved?" I grinned.

"Uh-huh. It's called the *Dirty Dozen*. It's twelve kilometer throu—"

"Twelve kilometers?"

Abby's smile seemed tight. "Yes. *Twelve.* Through mud and over obstacles and stuff. It's supposed to be fun to—"

"Seriously?" I raised my eyebrows. "You know I haven't been running in years."

"You could train. It's not until August."

I frowned. "It's not going to clash with our trip is it? Did you check?" To be honest, when I told Abby about Europe her reception had been so halfhearted, I wondered if I'd talked in Swiss-German, maybe I'd described the trip as a voyage to a nudist colony for seniors. My wife, it seemed, needed a Promethean effort to be impressed. Sarah, on the other hand, had shouted, "That is *sick!*" which I gathered meant good, then rushed off to text Claire.

Abby was looking at me. "Of course I checked, and no, it won't clash. And you might even enjoy the mud run. Shall I sign you up for it or not?"

"Err...no." I laughed. "Thanks anyway. I'll stick to volleyball. But you go ahead." I saw her hesitate, spin her wedding ring on her finger. "What's wrong?"

She smiled again. "Uh, well... Liam and I chatted earlier. Before you came home."

"Hold it a second." I sat up straight and held my hands out, palms facing Abby, in what I hoped resembled afternoon soap-opera effect. "You mean you and him have had a—" Abby's eyes widened a little "—*conversation?*" I laughed, and after a second or two she joined in.

"Yes. In the garden. We talked about Barbara's petunias."

I covered my eyes with one hand. "Dear god, not the *petunias?*" I thought it was funny, even if Abby's lips barely curved into a smile. "So is Nancy up for this muddy madness? She hasn't mentioned it."

"We only just talked about it. Liam doesn't think so. It's not her thing, you know?"

"Absolutely. She's sensible. Like me."

"But Liam's done a couple of mud runs before, and I bet he's like bloody Spider-Man on the obstacles. So I need to train a bit more. And I know you don't like me running alone."

"No, I don't. So you two should go for it."

She cleared her throat. "Then you don't mind me training with him? He thinks some of his colleagues might come, too."

I shrugged. "Why would I mind?"

"Well, it would bother some guys if their wife was working out with other men."

"You mean the way it would bother some wives if their husband helped other women redecorate?"

"Touché." Abby slipped her arms around my waist and plonked a brief kiss on my cheek. "That's sorted then."

As she'd walked away I'd thought about how Abby's displays of affection were an even rarer commodity these days.

The noise of a loud sigh along with the smell of damp paint ripped me away from the memory of my wife and back to Nancy and the freshly decorated room. I kneeled down and started peeling away the masking tape from the door frame while Nancy sat on one of the chairs we'd covered with a plastic tarp, a dreamy look in her eyes.

"You okay?" I said.

"Wonderful." She wiped her forehead with the back of her hand. "Completely exhausted, but wonderful."

I laughed. "And you've got paint all over your cheeks."

"Oh, no." She pulled a face. "There I was, thinking I looked all casual and interesting. I'm a complete mess."

Before I could stop myself I said, "Nah. You're beautiful."

To be fair, it was true. Her cheeks, still a little flushed from the effort of painting, were turning redder by the second, and most of her hair had loosened from her ponytail. But she looked, well, *hot*. It wasn't the first time I'd noticed, obviously. But noticing it and saying it, particularly to her directly, were two entirely different things.

As we stared at each other, something shifted in the atmosphere between us. The air felt close, the way it does before a cracking thunderstorm, when you know it's coming and there's no stopping it—all you can do is run for cover. Nancy took a few steps forward, then stopped.

I swallowed. We were alone in the house. Zac was out, and Liam and Abby were somewhere in the woods, probably leapfrogging over trees or doing countless sets of burpees or fartees or whatever the hell they were called. The point was we both knew none of them would be back. Not for ages.

Before either of us did anything stupid, I had the opportunity to clear my throat, make a joke or do something completely inappropriate, like break wind. But instead I stared back at Nancy. And then we were moving toward each other, ending up so close our thighs and chests touched. I raised a hand, ran my fingers down her face. Then she stood on her tiptoes and softly touched my mouth with hers.

It was strange, kissing another woman. My lips had only known Abby's for so long it was as if they were genetically programmed to connect solely with hers. Nancy's mouth was soft and her breath minty, with a slight hint of coffee. She gently parted my lips with her tongue and searched for mine. As she wrapped her arms around my neck, my hands went under her T-shirt. Seconds later I felt her tugging at my belt.

I wanted her, no point in denying it, my practically instant hard-on a testament of how close I was to ripping her clothes off—with my teeth if I had to—and taking her right there on the floor. Or pressed against the ladder. Or bent over the kitchen table. Anywhere, but—

"Wait, wait," I said, pulling away, telling myself to Stop. Kissing. Her. "We can't do this."

"Oh, Nate," Nancy whispered, "I know we shouldn't but…" She kissed me again, pressed her chest against mine, and I felt my resolve crumbling. Her breasts felt like soft pillows, and they were sending an overtly macho message to my penis that went something like, "Oh, fuck, *yeah!*"

"Nancy…" I pulled her back toward me, slid my mouth down her neck.

"I need you," she whispered in my ear, "I need you so much."

I wanted to tear off her bra, run a thumb over her nipple before covering it with my mouth. But before I did, my brain must have given my raging libido a stern talking-to because I put my hands on her arms and gently pushed her away. "We can't."

"We can..."

"*No.*"

Nancy took a step back, then looked at me. "You don't want me?"

I closed my eyes. Not seeing her made her easier to resist. "You have no idea how much I want you right now, believe me. But..."

When I looked at her again she was pulling her shirt down, then smoothed her hair with a hand. "Right then," she said.

"I'm so sorry. I, uh, we—"

"I think you should go." She looked away.

I felt bad. The downright look of rejection on her face almost made me change my mind. *Almost.* "Nancy—"

"You go. I have to finish cleaning up."

"But you can't lift that table alone. I'll help you."

Nancy looked at me for the first time in what felt like forever, but said nothing.

"Just the table. Then I'll go."

She exhaled loudly, then tried a half smile. "You know. I honestly wish I could say no because right now I want a meteorite to come crashing through the ceiling and squash me."

"Don't be silly. It'll ruin the paint job."

Nancy laughed and covered her cheeks with her palms. "How do you do that? You always know exactly what to say to make me feel better."

As we shifted the table and then the sofa around a few times before Nancy felt the result was the look she'd envisaged, I thought the electric current in the air evaporated, and whatever sexy vibe we'd had going between us all but disappeared. It was odd. As if we'd dangled a toe over the point of no return only to find no, thanks very much, we'd pass. I exhaled, relieved whatever the hell I'd been thinking had beaten a hasty retreat. It was over.

But then Nancy said, "Can I make you lunch as a thank you?"

I watched as she dusted off a blue-and-white-striped lamp shade the size of a baby hippo, and wondered if "lunch" was subtext for sex, like "coffee" at the end of a date. "Well, uh…"

"Relax." Nancy winked. "We've had our—" she made quotation marks with her fingers "—bizarro moment. Got it out of our systems. We can be normal neighbors from now on."

"Yes. Normal neighbors. Got it."

She smiled, then opened the fridge. "Cheese and pickled onion?"

Cheese and pickled onion? Definitely *not* subtext for sex. I bit back what felt like a surge of disappointment and said, "Yum, great."

And just like that, we went from almost shagging each other senseless to setting sandwiches, packets of salt and vinegar crisps and a large green plastic jug of water on the table before sitting down on opposite sides—a sort of buffer in case things derailed.

"Can we…can we keep this between us?" Nancy said before picking up her sandwich.

I hesitated. I didn't want to keep secrets from Abby. In fact, I'd only ever kept one thing from her and had always sworn I wouldn't add to the list.

Nancy must have seen my reluctance because she quietly said, "Please?"

What was the point in telling Abby about a snog? There was nothing to say, was there? Nancy had made a pass at me— or was it the other way around?—but it wasn't as if I'd dropped my trousers. I didn't bend her over the kitchen counter and shag her to Scotland and back. And Abby seemed to actually like Nancy and Liam these days. Telling her I'd kissed the neighbor would be bloody awkward, not to mention Nancy was married to G.I. Joe.

"Let's forget it ever happened. I'd rather not get punched in the face by Liam anyway."

"Thanks." Nancy's shoulders dropped. "Although I'm not sure he'd care, to be honest."

I frowned. "What do you mean?"

"Oh, come on, Nate." Nancy put her sandwich down on her plate. "If things were that good between us, do you think I would have...you know...with you?"

"Ouch." I grinned. "And I thought it was my irresistible James Bond–esque charm."

Nancy laughed. "Oh, you're definitely charming, Nate. That's also why I... Anyway. Look, Liam and I have been together for over eighteen years." She sighed. "It's not that I don't love him, but...well...to be honest, things aren't brilliant."

"Oh?"

"Yeah." She paused. "He's been distant. Cold." I didn't really know what to say, but she shrugged and added, "And sometimes I feel I don't know him, not completely." She shook her head. "I'm not making any sense, am I?"

"Actually, yes, you are."

She stared at me. "Wait a sec. Is that what Abby tells you, too? You bloody men."

I smiled. "No, it's the opposite. It's, uh, how I feel about Abby sometimes."

"Do you?" Nancy frowned. "But you two seem happy. You must be." She smiled coyly. "You turned me down, and

I mean, look at me." She gestured to herself. "I'm gor-*geous*, especially with paint on my face."

"You are gor-*geous*, with or without paint. And smart and funny."

She sighed again. "Can you tell Liam? Perhaps he'll notice we live in the same house."

I wasn't sure I liked the fact that I'd gone from wanting to rip her pants off to becoming her agony-uncle. "Uh." I scratched my head. "I don't think I have the qualifications for girl talk."

Nancy waved a hand. "I don't need you to talk, just listen. Give me your perspective?"

"Sure, why not?" I folded my arms and stretched my legs out under the table.

Nancy took a sip of water, then said, "All right. Well, we'd only been going out a few months when I got pregnant with Zac."

"Oh?"

"It wasn't planned—"

"No, I figured."

She frowned. "I didn't get pregnant to trick him or anything. I'd *never* do that."

I held up a hand. "It's none of my business, Nancy, and—"

She didn't seem to be listening because she continued, "But as soon as I told Liam, he proposed. And that was that. Married and a mum just after my twenty-first birthday."

"Twenty-first? I didn't know you were so much younger than Liam."

Nancy looked at me, her face in one of her grins that made her eyes light up and put dimples in her cheeks. "Not sure if that means he looks young or I look old."

"The former, of course."

"Hah. Well, we're almost nine years apart. I'll be thirty-nine soon."

"So, uh." I squirmed in my seat, trying to adjust to my new role as confidante. "How long have you been unhappy?"

"Oh, no, no. It's not constant." She shrugged. "We've had our ups and downs. The worst was a few months after Zac was born. I swear he wanted to leave."

"Leave *you*?"

"Yeah. He went away for work." She waved a hand. "In the Cotswolds. God, he was in such a mood when he got back. I should have asked him what was going on, but I was scared."

"Of him?"

"Oh, god, no," Nancy said. "Nothing like that. Scared he'd tell me the work pretext was a pile of bollocks. That he'd been off on a jolly with another woman. That he was leaving."

"And did you ever ask him?"

"No." Nancy's voice was quiet again. "I never had the guts. I was a young mum, remember? I felt frumpy. Exhausted. Vulnerable. Then after a while things went back to normal." She paused. "He can be a great husband, but I wish he appreciated everything I do for him more. And sometimes I think he settled because he felt he had to, you know?"

I cleared my throat, flicking away the nagging thought that Abby had done the same with me in some way. She'd never said as much, but I'd always sensed it. How many times had I told her I loved her enough for the both of us? Probably plenty for it to become a self-fulfilling prophecy.

"Maybe I've got too much spare time on my hands. You know, before I had Zac I thought about going back to college and doing interior design," Nancy said.

"But you didn't?"

"No. At first I just wanted to be a good mum, then dreams

and stuff got put on hold 'cos I *never* seemed to have time."
She opened her packet of crisps and popped one in her mouth.
"Then I blink, my kid's almost a grown-up and that's that."

"You could study now. Go back to college."

Nancy huffed. "No, I couldn't."

"Why not? What's stopping you?"

She smiled and shrugged. "Self-confidence, I suppose."

"You should check with the Adult Education College here,
see what programs they have. Doesn't cost anything to ask."

"Do you think I should?"

"Yeah. I mean, look at the stuff you've done to this place."
I gestured around the room. "I think you're very talented at
this home decorating stuff."

Nancy looked at me, and I noticed her eyes glisten. "That
means a lot, Nate," she whispered.

"Oh, come on." As I shifted in my seat again I laughed,
trying to lighten the mood. "I'm sure Liam thinks so, too.
He's probably preoccupied with his job. More responsibility, isn't it?"

"Yeah, or a twenty-five-year-old bimbo with legs up to
her chin."

"He doesn't seem the type to have a fling. Honestly, he's
such a decent bloke sometimes I wish his halo would hurry
up and strangle him."

Nancy laughed. "All my girlfriends fell over each other to
get to know him. They kept telling me how lucky I was."
She paused. "And you're right. He's not the type to have a
fling. That's just it. If anything, it would be serious. And if
he's doing anything—"

"Which he isn't—"

"But *if* he is... I think it would be the end of us."

"That's understandable."

"I don't need this crap. I'm thirty-eight, I have an almost grown-up kid—"

"And a degree in interior design soon."

"Apparently." Nancy laughed again. "I'm just being paranoid but...could you do me a favor? Abby's spending a lot of time with him—"

"Wait, you don't think—"

"Oh, gosh, no." Nancy shook a finger, and I lowered my eyebrows. "I *love* Abby, she's *wonderful*. And you're devoted to each other." I smiled as Nancy continued, "And she's not Liam's type. He's always preferred—" she gestured to her chest "—the voluptuous type. No offense."

"None taken."

"No, I meant could you tell me if she ever mentions anything? You know, Liam always texting or calling, asking her to cover for him. That kind of thing."

I scratched my head, already deciding there was no way I'd even bring it up. After years of watching Paul's escapades with married women pre-Lynne, I knew better than to get sucked into that death trap. "Look, I'll try..."

"I know it's a bit awkward," Nancy said, "but I'd be really grateful."

"Don't worry. I'm sure you're imagining things. And he'd be a stupid twat to lose you." Then I sat back and watched Nancy smile, trying to figure out the distant, flashing warning signs going off somewhere at the back of my head.

NOW
NANCY

I LAY IN BED, listening to Liam's rhythmic breathing, letting my mind wander.

I hadn't meant for things to go that far with Nate, but when they had, I didn't want us to stop. The intensity of the moment—the sheer, animalistic lust—had caught me by surprise, and getting the attention I'd craved, being able to almost seduce the most devoted husband I'd ever seen, had been such a turn-on.

Every few seconds since Nate had gone home I found myself thinking about it. I could feel his fingers on my skin, see myself yanking on his belt, remember how aroused he'd become. And yet it made me angry, too. Nate was showing me the attention my husband should have been bestowing on me all along.

In the end it was only a kiss, but it had made me feel young, desired—*daring*. Something I hadn't felt for years, not since I'd traveled to exotic places, slept with exotic men—and one woman—before I'd met Liam and my sense of adventure had been replaced with an unmistakable desire to nurture.

I hadn't been truthful to Nate about our story; then again I hadn't told anyone about the evening when Liam and I had gone for dinner with my mother. How he'd held the chair out for her, gotten up when she'd gone to the bathroom and paid the bill in a swift, elegant, yet unpretentious gesture.

"He's a good one, Nancy," Mum had told me while he fetched our coats. "You'd better hold on to him. A girl like you will never get another one like that."

A girl like you. Although I'd heard them a million times, the words still burned like invisible branding on my skin. Mum never meant to be nasty, and if I'd called her on it she'd have been mortified to see me upset. Besides, I understood what she meant. Her expectations for herself had never been high, and those feelings had inevitably trickled down to her only child, drip, drip, drip, forming around me like a stalagmite.

Mum looked around, leaned in and whispered, "He still hasn't proposed then?"

"Not yet, Mum. I don't think he's ready."

"Men are never ready, dear." She patted my arm. "Not until us women help them along."

I'd looked at Liam when he came back to the table, watched as he helped my mother slip on her coat, genuinely complimenting her on how the cut flattered her figure. She was right. I'd never get another man like him.

It had been an easy decision. Simple to lie about my contraception and religiously flush it down the toilet—a thrilling sensation, like going behind the bike sheds at school with a cigarette—only feeling slightly guilty when I told Liam, with a well-practiced, astonished expression, that I was pregnant.

I shook the memories from my head and looked at the alarm clock that now indicated a few minutes before midnight, then wondered what Liam would do if I told him about

Nate. Would it be enough to make him jealous? Would he even care? He hadn't touched me in weeks, barely acknowledged my presence half of the time. His continual distance had sent waves of rage through my body, especially when I wondered if he was touching someone else instead.

Then again, I reasoned, taking a deep breath, Nate had a point about Liam's work. Better job, new boss, new location. It all added up but it was still unacceptable. He wasn't the only one working hard. What about all the renovations I was taking care of, as well as running the household and taking care of Zac while he'd had a rotten cold? But on top of working long hours, Liam still went for his workouts—some of them with Abby, who obviously neglected Nate as much as Liam did me—even though he'd repeatedly encouraged me to join them in their ridiculous training.

Telling Nate there was no way anything could be going on between his wife and my husband was another thing I'd fibbed about. With the amount of time they spent together, I couldn't help but wonder, and the mere thought made me oscillate between wanting to collapse in a heap, and gouge Liam's and Abby's eyes out with my bare hands.

I reminded myself Liam didn't have time for an affair, that'd he'd never go for a frigid stick insect like Abby, but what if he had? Or what if they were using each other for cover? Meeting their respective lovers and laughing about it behind our backs? I shook my head. I'd watched way too many bad soap operas and conspiracy theories on television.

Still, to be sure, I'd checked his phone when he was in the shower, looked through his social media for clues and searched his pockets a few times, but I hadn't found anything. Either he was extremely clever at covering his tracks, or his coldness really was because of pressure from work.

A short while ago I'd have told myself to be more sensitive to his needs. Now that sounded like something from a 1950s *Good House Wife's Guide*. Liam and I were supposed to be equal partners in everything, and yet it felt I'd always made most of the effort. I'd chased him, adored him, put him on a towering pedestal and openly begged him to reverse the favor. I was no better than a lovesick, attention-seeking puppy. And frankly, I was sick of it. I was sick of Liam's behavior toward me, but not as sick as I was of mine toward him.

I smiled in the darkness as it dawned on me that Liam's lack of interest felt less important now that I had my little secret with Nate. The way I saw it, my husband took me for granted, and Abby did the same to Nate. So the two of us were simply balancing things out with a little innocent spice. I'd backed off when he'd said no, made myself appear vulnerable, but I wasn't a fool. I could tell how difficult it had been for him to resist me.

As I thought about Nate I slipped a hand between my legs, imagining all the things my naughty neighbor could do to me. I didn't need my husband. Right now I had plenty to distract myself with, both in my mind, and in reality. And I wasn't done yet.

The more I thought about Nate the more it dawned on me how good he was. Humble, kind and generous. Sexy, too, although it had taken me a while to see it. If we were together, he wouldn't neglect me the way Liam did. Nate would worship me like a goddess, and in return I'd show him how grateful I was. *I* wouldn't take him for granted.

Liam didn't care about my closeness to Nate. But I did. And I'd be making damn sure Nate cared about it, too.

NOW

SARAH

Dear Diary,

You know how I hate girls who go gooey-eyed over puppies, babies and guys (the worst!)? Well, apologies for what I'm about to write, *but*...I went on a date with Brian today. A proper date. And, bloody hell, he's *fantastic*. I mean, really *fantastic*.

Ugh! I just reread that and want to slap my face, but I can't help it! I didn't see Brian for a while at school. Paranoid as I am, I figured he was avoiding me—came to his senses and regretted he'd flirted with me, and now needed to bail. But then I found out he'd been ill. And on Thursday, there he was, walking down the corridor and coming toward me.

He smelled faintly of menthol chest rub, his nose shone brighter than Rudolph's and I noticed his chest (those pecs!) heave up and down as he tried to hold in a cough. I asked if he was okay. On cue, his lungs exploded and he held up a hand, coughed again, then smiled (that smile!).

Turns out he had the flu. The flu! Not that I'm happy he was ill, but it explains why I hadn't seen him. Then he rubbed the back of his neck (Claire told me it totally means a guy's nervous) talked a bit about math class and...

Him: Uh... I was wondering if you'd like to go out with me?

(That's another thing Brian does—uses 'like' in the proper way, not the way I do, like, every third word.)

Me (thinking I'd misheard): On a date? Like, with you?

Him (smiling, and, oh, those dimples, kill me now!): Yes, Sarah. On a date. With me.

We decided to go to the cinema on Saturday afternoon because he volunteers at the pet shelter in the mornings. The pet shelter! How cool is this guy? Anyway, I told him I'd meet him there directly. I mean, if Mum knew I was going out with a boy she'd make the Spanish Inquisition look like a family-friendly picnic.

That was Thursday, so I still had to get through Friday and part of today. I'm not sure how I managed. But I wondered if Brian felt like that, too, even a little, although I couldn't imagine him feeling anxious or insecure, like, ever. Not until I saw him anyway. Then things changed.

He gave me a peck on the cheek when I got to the cinema, and after he bought the tickets and we sat down, he kept chatting about school (ready for university), his career (wants to be a lawyer) and about his parents (married for almost twenty years, *happily*!). Honestly, I could hardly get a word in. Then he stopped, practically mid-sentence, and glanced over.

Him: I haven't shut up yet, have I? I'm not usually this nervous.

Me (laughing): You, nervous? Don't you take a girl out every Saturday?

Him (wait for it...): Only the special ones.

I was about to reply when I saw Zac and Nicole a few meters

away from us with Cokes and a bucket of popcorn bigger than Zac's head. Actually I wished he'd put it *over* his head.

I introduced them to Brian, who said hi so politely. Nicole flicked her hair and looked away. Zac said, "S'up" and I wanted to slap him, but Brian just smiled until they took the hint and sat down a few rows ahead of us, Nicole still swishing her perfectly primped, pretentious hair.

The adverts came on, then the trailers, and Brian and I kept on whispering. Then the movie started, and I had to stop myself from glancing sideways to make sure Brian actually *was* next to me, not some figment of my overactive, amateur writer's imagination. But he put his hand on my thigh and I put mine over his. And we sat like that until the end of the credits, him stroking my hand with his thumb, me thinking Claire would never believe me when I told her.

And when we said goodbye he gave me the softest kiss on the cheek (even though I totally would have kissed him on the lips) and asked if he could take me out again.

Me = Swoon, gooey-eyes, swoon. Repeat, repeat, repeat. Gah! What's happening to me?

Later,

Sarah xoxoxo.

PS. Word of the day: *gimcrack*, noun.

a showy object of little use or value: gewgaw.

As in: *Zac and Nicole are a pair of gimcracks!*

NOW
ABBY

SATURDAY MORNING. I lay in bed with a grin on my face, watching the time tick toward 6:00 a.m., trying not to bounce out of bed. Reading Sarah's diary, finding out she'd gone on a date a week ago with a boy who sounded like a proper gentleman was only one of the reasons for my smile. The other was because in less than two hours, I'd see Liam again.

Both he and I had known Nate and Nancy wouldn't be interested in the mud run. That was the whole point. We'd come up with the plan at The Steam Room, not even half an hour after I'd called him. He'd been on his way back from work when I'd phoned, immediately turning the car around to come and meet me.

"Are you okay?" he'd said before he sat down. "What's wrong?"

I smiled. "Nothing's wrong. Liam, I...I..."

"I know." He reached over the table and put his hand over mine. "I miss you, too."

As I looked at him my shoulders dropped, and I left my

hand under his. "We can't jump into something. We have to be sure. I told you I won't have a fling."

"It won't be. It could never be just a fling."

"How can you be so sure, Liam? We—"

"Because I know—"

"—don't even know each other anymore."

"We *do*. We always have."

I looked at him, told myself calling him had been a bad idea, but he smiled and squeezed my hand.

"Look," he said, "let's spend some time together. Get to know each another again. *Properly* and—"

"Oh, no." I waggled a finger at him. "No sex."

He sat back in his chair and held up both palms in a surrendering gesture. "No sex."

That was when we'd come up with the mud run plan. It was simple. We'd spend time together, talk, figure out what we felt for each other, what we wanted from each other and, from there, what we were going to do.

When we went training the first time and Liam put me through bear crawls and burpees, push-ups and more sit-ups than I could count, I couldn't remember feeling so light-hearted and relaxed, or that I'd laughed as much in ages. After two hours of walking, jumping, running and sweaty groans completely unrelated to sex, we'd ended up sitting on tree stumps eating our lunch (had bread always tasted this good?).

We'd quickly decided attempting to fit years of stories into half an hour was like trying to cram the Atlantic into a thimble. We had to see each other again, and soon.

Back in my bed I watched the alarm clock take pity on me and finally change its ghostly green display to six o'clock. I pushed the blankets away and went to shower. When I came out of the bathroom Nate sat in bed reading.

"You're up early," I said.

"Couldn't sleep," he answered. "You look great. New Nikes?"

"Oh, yes." I dropped my shoes on the floor and quickly slid my hair into a ponytail, hoping he hadn't noticed I'd washed it, and had put on a little blush and mascara, too. "My old ones were worn through."

Nate laughed. "Now there's a surprise. Liam won't be able to keep up."

"I'm sure he will. He's very fit."

He put down his book on the bedside table. I thought a slight frown made its way across his face, but when I looked more closely it had gone. "You working out together again today?"

"Yeah." I shrugged. "You were right. I do feel safer running with someone."

"Even Liam?"

I clicked my tongue. "He's okay, I suppose. Not as much of a prat as I thought." I laughed, making sure it sounded natural and not overdone. "Still a prat, though."

"But a good-looking one," Nate said, keeping his gaze steady.

Did he know something? Could he tell? I made sure I blinked only once and didn't look away. "Yeah, not bad, I suppose. But he knows it. To be honest, it's a bit off-putting. He whistled at a woman last time." *Liar.*

"With you there?"

"Yup." *Double* liar.

"Ugh. No class." Nate smiled. "Unlike you."

I bent over and kissed him on the cheek. "I'll see you later. Not sure when we'll be back."

"No rush," Nate said. "I'm laying the carpet with Nancy."

I put my hands on my hips. "You know, with the amount of stuff you've helped her with, I'm wondering what she's doing to get so many favors." I raised my eyebrows and smiled.

Nate laughed, and a blush crept over his face. "Don't be silly. You know me, I'm Bob the Builder."

"Yes, you are." I waved at him. "Bye, Bob."

As I walked downstairs I imagined what would happen if Nate *did* like Nancy, or if there was the remote possibility they were actually having an affair. I waited to feel some kind of jealous pang in my gut, but it held still. Was it because I knew Nate wouldn't cheat or that I wouldn't be bothered if he did? After all, wouldn't it give me the perfect excuse to leave?

I thought back to what Camilla had said about waking up with the wrong person. But how could Nate be the wrong person when he was so good to me, when he'd do anything for me? Was I only attracted to Liam because of unfinished business? Or maybe it was an attempt to hold on to my youth? No. It was neither of those. I'd told Liam I had to be sure. But he was right. I already knew. I'd always known.

As I walked over to his house, their front door opened and Zac walked out with his usual sullen expression, and I couldn't help wondering what would happen if he smiled.

"Morning, Zac. You're up early."

"Saturday job at Boots." He coughed hard, covering his mouth with the side of his arm.

"Are you okay? You're very pale. Liam mentioned you had the flu?"

"Yeah." He looked at me. "It's been going around school."

"Well, I hope you feel better soon."

"Uh-huh. I'm late. See ya."

I watched as he meandered down the path, his long legs taking giantlike strides. He'd inherited his father's dangerous combination—good looks and that certain je ne sais quoi charm easily mistaken for arrogance. Girls probably couldn't decide whether to slap him or kiss him first. I knew he hadn't confided in Liam about his girlfriend, and when I'd casually mentioned Nicole and Brian to Camilla, for once she didn't have the inside scoop.

"From what Claire told me Nicole sounds like a proper little madam," she'd said before beaming widely, "but this Brian? Gosh. He sounds wonderful. And don't worry. I promise I won't tell Claire or Sarah you asked."

Sarah hadn't even told Nate about her boyfriend, and when I'd convinced him to ask her, jokingly and discreetly, if she was interested in anyone, he did it over dinner with me at the table. Sarah had looked straight at me, sniffed and said, "Well, you'd be the first to know."

I wished Sarah would bring Brian up in conversation, and I pictured us lying on her bed, me listening to her giggles as she described him, or her showing me pictures of him on her phone. No. That wasn't the kind of relationship we'd ever enjoyed.

Liam and Nancy's front door opened again, and Liam stepped out, making my stomach go into a wild flutter. His skin had browned slightly from spending time in the garden, and he'd had his hair cut since I'd seen him last. It suited him. No matter what he did or wore, it suited him. He could have walked down a runway in nothing but a bin bag and eclipsed David Gandy and David Beckham simultaneously.

"You're ready for this?" he said with a smile, and held up a rucksack. "I've brought plenty of water in case you need to revive me."

"Give over." I laughed as we walked to my car. "You know it'll be the other way around."

"*You* want to do fifteen kilometers today. *Fifteen*. You know it's called the Dirty *Dozen* for a reason, don't you?"

"Ha. You can handle an extra three kilometers, you big girl's blouse."

"Big girl's blouse? Just you wait, you'll—"

"Oh, I know. I'm already worried about the stuff you've got—"

"Pah! Come on, what's two hundred burpees between friends, eh?"

"Famous last words," I said as I unlocked the car and got in. "And if you make me do two hundred burpees again, Liam, I'll beat you to death with my new shoes." He snorted as he sat down, his long, toned legs stretched out in front of him. "Okay," I said, "start at Jubilee again?"

"Yes, ma'am," he answered as he pushed back his seat. "Lead the way."

The drive barely took ten minutes, and the parking lot was empty except for one solitary car. Apparently most people had more sense than we did, although, I decided, not nearly as much fun. We clipped our water bottles to our belts, and set off along the trails, walking at a steady pace that still allowed us to talk.

"How's work?" Liam said.

"Great, it's been a fun week."

"And your friend Camilla?"

"Oh, she's fine. They got the divorce papers, and Josh moved out."

"And she's still sure about it all?"

"Yeah. She says she's more certain about the divorce than she was about getting married."

Liam said nothing and picked up the pace a little.

"How was your week?" I said, but he didn't answer. "What's

wrong?" I tried to keep up with his increasingly long strides, almost having to break into a light jog.

"Nothing," he said, then added, "Let's run."

"Liam…"

"It's nothing. Nothing."

I stood still. "Hey. Tell me what's bugging you."

"You won't like it."

"Try me."

He turned and looked at me. "I've decided to ask Nancy for a divorce."

"What? Why?"

"What do you mean, *why*? Because I'm in love with y—"

"Liam, don't. We said we'd get to know each other before—"

"I know. But I know what I want. And it's not her." He started walking again so I followed and reached out to touch his arm.

"When are you going to tell her?"

"I'm waiting for the right moment." A small laugh escaped his lips, and he threw his hands in the air. "God that sounds pathetic. Why am I such a coward?"

"You're many things, Liam." I squeezed his arm. "But a coward isn't one of them."

Liam stared at me for a second, then shook his head and looked away.

I stopped walking again, and he turned toward me. "You're not a coward," I repeated. "You're a wonderful man. You're—" I kissed him, meaning for my lips to graze his cheek, but he turned and our embrace became so intense, so fast, I forgot we were on a path in the middle of the forest.

I should have pulled away, taken a step back and told him we had to head back to the car, that we were breaking our self-imposed rules. But I couldn't. The images of Nate that were protesting in my head never stood a chance as they were pulled, kicking and screaming, to the back of my mind. My hand slid down Liam's arms, then under his shirt and across his broad, smooth back.

"Abby," he whispered as he pulled away, "Abby."

"Shhhh." I put a finger to his lips. "Don't say anything. Please."

He looked at me, then took my hand and led me off the path and into the forest, where he softly pressed me against a tree and kissed me again. I pulled him toward me, tugging at his clothes with the unmistakable message of urgency. But Liam had other plans. He kissed my neck slowly, gently, every touch reigniting what we'd once had, and I closed my eyes, sinking into him. His hands wandered, slipping off my shirt and under my sports bra, stroking me with his fingers. I moaned and he silenced me with another kiss, another whisper of "I love you."

"I love you, too," I whispered, kissing him back, feeling he wanted me as much as I him. "I love you, too."

His mouth traveled downward, stopping at my breasts, then carried on until he was on his knees, getting rid of my belt and sliding my shorts over my thighs. We laughed as my underwear got caught on my new shoes—sports gear wasn't proving to be synonymous with sexy—but as soon as his tongue nestled between my legs, my giggles turned to sighs. And as he had done so many years before, he took me to the edge and back, but didn't let me fall.

"I want you inside me," I gasped, unable to wait any longer. *"Please."*

Liam stood up slowly, and I slipped my hand into his shorts, curling my fingers around him. He closed his eyes and gasped as I pulled him inside me, wrapping my leg over him. His fingers lingered, playing and touching, and we found our rhythm. As we both went over the brink, eyes wide-open, I felt as if I'd been magically woken from years of slumber. And as we held each other, our hearts pounding, I wondered how I could even begin to imagine spending another day without him, how I could possibly take another breath without Liam by my side.

He kissed me again. Gently, slowly. Then whispered, "I've waited seventeen years to do that again. Seventeen long years."

I clung to him, the memories of the last time we'd been together flooding my mind, rushing forward from the depths of my brain. And this time, I set them free.

THEN
ABBY

"HAVE A GREAT TIME, LOVE. See you Friday." Nate kissed me gently before sliding my sports bag in the back of my colleague's souped-up Corolla.

I kissed him back and got into Olivia's car. "Bye."

"Nate's such a sweetheart," she said, and I watched as she checked the rearview mirror a third time, getting another glimpse of my husband. I'd always thought she fancied Nate a little, ever since he'd picked me up at Hoskins for lunch a few weeks after I joined years ago.

"Yeah," I answered, plucking a bit of fluff from my trousers. "And thanks for picking me up, Liv. I appreciate it."

"No problem." Olivia reached over to pat my knee and smiled with her immaculately painted lips. Her grooming habits reminded me a little of my mother's. Although that's where the similarities ended. Mum had always turned her nose up at tattoos, fast cars and motorbikes. "You know me," Olivia said, "any excuse to drive. Hey, did you get the skinny on what we're doing?"

I fished a bottle of water out of my bag and cracked the

seal. "Team building in the Cotswolds is all I know. I bet we're paintballing or something."

"Oh, I hope so." Olivia laughed. "We can gang up and shoot Ben in the ass. Make it all purple with bruises. I can't believe how button-lipped he's been. You'd think we work for MI6, not Hoskins bloody Insurance. Mind you, I won't be complaining if Pierce Brosnan shows up." She giggled. "I'm gagging for a shag." She laughed even harder as I choked on my water.

"You told me you slept with the stationery supplier two days ago."

"Yeah." She grinned. "Exactly."

"I'm kind of looking forward to the next few days," I said, thinking I was actually mostly looking forward to being away from Nate. Not that he'd done anything wrong. He was still too busy trying to make everything perfect.

As if she'd read my mind, Olivia said, "So…how are things with Nate?"

"Fine." When I caught her sideways glance, I turned up my *It's A Wonderful Life* expression. "Everything's absolutely fine."

Olivia wagged a finger. "Absolutely bullshit, more like—"

"No, I—"

"Uh-huh. I can tell by the way your voice went all pitchy."

I took a deep breath. "Nothing's wrong."

"That's not what you said last week. Have you made a decision about moving?"

"No. I mean I know the new job's a fantastic career move for him, but like I told you, I've been in Wembley for five years now. I feel settled." I paused. "To be honest I was surprised when he suggested moving. I mean, we only bought our house a year ago. But you know his dad died, so I wonder if that's got something to do with it."

"Like he's running away, you mean?"

"Yeah, maybe. But I like my job and the people—"

"Awww...thanks, darling..."

"—and I've worked hard to feel...like I'm at home somewhere. Like I belong. Does that sound stupid?"

"Nope. Not at all." Olivia looked over her shoulder before she eased onto the highway. "But what does Nate say he wants?"

I waved a hand. "Well, the job, obviously. He says this Kevin guy has a great reputation in the recruitment industry and he's flattered he specifically headhunted him. But he insists I have to decide. He says all that really matters in the end is that I'm happy."

"Well, that's nice, isn't it? More blokes should think like him."

"Yeah, 'course." I paused, unable to explain how Nate's thoughtfulness could sometimes feel as if he were holding a pillow over my face. It didn't sound fair when I said it in my head, let alone out loud. "It's lovely." I could feel Olivia's gaze burning a hole in the side of my face but refused to move my head until she concentrated on the road again.

"When you made that comment the other day, the one about not being happy," she said, "did you mean because of the move or with Nate?"

"The move, of course."

"You sure?"

"Yes. Absolutely. A hundred percent." I looked out of the passenger window, staring at the horizon.

She clicked her tongue. "So what are you doing to—"

"Actually, do you mind if we don't talk for a bit? I'm knackered." I stole a sideways glance and saw Olivia suck in her cheeks, but she said nothing. I closed my eyes, grateful for the opportunity to sit back and rest. I hadn't appreciated how much energy finishing my finance degree would sap out of me, but soon I'd be fully qualified. Finally. No more staying up until stupid o'clock to study for a test. I'd be able to read all the books I'd stashed away in the drawer of my bedside table, starting with the new *Harry Potter* when it came out.

I sank into my seat. Sun rays flowed through the window, collecting at the top of my chest. When Olivia turned the radio on, my foot tapped to Oasis's "All Around The World," but soon stopped as I drifted off to sleep.

When a bump in the road jolted me awake it felt like I'd only just shut my eyes, and for a split second I couldn't remember where I was. I stretched out as far as the confines of the car would allow and yawned loudly.

"You've been asleep for ages." Olivia smiled as she looked over. "Almost two hours."

"Oh, sorry, Liv. I'm crap company."

"Don't worry about it, we'll be there soon."

I looked out of the window, perusing the scenery, which had turned from cityscape to green fields, trees and bushes. "Where are we?"

Olivia held up a map. "Somewhere between Newbury and Swindon. I think the exit's coming up soon. I'll need your help then. Ben said the place is in the middle of nowhere, and I'm expecting to be chased down the road by a bull or something."

"Spoken like a true city girl." I stretched and yawned again. "Anyway, he said being in the middle of nowhere is the whole point for these team building things."

"*Why?*"

"You know, be out of your comfort zone, get away from everything and minimize distractions. Blah, blah, blah."

Olivia grunted. "I'm hoping Martin will distract me."

"Down, Liv." I laughed. "He's married."

"Yeah, I know." She grinned. "But that doesn't stop me from looking at his bum."

A little while later we made it to the Bella Vista Conference Centre on the outskirts of Cirencester, but not before a few wrong turns caused by my adamant protests of, "It can't possibly be this far. The directions must be wrong."

The promise of views didn't disappoint, though. The blue skies and green fields stretched for miles, and were even enough to win over Olivia, who oohed and aahed every few seconds, sounding like an old grandma on her annual trip to the seaside.

The stone conference center at the end of a long driveway looked as if it belonged in a period drama, with its immaculate brickwork, intricate leadlight windows and peaked roofs.

Olivia peered up at the building. "Bloody hell. I should have packed a corset."

The woman at the reception, whose name tag said *Shirley*, beamed at us, her red fingernails clicking across the keyboard beneath her ample chest. "Welcome to Bella Vista," she said. "May I check you ladies in?" Shirley took our information, then handed us heavy, metal keys the length of our palms. "Miss Brewer," she said to Olivia, "you're in room 306. And, Mrs. Morris, you're in room 209."

"At least that way I won't hear you seducing Brosnan," I whispered to Olivia, who bit her lip and had to turn away for a second.

"Your group is set to have dinner at six thirty," Shirley said with another smile. "The restaurant is down the hallway, first on the left."

"Thanks." Olivia turned to me. "It's only twenty to five.

I'm going to have a nap. Meet you here in an hour, and we can have a wander around or something?"

"Sure." I smiled at the prospect of spending some time alone. "See you later."

I walked to my room, down a long red carpet-covered, wood-paneled hallway, hoping for a large, comfy mattress and a TV I could sneak up and watch after dinner. I pushed open the door and instantly wondered if they'd checked me into the broom cupboard.

The room didn't have a TV. Or a radio. Instead, it had a single bed, a desk the size of a tea tray, a tiny chair and a wardrobe with three hangers. I remembered what Ben had said the week before.

"The rooms are pretty basic. The whole point is to force people to spend time together."

No kidding, but unlike Olivia, I wasn't about to pounce on an unsuspecting guest to pass the time. I brushed my teeth and freshened up, then dug around in my bag for my newspaper before remembering it was still sitting on the sideboard at home. Cursing my usually impeccable memory, I shoved my bag under the bed and left the room. A stroll outside would do fine, and I walked back to the lobby and out the front entrance. The slightly cooler air had the inviting smell of lilacs, but a jacket would probably be a good idea. Without looking I spun around and collided straight with someone's broad chest.

"Oh, shit. I mean, sorry, I—"

"Abby?"

I looked up. Straight into those eyes.

"Liam?" The word came out as a strangled whisper.

He smiled broadly, grabbed hold of me and hugged me, then let go only to hug me a second time. "Christ. What the hell are you doing here?"

I swallowed, trying not to breathe in the familiar scent of his aftershave, but feeling dizzy all the same. "Work." It sounded more like a squeak than an actual word. "Uh, I'm here for work."

"Me, too," he said. "Wow, Abby. How are you? I always wondered what happened to you. You seemed to...well, *disappear*."

I looked at him, studied his face, his square jaw, his gray eyes. It was him, it really was. Feelings I had pushed down to the very bottom of my heart and wrapped in the biggest chains possible were rattling, struggling to be freed. I could feel them making a break for the surface, traveling throughout my entire body, and I had to get them back under control.

"How long are you here for?" he said, still looking at me.

I cleared my throat. "Until Friday."

"Me, too."

"It's a bit far from Preston, isn't it? Did you move away?"

"No. I was in Birmingham for the week. HBT has its headquarters there."

"HBT?"

"The bank I work for."

I couldn't stop looking at him. It felt strange, knowing Liam would be in the same building, walking down the same corridors, sitting in the same restaurant. I imagined him lying alone, underneath the cool sheets of the hotel bed and... "So," I said, before the dirty pictures took over.

"So..." Liam smiled, stopped and stared at me. "God, it's good to see you. I really can't believe it's you and—"

"Liam!" A guy the size of an industrial fridge walked up, the gravel scrunching loudly underneath his feet. He gave Liam a thunderous clap on the shoulder. "We made it."

"Francis." Liam shook his hand. "Good to see you again."

Francis looked at us both, so Liam added, "Uh, Abby, this is my colleague, Francis Wilkinson. He's from our Birmingham office. Francis, this is Abby."

"Good to meet you," he said, grabbing my hand with a massive paw bigger than the hubcaps on Olivia's Corolla. "I don't think we've met before. Are you new?"

"Oh, no," I said. "Liam and I, we, er..."

"We go way back," Liam jumped in. "School."

"Say no more," Francis said. "Liam, before I forget, can we talk about the brief we got yesterday? I've had some ideas I'd like to run by you."

Liam's eyes went from mine to Francis's. "Okay. Meet you at the bar in a few minutes?"

"Absolutely. Pleasure to meet you, Abby," Francis said and bowed slightly before he left.

"I should go, too," I said. "Got plans and, uh..."

"Abby." Liam stuffed his hands in his pocket. "I want to say so many things. Ask you all about where you've been, what you're doing."

No. No. No. "I don't think there's much to say."

He looked at my left hand. "Well, I do. Meet me for a drink after dinner?"

"I don't drink anymore. Haven't since—"

"Of course, of course. Coffee then, we—"

"It's not a good idea, Liam."

"Abby, look, I haven't seen you in almost six years. We can't ignore—"

"Yes, we can." I looked at him, willing determination into my voice. "Sometimes it's best to leave things alone."

He crossed his arms, smiled at me. "What's the worst that could happen?"

I might tell you I still love you, I thought, then pounded the feeling as if it were a game of Whack-a-Mole. "I have to go. I'll be late."

"You can't avoid me completely for the next two days. I'll get you to change your mind."

"No, you won't," I said, and ran to the ladies' room, ignoring the young couple who gave me a huffy look as I pushed past them and covered my mouth with one hand. I barely made it to the bathroom in time, where I knelt in front of the loo, retching over and over. And after I thought there was nothing left to bring up, it happened again.

An hour later Olivia bounced down the hallway looking like an exotic flower in her flowing, multicolored dress that showed off the multiple pixie and fairy tattoos on her arms.

"You look happy," I said with a smile, feeling much better after two glasses of water.

"Oh, *yes*." She grinned slyly. "A bloke asked me for my number."

I laughed. "You've only been here an hour. What did you say?"

She winked. "Gave him my room number."

"You did *what*?"

Olivia shrugged. "He's single. I'm single. Where's the harm?"

"What's his name?" I laughed, thinking perhaps I should introduce her to Paul. Although the world might implode if their sex drives collided. "Please tell me you at least got his name?"

"Francis," she said with a raised eyebrow. "Wilkinson."

"Hold on a sec," I said. "I met him. Big guy, huge hands and—"

"That's him." Her face fell. "Oh, no. Did he try to pick you up, too? The—"

"No, no, no." I quickly waved my hands around. "He works with someone I, uh, used to know."

"Oh, yeah?" Olivia smirked. "Who?"

"No one. Someone from school, years ago. But anyway, Francis seemed nice."

Olivia nodded. "Handsome, too. And you know what they say about men with big hands."

"Big...*gloves*?" I offered.

"Ha! Yeah." She winked again. "That, too."

After the rest of the Hoskins Insurance team arrived, ten of us settled down for dinner in the restaurant. As our appetizers, daintily arranged towers of mozzarella, sweet tomatoes and crisp basil were brought out, Liam walked into the room, and my appetite disappeared faster than Olivia's second rum and Coke. He'd changed from his business suit into a pair of jeans, a tailored white shirt and brown loafers. His hair was longer than I remembered and it softened his strong features. If Olivia hadn't had her back turned she definitely would have wolf-whistled.

"What do you think, Abby?" Ben said.

"I'm sorry, what?" I tore my gaze away from Liam. "I was miles away."

"Martin's proposal to reduce admin overhead?" Ben said with a frown.

"Oh, I, er, think it's good." Ben looked at me, and I felt my ears starting to burn. "It makes sense," I continued, thankful Martin had been bragging about his ideas to anyone who'd listen for the past month. "And sending the forms to people before their appointment would help, too. Especially if they have email."

"Excellent idea," Ben said. "See? The team building's working already." He smiled. "So how's the food? And what do we think of..." Ben started talking about another of his plans.

"What's up?" Olivia whispered. "It's not like you to lose focus."

"I was thinking about Nate," I said, wanting to stab myself in the thigh with my fork for using him as an excuse.

"You're so sweet." Olivia grabbed my arm. "Look, that's him," she said, nodding toward the door. "Francis." I watched as the big man scanned the room, locked eyes with Olivia and gave her a wide smile. "Oh, I've gone all funny inside," she said. "He's lovely."

"I know how you feel." I looked at Liam who was talking to the waitress. A delicious, tingly shiver slowly traveled down my spine and all the way back up again.

"Aww." Olivia reached over and patted my hand. "You'll see Nate on Friday."

"Yeah." I smiled as I continued to stare. "I'll see Nate on Friday."

I managed to eat half of my beef Wellington and roasted vegetables. But although the dessert, a beautiful arrangement of delicate pastries, looked as if it would melt in my mouth, I refused the plate regardless.

"You're so good," Olivia said as she dug into her profiter-oles. "You've got so much willpower."

I looked over at Liam. "It's habit. If you tell yourself often enough you don't want something, you convince yourself it's the truth."

Coffee and Calvados followed, and we all decided while the rooms might only be a step up from prison cells, the chef certainly knew his way around the kitchen. By the looks of things, all of my colleagues knew their way around a few bottles of wine, too.

"Are you sure you don't want any?" Martin said, hovering the merlot over my glass. "Go on, have some."

"No thanks."

"Wait a second." Martin grinned, his eyes slightly glossy. "Are you pregnant? Oww." He leaned over and rubbed the bottom of his leg. "What the hell, Liv?"

"Don't be rude, Martin," she said, then winked at me, and I felt glad I'd confided in her about Tom's death, although in my version we'd been hit by a drunk driver. I'd become a master, it seemed, at avoiding judgment, as if I were continually crossing a river over a set of badly placed, mossy stepping stones.

"But seriously," Olivia said to me once Martin was arguing with Ben about which team would win the World Cup this year. "Are you yet?"

"What?"

"Pregnant?"

I deliberately let my gaze drop to my lap. "Not this month."

"It'll happen for you, I'm sure it will," Olivia said as she squeezed my hand, then turned to tell Ben he was out of his mind, France would never, ever, not if all the cows came home wearing ice skates because hell had frozen over, win the World Cup.

I switched off and let my thoughts drift. How *could* I be pregnant? I was still taking the pill despite having told Nate I'd stopped over eighteen months ago, hiding them at the back of the medicine cabinet, behind my bottles of makeup remover and deodorant.

Truth was I still didn't feel ready to have a baby. I didn't trust myself to look after a houseplant, let alone another living, breathing human being. But lately Nate had talked about getting some tests done—him not me, he'd said, he didn't want to put me through that—so I knew I'd soon have to make a decision. And Nate had been ready for a child almost as soon as he'd proposed.

"Why wait?" he'd said as we lay in bed one Sunday morning.

"You're funny." I draped one of my legs over his. "I'm only just back at college, loving Hoskins and I'm twenty-*three*."

"So?" He rolled onto his side and propped himself up with one arm. "The younger you are, the easier it'll be to get your figure back." He covered his head with the blankets.

I laughed, pulling them back down. "Such a romantic, aren't you?"

"A hopeless one." He paused and smiled at me. "And you're sure you're happy with the wedding plans?"

I nodded. "Yes. Just the registry office."

"And only close family and friends?"

"Only *your* close family and friends."

"You're still not going to invite your mum?"

"Nope."

"And nobody from Preston? No best friend from school or people you worked with? Stu from the Kettle Club? Or—"

"*No.*"

"Abby…"

I shook my head. "No. That part of my life's over, Nate. Done and dusted. You're my family now."

Nate pulled me close. "Well, once you're Mrs. Morris we can start making Little Morrises. I'm the only one left to carry on the family name you know."

"Aren't you forgetting someone?" He gave me a blank look. "Paul. Your *brother*?"

"Paul? God no, he'll never have kids, mark my words.

That's my job. When you're ready we'll build the family you should have had."

I'd kissed him, thinking at any moment someone would be along to ordain him a saint.

"I'm going to bed," Olivia said, pulling me out of my thoughts. "Are you staying here?"

Liam's table was almost empty. He and Francis were the only ones left, deep in conversation over what looked like glasses of cognac. What harm would sitting and watching him do? I hadn't seen him in almost six years. Another six minutes wouldn't make any difference.

"For a while," I said to Olivia. "Maybe I'll have another glass of water."

"Uhh," she said, patting her stomach. "I'm so full I could burst. And I'm so tired. I'll see you tomorrow." She yawned, but I could tell she was faking it. Olivia was the mother of all night owls, regularly sending emails at two in the morning. At this hour she was barely getting started. "Night," she said to Ben and Martin, the only ones from our table who hadn't yet left.

I smiled at her. "Sleep well."

Olivia walked out of the dining room, and I watched as she turned her head toward Francis. He was openly gazing at her, taking in her every move. I saw her nod at him, and he winked, nodded back. He said something to Liam and two minutes later got up and left.

Liam's eyes met mine again, adding kindling to an already raging fire in my belly. His wolf eyes were full of loneliness and longing; I worried he could see exactly the same in mine. I dropped my gaze and turned to Ben and Martin.

"What's the plan for tomorrow?" I asked. "Or is it still classified?" As I half listened to Ben talking animatedly about the upcoming training, I sneaked a glance across the room only to find that Liam had gone.

"Grab a chair," our event organizer, a short, stout, bald man called Justin, said the next morning. "Come on, all of you, arrange them in a circle."

"What's this?" Martin said as he sat down, leaning back and putting his hands behind his head. "Are we going to sing 'Kumbaya'?" He hummed a few bars of the tune.

Ben elbowed him in the ribs. "Very funny."

"I thought we'd start by getting to know each other better," Justin said.

Martin looked around. "We need beer for that. Don't we guys?"

Justin laughed. "Later, promise. For now, I'd like you to share something the others wouldn't be able to guess. Something you feel comfortable saying, of course. We don't need to know about your secret Batman collection in the attic." He looked around the circle, but nobody spoke and he grinned. "Okay, looks like I'll go first. I'd love to give ballroom dancing a go, but my wife flatly refuses. She thinks I have the coordination of a drunken bear and weigh about twice as much."

Snorts of laughter erupted as we imagined Justin attempting the fox-trot, then Amanda from accounts had a turn followed by Sue. As Andy started talking, Olivia whispered in my ear, "The sex last night was the best I've ever had."

I just about managed to change my laugh into a cough and put my head down to stifle another giggle.

"I've been to see Depeche Mode six times," Martin said, his eyes lighting up. "And the fifth time they let me go backstage, and I met the band." He beamed. "I touched Dave Gahan's hand and didn't wash it for three days."

"Ugh," Olivia said. "Gross."

"Yeah," Martin said. "It was a bit."

As the rest of the group took turns, my mind seemed to run off in all directions, trying to come up with what I'd say.

My dad left when I was ten, and I haven't seen him since. No, way too personal.

My husband thinks we're trying for a baby, but I'm taking the pill. No, absolutely not.

Sometimes I want to run away and never come back. Stop, just stop.

I think I'm still in love with my ex-boyfriend. What the—

"Abby?" Justin said, and I felt everybody's eyes on me. "Want to share anything?"

"Uh." I pushed myself up. "I don't think the Wellington agreed with me."

As I rushed into the corridor, I heard Ben say, "Not quite what we had in mind but cheers."

I ran down the hallway, thinking I'd hide in the loos for ten minutes so Justin would move onto another exercise. But as I turned a corner I slammed straight into the person coming the other way.

"Oh, gosh. I'm sorry." I looked up. "I—"

"We've got to stop meeting like this." Liam smiled at me, and my knees went soft.

"I...I..."

"Are you okay?" Liam steadied me with one hand. "You look a bit...flustered."

"I'm fine. Fine. Taking a break."

He hooked his thumbs into his jeans. "So how's it going? Having fun?"

"It's okay." I shrugged. "We were supposed to share something about ourselves."

Liam rolled his eyes. "Bloody hell. They boilerplate these things, don't they?" I frowned and he added, "We did the exact same exercise yesterday. So what did you say?"

"I didn't. I made a beeline for the loo."

"Sounds sensible." He laughed, and the sound felt like a blanket wrapping itself around my body, something I could find comfort and warmth in, a place to stay forever. Liam smiled again. "But you know you could've made something up."

I laughed, lowered my shoulders. "Yes, I should have. What did you tell them?"

"I wanted to say that I met the love of my life on New Year's Eve."

I caught a glimpse of the gold band on his finger. "You met your wife on New Year's Eve?" A surge of raging envy hit the pit of my stomach.

"No, Abby." He sighed. "I met her at an airport."

I took a step back. "I'd better go." I turned around.

"Wait." He took hold of my arm, pulled me toward him, making every part of my body tingle. We were so close I could feel the beating of his heart. "Have dinner with me. Just dinner."

I pushed him away. "I can't. I'm here with my colleagues."

"Meet me after. There's so much to say. Please. Then you never have to see me again."

I paused. It was true, there were things we needed to say. Things I'd been carrying around with me for six years. A bag of guilt, a suitcase of remorse. Maybe talking to Liam would give me the opportunity to set them down and leave them behind. Then again...

"Okay. But not before ten thirty."

I felt his eyes follow me as I walked away, and I willed myself not to look back because if I did, I wasn't sure I'd keep going.

Liam and I sat at the empty bar later that night, him with a glass of Bordeaux, me with my usual water and lemon. Thanks to Francis and Olivia, the respective groups from HBT Bank and Hoskins Insurance had merged after dinner, sharing jokes and work stories, banking tricks and insurance tips, and I'd been able to spend part of the evening sitting closer to Liam. We'd stuck to our "old friend from school story," which nobody cared enough about to question. And, one by one, Ben, Martin and all the others admitted defeat after another booze-laden night. Francis and Olivia hadn't even waited for dessert.

"I wasn't sure if I'd see you at all tonight," Liam said, then drank some wine.

"To be honest I almost changed my mind."

"What stopped you?"

I looked at him. "You're right. We need to talk, but I don't know where to start."

"With you," he said. "Where are you living now?"

"South London area," I said, waving a hand.

"That's pretty vague. Want to narrow it down?"

I shook my head.

"Okay, maybe later. I spy a ring on your finger. You're married?"

"Four years," I said, absentmindedly spinning the gold band and matching solitaire around my finger. "Nate."

"Nancy," Liam said. "My wife's name is Nancy. Kids?"

"Not yet. Maybe someday. When the time's right. You?"

"A boy," he said, and I immediately wished he hadn't. "Zachary. Four months." Liam pulled a picture from his wallet and handed it to me. The toothless baby had a wide smile, tufty brown hair and was busy cuddling what looked like a slightly damp blue rabbit.

"He's beautiful. He has your eyes."

"Do you love him?" Liam stared at me.

I laughed, sliding the photograph back across the bar. "Steady on. He's cute but—"

"You know who I'm talking about."

My smile faded. "Yes. I love Nate very much."

Liam's jaw tightened, and we sat in silence for a while. I kept my hands on my glass to make sure they weren't moving closer to his.

"Why did you run?" he said abruptly. "Why did you push me away?"

I fiddled with my ring again. "Those are complicated questions and—"

"They're important questions," Liam said loudly, then added, more quietly this time, "And I feel I have a right to know."

I leaned back as far as the leather bar stool would allow. "I didn't think I deserved to be happy. I didn't think I deserved to be with you."

"And now?" I didn't answer, and Liam looked away. "It wasn't your fault."

"So people keep saying. Maybe I'll believe it in time but—"

"I loved you, Abby. I still—"

"Don't." I leaned forward and put a finger to his lips. "Please. You're married. So am I."

He gently pushed my fingers away. "To the wrong people."

"You can't say that."

"I just did. And I'll say it again. To the *wrong* people."

"You don't even know Nate. He's good to me. I owe him—" I sighed "—*everything.*"

We sat in silence for a while until Liam spoke again. "Did you know I went to see your mum once, after you left?"

"My mum? Why? She only met you the one time, and she was so rude."

Liam laughed. "You know I never took it personally. She was only ever nice to Tom." He grinned at the memory of my brother. "Anyway, she let me stand on the doorstep for all of thirty seconds but refused to tell me where you were. Didn't she tell you?"

"We rarely speak."

"The only thing she said was that you'd moved away and married the man who saved you. Is that true?"

I picked up my glass, swirled the ice cubes around. "Yes. That's Nate."

Liam's face clouded over with an expression I'd never seen before. Was it hatred? Jealousy, perhaps? I couldn't tell. He looked away. "And nothing ever came back about that night?" he said quietly.

I shook my head. "No. I gave up trying to remember. What's the point? It'll never bring Tom home. Nothing will."

Liam flinched, his brow furrowed. "I miss him."

"Me, too," I whispered. "Every day. Every single day."

"You weren't at the funeral. You never returned my letters, my calls and—"

"I couldn't, I—"

"—sometimes I stood across from the Kettle Club, just to see you."

I nodded. "I know."

"And then, zap." Liam snapped his fingers. "You disappeared. Off into the sunset, well, South London area anyway, with your knight in shining armor."

"I couldn't stay. It was too hard."

"I should have been there for you." He rubbed his eyes. "You shouldn't have gone through it all alone."

I put a hand on his arm. "I pushed you away, remember? And I wasn't alone."

Liam looked at me with such sadness in his eyes, such pain and hurt, it made me want to shrivel up into a speck of dust and fall to the floor, ready to be swept away.

"And you're happy?" he said. "With...*Nate*? As happy as we were?" He looked at me, and I imagined his fingers sliding down my bare skin, his lips on mine, our limbs entwined. I didn't have to try to remember how much I loved him. I didn't need to. It had never gone away.

I cleared my throat, drained my glass. "Yes." There was no alternative. "We're happy."

Liam remained silent for a moment. "And what did he think about stealing you away from me? Did he at least have the decency to feel bad?"

"I never told him about us."

"Didn't you? Why?"

I shrugged. "I couldn't. It was too hard to talk about you. I said I'd split up with a boyfriend a while before the accident. I never told him your name." I paused. "What about you? Did you tell your wife about me?"

"No. Those memories are mine. They're...they're not something I want to share. I don't want to answer her questions." He got up, and for a moment I thought he was going to thank me for my company, wish me a nice life and leave. But instead he grabbed my hand. "Let's get out of here. Pretend the last six years never happened."

I pulled a face. "Liam..."

"Just for a little while," he whispered, squeezing my hand. We wandered outside into the chilly air. When Liam put his arm around me and I rested my head against his shoulder, I felt his muscles tense and could smell his deodorant. I breathed in his scent as I closed my eyes for a second, letting his movements guide me. As we walked around the conference building and into the gardens at the back, a distant church bell struck midnight. The earlier rain shower and cooler temperatures meant we were the only ones outside. We made our way over to a bench and sat down, leaning back and looking toward the sky.

"It's so quiet here." I half closed my eyes and listened to the crickets. "Peaceful."

Liam kissed the top of my head. "I wasn't looking forward to being here," he said as he pulled me closer. "Now I wish I could stay."

"What time are you going tomorrow?"

"Around eleven," he said quietly. "Eleven thirty at the latest."

"I've got meetings from eight thirty until lunchtime... Maybe we can meet before breakfast. To say goodbye?"

"We can spend the whole night saying goodbye, Abby."

"Liam, we can't..." I put a hand on his chest and felt the beating of his heart. As I raised my head and looked at him, whatever words I had planned to say got caught in my throat. My eyes wandered over his face, taking in the ruggedness of his cheekbones, the gentle curve of his mouth. His breath had the sweet scent of wine, and his two-day stubble was so close, it almost grazed my chin. And as he sat up and his lips came nearer, I closed my eyes, letting the last few images of Nate I'd been clinging on to slip away like sand through my fingers.

We didn't speak again until we were in Liam's room, where we slowly lay down on the tiny bed. "I've missed you Abby," he whispered. "God, I've missed you."

He undid my blouse, one button at a time, without taking his eyes off mine. His hands slipped under the fabric, his fingers over my skin. I closed my eyes as he kissed me, and as I felt his mouth slide down my neck I moaned, wanting him to touch every part of me. Liam eased off my bra and cupped my breasts with his hands, then lowered his head toward them. Back arched, I pulled him up toward me, grinding my hips against him, feeling how ready he was.

"I need you," I whispered in his ear as I reached to unbuckle his belt. "I need you now."

And finally he was inside me, our bodies fitting together so perfectly, moving with such familiarity, it was as if we'd never spent a single moment apart.

"I still love you, Abby," Liam whispered as he held me afterward.

"I still love you, too." The words spilled out of me as the tears rolled down my cheeks, settling in a damp little pool on the pillow. Tears of happiness at first, the ones you cry when you realize you're finally, at last, exactly where you should be. But then they were replaced by tears of sadness because I knew it wasn't somewhere I could stay.

After we'd made love again, slowly this time, and Liam had fallen asleep, I stayed awake, listening to the steady rhythm of his breathing, forbidding myself from drifting off, too. I needed time to stand still or, at least, slow down. I wanted to relish every second that passed. Because I already knew I'd never see Liam again. Could *never* see him again. I told myself over and over this was the closure we'd never had. From now on we'd be walking two distinctly separate paths that would never, ever cross again.

It was three in the morning before my body betrayed me

and gave in to exhaustion, and I fell asleep wrapped in Liam's arms, thinking I couldn't possibly feel this safe again.

Timid sunlight made its way through the gap in the curtains when I woke up, my legs and arms still entwined with Liam's. I slowly managed to untangle our bodies without him stirring, and I stood there for a moment, watching him sleep, his mouth slightly open and a hint of a smile playing on his lips. It was one of those moments where everything was perfect, where everything would remain perfect, as long as nobody moved. But as I slowly bent over to pick up my clothes, the illusion began to waver, then shattered around me.

As I dressed, I willed myself to feel terrible about what we'd done. I wanted my heart to fill with guilt toward Nate, anger toward Liam and hatred toward myself. But instead a sadness so heavy pulled at me, I thought it might rip me straight through the floor.

Standing in the middle of the bedroom I forced my gaze away from Liam's face, gathered my bag and shoes and tiptoed toward the door. I barely made it two steps before he spoke with sleepy confusion in his voice.

"Abby?"

I turned around, clutching my things against my chest. Tears prickled my eyes because I could see what last night had meant to him, to me, to the possibility of us.

"Don't leave yet." Liam held out his hand. "Come here."

"I have to go. I can't risk anyone seeing me."

Liam sat up. "Leave him." His voice was loud, determined. The voice of a man on a mission who had no time to waste. "Leave Nate."

"Liam, I—"

"I'll leave Nancy."

"But you—"

"No. I don't want to be with her. Not when I can be with you."

"We can't—"

"We *can*. We can move anywhere you like. *Anywhere*." Liam held out his arms toward me. "We'll start again. Just you and me."

"But...but...it's not just you and me, is it?" I said. "There's Nate and Nancy and—"

"They'll cope, they—"

"And you have a *son*, Liam. A *son*."

"And I'll support him. I'll be there for him, whatever it takes. And when we have kids of our own he'll have half sisters or brothers. Don't you see it's—"

"No," I said. "You can't ask me to do that."

Liam stood up, naked and vulnerable. "I want to be with you, Abby. And I know you want to be with me."

"*No,*" I said, more loudly than I'd intended. "I can't do this. You're a father now. A *good* father. I won't be responsible for breaking up your marriage and—"

"You won't be responsible. *I* will."

"*No.* My dad left Tom and me and look at me." I tapped my chest, the heel of my shoe digging into my ribs. "It screwed me up. You, of all people, should know and—"

"Abby, you're not your dad, you—"

"Then don't ask me to make you be like him." I shook my head. "I can't. I *won't*. We've both made our choices." My hand grabbed hold of the doorknob, but I wavered, confused about whom I should listen to—my mind telling me to go, or my heart screaming to stay, stay, *stay*.

"Abby. Please."

"This was a mistake," I whispered, unsure of whom I was

trying to convince more. "Last night should never have happened."

Within half a second Liam had his arms around my waist and held me tight. "You leaving is a mistake and you know it. So don't. Please don't."

"I have to. And you have to let me." I pushed him away and opened the door.

"Wait! You haven't told me where you live. I don't have your phone number."

"It's better this way. Believe me, Liam. It's better for both of us."

I closed the door behind me, but it took every fiber of my being, every iota of self-control I'd ever possessed, to stop me from opening it again. Forcing one foot to move in front of the other, I scurried back to my room, where I stripped down, stood in the shower with the water as cold as I could bear and sobbed until no more tears came.

I shivered and assessed the damage in the mirror—dark circles under my swollen, bloodshot eyes, and tear-streaked cheeks. It was already seven. Even if I skipped breakfast to avoid bumping into Liam and exchanging pleasantries over the croissants and fruit salad, I'd have to join Olivia and the rest of the team by eight thirty. In an hour and a half I'd be sitting in a conference room with my colleagues discussing feedback charts and company procedures.

"Get through the morning," I told myself as I reached for my foundation and started the process of erasing the night before. "Get back home and you'll be fine."

Five hours later I stood at the reception.

"How was your stay?" Shirley beamed at me. "I do hope you enjoyed yourself?"

"Great." I smiled tightly as I handed over the room key.

"Excellent," Shirley said. "Oh, before I forget, Mr. Jefferson left this for you." She slid a hotel envelope toward me and leaned in, her ample chest resting on the desk in front of her. "He insisted I give it to you personally." She sat back, apparently satisfied she'd completed her assignment. "He's such a nice man." Her gaze flickered to my left hand and I quickly moved it behind the counter. "A very nice man indeed."

I grabbed the envelope, muttering a quick thanks as I tore it open, my heart tightening as I read Liam's neat handwriting.

Abby,
We know we belong together. We always have.
    Please contact me. I can't let you run away from me again.
I love you.
Liam x

I rubbed my thumb over the phone number and email address he'd added at the bottom, contact details I immediately and irrevocably swore I'd never use.

"Abby!" Olivia waved from across the hallway and sauntered up to me as I stuffed the letter back into the envelope. "You okay? You've hardly said anything all morning."

"I didn't sleep well."

"Nothing like your own bed," Olivia said as we headed for the door. "But that was a fun evening, wasn't it? That Liam seems nice. Funny how you ended up seeing an old mate, eh?" She leaned in closer. "I spent the night with Francis again. I know it sounds over the top, but I was gutted when he left."

"Oh, well." I shrugged. "Plenty of fish but not enough time. That's what you always say."

She stopped walking and put a hand on my arm. "Abby, I think he's *the* fish."

"*The* fish?" I tried to keep my voice neutral and stop it from going up a couple of octaves.

"Uh-huh. This wasn't just a shag, Abby, not for me, and from what he said, not for him either. But we live hundreds of miles apart," she grumbled as we went outside to the car. "For god's sake. Why does life have to be so bloody complicated?"

"I have no idea, Liv." I shoved my bag onto the back seat. "Not a sodding clue."

"Well—" she popped her sunglasses onto her nose "—he said he'd call me tonight." Olivia suppressed a squeal, and my heart raced as I processed the information.

"This doesn't sound like you. I mean, how serious can it be already?" I said.

"I'm going to Birmingham to stay with him in two weeks." Olivia's face lit up and I recognized the look. I used to have it whenever I thought of Liam. She sighed. "I can't wait."

"Give me a second. I need the loo before we set off." Back inside I splashed my face with cool water and gulped in a lungful of air to slow my breathing. If Olivia and Francis were in contact, Liam would know how to find me. I couldn't let that happen. I *wouldn't*. And to make sure I kept my end of the bargain, I pulled Liam's letter out of my pocket and threw it away.

NOW
ABBY

NOT EVEN A week had passed since Liam and I had made love in the forest. After we'd pulled our clothes back on, and despite knowing it was absolutely inappropriate considering what we'd done, I'd started to giggle. Quietly at first, but then a loud belly laugh escaped from deep within me, a sound I didn't recognize at first because I'd suppressed it for years.

A giddiness invaded my heart, like a child who'd been invited to live in Disneyland forever. It felt as if I'd been opened up, freed from some invisible, twenty-year-old shackles that had restrained me, keeping me firmly on the ground.

"What's so funny?" Liam said, and his face broke into a grin, too.

"I...it's not..." I tried to compose myself as I gestured with my hands. "This isn't..."

He wrinkled his nose. "Not quite the romantic setting you had in mind?"

I laughed again. "Not really, no."

"Up against a tree," he said, his shoulders shaking, "like a pair of lusty teenagers. The least I could have done is bought you a bag of chips first." I put my arms around him, and he looked at me, his smile fading like a sunset. "So now what?"

"Oh, god, Liam." I sighed. "I know I should hate myself for this. And I know I should feel guilty. But I feel guilty that I don't."

"If it's any consolation, I don't either. Not yet. Christ. Are we bad people or what?"

Nate's and Sarah's faces popped into my mind, and my face fell. "Yes," I whispered, "despicable. And we can't do this again. We said we wouldn't."

"Abby, we—"

"Wait. I was going to say not until we figure out what we're going to do."

"Well, that's easy. We'll be together."

I closed my eyes. "Yes, I know b—"

He kissed me. "Don't even think about saying *but*."

I smiled at him. "I won't. *Although*...we have to be more respectful of Nate and Nancy, and the kids. It's not right." He pulled me back toward him, buried his face in my neck, so I gently pushed him away. "No, listen to me. There can be no more of this. Not until we've decided. Not until we've made a plan. Okay?"

"Okay." Liam exhaled. "Okay. I can wait."

But it was me who couldn't. Instead of doing our Wednesday evening training, I told Liam to drive to a hotel in Guilford, where we now lay on the bed after making love twice already, whispering how much we'd missed each other, how we couldn't bear to be apart.

"We broke our resolution again." Liam smiled as he stroked my hair. "You can't keep seducing me like this, you know."

I gently slapped his back. "Yeah. And you said no how many times? Let me see...hmm...oh, that's right...*none*."

He grinned and rolled off me onto his back, putting one hand behind his head, the other around my shoulder. I pulled the hastily discarded sheets over our bodies and closed my eyes with a sigh.

"You okay?" Liam murmured.

"Yes." I smiled. "More than okay. I know everybody's about to go through hell, I know it's going to be really hard, that we're going to cause people pain...but I haven't been this sure of what I'm doing in...well...*ever.*"

"Everything's going to be all right," Liam said. And as I snuggled up closer to him, I tried to silence the quiet whispers warning me to be careful, reminding me true happiness wasn't something I deserved.

"We can't go to sleep," I said. "Okay? Nate's working late, but we have to leave soon."

"Mmmm," Liam murmured, and I couldn't bring myself to break the fragile cocoon we'd made any earlier than I absolutely had to.

NOW
NANCY

IT HAD HAPPENED by accident the night before, an hour or so after Liam had come back later than usual from his training. I wasn't even the one who'd found it. It was Zac.

"Hey, Dad," I'd heard him say as I sat at the kitchen table, getting my shopping list ready for the morning. "Who's this?"

"Where did you find *that*?" Liam's tone was tense, and I wondered what they were talking about for him to sound so alarmed. I tiptoed out of the kitchen and stood quietly in the hall, far away enough that they couldn't see my shadow on the wall, but close enough for me to hear. Looking through the crack of the doorway, I saw Liam practically snatch a photograph from Zac and stuff it in the back pocket of his jeans.

"Floor upstairs," Zac said.

"Oh. I moved the box of old photographs earlier. Must have fallen out then," Liam said, but I knew it was a lie. That box had been in the spare bedroom cupboard for weeks.

"Who is it?" Zac insisted, and I secretly praised him for his curiosity.

"You wouldn't remember them. Francis and Olivia. I used

to work with him, years ago. Hey, do you want to watch something with me? An action movie?" Liam said.

Zac shrugged, flopped down on the couch and turned on the television. "Sure."

My heart pounded in my chest. Francis and Olivia. Liam was right about Zac not remembering them, he'd only been a baby when we went to their wedding. I'd never forgotten the story about how Francis and Olivia met. On a corporate retreat, the one from which Liam had come back moody and withdrawn, the one after which I'd wondered if he'd been cheating.

Why on earth did he still have a photograph of them, when we hadn't met in over a decade and a half? And why had Liam lied about it? I took a step toward the living room, ready to confront him, but something told me not to. I swallowed and crept back to the kitchen, my heart going into overdrive, my head telling me to address the situation with cold, surgical precision.

I forced myself to watch television with Liam and Zac, pretending I hadn't heard their conversation. After Zac went to bed I cheerfully told Liam I had a couple of episodes of some period drama to watch, and that I'd be up later, careful to react normally when he kissed me good-night with what, I decided, could only be described as a guilty peck on the cheek.

An hour and a half later, once I was sure they'd both be asleep, I tiptoed into our bedroom, grabbed Liam's jeans and sneaked into the hallway. My temples throbbed as I felt around in the pockets, my pulse quickening with each second that I was unable to locate that picture.

I wanted to throw the jeans on the floor and stamp my feet. The fact that the photograph wasn't in his jeans only added to my certainty that it meant something. That I'd finally have proof of an affair all those years ago.

I stopped for a second, trying to remember what Liam had done before he'd gone to bed, attempting to picture his movements in sequence. He'd checked his emails, so I searched his laptop bag, and, for good measure, the pockets of his jacket and his blazer, every unsuccessful attempt infuriating me further still.

What else? I snapped my fingers. He'd read, like he did every evening. Holding my breath I moved stealth-like back to the bedroom, picked up his book and returned to the hallway.

And, suddenly, there it was. The photograph. Wedged in the middle of the pages, and as I looked more closely I almost screamed.

I'd been stupid. Pathetically, embarrassingly *stupid*.

I considered my options. Wake him up, shout accusations, which he'd surely deny. I didn't have much to go on. The evidence was grainy and coincidental at best. No wonder Zac hadn't made the connection. And yet, I knew. I *knew*. My intuition hadn't been wrong after all.

The woman in the photo—standing at the bar with Liam, behind Francis and Olivia—was Abby.

Beautiful but awkward, quiet and nonthreatening, Abby. Friendly neighbor, Abby. Conniving, husband-stealing, slut, *Abby*.

I had to cover my mouth with both hands to stop the blind rage that tore through me from escaping from my mouth in an earsplitting shriek. Breathing heavily I slid to the floor, rested my head against the wall in an attempt to stop myself from falling down completely.

One old photograph might not be enough ammunition to

blow the whole thing wide-open, but it was a start. And I wanted to destroy Abby. Extinguish both of her relationships, if that's what they really were. Then I'd swoop in to claim what I now realized I truly wanted—no—what I *deserved*.

But it would only work if I played the game carefully, tactically.

And I knew exactly what to do.

NOW
NATE

IT WAS FRIDAY AFTERNOON. I'd made another two deals and left the office early as a reward. Abby had said she'd go training straight from work, and Sarah was spending the night at Claire's. The thought of my daughter made me smile. She was so happy these days, laughing and joking around—with me, not Abby, although that was nothing new.

As I pulled up to our house I decided to pop over and help Nancy with the final touches of their main floor transformation. She smiled when she opened the door, but it looked forced.

"How was your week?" I asked once we'd settled at the kitchen table with mugs of coffee.

Nancy shrugged. "It was okay."

"That good, eh?"

"It's nothing." She blew on her coffee for the third time.

I put my cup down. "Nancy, what's up?"

With a sigh, she said, "The stuff with Liam's bothering me. He's still distant, more so, actually. I've asked him what's wrong, but he always says he's fine when clearly he's not." A quick shrug. "We're going out tonight. Movies and dinner."

"Well, there you go, if he organized—"

"Don't be daft, it was my idea. I thought maybe I could get him to open up." She paused, her eyes glistening. "I wish he'd talk to me. I don't suppose…has Abby mentioned anything?"

I shook my head, thinking about Abby telling me he'd whistled at another woman. But that hardly counted. "Like you said last time, I'm sure it's a phase."

"I hope so," Nancy said. "Because I've decided I'm not hanging around if he's having an affair. I couldn't. My trust would be completely broken, you know? Then again… affairs happen all the time, don't they? And couples recover? I mean, what would you do if Abby cheated? Would you stay with her? Try to work things out?"

I shook my head. "I don't know… I don't think so."

"Well, it's a bit of a silly question." She smiled. "She'd *never* do that to you. Why would she? You're such a wonderful husband."

"Stop it. Actually, no, don't. I like it," I said, wishing Abby were as generous.

Nancy laughed. "I'm sure Abby knows exactly how lucky she is. She'd be crazy not to. You're one in a million, Nate, you must know that. Anyway… I want to invite you all over for dinner. As a thank you for the work you've done. How about tomorrow or Sunday?"

"Uh, we can't," I said quickly. "Got plans for the weekend."

"Oh?" Nancy looked annoyed for a second but then quickly grinned. "No doubt something romantic. Monday then?"

I nodded. "Great. Our turn to bring booze and dessert."

As I walked over to our house I wondered if it would still

be standing come Monday, considering I might have kicked off World War III.

Abby's mother had called two days ago. I'd sat at my desk, poring over a sales report, when the phone rang. The unfamiliar number flashed with insistent determination, and I let it go to voice mail. I had a sneaking suspicion who it was, and sure enough, I sighed loudly as I half listened to Dolores informing me in her usual clipped tone that she needed to speak with me *immediately*. Maybe she'd meant to call the house. Then again, Dolores had left a few messages on our machine at home, but Abby had never mentioned they'd spoken.

I decided Dolores could wait. I was in no hurry considering the last words I'd uttered to her years ago, when she'd left Abby on the phone in tears again, were, "Happy fucking Christmas, Dolores."

My mother-in-law was the kind of woman you wanted to ignore, but it wasn't easy, I'd give her that. It had taken me a decade to master the art of letting her stinging comments roll off my back, and not go after the bait so fast it would've made *Jaws* look like a goldfish. She was persistent, too, because, sure enough, a minute later the phone rang again, and I gave in.

"Nate Morris," I said in my best singsong voice.

"Nate. It's Dolores. How are you?"

"Uh," I cleared my throat. "Hello, Dolores. I'm well. You?"

She paused. A long-drawn-out silence I'd normally jump in to fill. Finally she said, "I have to see Abigail." The desperation in her voice was unusual and sounded scarily genuine. "I need your help. She won't return any of my calls."

I let out an exasperated sigh. "Well, surely it's not a surprise, you—"

"Please, Nate," Dolores said quietly. "For once, I don't want to pick a fight. That's not why I called you."

"No? Then why did you?"

"I need to see Abigail face-to-face," she said. "Ask for her forgiveness. And for yours, too."

I laughed. "Christ, it sounds like you're dying or something." When she didn't answer I said, "Dolores? Is...everything okay?"

"No, Nate. It's not. That's the other reason for my contacting you."

And by the end of the conversation we'd arranged everything, and against my better judgment I'd agreed to keep her upcoming visit a secret. What other choice did I have?

Once I'd gotten back from Nancy's I decided to have a shower. After I'd finished and stood in the bedroom putting my clothes on, I heard a car pull into our driveway. Abby and Liam were back from their run. I was about to knock on the bedroom window and wave down at them, but something stopped me. I felt my eyes narrow as I watched them. The way she smiled at him, head tilted to one side. Him throwing his head back as he laughed at something she'd said, how he put his hand on her arm.

There was no kiss, no embrace of any kind. But as I remembered Nancy's comments, and although my flirting radar belonged on the scrap heap, a cold trickle of sweat pooled at the bottom of my back. I watched my wife give Liam a breezy wave goodbye before turning toward our house. I swallowed. Had I really seen anything at all?

I wondered if I should call Paul and have a heart-to-heart. Then again, they were in the throes of packing up the entire house, getting ready for their big move, so he'd hardly have the time to listen to my probably—*definitely*—unfounded woes.

"Anybody home?" Abby called as she came in the house,

and I heard her bound up the stairs. "Oh," she said as she saw me in the bedroom. "I didn't know you were here."

"Did you have a good time? With Liam?"

"Yeah." She shrugged. "It was fine. Beat my record over five kilometers."

"Is that so? Anybody else go with you?"

"Not this time." She crossed over to the bathroom. "I'll hop in the shower."

I stared at the closed door for a while, telling myself I was being stupid. Abby wouldn't. She *wouldn't*. There was no way. But just in case, I told myself quietly and resolutely, when we went for dinner at Nancy and Liam's on Monday, I'd be watching.

NOW

SARAH

Dear Diary,

I saw Brian today... Mum and Dad were only out for a few hours, but at least we had the house to ourselves for a while.

We snuggled up on the sofa and it felt so right. Like it always does. It's hard to explain, but it's like Brian totally understands me, *all* of me. He laughs at my stupid jokes, even when they're not funny. And he's not laughing to be polite, but because of the way I tell them. He's polite, opens doors for me, not in a "you're a weak girl, let me save you" way, but as a gentlemanly gesture, which I never thought I'd like, but I do. When he said the LGBT piece was the best article he'd ever read, I knew he hadn't said it because I'm his *girlfriend*.

When the movie finished I took him by the hand and led him to my bedroom. I knew he'd bought condoms so I didn't have to worry, and he undressed me and then...well...you're not getting those details. I'm keeping them all to myself.

Later,

Sarah x.

PS. Word of the day: *beatific*, adjective.
1: of, possessing, or imparting a state of utmost bliss.
2: having a blissful appearance.
As in: *Being with Brian made me feel utterly beatific.*

NOW
ABBY

MY HEART RACED as I slammed Sarah's diary shut. All I'd wanted to know when I'd started sneaking peeks into her personal life was if she felt anything for Zac. And despite it being clear for weeks that she didn't, I'd been unable to stop my prying, needing to read her scribbles like a soap opera addict who couldn't go without her fix. But *that*? Her sleeping with Brian in our house? I didn't want to read *that*.

I felt like slapping my own stupid face for reaching this all-time low in my relationship with Sarah. *Relationship?* Please. We were barely speaking to each other, but instead danced around like boxers with our guard up, waiting for our opponent's jab.

And now she was having sex with her boyfriend—*in our house*—and I had to pretend I didn't know. A pregnancy didn't worry me too much, they were obviously being smart, and heavy cycles meant she'd been on birth control for a year now, too. But how was she *feeling*? I needed to talk to her—she'd seen Brian a few days ago already—but how could I ask her without her suspecting I'd snooped in her things?

Over the past week I'd been worrying so much about how Sarah would cope living without Nate. Now I worried how I'd live without her, because surely when she found out what I'd done she'd never choose to stay with me.

It was something else Liam and I had discussed Wednesday night, how we'd extricate ourselves from our current lives.

"We have to tell them we knew each other in Preston," I'd said. "I think it'll make it easier for them, knowing it's not a recent thing. They have to know we've loved each other for years."

"Don't you think it'll make it worse? And what about the Cotswolds? Do we tell them what—"

"*No!* Definitely not. That's too much for anyone to bear."

And so we'd continued discussing, made love, then debated again how we would—because the word *could* had disappeared—untangle ourselves with the minimum amount of collateral damage.

Back in Sarah's bedroom, as I attempted to bring some form of order to my thoughts, the doorbell rang. We weren't expecting anyone, and I knew it wouldn't be Liam. He and I had continued to be careful when we were at home, wary of every look, gesture and comment whenever we saw each other.

When I opened the front door I expected the postman with another Amazon package for Sarah—Brian didn't seem to be influencing her gaming habit—but the person on the front step was my mother.

"Mum." I tried changing my confused expression to a happy astonished face.

"Hello, Abigail." She leaned forward for a kiss, almost touching my cheek. "I'm sure this is a surprise."

"Well, uh, I wasn't expecting you."

She smiled, a gesture that never quite managed to reach her eyes. "May I come in?"

As my mother walked past me I noticed her small suitcase. Exactly how long was she here for, and, more to the point, *why*? I watched her eyes travel around the hallway, then settle on Tom's photograph.

"Why didn't you phone?" I said. "I would've—"

"I did, Abigail. But when you ignored all of my messages, I called Nate."

"*Nate?* Hold on. He knew you were coming? He didn't tell me."

"I asked him not to."

"Why?"

"Because I wasn't sure you'd agree."

I frowned. "He told me to keep the weekend free. I thought he'd planned something."

"He did. And I'm sure this is a disappointment."

It wasn't. Actually it was a relief. I'd worried Nate had orchestrated a romantic getaway with a four-poster bed and a couples massage. I hadn't been intimate with him since well before Liam and I had been together in the forest. I shook my head, returning to the matter at hand. "Why are you here, Mum?"

"Because, Abigail. We need to talk."

"Talk?" We hadn't spoken properly for years, or seen each other for even longer. Yet here she was. The unfathomable Mrs. Sanders, dressed in a starched blue-and-white-striped shirt, her black trousers ironed with such precision they could have sharpened knives. She was in her early seventies now, and while her figure no doubt caused envy among her friends— if she had any—the lines around her mouth and eyes easily aged her by at least a decade.

"I'm glad you were in," she said. "The taxi driver didn't know the way very well, and I couldn't remember, it's been so long."

I resisted the urge to defend myself. "Nate's gone to pick up Sarah. I'm sure she'll be pleased to see you."

"Will she?" My mother looked at me with a blank stare. "She never speaks to me, never calls."

I winced as I dug my nails into the palm of my hands, hard. Didn't she know the phone worked both ways? I opened my mouth and at the last moment said, "Would you like a drink? How was your trip?"

"Fine, thank you. I caught the first train. And water with lemon, please, if you have it."

We entered the kitchen, and I waited to hear her suck in her breath at the pile of clothes in the laundry basket. It was only one load, still warm from the dryer, but I knew my mother. She whipped out the ironing board for every shirt, skirt or stray sock she could find. But she commented on how she liked what we'd done to the kitchen instead, so I poured our drinks and took them to the conservatory.

"If I'd known you were coming I'd have made a cake," I said as we sat down.

She waved a hand. "Dear god, I haven't eaten cake since the sixties. And I came to talk."

"So you've said. About what?"

Mum hesitated, touched the ruby-red teardrop pendant around her neck. "You. Me. Us." As I stared at her she added, "This is hard for me, Abigail." Again I stayed silent until she quietly said, "I'm ill."

I frowned. "What do you mean, *ill*?"

"I had breast cancer four years ago—"

"Breast cancer? I had no idea, you never—"

"Told you?" She shook her head. "I don't fare well with pity, so I dealt with it alone."

"But you're okay?" I said quickly. "You're in remission?"

"I was." She hesitated, took a sip of her water. "But recently I've felt tired and had headaches. So I went for some tests." Mum tapped the side of her head. "It's in my brain. I have another nine months."

"Nine *months*?"

"Perhaps a year at best."

"Wait, *what*?" She was so matter-of-fact, so blasé. She must have been feeling something? Surely my mother, the irrefutable Ice Queen, couldn't be that cold. "I can't believe it."

"Look—" she smoothed down her shirt "—I need to say goodbye. I'd like us to spend some time together before I... go." She sighed. "I want to bury the hatchet. Forgive you—"

"*Forgive* me? Well, that's rich—"

She spoke louder, holding up a hand "—and ask you to forgive me." As my mouth fell open while my mind scrambled to process her words, she said, "And we need to talk about your father."

"Dad?" My heart quickened. "What does he have to do with it?"

She exhaled. "Everything, Abigail. Absolutely everything."

I folded my arms across my chest. "I don't understand."

Eyes lowered, she said, "You deserve to know the truth."

"The truth?" I frowned. "What do you mean?"

My mother pinched the bridge of her nose with her thumb and index finger, then lowered them and looked at me again. "First of all you have to understand I loved your father, Abigail. More than life itself. He was a wonderful man—"

"Sorry, but how can you say that after what he did?"

She exhaled. "I would have done anything for him. But

his betrayal...it *broke* me. I was never the same after he left me for...for..."

"Another woman?" I wanted to add if she'd not been a constant nag, if she'd been emotionally available, had an ounce of a heart, then maybe Dad would never have walked away. But I kept my mouth shut. Over the last few months I'd come to understand relationships were rarely as simple as they appeared.

"Yes," she said. "Did I ever tell you she was American, and at least ten years younger than me?" I shook my head. "It made me feel so old, so...*discarded*. And I was only thirty-six when he left, hardly past my prime. But of course age had nothing to do with it. He loved her as fiercely as I loved him. Followed her to Boston."

"*Boston?* You always said you didn't have a clue where he was."

"I don't think he's ever been back to England." She paused. "But they're still together. They have three children. And grandchildren."

"*What?*" I sat up straight. "How do you know all this?" When she refused to meet my eyes I insisted, "Mum? How do you know? Did you contact him?"

After a long moment she said, "No. He contacted me."

"What?" I whispered. *"When?"*

"This is the part where I need you to try to understand. What I did was wrong but..."

"Mum..." I eyed her, watched as her face turned ashen. "What did you *do*?"

"I'm so sorry, Abigail." She took a deep breath, and when she spoke again her voice was so low I had to lean forward to hear. "He called the house many, many times after he left."

"He did *what*?"

"At first I told him you were too upset to talk—"

"Hold on, you can't be—"

"—then I said you and Tom didn't want anything to do with him."

"But you never said any—"

"I know—"

"And you had our number changed. You said it was because Dad gambled, that he owed people money. You said they were harassing *you*."

She wrung her hands. "It was a lie," she whispered.

"What?"

"Your father didn't owe a single penny."

I stared at her. "Then what happened?" She didn't look at me for a while. *"Then* what?"

"He wrote."

"He *wrote?*"

"At least once a month. He sent cards for your birthday. For Christmas." Hands trembling, she opened her black leather purse and pulled out a thick wad of envelopes tied together with a wide, red satin ribbon.

"Jesus Christ, Mum," I said as she passed them to me. "What the hell have you done?"

"He's written every year—"

"Oh, god—"

"—to make sure you had his most recent address in case you wanted to—"

"Mum, what the—"

"—contact him. And in the last one he asked if you're on Facebook or the Twitter thing. And I was glad you'd inherited your discreet side from me." When her eyes met mine again I stared at her, the words unable to travel from my brain to my mouth. "Talk to me, Abigail. *Please.*"

I opened and closed my mouth a few times, sentences whirling through my head like mini-tornadoes, but still none of them made it past my lips. "Why would you do this?" I managed at last as I ran a fingertip over my father's neat handwriting. *"Why?"*

Her voice came out barely a strangled whisper. "To punish him. Hurt him."

"But you hurt us, too. Me *and* Tom. We thought Dad didn't care. We thought he'd forgotten about us. We thought he'd *died*. Does he even know about Tom?"

"I sent him a letter a few months after the accident."

"You did *what*?" I threw my hands up in the air. "I'm sorry, but who the *hell* gave you the right to? Who do you think you—"

The last time I saw my mother cry was when she'd stood in my hospital room, moments before she told me how much she hated me. I wanted to loathe her, detest her, but all I saw in front of me was a tired, lonely, sick old woman. It had been years since I'd looked at her for more than a few seconds. Her hair, which should have been silver by now, was still a rich shade of strawberry blonde, pulled back into a tight bun, making her cheekbones higher and more prominent. I noticed her rod-straight back, how she sat perched perfectly on the end of her seat, her knees and feet together, as if she were ready to meet the Queen at a moment's notice.

As I stared at her I realized she'd never felt good enough, always inferior, constantly on her guard with defenses so strong, she'd alienated her husband, children and everybody else around her. She had nobody left. And now she was dying. Alone.

"I don't know what to say," I whispered.

"What I did was wrong, Abigail. I know that." She retrieved a tissue from her bag and wiped her eyes. "But when your father left... The thought of losing you and Tom, too, that you might go with him... I was so scared." I watched another tear slide down her cheek, leaving a streak of mascara in its wake. "I was so worried I'd lose you both. And then it happened anyway."

"But you didn't *lose* me. You pushed me *away*. After Dad left you were so cold, and when Tom..." I pressed my palms over my eyes for a second. "The things you said at the hospital... But I know how much Tom meant to you."

"I loved you both the same, Abigail."

I half smiled. "I thought you said you'd tell the truth."

She sighed. "I saw so much of myself in Tom—the good parts, before you say anything. But you..." She paused. "Well...your father and I used to joke how much you were like him."

"What? A lying, cheating bastard?" Not that I could really argue.

"No, Abigail," Mum said. "Smart, independent and funny. Stubborn and opinionated, too, but I loved that about him. And when he told me he was leaving, that he'd met the love of his life and couldn't live without her, I thought I was going to die because that's how I felt about him."

"I had no idea. None."

"I know this is so much for you to take in, but I had to tell you before I..."

I looked at her, feeling like I was a child again. "But what do we do now?"

Mum reached over and put her hand on mine, and for the first time in years I didn't shake off her touch. "Read the letters. Contact your father. But most of all, Abigail, *Abby*, I want you to let go of the guilt."

I covered my mouth with a hand and closed my eyes for a second, then swallowed hard. "I can't, Mum. I just can't."

"You *can*. Tom's been gone for so long… I stopped blaming you. You never meant for it to happen." She sat back in her chair. "You have to stop blaming yourself, as well."

"It's not quite so simple, is it?"

"Promise me you'll try. Life's too short, believe me. And you have a wonderful daughter and a husband who worships you." She looked at me. "I envy you."

I laughed. "You've no idea what you're talking about."

Mum frowned. "Why? Is something wrong?"

"How can you possibly think you have the right to ask?" I closed my eyes, exhaled and opened them again. "I'm sorry."

"No, I deserved that, and more." She got up. "I should go."

"You can stay here," I offered. "We have the spare room."

Mum smiled. "I booked a hotel. I thought I'd give you some time to…" She gestured to the pile of envelopes still in my lap.

"No, Mum. Don't go. I'd like you to stay."

She looked at me for a moment. "Well, in that case," she said, "I'd like to stay, too."

NOW

NATE

"GRANDMA SANDERS IS HERE?" Sarah said on the drive home after I'd picked her up from Claire's. "And Mum didn't know?" She whistled. "You are *so* dead, Dad. So very, *very* dead."

"I know," I said. "I know."

"Well, holy shit," Sarah said, and I didn't have the energy to reprimand her for her choice of language. I couldn't have put it any better myself.

"How are things going with you?" I asked instead. "School's okay?"

"Yeah, great. Got 115 percent on my latest math test."

"Woo-hoo. Awesome. That's my girl."

"Dad." She rolled her eyes and laughed. "You know you can't get away with saying *Woo-hoo* or *awesome* anymore, right?"

"Is that so?"

"Uh-huh."

I grunted. "What else is going on then? Mum's been asking me about you and boys again."

She sat up in her seat. "I bet she has."

"What do you mean?"

Sarah shrugged. "Like, she's never wanted me to have a boyfriend, not unless he meets her ridiculous standards. And she's always checking up on me. I hate it. She needs to mind her own business."

"She cares about you, Sarah. She loves you more than anything."

"So do you, and *you* don't..."

"I don't what?"

"Nothing."

"We're parents. Checking up is what we do." I glanced at her, but her face was in a determined pout. "And I wish you two would get along. Or at least try."

"Why don't you tell *her* that?" she fired back. "Instead of always giving in to what *she* wants."

"Careful, Sarah." I cleared my throat. "Anyway, are you looking forward to our trip?"

"Uh-*huh*." She grinned. "It's going to be the best trip ever. Zac's *so* jealous and—"

"Zac? I thought you said, and I quote, 'I, like, totally hate him. OMG, like, he's like the worst *ever*.'"

"Pfft, good impression," she said quickly. "And yes, he is. That's exactly why I told him."

"You're sneaky," I said with a laugh. "And a little bit scary."

"Yup." She grinned. "Totally devious."

The house was quiet when we got back. Sarah went to the bathroom, and when I walked into the conservatory I wondered if I was going to find dead bodies with multiple stab wounds. But Abby was lying on the sofa fast asleep, her head in Dolores's lap, envelopes and letters strewn across the floor in front of them.

"Thank you, Nate," Dolores said as she looked up.

"No problem."

"I meant for letting me come."

I smiled. "I know."

NOW
SARAH

Dear Diary,

It's Sunday. Grandma left today. I can't believe it'll be one of the last times I'll see her. Part of me is sad, the other part, well, I hardly know her, so how can I be upset? And that makes me even sadder.

It got me thinking, too. A lot. About what Dad said about Mum and me. About how we snap at each other and fight, or ignore each other, sometimes for days.

And about the lies.

I don't want us to end up like her and Grandma. I *don't*.

But I'm not sure what to do about it. Or if it's too late.

I think I'll talk to Dad. About everything.

Dad always knows what to do.

Night.

Sarah x.

PS. Word of the day: *decimate*, verb.

1: to select and kill every tenth man.

2: to reduce drastically in number.

3: to cause great destruction or harm to.

As in: *I should talk to Dad so we can all stop decimating this family.*

NOW

NATE

"NO THEY DON'T." I tapped my index finger on Nancy and Liam's table.

"Yes, they *do*," Nancy insisted with a smaller laugh than usual.

"Nope." I crossed my arms and smiled. "Sorry, but opposites only attract in the short run."

The four of us sat around their dining table following Nancy's "Thank you for the help" dinner. Sarah and Zac had declined to attend, and at some point over dessert the discussion had switched to mismatched couples.

"Pah!" Nancy sniffed. "You're wrong."

"I'm with Nate on this," Abby said. I squeezed her hand, but she picked up her glass without touching me back and smiled at Liam. *Strike one.* "I mean," she continued, "what about Katy Perry and Russell Brand? Angelina Jolie and Billy Bob Thornton? Marilyn Manson and—"

"Anybody?" Liam said with a laugh.

"Exactly," she answered, beaming at him again.

Was that strike two? Abby had been so happy since finding out about her father over the weekend, it was difficult to tell. Jesus, maybe I was being a paranoid old fart.

"Mind you," Abby said, "it's Hollywood, so who knows what the truth is."

Nancy shrugged. "I suppose. But we've known couples you'd never put together, not in a million years." She turned to Liam. "Like Francis and Olivia? Remember them, honey?"

Abby, who was reaching for the jug of water, knocked over Nancy's glass. "Oh, shit, sorry, Nancy." She dabbed at the spill with her napkin. "Argh. I ruined my piece of cake."

Since when did my wife eat cake?

Liam cleared his throat. "Let me cut you some more. What did you say it was again?"

"Yogurt cake," Abby said. "With fresh cream."

"It's great." As if to demonstrate, he cut himself another slice, too.

"Oh, good," Abby said. "I'm glad you—"

"I'll get the recipe from you," Nancy said loudly. "Anyway, Liam worked with this Francis guy for a while, but then he was made redundant, poor thing. It was only a week after they'd all been on this big corporate team building thing, too. Cruel, huh? Remember, *honey*?"

"Not really," Liam said.

"You went to the Cotswolds," Nancy said and paused. "Surely you haven't forgotten?"

Liam cleared his throat. "Oh, yes. Anyway, Nate, how's business?"

"*Liam.*" Nancy shot him a look. "I was in the middle of a story. Anyway, Francis could have had a pet giraffe, he was so huge. And such a nice man, too, a real softie, and eloquent. Kind of old-fashioned, in a way."

Liam and Abby were very quiet, so I said, "Okay…" to indicate at least somebody was listening.

Nancy continued, "Well, Francis goes to this team building thing, has what I'm pretty sure is his first ever one-night stand, gets fired and three months later, bam!" She clapped her hands. "They're getting married." She sat back in her chair and waggled a finger. "And this Olivia? She was the complete opposite to him. Short. Tiny actually. A biker chick with lots of tattoos. Remember, hon?" She laughed and patted Liam's shoulder, but he didn't answer. "There you are, Nate, I rest my case. Opposites attract."

"Are they still married?" I said. "Your theory won't work otherwise."

She pulled a face. "God, I don't know. We haven't seen them in years, have we, Liam?"

"We haven't," he said. "Anyway—"

"I could find them," Nancy said, sipping her wine. "What was his last name again?"

Liam shifted in his seat. I'd never seen him so uncomfortable. It was odd. He was paler, too. Maybe he'd fired the guy. Benefited from his departure or something, or…

"Oh, come on, Liam," Nancy said. "Surely you remember his name? You guys worked together for ages. I think it was Wilkinson. But I remember Olivia telling me she was keeping her maiden name. What was it…uh…"

"Nancy," Liam said, smiling at her. "I don't think anybody cares."

She laughed, then looked at Abby and me. "Sorry. But don't you hate it when you've got a name on the tip of your tongue? Argh. I can see it on the wedding invite. God, it's going to bug me all night now. Brennan. No. Bre…Bre…"

Nancy threw her hands up in the air, then let them settle in her lap. "I give up."

"It's getting late," Abby said, despite the fact that it was only eight thirty. "We should probably go, Nate." She pushed back her chair and got up. "Thanks so much for dinner. It was lovely."

As we all shifted toward the door, Nancy snapped her fingers. "Brewer. Olivia *Brewer.*"

"Olivia Brewer?" I repeated, then looked at Abby. "You worked with an Olivia Brewer."

"Really?" Nancy looked flustered for a second. "Surely it can't be the same one? Wouldn't that be funny?"

"Very. Did you stay in touch with her, Abby?" I looked at my wife, but she appeared to be drawing a blank. "Olivia. She had the jazzed-up Corolla and a bike?"

"Oh, *that* Olivia," Abby said, as she smiled and patted my arm. "*Brewster.* That was Olivia *Brewster.* You and names, eh?"

I looked at Abby but couldn't quite smile back. Because I remembered Olivia Brewer. Short, slim, dark hair. We'd met at Abby's office a couple of times, and she'd dropped off some files at our house once, proudly showing off her Kawasaki Ninja and new pixie tattoo.

An uneasy feeling crept into my chest, twisted itself around my heart and squeezed.

Abby lying to my face was strike three.

NOW
NATE

I SAT AT my desk in the office after a packed lunch that had mainly gone uneaten. For the last hour or so I'd tried to focus on the sales reports Kevin's assistant had sent me, but every few seconds my mind slipped back to last night's conversation. For the umpteenth time I glanced at my Facebook account to see if the friend request had been accepted, then stood up and slammed my palms down on my desk, breathing heavily.

While I'd been an early social media adopter, I rarely posted anything. I'd never been a fan of sharing my life stories on the internet for everyone else to judge. For a long time I'd thought if people spent as much time caring about each other as they did posting their narcissistic selfies, the world would be a better place. But today? Today I thought I might be grateful for the "look at me" trend.

I hadn't been able to shake last night's uneasy feeling. When we got home Abby had said she wanted to go through her father's letters again, then sleep on it and decide what to do in the morning. And after she'd taken the pile of envelopes and headed to bed, I'd fired up my laptop and searched.

Within seconds I'd found a few people called Olivia Brewer on Facebook. The one I remembered practically zoomed off the screen—there she was in her profile pic, proudly sitting on a Harley, her arms even more colorfully decorated than I recalled.

That's where my investigation came to an abrupt end because Olivia didn't seem to welcome snoopers, and her privacy settings were tight. Except for the indication she was married, liked watching *Friends* reruns and reading mystery novels, there wasn't much to go on.

I immediately sent Olivia a friend request, hoping she was, or soon would be, online. At three o'clock I admitted defeat and went to bed, tossing and turning next to my soundly sleeping wife until it was time to get up. And now I was at the office, hours later; my request still remained frustratingly unanswered.

Perhaps Olivia didn't remember me. And perhaps I was being stupid. Maybe Abby had simply mixed up the names. It was possible, wasn't it? But I couldn't shake the gnawing feeling, no, the *certainty* that something was wrong.

I knew how organized my wife's brain was. Her attention to detail had saved my behind, and Sarah's, on numerous occasions when we'd forgotten appointments, birthdays, piano practice and homework. No, Abby wouldn't have made a mistake like that.

As I rubbed my hands over my face my computer made a quiet ding, indicating a new message. It was from Olivia.

Hi Nate,

What a lovely surprise to hear from you! Such a shame we lost touch.

I remember thinking a while back I should look you and Abby up, but then—are you sitting down?—I found out I was pregnant. Can you believe it? I'm 43 and six months gone already. Needless to say my brain is mush and Francis is still in shock.

Actually, I don't think you ever met Francis, did you? I was so disappointed when Abby said you couldn't make it to our wedding. We're still married (bliss) and live in Brighton now. We've got two kids already. Bobbi will be fourteen soon and Helena is twelve going on eighteen. They're half-grossed out, half-delirious about the new baby coming.

How about you guys? Please say hello to Abby and let's organize something soon (before I'm up to my eyeballs in baby wipes again). I'd love for us to catch up properly.

Hugs,

Liv xxx

I read her message, then went straight to her profile, looking through the photos. Nancy was right—Francis was a beast of a man who looked like he'd be more at home in a Mexican wrestling outfit than a suit.

I waded through the pictures, not exactly certain what I was looking for, but sure I'd know once I found it. I didn't think it would be in the album marked "Florida vacation," nor the one labeled "Biking gone bad," but I went through all the photos anyway. Cheesy grins at Universal Studios, a serious case of road rash. By the time I'd been through four of Olivia's folders I felt like we were BFFs.

My search continued. Scroll, click, scroll, click, click, scroll. Until I found an album marked "Throwbacks." I leaned in, my nose almost touching the screen.

The fourth picture was a scanned, pre-digital snapshot of Olivia and Francis. He took up two-thirds of the frame with tiny, pint-size Olivia next to him, staring up in total adoration. She'd added a caption. "Best Hoskins team building event ever—Cotswolds." Even labeled it "June 10–12, 1998." My stomach lurched.

Click, scroll, click, click.

I wobbled the cursor across the screen as I continued flicking through the photographs. And then, three shots later, there it was.

Olivia and Francis in the same clothes as the first picture. I focused on the people standing behind them in the corner by a bar, apparently unaware a photograph was being taken.

And I recognized them. *Both* of them.

Much younger versions of Abby and Liam.

Abby and *fucking* Liam.

It could have been a business encounter, I rationalized. They'd spoken a few words, then gone their separate ways, but something told me that wasn't it. The way they looked at each other, the way they stood so close. His hand resting on her *shoulder*, for fuck's sake, and she was leaning toward him, smiling. And that look—it was the one she'd given him when I'd watched them from our bedroom window just days ago.

Abby had lied about Olivia last night, and years before she'd turned down their wedding invitation she'd never even told me about. My lungs reminded me to breathe, and I gulped in air. I hadn't been *paranoid*. I'd been an *idiot*.

Abby and Liam hadn't met when he moved in. They knew each other from before, *way* before. Whatever was going on between them hadn't just *begun*. I wanted to scream as the wave of realization hit me in the gut. Nancy hadn't been imagining things. How could I have been so ignorant, so goddamn trusting, so *naive*?

And as I sat there next to a half-eaten sandwich and a sodding Kit Kat, the jigsaw puzzle pieces fell into place. I felt as if someone had removed a filter that had been in front of my face the entire time, but one I hadn't even noticed was there.

I remembered Liam's odd look when I told him Abby's name. How she'd all but fled when she'd been introduced to him. And the next morning…the morning when she'd asked me, no, *ordered* me to *fuck* her. The recollection made my entire world cave in, burying me in the middle of my office as I finally understood Abby hadn't wanted *me*.

Abby was a liar. She'd lied about not knowing Liam, about not liking him. About training for the mud run, selling it to me under the pretext I didn't like her running alone. I imagined him, his six-pack glistening with sweat as he *fucked* my wife, her crying out *his* name, fingernails digging into *his* back. I heard them laugh at Nancy and me, at our trusty stupidity, saying how clever they were to be living next door to each other, fucking and fucking and *fucking* whenever they could.

How long had this been going on? *How long?*

And over and over I kept thinking June 1998. June 1998. June *fucking* 1998.

A loud bellow echoed around my office as I swept my hands across my desk, sending my phone, files, keyboard and lamp crashing to the floor. It took me a few seconds to comprehend that the howl—because it truly sounded like an animal's—came from me. And finally the seed of suspicion I'd been carrying around in my belly for so long took over, digging in roots and spreading throughout my entire being like poison ivy.

Because I knew. Something I'd suspected but had chosen to ignore.

I knew.

Sarah wasn't mine.

THEN
NATE

WHEN ABBY HAD set off for her work thing in the Cotswolds it had felt a little strange without her. Since she'd moved to Wembley we'd never spent a night apart. At first she didn't like to be left alone, and I felt pretty sure her nightmares were always about the accident, although I suspected she sometimes pretended it had been something else.

At least she didn't wake up crying or screaming as often as she used to, and over the years she'd stopped cowering at the bottom of the bed, shouting for her brother.

Six years had passed, and at times, the inner workings of my wife's brain were still a complete mystery to me. She said she loved me, and I believed she did, in her own way. But after a few years of being together I'd accepted there would always be a part of her heart and a part of her mind that were out of bounds, completely closed off to everyone, including me.

Could I blame her? Not really. Her father had walked out. Her brother had died and her mother practically disowned her. It didn't take a genius to work out there were abandonment issues, and I knew she still wrestled with the guilt of Tom's death every day.

Pushing the thoughts aside, I fetched my tool belt. Abby didn't know, but I'd managed to take two days off to do some work around the house. Things I'd been planning on doing since we'd moved in, but hadn't got around to. From our last conversation it was pretty obvious we wouldn't be leaving anytime soon. I'd have to turn Kevin's job offer down. It was a bummer, but then again, if Abby was settled, the sacrifice was worth it. There would be other opportunities.

Besides, I didn't have time to dwell on that job. I had work to do. Yesterday, I'd repainted the bedroom in the off-white color Abby had pointed out in a magazine. And this morning I planned on redoing what she called the "family" room. As I opened the can of paint, it dawned on me having a family room implied one should have a family to put *in* it.

"Maybe it's nature's way of telling me not to procreate," Abby had said over dinner one evening, after she'd told me things hadn't worked out again for us that month.

"I don't believe that for a second. You'll be a great mum."

She put her fork down. "But what if I'm not? What if I can't take care of a baby, like I couldn't take care of...?" Her voice trailed off.

I almost wanted to shout at her, say Tom didn't have to define every bloody thing about our lives from his grave. Instead I said, "You'll be great."

But more months had passed, and I began to wonder if Abby not getting pregnant was in fact nature's way of telling *me* not to procreate. And three weeks ago, I'd secretly made an appointment for a sperm test.

It had been a bit of a peculiar experience, to say the least. I'd imagined a room full of porn magazines and videos, fantasized about a hot receptionist offering to do a sexy striptease to get me in the mood. Instead, a hundred-and-fifty-kilo, possibly hundred-and-fifty-year-old woman named Bertha handed me an orange plastic cup.

"Do I have to fill it?" I said with a stupid laugh.

Bertha stared at me. "A larger cup helps with the aim. Sir."

My face burned as she directed me to a room the size of a broom cupboard, filled with medical supplies. Not exactly what I'd had in mind. Once I'd closed the door I'd stood there for a while, thinking this was a bad idea. A really, *really* bad idea.

What if the room had hidden cameras? Or what if someone walked in while I was standing there jerking off with my boxers around my ankles, caught out like a spotty teen? And then I thought about Big Bertha, who knew exactly what I was doing. I might as well have opened the door with my cock in my hand and said, "Ta-daaa!" like a magician at the circus. Not that magicians yanked their cocks out at the circus. At least I hoped they didn't.

I swiped a tissue from the box on the shelf and dabbed my clammy forehead. Then I checked the door again, ensuring it was locked properly, and searched the dark corners, looking for cameras. Basically buying myself some time before I, inevitably, had to do the deed.

On the drive over to the clinic I'd decided *not* knowing if my swimmers were indeed *swimming* was good. Ignorance was bliss. Not getting your partner pregnant in months and months of regular sex was pretty common, wasn't it? Not everyone got a girl knocked up in a drunken stupor at a party. There was nothing to worry about.

But then I'd told myself to man up, face reality head-on. Besides, I'd have to get tested eventually if I couldn't get Abby pregnant, and then what would I do? Cough, stutter and feign surprise when the doc told us I had useless spunk? Or fess up and tell her I'd known all along, then risk her thinking I was some kind of weirdo who actually enjoyed masturbating into an orange plastic cup in a room the size of a shoebox.

I took a deep breath and decided I had to get on with it. Jackin' the Beanstalk (as Paul had once so eloquently put it) wasn't a massively regular occurrence for me, but it was always a pleasurable one. Hang on, had I thought about my brother? Damn it. This was going to be harder, or should I say more *difficult,* than I had imagined.

A knock on the door made me jump.

"Everything okay, sir?"

Shit! It was Big Bertha. How long had I been in there? Were her other clients…*faster*? What did she want? The last thing I needed was the image of her face looming over me.

"Uh, yeah," I said. "I'm, uh, fine."

"Okay." I swear I could hear a grin in her voice. "Take your time."

I groaned, but not in a good way. Then I unzipped my fly and pulled out my penis, which seemed to be withering away faster than I could say Weed-B-Gon.

"Come on," I said, looking down, willing it to cooperate and spring to attention. I cursed myself for not coming prepared with a handful of *Playboys*, preferably the one Paul had shown me with the centerfold of Nikki Schieler (man, she was *hot* and…*shit*, I'd thought of Paul again).

"Come on," I repeated to my penis that hung limply in my hand. "Don't let me down. We can do this."

As I stroked and huffed and puffed for a bit I relaxed and thought about Abby. Her long blond hair, her elegant neck, her gorgeous eyes…and then increasingly dirty thoughts I'd never dare tell her about. Her firm ass slapping against my thighs, my hands on her tits and then her going down on me, expertly teasing and playing, until I couldn't wait any longer and…

"Uh-oh," I yelped and held the plastic cup up to myself just in time, thinking if it were any smaller, I might have missed.

Back in the family room, I shrugged off the somewhat disturbing masturbation thoughts, remembered I was behind with my painting plans and finished the first coat in double-time. Abby would be home later that afternoon, and I wanted to get the furniture back where it belonged before she arrived. I was close to finishing the second coat when my mobile rang.

"Nate Morris."

"Mr. Morris, this is Dr. Messer from the sperm clinic. How are you today?"

I cleared my throat. "I think that will depend on what you tell me."

Dr. Messer half laughed. "Well, I'd like you to come in to discuss your results."

"That sounds ominous. Why don't you tell me over the phone?"

"We usually prefer couples to come together," Dr. Messer said, "if that's feasible? To, uh, discuss options, if need be."

"Look, my wife doesn't know I had the test done," I said. "So I really would prefer if you told me what's going on."

"I see," Dr. Messer said. "How…unfortunate."

"I'm a big boy. I can handle it."

"All right, Mr. Morris," Dr. Messer said slowly and deliberately, as if he were talking to a child. "The test showed you have a normal sperm count, but I'm afraid motility is low."

"Mobility?" I said. "As in…they don't move?"

"Mo-ti-lity," Dr. Messer said. His bedside manner clearly

needed some work. "Yes, they move, but not the way they should."

I sat down, leaned against the wall. "Can...can I have kids?"

"Almost certainly," Dr. Messer said. "But doing so naturally will be difficult and may take a long time. The most common treatment in this instance is IUI or possibly IVF." He explained each of them briefly, and both sounded like a bad science experiment. "This removes the need for the sperm to travel far or even at all, you see," Dr. Messer concluded. "We give it a head start, so to speak."

"Are there other options? Any that don't involve my wife."

"Mr. Morris," Dr. Messer said in a school principal tone, "generally getting pregnant involves two people."

"Yes, I'm familiar with the concept," I snapped. "But what can I do if I don't want to tell her I have lazy sperm?"

Dr. Messer exhaled loudly, and I thought about telling him to be more sodding considerate, but he said, "You could try boosting your vitamin and mineral intake. Cut down on alcohol and—" I heard him rifle through papers "—I see you indicated you don't smoke, which is good."

I scratched my head. "What do you suggest I do next?"

"Talk to your wife, Mr. Morris," he said. "That's my recommendation. Then come and see me. *Together.*"

I hung up and stared at the ceiling for what seemed like ages, thoughts swirling around in my mind. I'd promised I'd take care of Abby. Do whatever it took to make her life stable, build a home, a family, a future. And now, not only was I asking her to move, but I'd also found out I had swimmers who couldn't be bothered crossing the finish line.

"Sodding *shit*," I said, getting up and finding my shirt had stuck to the wet paint on the wall. "Sodding, bollocking, *shit*!"

"What's going on?"

I turned around. Abby stood behind me, suitcase in hand. "Are you okay?"

"Oh, I'm fine." I plastered a grin on my face. How long had she been standing there? "I didn't hear you come in."

"Were you on the phone?"

"Oh, uh, work. A deal fell through." I waved a hand and walked over to hug her tight, kiss her gently. It had only been two nights, but, god, I'd missed her. "How was it?"

A shadow crossed her face, or maybe it was the way the light reflected off the new paint. She smiled at me. "Fine. It was fine. You know how these things go."

"Let me guess. You had to say something interesting about yourself."

Abby laughed. "How did you know?"

"Not my first time at the rodeo, missy. What did you tell them?"

She looked at me, seemed to hesitate, and then said, "The love of my life met me at the scene of an accident." She smiled. "And I've been thinking. You should take the job with Kevin."

"But what about—"

"No. You must. You deserve it. I don't mind moving, and I'll find another job. It'll be fine. To be honest, I'm a bit fed up working with Ben and Olivia anyway."

I took the bag out of her hand, placed it on the floor and kissed her slowly. And then I made love to my wife on the empty family room floor, next to the tins of paint, rollers and brushes, thrusting into her as deeply as I could, ordering my stupid, lazy sperm to hurry up and get to their destination.

Six weeks later, when Abby shakily held out a pregnancy test, I racked my brains, trying to remember every detail of the conversation with Dr. Gloom aka Messer. He'd said "difficult," not "impossible." It may only have been a few weeks, but since talking to him I'd cut down on beer, eaten more veg and even gone for a run.

I looked at my smiling wife. She was pregnant with my child—*my* child. A grin wider than hers spread across my face, then I picked her up, carried her to the bedroom and made love to her twice before dinner.

NOW
NATE

KEVIN BURST INTO my office, his mouth open wide as his eyes darted across the room, taking in the debris on the floor. "What the blinking hell is going on in here?"

"Not now, Kevin." I grabbed my jacket and bent over to retrieve my keys. "I'm leaving."

"Nate, hang on. Is everything okay?"

"Does it look like it, Kev? What do you bloody think?"

Kevin held his hands up in a defensive gesture. "Whoa. Whatever's pissing you off, you can tell me."

"All right, Kev." I crossed my arms. "You really want to know? Okay. My wife's screwing the next-door neighbor."

"She's what?" He shook his head. "Nah. Not Abby. No way."

"Yes, fucking way. And they've known each other for years. *Years*, Kevin!" I panted, took a big gulp of air. "They pretended they didn't know each other, but I saw them." I pointed to my screen, the only thing left on my desk. "On Facebook. One of Abby's colleagues posted a picture when…" My voice tailed off, and for a few moments I couldn't speak.

"Mate," Kevin said. "These things...they happen, you know? But you can—"

"You don't get it, Kevin. It was an *old* picture. From before Sarah was... I don't think she's... My girl's not..." I felt a tear trickle down my face, and I brushed it away angrily with the back of my hand.

"Jesus Christ," Kevin said. "You're sure?"

I pressed my lips together to stop myself from crying again, then said. "I don't know. I just don't know."

"Look, Nate, you can't—"

"I have to go. I have to sort this out." I looked at him. "You have a problem with that?"

Kevin took a step toward me. "Why don't you sit and calm down for a bit?"

"Sit and—" I ran both hands through my hair. "Didn't you hear anything I just said? *Calm down?* Are you *kidding* me?" I punched the wall, leaving a neat, knuckle-shaped dent in the plasterboard, not registering—or caring—if it hurt my hand.

"Jesus, Nate. Listen to me—"

"I'm going home to—"

"*Wait.* Don't leave in this state. You'll do more harm than good. Trust me. When Felicity found out I'd—"

"Oh, please," I spat. "Don't give me the story of when you shagged the assistant. Naomi, Nathalie, Nadia or whatever her name was. I don't want to hear it."

Kevin stuck his hands in his pockets. "Gotcha. But simmer down before you do something you regret, okay? Go and have a drink. Walk around and get some fresh air. Whatever. I'll come with you."

"No," I said quietly, my fists clenching and unclenching as if they had minds of their own. "I don't want a fucking *drink*, Kevin. Or a walk. I need to go and see my *wife*."

As I walked out, I tried to ignore the looks of my coworkers who—how very English of them—pretended not to stare, but who were burning holes in the back of my head just the same.

NOW
ABBY

"ABBY? IT'S KEVIN."

"Kevin? Is everything okay? Is Nate all right?" My phone seemed to rattle around in my palm until I tightened my grip. "What's wrong?"

"Nate's on his way home," Kevin said quickly. "He seems to think you've been…"

"What?" Silence. *"What?"*

"Uh, sleeping with your neighbor." The words hung between us, dripping with all the indecency and the squalid lewdness of how an affair could appear from the outside.

I swallowed. "He said that?"

"Yeah. He thinks it's been going on for a while, too. Said he found a photo on Facebook. A colleague of yours or something. And—"

"But there isn't… It's not like that, Kevin, I—"

"Abby," he said. "It's none of my business. I wanted you to know he just left, and he's livid. I've never seen him so…" He exhaled deeply. "He also, uh…he said something about maybe not being Sarah's dad."

"*What?*"

He cleared his throat. "Anyway, I had to warn you, okay?"

"Yes," I whispered. "Thank you." But Kevin had already hung up.

Liam had only left me a short while ago. We'd both arranged to work from home while Nate was at the office and Nancy had gone shopping. Sarah had told me earlier she didn't feel well, but I'd insisted she go to school. Liam and I had only intended on having coffee and finalizing our plans, but the bed upstairs was still warm. I hadn't yet been able to bring myself to strip the sheets and put them in the wash.

A few moments ago we'd been wrapped up in bed, safe in our little world, Liam's hand stroking my legs as we agreed on the last details. We'd wait until the weekend, then sit our respective partners down and tell them the truth, right from the beginning.

We'd move out, and until we found a house we'd stay in an apartment a few minutes away, so we could still be close to the kids. Liam was going to sign the lease for the flat this week. He'd even started packing a suitcase. Everything was going to be okay, even with Sarah, *especially* with Sarah. Liam and I had promised each other it would all be okay. "No it won't," a spiteful little voice said in my head, "and you'll finally get what you deserve."

My fingers trembled as I dialed Liam's number. "Abby," he said as soon as he picked up. "I miss you, too, but I can't—"

"You have to come over, Liam. Now. *Please.*"

"Sweetheart, what's going on?"

"Nate knows. He *knows.*"

"I'll be there in twenty seconds."

It took him ten.

"What happened?" he said as he led me into the living room. "How does he know?"

When I heard myself talk it sounded as if my voice—high-pitched and grating—didn't belong to me. "Nate's boss called." I rubbed my arms, trying to get warm. "Nate found a photograph on Facebook and—"

"What photograph?"

"I don't know. I don't know how he…" My mouth dropped open.

Liam looked at me. "What?"

"Last night," I said. "It must have been. When Nancy talked about Francis and Olivia. I saw his face when I said he'd got her name wrong. He knew I was lying. He *knew*."

"Jesus, *that* picture."

"Which one? What are you talking about?"

"The one of Olivia and Francis with us in the background."

"What?"

"When Francis showed it to me I asked him for a copy. He thought I was joking." He exhaled. "I've always kept it. I dropped it the other day, but luckily Zac found it and he didn't recognize you. I thought that was that. *Shit!*"

"But what if Nancy found—"

"Look, either way it forces our hand. It wasn't how we'd planned on telling them but… Anyway, I'm staying here. We'll speak to Nate together. It's going to be all right."

"You don't understand." I started to cry. "He knows everything. *Everything*."

Liam looked at me, his eyebrows raised. "What do you mean *everything*?"

"About Sarah." I swallowed.

He spoke slowly. "What about Sarah?"

"I'm sorry," I said as my chest heaved. "But I couldn't do that to him."

"Do what, Abby?" When I didn't answer he said, "Do *what?*"

I looked away. "Tell him she might not be his."

He drew a deep breath. "Hold on. You said you were pregnant when we..."

"I wasn't..."

"But I did the math. She can't be mine, she—"

"She *can*," I whispered. "She came early."

Liam grabbed hold of my shoulders. "Is Sarah my daughter?" I opened and closed my mouth, but no sound came out. "Abby? Is she?"

"I don't know." Liam's face contorted into an expression I'd never seen before. "I don't *know*. It could be either of you."

And then a loud gasp to my left made both Liam and I turn. Sarah stood in the doorway, her mouth and eyes wide-open, her face a shocking tone of gray, and I realized she must have felt unwell at school and had come back early. I hadn't heard her come in.

"Mum?" Her voice sounded like it did when she'd thought I'd left her in the middle of Asda when she was three. "It can't be... You're lying... You..."

"Sarah." I moved toward her, holding out my arms. "I can explain."

She took a step back. Her gaze moved from my face to Liam's and back again. "Is it true?" The words came out as a strained squeak. "Is it?"

"Sarah, I—"

"*Is it true?*" She was shouting now, the veins on her forehead more prominent, a speck of spit in the corner of her mouth. "Is *he*—" she pointed at Liam "—my dad?"

I held my breath.

"Is he?" she yelled, the words bouncing around the room. *"Is he my dad?"*

"I'm not sure," I whispered as I covered my mouth with a hand. "I'm so sorry, baby. I'm so, so sorry, but I'm not sure."

"How could you do this?" Sarah clenched her fists, then tugged at her hair. "This is so messed up." She let out a wail, sounding like a wounded animal as she paced two steps to the left, three to the right, over and over. "It's *fucked* up. Oh, my god. I have to tell him."

"Sarah, please." I moved toward her again. "Dad's on his way home. Sit down and we—"

"You don't understand what you've done," she shouted, looking at me, eyes protruding from her skull and wild with anger. "Oh, my god. What have you done?" Her arms dropped.

When Liam spoke, I jumped. I'd almost forgotten he was there. "Sarah," he said gently, "we'll sort this out."

"Shut *up!* Don't you dare talk to me," she yelled. And then she stared at me, raised her chin. "I slept with him. I *slept* with him."

"With who?" I looked at Liam, then at Sarah. "Honey, no. No. He *wouldn't* have."

"Not him, stupid," Sarah screamed, pointing at Liam again. "With—"

"It's okay, it's okay. I...I read your diary. I know. With Brian."

Sarah laughed; it sounded cold, hollow. "You really are a stupid cow. We both knew you were snooping. I made Brian up, *Mum*. He doesn't exist."

My lips quivered as I spoke. "What?"

"I *lied*. Made up the perfect boyfriend. One you'd want

me to go out with, one you'd approve of. It was his idea, and he helped me."

"Who are you—"

"So did Claire. I wasn't sure you were reading my stuff. Not until you asked Camilla about Nicole and Brian. Then I knew… But it was lies because I knew you didn't like him." Tears slid down her cheeks.

"Didn't like who?" I said. "Sarah, tell me who you're talking about."

"Zac, Mum," she whispered, craning her neck toward me. "Zac's my boyfriend. Zac."

Liam draw a sharp breath. "Oh, Jesus, no."

"I slept with my *brother*," Sarah said, laughing again. "My brother."

I tried to keep my voice level for her sake as much as my own. "We don't know. We—"

"It all makes sense now," Sarah sobbed. "Why we get along so well. Why we like the same things. It's because we have the same father. Oh, my god. Oh, my god." She put a hand to her mouth. "I hate you," she said when she took it away. "Do you hear me, Mum? *I hate you!*"

And then she ran.

"Sarah," I shouted. "Sarah! Wait. Wait."

"Abby, let her go." Liam grabbed my arm. "Give her time. Nate will be—"

"No!" I shouted. "I won't leave her." I shook off his grip and followed Sarah, spotted a flash of her red jacket and sprinted faster.

As she ran up the road I managed to gain some ground. I turned back and saw Liam running after us, too. It didn't take me long to catch up with Sarah, and when I did I managed get ahold of her arm and she spun around.

"Don't touch me," she seethed, her eyes red and her cheeks streaked with tears. "Don't."

"Honey, please." I held on to her arm again. "Let's—"

"I said *don't touch me*." She yanked herself away and ran into the road.

"Sarah! No! Don't—" I lunged forward and pushed her out of the way of the van hurtling toward us. But whatever else I wanted to say got lost in the squealing of the brakes and the dull thud when the front of the vehicle slammed into me.

NOW
NATE

I WAS ALREADY on the train by the time I realized I'd left my phone at the office, probably under the pile of stuff I'd scattered over the floor. But I wasn't going back. I wondered if I'd *ever* face going back when everybody would be openly pitying me, or secretly laughing at me telling the story about how my wife had been shagging the neighbor.

I could feel my pulse throbbing in my neck as I sat on the train, thoughts peppering my brain so fast it felt like an electric storm in my head. I pulled out my wallet and dug around for the pictures of Sarah. I peered at her, examining every detail, every angle of her face, every freckle. Did she look like him? Everybody always commented on how much she looked like Abby. But did she look like *him*?

I started telling myself that maybe I'd gotten it all wrong. The picture meant nothing. Abby and Liam really hadn't recognized each other when he'd moved in next door. The glances and the gestures were figments of my imagination. Even Abby's mistake with Olivia's name was genuine. Liam was banging some big-breasted twenty-five-year-old instead.

But, I decided, if it walks like a duck and talks like a duck, then guess what? Your neighbor's probably screwing your wife. So then the question became, now what?

Despite what I'd told Nancy, by the time I'd gotten in my car I'd decided this wouldn't be the end for Abby and me. It didn't have to be. People recovered from affairs all the time. And it couldn't be serious. Liam had only moved in next door a few months ago. There was no way they'd been carrying on before. They'd lived miles away. When would they have found the time?

And, fuck it, besides all of that, I still *loved* her.

There was a reason for what had happened, I decided as I drove over the speed limit, drumming my fingers on the steering wheel. Maybe she was going through some kind of crisis. Maybe I hadn't taken care of her the way I should. Or maybe I was too bloody *nice*. But we'd figure it out. I'd fight for her. I'd fix it. I'd pound Liam into the ground if I had to.

And if—*if*—Sarah was his, he'd never take her from me. I'd raised her, loved her, always been her father. That would never change. We'd move away, far away from the Jeffersons. Hell, I'd call Paul and see what Switzerland could offer. Anything to get us away from *him*. I would not lose my family. He would *never* split up my family. I had to be strong, be calm. Show Abby I could forgive her and we could move on. I took a deep breath as I turned the last corner.

But then I saw the flashing lights of the police cars, one of which was in our driveway.

It's strange how easily a person can slip into survival mode. A police officer tells you your wife has been seriously hurt, that she's on her way to the Princess Royal Hospital with your daughter, and they'll take you, too. All I could say was, "Will you move your car out of my driveway so I can park, please?"

I don't remember the name of the policeman, only that his brown eyes kept checking on me in the rearview mirror. At the hospital, with his hand on my shoulder, he escorted me to one of the waiting rooms, and when we got there, I still hadn't spoken another word.

"Dad!" Sarah hugged me tight and buried her face in my shoulder as I wrapped my arms around her. "Mum got hit by a van and..." Her sobs muffled the rest of her words.

"Nate... I—"

"You!" I shouted as I saw Liam, who'd been standing in the corner behind Sarah. I let go of my daughter and pushed her out of the way. "You *bastard*." I got two punches in—one in the face and one in the gut—before the doe-eyed police officer held me back, releasing me only once I'd promised I'd calm down.

"I'm so sorry," Liam said as he rubbed his reddening cheek, and I realized he hadn't even put a hand up to protect himself from my blows. "I'm so sorry."

"Fuck you, Liam," I growled. "*Fuck* you, you—"

"Dad." Sarah's voice sounded small, insignificant. Scared. "Please." She put her arms around me again as I hung my head.

"Mr. Morris?" A petite woman in a white coat, red stethoscope around her neck, stood in the doorway, her face the smooth perfection of a porcelain doll. She looked at me, Sarah, then Liam. "Mr. Morris?"

"Yes," I whispered. "Where's Abby? When can we see her?"

She came over to me, her head barely reaching my shoulder. "I'm Dr. Khan." She swallowed. "Your wife...I'm afraid

she suffered massive internal trauma. The bleeding was so se-
vere we couldn't—"

"No," I said. *"No."*

"Dad?" Sarah gripped my arm. "Daddy?"

"I tried… We tried…" Dr. Khan said, looking up at me.
"I'm so sorry, Mr. Morris, but your wife passed away. She—"

"No!" I shouted. "No! You have to do something. Please.
Can't you *do* something?"

Dr. Khan shook her head. "I'm so sorry… She's gone."

I watched as Liam pushed his way past everybody, running
down the corridor, and Sarah crumpled to the floor, sobbing.
"It's my fault, it's my fault," she cried, her shoulders shaking
hard. "It's *my* fault."

"Shhh." I knelt down and scooped my little girl into my
arms, rocking her and kissing the side of her damp head.
"Shhh. It's not your fault. It's not."

"It is." Sarah looked at me. "I ran into the road, Dad,
after…after I heard them talking," she whispered. "Mum
said…she said…she doesn't know if…if you're my…"

"I know, sweetheart," I said, pulling her closer, our tears
mixing together as they dropped into our laps. "I know. But
everything will work out. Everything will—"

"No." Her face scrunched up as she whispered again, "No
it won't, because, because…"

And as I listened to my baby girl tell me about Zac, the tiny
piece of my world that hadn't yet fallen imploded entirely.

NOW
NATE

"NATE," LIAM SAID when I opened the door a few days after Abby's accident. "Are you alone?"

I didn't answer.

"Can we talk?" he said. "Please."

The exhaustion on his face told me he'd had about as much sleep as me, and his eyes were a shade of pink I'd never seen before. He looked like he hadn't touched a razor for days, and his clothes were badly crumpled. But most noticeable was the shiny bruise on his left cheek. It made me want to give him a fresh one on the other side.

I didn't want to look at him, let alone hear him speak. But he had answers. And I needed them. I turned my back but left the front door open. I crossed the hallway, walked through the kitchen filled with food and other goodwill gestures people had dropped off, past Abby's sneakers I couldn't yet touch. I sat down but Liam chose to stand, and I watched as he fiddled with the cuffs of his shirt.

"Is Sarah…?"

"She went to Claire's. Needed to get out of the house."

He nodded. "That's probably for the best. How are you?"

A snort escaped my throat as I stared him down. "What the hell do you care?" I paused. "Man, you look like shit."

"Yes."

"I hope you feel like shit, too."

"Far worse."

"Good. I hope it lasts forever."

He lowered his eyes. "I deserve that. I deserve all of it."

I shrugged. "What do you want? Paul will be back soon, so whatever you're here for you'd better get on with it. He'd be quite happy to beat the crap out of you, too."

Liam looked at me. "I want to tell you the truth about what happened."

I laughed. "Come to off-load your guilt, have you?"

"It's not that."

"Well, let me spare you the trouble." I said. "You and Abby met in the Cotswolds. You fuc—" I closed my eyes, took a deep breath, then opened them again. "And then my daughter was born. Voilà."

He looked away and swallowed.

"Don't tell me there's more," I spat. "There can't possibly be anything else."

"We knew each other before. Before the Cotswolds."

I could feel my pulse thumping in my neck. "The hell are you talking about?"

"We were together before she met you. Before the accident when...when—" I opened my mouth—in shock or to speak I wasn't sure—but he continued "—when I killed him."

"Who? What are you talking about?"

He took a deep breath. "*Tom.* I was the one driving that night. It was *me.*"

It felt as if the air had instantly been sucked out of the room.

I was unable to move any part of my body, including my lips, rendering me incapable of saying anything at all. Part of my brain wondered if I'd misheard, trying to decide if I found myself in the middle of a continuous nightmare, but Liam spoke again, every word revealing my new reality.

"Abby and I had been together for months. We were in lo—" His eyes darted around the room. "That night...I met them outside the pub just as they were leaving. They were both wasted, so I said I'd drive and we'd take Tom home first instead of him getting a cab." He gulped. "But a deer ran into the road and...and I swerved. I lost control." He was sobbing now. "Neither of them were moving. I thought they were dead. And I'd had a few drinks earlier...so...so I panicked and ran. I fucking *ran*."

More seconds passed before he looked at me, and my voice finally returned. "You left her in the *middle of the road*? Deserted her brother who was trapped *inside the car*?" I tried to get up, wanted to punch him in the gut repeatedly, but my arms and legs still felt like dead weights, and I was sure I'd collapse before I even got to him.

"I was scared," Liam whispered. "I'd already lost my license once before. I thought I'd be locked up. I'd lose my job. I thought I'd already lost Abby. But I was selfish...so bloody selfish. And I'm sorry." His eyes were pleading with me now. "Christ, I'm so, so sorry."

"But that means..."

"It wasn't her fault," Liam said. "None of it was *ever* her fault."

"Jesus." I managed to get up, pressed the palms of my hands over my face for a few seconds to stop the room from spinning. "I don't know what to do with this information. I can't—"

"I loved her, Nate," Liam said, and I forced myself to unclench my fists before they connected with his face. "We were going to move in together, but after the accident..." He exhaled. "She left me anyway. She said she couldn't be with me."

"And so you *punished* her? Let her think she'd killed her brother? What the f—"

"No! You've got it wrong." Liam drew a breath.

"Oh, please. You say you loved her! How could you do that to her? How?"

"I wanted to tell her. But I knew she'd never forgive me. If I told her, we wouldn't stand a chance. I thought if I gave her time...enough space... But then she left—"

"With me." I laughed bitterly as I paced the room. "And I took care of her, put her back together. And all these years, all this time, she blamed herself when all along it was *you*."

"Yes," he whispered. "And I've wanted to make it up to her every single day ever since. I thought you should know. I thought it might help you understand why—"

"Oh, *fuck* you, Liam." I pointed at him. "You'd never have told her the truth, would you? You'd have let her believe she was responsible forever. Christ, your *fling* with Abby was built on nothing but lies, you manipulative coward." I planted my feet on the ground, dug my fingers into the back of my chair. "Get out of my house."

He swallowed and looked at his feet. "Nate, I need to know about Sa—"

"What? Taking Abby from me wasn't enough? Now you want my daughter, too?"

Liam's head snapped upward, and he met my eyes. "No, I'd never—"

"But you want to know if she's yours." I stared at him. "Don't you?"

"If she's mine," he said, aging a decade with every passing moment, "then she's the only part of Abby I have left."

"You have nothing of Abby left. And Sarah's mine," I said through gritted teeth. "She's *mine*."

"Nate, it's not just about us. Zac...he's a mess. The kids... they need to know."

"What about your wife? Where does she fit in? I haven't seen her around lately. What did you do, kill her, too?" I stared at Liam, momentarily satisfied when I saw him flinch.

"Nancy's devastated, Nate, she's beside herself. She, uh, she took Zac to her mum's. We're selling the house. Getting divorced."

I stared at him. "Is that what Abby was going to do, too? Divorce me? For you?"

Liam closed his eyes and kept his head down.

"Jesus Christ, this keeps getting better and better. You're such a bas—"

"I loved her, Nate," he said quietly. "From the first moment I saw her. I loved her."

"Yeah," I said with a shrug. "She had that effect on people."

"She loved you, too. She told me you—"

I shook my head, my voice a growl. "No. Don't you fucking dare." I closed my eyes. "You need to leave, Liam. Get out *now*. Before I do something I won't regret."

NOW

NATE

IT HAD BEEN two weeks since the funeral. Abby's father, Patrick, flew over from Boston, and Sarah and I recognized him instantly when we picked him up at the airport. His face looked like Abby's, but by the way he walked we'd already suspected he was her dad, and his sad smile confirmed it well before we shook hands. He sobbed as he hugged Sarah and me, whispering over and over how sorry he was, and we clung to him like drowning men to a lifeboat.

I respected both Patrick and Dolores immensely to have put what must have felt like insurmountable differences aside, at least for one day, so they could say goodbye to their daughter. But now Abby's parents, Paul, Lynne and the girls had all gone home, resuming their normal lives, and Sarah and I had to start our own.

My daughter and I sat in front of my laptop. The light gave her skin an eerie, bluish tinge making the rings under her eyes darker still. I was glad it would be the end of the school year soon. We were going to Europe next month; both of us had decided we had to get away, make some new memories, just the two of us, and then with Paul and Lynne in Switzerland. Kevin had already arranged it all, no expense had been spared. But before that, we had something else to take care of.

"You're sure about this?" I said, the cursor hovering over the Submit button. "You're absolutely sure you want to do this?"

"Dad," Sarah said. "It's not about *him*." She still refused to say Liam's name. "You're my dad. You always will be. But I have to know about Zac." She squeezed my hand. "I have to."

"But he'll be at university soon," I said quickly. "And the house will sell. You never have to see him again. We'll never see *any* of them again."

"Dad," she whispered, then swallowed and said, "I need to know."

The package from GeneTech arrived in a plain envelope a few days later. "Don't make me do the cheek swabs, Dad," Sarah said as we went through the instructions. "Please don't make me feel like a criminal."

I hugged her. "We'll use hair samples instead," I said. "Will that be okay?"

She nodded, her eyes welling up as she looked over the rest of the pamphlet. "It says it's better if we send a sample from Mum, too." Tears spilled over her cheeks. "How do we…?"

"I'll take care of it." I kissed the top of her head and went to our—my—bathroom, opened one of the drawers and stared at Abby's brush. I picked it up, pulling and unraveling the long blond strands, my pounding heart filling with hatred and anger.

Sometimes I thought if she were still alive I'd want to kill her. Slip my hands around her dainty little neck and squeeze until I watched the life seep out of her. But before that I'd shout and rant at her, yell about how I'd tried to make her happy every single day since I'd laid eyes on her in the middle of that godforsaken road. I'd tell her I should have left her to die, like her precious, perfect Liam had.

But then the anger vanished and was replaced by a feeling of absolute, drowning despair, and I whispered a pathetic "sorry" to my dead wife, apologizing for the terrible thoughts over and over, begging her to come back, to lie down next to me so I could tell her I still loved her. Grief, I knew, was a slippery, fickle little bastard, difficult to get hold of, almost impossible to tame.

I took a deep breath and went back to the kitchen, put Abby's hair into the envelope and hugged my daughter.

She looked up at me. "What do we do now?"

"Now?" I said with a faint smile. "Now we wait."

NOW
SARAH

Dear Diary,

It's been a year—twelve months exactly—since the Jeffersons moved in next door.

It feels more like twelve years.

My therapist says I'm doing well. He thinks I'm "making progress in accepting your mother's death wasn't your fault." I smiled and thanked him. It's easier that way.

Zac tells me it's not my fault either, it's his father's, whom he still refuses to see. Zac emails me every day, tells me he wants to see me again. He wrote "I love you" today, and said what happened between his father and my mother shouldn't keep us apart. He said we're meant to be together. And it makes me cry because I feel the same.

Dad cries a lot, too. He doesn't know I can hear him, but I do, late at night, when I can't sleep either, when I'm lying in bed, thinking about everything that's happened.

When Dad saw the DNA results his tears were different, because he was smiling, and he hugged me so tight I felt like I couldn't breathe. He whispered that everything was going to be okay. He promised from now on everything will be all right.

And I asked him what he'd have done if the results were different, and he said it wouldn't matter, he loved me no matter what. But he was lying, I'm sure he was. When I looked into his eyes I knew I'd made the right decision. I mean, what other choice did I have?

And I'll never tell Dad the truth.

He'll never know how I sneaked into Zac's house and took his father's hair the day after my mother died. That I sent two packages to GeneTech, both with Dad's name, but one with my signature a tiny bit different so I could tell them apart... Or that I shredded the results from the test with Dad's sample.

I *had* to. It would destroy him if he knew he's not my real father. And he'd stop loving me, I know he would. How could he still love me, knowing I'm half of Lia *him*.

But Dad will never know. Nobody will *ever* know. My mother might not have been able to keep her secrets properly, but I will. Which is why, Dear Diary, tomorrow morning you'll be a smoldering pile of paper.

Ashes to ashes.

Dust to dust.

Lies stay secret.

And so they must.

Later,

Sarah x.

PS. Word of the day: *risorgimento*, noun.

1: often capitalized: the 19th century movement for Italian political unity.

2: a time of renewal or renaissance: revival.

As in: *It's time for my own risorgimento to begin.*

* * * * *

ACKNOWLEDGMENTS

Many people helped shape this novel, and I will be forever grateful to every single one. But first, I want to extend my gratitude to you, the reader. You picked this book when there are so many others vying for your attention. A million times thank you.

To Cassandra Rodgers and Sam Hiyate from The Rights Factory; you saw something in my early writing and took a chance on me. Thank you for putting up with all my questions, for your continual support, advice and all-around agent awesomeness.

Michelle Meade, my brilliant, generous, insightful and inspiring MIRA editor. Working with you is an absolute pleasure, and the editing process a dream. Your invaluable guidance did wonders for this story, and I'm so excited to be on this journey with you. Long, long may it continue, with many more books to come.

The rest of the MIRA team—Nicole Brebner for loving the manuscript enough in the first place, and the outstanding marketing, PR, art and production teams. You all work incredibly hard, and I'm so fortunate my novel found its way into your capable hands.

A massive thank you to Mum and Dad for believing in my writing from the beginning, to Joely, my (little) big sis whose no-nonsense approach and practical advice keeps me grounded, and to Becki, who's championed everything I've done for over twenty years.

To Brian Henry and my QuickBrownFox writing group colleagues; Adrienne, Bieke, Brian C., Cat, Dave, Donna, Ginelle, Glen, Gord, Janis, Lena, Linda, Lorie, Lyanne, Maggie, Marilyn, Nancy, Nydia, Pat, Patricia, Ray, Rob, Sally W. and Sheila; thank you for your fabulous suggestions and, of course, the regular fits of laughter.

Where would I be without my fantastic beta-readers? Emma, Mary, Michelle S., Nick, Reena, Sally B. and Shauna—I'm so lucky to have you. Thank you for reading an early draft, telling me the good, the bad and the downright ugly, so I could make the story so much stronger.

To Matt Cascio and Sean Joyce; thank you for making time in your busy schedules to answer my legal questions on both sides of the Atlantic.

To Elie, who I miss every single day and who resembles Tom in so many ways. I wish you were here to celebrate with me. I shall raise a glass (or two) to you, and carry you in my heart forever.

Finally, to my incredible husband, Rob, and to our wonderful boys, Leo, Matt and Lex; thank you for keeping me on track and for telling me everything will work out in the end (you were right!).

DISCUSSION QUESTIONS

1. What do you think was the most impactful event in Abby's life? How did it shape her in the short- and long-term?

2. Abby blamed herself for Tom's death and pushed Liam away to deny herself true love. Do you know anyone who has punished themselves in similar ways? How has that affected them?

3. What was behind Nate continually trying to "fix" his wife and restore her happiness? How do you think this impacted his decisions regarding himself and Sarah? Would he have been happier with someone else, and if so, why?

4. When Liam and Abby meet on the retreat, he tells her he still loves her, and that they're "married to the wrong people," but Abby says she owes Nate "everything." Did that situation justify Liam and Abby having an affair? Why?

5. What do you think would have happened if Liam had immediately confessed he'd been driving? Or if Nate had

told Abby about his sperm test results? How would it have affected the characters and their stories?

6. Camilla tells Abby one in two marriages end in divorce because people pretend to be something they're not when they first meet. Do you know anyone to whom that has happened? What did it do to their relationship?

7. What scene did you think was the most pivotal in the story? How would the novel have changed if that scene had been different, or hadn't taken place? What did you expect to happen?

8. All the women in the story have deep-running, emotional issues. What could they have done to help each other, and how could that have changed their outcomes? Do you think women in general support each other enough? What more could be done?

9. How did you feel when Abby died? Did your feelings change when you found out she wasn't responsible for Tom's death? If so, did that change surprise you?

10. How can Nate deal with his grief, but also try to come to terms with the lies Abby told, and the secrets she kept from him?

11. Do you think Sarah can keep the secret about Nate's paternity? What would you advise her to do? How will her decision shape her as an adult, and do you think she'll see Zac again?

Q & A

What was your inspiration for *The Neighbors*?

Most of my stories start with a single question, and The Neighbors was no exception. In this case it was: What if an ex-boyfriend moved in next door? I played around with the idea for a while, imagining how awkward it could become. I wondered if the main character would tell anyone, and if not, why? Then I imagined the secrets each person could be keeping. Basically, I kept making the situation worse and worse for my characters. That's one of the fun parts about writing. You can be as manipulative as you please, and the cast will still show up the next morning without bearing any grudges.

What was your greatest challenge writing this novel? Your greatest pleasure?

This is my second novel, so the first obstacle was finding out if I could write another. The next challenge was working with a non-linear timeline—jumping about in time can become very confusing for everyone—and having multiple viewpoint characters. The latter definitely pushed me because I had to ensure each character's voice was distinct from the others.

My greatest pleasure was building the story; editing and layering before anybody got to see the full manuscript. My initial drafts are awful, truly pitiful, but I have to tell myself the story in its most basic form first, then go over it repeatedly, adding complexity and depth with each round. Seeing it all come together, feeling the manuscript was beta-reader- and agent-ready was the most rewarding part of that process. Of course, that's also when the real editing work began!

You mentioned the four different viewpoint characters. Did you have a favorite to write, and if so, which one and why?

I enjoyed writing all of them very much. Abby's because she's so emotionally damaged and complex, my heart aches for her. Nate's because he's a lovely man who tries to do the right thing but loses sight of his own happiness in the process.

Nancy's transformation from overlooked housewife to cunning manipulator was the suggestion of my editor, Michelle Meade, and such fun to write. Sarah's chapters felt almost nostalgic, and I listened to a lot of '80s music to capture the teenage mood (thankfully no leg warmers or a perm were required).

I loved writing the happy scenes with Abby and Tom, too. Their relationship almost made me jealous, and I don't even have a brother!

Can you tell us about your writing journey so far?

I started writing mid-2011, but instead of working on short pieces to develop my skills, I wrote an entire novel, Time After Time. The *trouble was that while the premise caught people's interest, the execution was flawed. I stuck with it, though, had the novel critiqued (eye-opening!), and took a number of writing courses both locally and online with Curtis Brown Creative UK. After that course I secured representation with Cassandra Rodgers from The Rights Factory.*

We worked on the novel for a few months, after which she quickly sold it to HarperCollins UK's digital arm Maze, and Time After Time *was published six months later, in June 2016. Going through the whole pitch to publication process was enlightening, and it taught me so much about the business.*

I'd already been working on The Neighbors *at that point—I needed something to distract me during the submission process, or I was going to go mad. Both Cassandra and I were hoping for a traditional print deal for my second novel, and when MIRA offered a two-book deal I jumped up and down with my dad in my parents' living room, shouting, "I did it, I did it!" Meeting Michelle and the MIRA team for the first time was wonderful. I felt—still feel—incredibly lucky and privileged, and often don't quite believe it's actually happened.*

Your first novel, *Time After Time*, was a lighthearted, romantic read, whereas *The Neighbors* is firmly in the domestic suspense category. What made you switch genres, and what challenges did that present?

You're absolutely right. Time After Time *is a romantic tale of roads not taken—it's the love child of the movies* Groundhog Day *and* Sliding Doors*—and the idea for the novel from start to finish was crystal clear from the beginning. Having said that, I wanted to write something darker and grittier for my second book, with more complex characters and shades of truth. I realized the genre wasn't the same, but wasn't particularly concerned.* Time After Time *hadn't* *yet been submitted to publishers when I outlined* The Neighbors, *so I kept going. After all, there was no guarantee any of my novels would be picked up.*

Later, when Michelle and I spoke about The Neighbors *suiting the domestic suspense category, I realized it's where I wanted to be going forward. I'm drawn to messy stories where things don't necessarily work out well, where characters are flawed, imperfect and achingly human.*

Do you have a specific writing routine you like to stick to?

I try, but with three boys I have to be flexible. Most days I write in the morning for a few hours, go to the gym for a break (treadmill = idea generator, I'm sure of it!) and usually write again in the afternoon. As soon as the kids come home that's it—author hat comes off, mum hat goes on. I tend to keep the weekends free for the family unless I'm finishing a manuscript or I'm in the final editing stages, when I'll often work well into the night. My characters keep me from sleeping and cause terrible parasomnia anyway, much to my husband's amusement!

Do you read when you're working on a project? Or does it distract you from your stories?

I love reading fiction, and rarely find it to be a distraction from my work—except when the book is so brilliant I'd rather be reading it than working on my own manuscript! But when I'm stuck on one of my chapters or frustrated with edits, I pick up a novel and lose myself within.

I read one book at a time, usually in the evenings and always before bed, a habit my eldest son has picked up, too. Even if it's only a few pages, I find it relaxing and it gives me ideas and inspiration for my own work.

I'm rarely upset when the weekend forecast is terrible—it gives me an excuse to curl up on the sofa and be instantly transported to another place without needing an umbrella.

9 780778 311003

CPSIA information can be obtained
at www.ICGtesting.com
Printed in the USA
LVHW040047251121
704426LV00006B/813